SMALL ACTS
of
KINDNESS

Published in the UK by Universe
an imprint of Unicorn Publishing Group, 2022
Charleston Studio
Meadow Business Centre
Lewes BN8 5RW

www.unicornpublishing.org

A catalogue record for this book is available
from the British Library

5 4 3 2 1

ISBN 978-1-914414-99-2

Cover design by Unicorn
Typeset by Vivian Head

Printed and bound in Great Britain

SMALL ACTS
of
KINDNESS

A Tale of the First Russian Revolution

Jennifer Antill

UNIVERSE

CONTENTS

For my sons,
Matthew and Thomas

Acknowledgements

Many thanks to my husband, Nick, for his constant support and forbearance.

To the 'godparents' of *Small Acts of Kindness*, Julia Payne and Alison and David Carse.

To the following people for valuable encouragement and help: Hugh Belsey, Susan Davis, Simon Edge, Ken Farmer, Andrew Fleming, Claude Forthomme, Vicky Hamill, Angharad Hampshire, Gill Knight, Ellina Konovalova, Arabella McKessar, Brian Moody, Philip O'Loughlin, Maggie Potter, Hilary Taylor, Tessa West, Seb Wheeler, Angela Winwood.

And also Ian Strathcarron and Unicorn Publishing Group. Ryan Gearing, Lauren Tanner, Felicity Price-Smith and Rollin.

To those who inspired and encouraged my enthusiasm for the Russian language and culture at the School of Slavonic and Eastern European Studies, UCL, and the Annual Cambridge Russian Summer School and beyond, including Rachel Morley, Nick Brown, Arnold McMillin, Svetlana McMillin, and Tanya Yurasova.

And finally, to the staff and volunteers at Sudbury and District Citizens Advice, where great and small acts of kindness occur every day.

About the Author

Jennifer Antill studied Russian Language, Literature and Politics, at UCL School of Slavonic and Eastern European Studies, and has travelled widely in the country, often staying with Russian families. She gives talks on Russian cultural topics to a wide variety of organisations. In a former life, she worked in the City of London as an investment analyst, and for the last eleven years she has served as a local councillor. Jennifer is married to Nick, has two sons, and lives in Suffolk.

Small Acts of Kindness is her first novel.

For information about Jennifer's talks, publications and access to her blog go to: www.jenniferantill.com

Who's who

The Belkin and Bogolyubov Families

Vasily Nikolayevich, Count Belkin (Vasya).

Alexander Petrovich, Count Belkin (Sasha): Vasily's and Katya's uncle; Nikolay's older brother. A senior civil servant in the Ministry of the Interior.

Ekaterina Nikolayevna, Princess Polunina (Katya): Vasily's sister.

Maria Vasilyevna, Countess Belkin: Vasily's and Katya's mother; cousin of Antonina Stepanova, Countess Laptev.

Nikolay Petrovich, Count Belkin: Vasily's and Katya's father; Alexander's brother; (died 1812).

Yevgenia Alexandrovna, Countess Belkin: Vasily's and Katya's grandmother; Nikolay's and Alexander's mother.

Dmitry Vladimirovich, Prince Bogolyubov (Dima): Alexander Petrovich's former superior officer and mentor, landlord, friend and partner.

Konstantin, Prince Polunin: Katya's husband.

Nikolay Konstantinovich Polunin: Katya's baby son.

Servants (Belkin and Bogolyubov families)

Yakov: Vasily's manservant.

Matvey: a kitchen boy.

Karl Feodorovich: former German tutor and steward on the Belkin estate, now retired.

Grigory: a coachman.

Venyamin: an old servant.

The Laptev Family

Elizaveta Gavrilovna Laptev (Lisa): an heiress.

Gavril Ivanovich, Count Laptev: Lisa's father.

Antonina Stepanova, Countess Laptev: Lisa's mother; cousin of Maria Vasilyevna Belkin.

Nadezhda Gavrilovna Laptev (Nadya): Elizaveta's younger sister.

Madame Darya Stepanova Svetlov: Antonina's older sister; cousin of Maria Vasilyevna Belkin; a widow; chaperone to Elizaveta Laptev.

Laptev family servants

Boris Abramovich: a serf artist.

Petya: Boris's son.

Yevgraf: the estate steward.

Vera: Lisa's maid.

Other characters

Colonel Pavel Pavlovich Kalinin: a diplomat.

Irina Pavlovna, Baroness von Steiner: Pavel Pavlovich's sister.

Georgy Mikhailovich Kalinin: Pavel's and Irina's cousin.

Frau Margarethe Geyer: companion to the Baroness.

Mikhail Alexandrovich Stenovsky (Misha): a cornet in the Chevalier Guards.

Nikita Alexandrovich Stenovsky: Mikhail's older brother; a staff captain in the Guards General Staff.

Ivan Alexandrovich Stenovsky: Mikhail's younger brother; Vasily's school friend; now fighting in the Caucasus.

Madame Stenovsky: Mikhail's and Nikita's mother; a widow.

Mr. Thomas Maltby: an English tutor.

*Kondraty Feodorovich Ryleev: a poet and political activist.

Kuprin: Prince Bogolyubov's neighbour; a newly made noble from a merchant family.

Leonid Sergeyevich, Count Fedulov: former army captain; Collegiate Assessor (later promoted to Court Councillor) in the Ministry of the Interior.

*Mikhail Bestuzhev: a staff captain in the Moscow Regiment.

*Konstantin Chernov: a lieutenant in the Semenyovsky Guards Regiment, Ryleev's cousin.

*The Grand Duke Mikhail Pavlovich Romanov: youngest brother of the Emperor.

Antonov and Bortnik: private agents.

Sergey Ivanovich Chudov: Titular Councillor; head of the Oryol and District office of the Ministry of the Interior.

Collegiate Secretary Komarov: Chudov's second-in-command.

*The Governor of Oryol Province.

Vladimir Vladimirovich Golovkin: a writer, journalist and teacher.

Colonel Strogov: Chief of the Gendarmes in Oryol Province.

Krylov: a fugitive.

*Count Sergey Kamensky: a theatre owner.

Yevgeny Filipovich, Prince Uspensky: a yunker in the Pavlogradsky Hussars.

Supporting cast:

Priests, soldiers, field and house serfs, agents, police, gendarmes, bureaucrats and scribes.

*Emperor Alexander I; *Baron Andrey Rosen; *Count Benkendorf; *Emperor Nicholas I; *Count Arakcheyev.

*Historical figures

'The historical value of revolutions depends upon three conditions: upon what they destroy, upon what they create, and upon the legends that they leave behind... The Decembrists have not destroyed anything or created anything. The value of their accomplishment consists entirely in their legend. But that is sufficient.'

Aldanov, *Memories of the Decembrists*, 1926

PROLOGUE

—

12 December 1825, The City Barrier, St Petersburg

'Open up!'

Sparks spiral skywards through the dark frozen air. The sentry thrusts his blazing torch into the sealed wagon. Revealed in an arc of light, the prisoner shields his eyes. He staggers back and falls, unbalanced by his chains, and his head slumps onto his chest.

'Let's be seeing you!'

The man looks up, is dazzled, blinded.

'You'll do.'

An officer in the guardhouse scans the documents, stamps them, and hands them up to the driver, who, clumsy in his heavy furs, stuffs them into his boot. The city clocks strike midnight.

The door slams with a metallic clang; the bar drops; darkness returns. The wagon sways away into the night, taking the road towards Moscow. As the surface roughens, the vehicle bucks and judders. The prisoner is jerked back and forth, his body driven repeatedly against the rigid side. There is straw on the floor. He pulls a bundle towards him, trying to bury himself. The cold seems to dissolve his flesh, invade his bones; his throat is sore and very dry. They have left him a flask; he gropes for it. The water tastes of salt, of old leather. There seems to be bread too. He tries to eat. He cannot swallow.

He must think, must focus, and try to grasp what has happened, what damage he might have done. He had been with his friend the Englishman, opening the Madeira, enjoying the warmth of the fire when they had come for him. And now, suddenly, he is here, shivering, shackled, alone. Has he been deceived? Tricked? Are they, after all, taking him to the fortress?

The wagon picks up speed and achieves a smoother rhythm. He shuts his eyes and drifts into the past.

PART ONE

—

'Between the tyrant and the slave there can be no reconciliation, there is nothing conditional. It is blood, not ink, that is needed. We must act with the sword.'

Kondraty Ryleev

CHAPTER 1

July 1825 – St Petersburg

THE VOYAGE HAD been tranquil. Blown by a steady south-westerly, the English merchant vessel *Virtuous* had made swift passage to the Gulf of Finland. Vasily leant against the rail, elated by the cries of the seabirds, the lapping and overlapping surface of the sea. In the early sunlit haze, he could make out the trees, grey boulders, and buff-coloured sands of the Russian shore. Soon they would reach Kotlin Island and the town of Kronstadt, where the captain would pause for customs checks before sailing on overnight into the city of St Petersburg.

The rigging creaked and the smell of tar rose from the warming deck. He looked towards the prow, brushed his hair aside, and blinked against the sun. There were some small islands in the distance, but they were not yet close to Kronstadt.

He was considering going below to fetch his sketchpad when he heard footsteps. A tall, broadly built man was approaching along the deck, throwing a long shadow behind him. He wore a dark broadcloth coat and a peaked cap pulled down over his eyes. Vasily had noticed him in Stettin, standing at the head of the gangway, closely observing the new passengers as they embarked. After that, he had only seen him fleetingly. He hadn't appeared for meals in the general cabin.

The man joined him at the rail and said, in Russian, 'It seems we're almost home.'

'Yes, indeed.' Vasily acknowledged him with a short bow. 'Vasily Belkin.'

'Pavel Pavlovich Kalinin. Are you Count Alexander Belkin's

son? I wasn't aware that he had one.'

'Alexander Petrovich is my uncle. My father – his brother Nikolay – died during the war. You know my uncle?'

'We've encountered one another from time to time.' Kalinin paused. 'You came on board at Stettin?'

'Yes, Berlin was the end of what I suppose you could describe as an educational journey.'

'You've been travelling in Europe?'

'In France and Austria, as well as Prussia. I've seen and done a good deal over the last year, but I'm not sure that my patron will think my formal education much progressed.' Vasily looked down. A glimpse of black lace floated into his head, a carefully placed gardenia on the palest of skin; his trip had been intensely self-indulgent. He forced the vision away.

'And you?'

The man was studying him, smiling slightly. His hair was an unusual shade of dark auburn and his skin very pale. He must have been close to forty. 'I've come from England,' he said. 'I've been working at the embassy in London for some years and go back and forth on occasion.'

'How do you find the foreign service? My uncle hopes that I'll join shortly if all goes to plan.'

Kalinin considered for a moment. 'It's absorbing enough, but if times were different I'd rather still be a soldier.'

'You fought Napoleon?'

'Yes, chased him all the way to Paris in '14.'

'But you didn't stay in the army?'

'No. Once the war was over, I soon resigned my commission, retired with the rank of colonel. I wasn't prepared to waste my time on the parade ground, fretting about guard duty and the like. For many, that's all soldiering is about these days.'

'When I was a child, I was desperate to join the army,' Vasily said. 'But the plan has always been for me to follow my uncle and grandfather into government service.'

'I wouldn't have too many regrets. The army has a fine reputation, of course. It's still basking in the reflected glory of the war. But the truth is that you'll have avoided hours of boredom. Young officers these days seem to spend most of their time drinking, fighting duels over women, and gambling away what's left of their fortunes. Government service may not seem exciting, but it can be rewarding.'

'I hope it will be. I'd like to make some sort of mark on the world, make it a better place.'

The Colonel scrutinised him with apparent interest. Vasily turned away and looked out over the water. Perhaps he'd sounded a little eager, overzealous. 'I think we're approaching Kronstadt.' He pointed to a smudge low on the horizon.

'In that case, I must go below,' Kalinin said.

'Aren't you going to watch us sail in?'

'There'll be time to take in the view of the harbour later. But you should stay up here if it's your first time. There's plenty to see. I'm dog-tired, actually. Some fellow in the cabin next to mine spent most of last night carousing with the ship's cook, or he would have done if I hadn't told him to hold his peace. Don't know who it was…'

Vasily winced. 'I'm afraid that was probably my man.'

'What, you bought your servant a berth? How very liberal of you! My man's in steerage.'

'I'm sorry he disturbed you, sir, but Yakov's a special case. We're the same age, and he's been with me since childhood. He came with us when my family moved to Petersburg from

Moscow. He wasn't keen on a sea trip and has hardly left his cabin since we left Prussia. It didn't seem right to make him travel in steerage, not after all we've experienced together over the past year.'

'But you'll still expect him to carry your baggage off the boat, I assume? He'll have to get used to different ways now you're back in Russia. So, what are your plans? Straight into the Service?'

'That's what's expected, but before I start, my patron, Prince Bogolyubov, thinks I should learn some English. There was no time to visit on this trip. He may have appointed a tutor for me already.'

'Ah yes, English. A barbaric language, in my opinion. But the Prince is right. It is increasingly useful.' The Colonel's eyes gleamed; he seemed to be enjoying some private joke. 'If no tutor has yet been engaged, there's a man I know who would be an excellent choice. You could do no better than employ him. He'll agree with your democratic instincts, too, I dare say. Shall I ask him to call on you?'

'That would be kind. I can be found at the Bogolyubov Palace. My family has rooms there.'

'Good. Well, *au revoir*, Count Belkin. Perhaps our paths may cross in Petersburg. I shall be here for a few months, I think.' Colonel Kalinin turned and walked away.

Vasily looked up ahead. The *Virtuous* was still making good progress. They passed the wooden Tolbukhin lighthouse, and within half an hour, the ship was reaching along the passage that skirted the edge of Kotlin island. The crew dropped anchor between the three-tiered wooden fort that stood high out of the water and the citadel on the shore. A confusion of masts and shrouds rose above the Merchants' Harbour.

The noise of construction, sawing and hammering, sounded across the sea. There were signs of breaches in some of the wharves, damage caused by the great flood which, eight months before, had inundated not just Kronstadt, but also the city of St Petersburg itself.

He watched as vessels came and went through the busy waters. Lighters and skiffs clustered around the large ships anchored offshore. After an hour or so, a boat approached the *Virtuous* and a group of customs officials boarded. Later, another vessel arrived, delivering two dark-uniformed officers, the pilots who would take the ship the last thirty *versts* up the river.

Vasily was content to contemplate the scene until late morning when Yakov came looking for him. The captain needed their passports and papers to complete the formalities of arrival. Reluctantly, Vasily took one last breath of fresh air before following his servant below.

When Vasily walked up on deck the next morning, the *Virtuous* lay at anchor in the Neva River. Across the wide expanse of water, the buildings of St Petersburg glistened, floating bright tablets of colour above the granite embankments. The spire of the new Admiralty blazed gold against the sky. The heavy walls of the fortress today shone, innocuous in the sunshine.

An hour or so later, a lighter came to ferry the passengers to the Customs House. The captain was on deck. He had made his bows and farewells, relieved, perhaps, to be disembarking the more troublesome part of his cargo. Colonel Kalinin stood at the top of the gangway, his face shaded by his cap. He was observing the passengers as he had in Stettin and nodded to Vasily as he passed.

Vasily climbed down into the boat while Yakov organised their boxes. As the oarsmen pulled away towards Vasilyevsky Island, he took off his hat and looked up at the comfortable curved bulk of the *Virtuous*, briefly regretting the end of the voyage. Kalinin still lingered on the deck. He seemed to be watching them depart. His eyes remained fixed on the boat as it crossed the light-dappled water and reached the embankment below the columns of the Exchange.

It was a short drive to the palace. They crossed over Saint Isaac's bridge towards Senate Square and headed at a spirited trot to a smaller thoroughfare nearby. The city air carried a taint of fetid water. The wide streets and vast squares were almost deserted. Most of the gentry were away, gone to their country estates or dachas in the nearby countryside. The carriage pulled up outside a russet stone mansion with square windows faceted in white, granite columns and a balcony above the portico.

Vasily banged on the roof. 'You can take us into the yard if you like, Grigory.'

'The Prince says you're to go in through the front door today, sir,' the coachman replied.

Vasily looked up to the familiar varnished doors, two steps up from the dusty pavement. A liveried doorman pulled them open. 'Welcome home, Vasily Nikolayevich, sir!'

It felt cool in the small vestibule. Vasily ran up the flight of stone steps that rose in a great sweep to the entrance hall on the first floor. Dmitry Vladimirovich, Prince Bogolyubov, was waiting, two small dogs bouncing at his feet. He embraced Vasily, patting him on the back.

'Well, Vasya! Home from your travels! I want to hear all about them.' He held Vasily at arm's length. 'You look healthy enough!' His round head nodded under his sparse greying hair. 'You've filled out a bit. Not a bad thing. Not any taller, though!'

Vasily laughed. 'Sadly, sir, you're right. But I'm indeed very well and pleased to be home.'

Behind him, he could hear Yakov shouting instructions, and the slap of feet on stone as house serfs ran down the steps to fetch up his boxes. He looked up at the benign face of his family's benefactor. They embraced once again.

'Come along!' The Prince took his arm.

Trailed by paws skittering on the wooden floor, they walked through the anteroom and along the enfilade of formal reception rooms. Nothing had changed: the clean-lined French furniture; the gilt mirrors, some slightly crazed; the deep-pleated drapery at the windows, all once opulent, now slightly faded. The Prince paused when they reached the divan room and sat down. Vasily knew he wouldn't escape until Dmitry Vladimirovich had told him the family news.

'You know that Alexander Petrovich, your mother, and most of your servants, are at Dubovnoye on the estate?'

'Yes, my uncle wrote to me in Berlin.'

'The estate manager wants to retire, so Alexander went down to meet a possible replacement. He's written that your grandmother is well, still supervising everything in her particular way.'

'I'm pleased to hear that. I hope she received my letters from abroad.'

'Oh, and your sister, Katya, is expecting a baby! She and Prince Polunin are out at Tsarskoe Selo this summer. You might like to go to visit them? The Court is there, as usual, of course, but the Emperor himself is travelling in the south.'

'I don't think so, sir.'

'No, well, I can't blame you. What other news is there? You know that your uncle has been promoted again? He's now a State Councillor. We have to treat him with great respect! And your mother has written to warn us that some female cousin of hers is coming to town with her niece to stay with Katya. I think the aim is to introduce the girl into society...'

The Prince continued for some minutes.

'I'll leave you here to get settled in, Vasya.' He rose to his feet. 'I've sent two men up to look after you. I hope one of them has aired your rooms. I want to hear every detail of your trip. You did well with your purchases, by the way. I was very pleased with everything. The drawings and paintings, and the Sèvres for your sister, arrived safely. No rips or breakages. I've got everything out downstairs; we can take a close look after dinner.'

'I should like that, sir.'

'I much admired your portrait that we commissioned in Paris. It's a good likeness. I wanted to keep it myself but thought we'd better hang it in your uncle's study. You've got some work of your own to show me, I hope?'

'Yes, sir, I've produced a good deal. Mainly drawings, but some watercolours, too.'

'Good, excellent!'

Vasily watched the bulky form of Dmitry Vladimirovich retreat towards the staircase, the dogs at his heels. It was good to see him again. Since the Prince had taken Vasily and his mother and sister into his house after Vasily's father had died, he had treated them like his own kin. Without this support from his uncle's friend, their life would have been far less comfortable.

Clicking open a door concealed in the panelling of the divan room, he entered his family's apartment, which occupied a wing at the back of the house. He felt dispirited and a little disorientated as he walked into the silent hallway, but it was true: it was good to be home.

Colonel Pavel Kalinin stood on the deck of the Virtuous, his eyes fixed on the lighter that had taken Vasily Nikolayevich ashore. He roused himself. He must ensure that the official boxes and dispatches from London would be taken directly to the Ministry of Foreign Affairs. Once that business was complete, he, too, could disembark.

The Colonel's St Petersburg home occupied a bright maze of rooms on the upper floor of a former merchant's residence. The house stood on the English Embankment and looked out over the ever-changing river.

'Is my sister here?' Kalinin asked the doorman as he arrived.

'No, Colonel, sir, she's out with her maid. She should be back presently.'

He ordered a bath to be prepared and then drank tea as he scanned the newssheets. Making his way to his study, he surveyed the orderly piles of paperwork on his desk. He glanced at the communications from his steward on his estates in the south. The stack was interleaved with notes in Irina's clear hand. His personal letters remained unopened. There were not many, and he set them to one side. There was nothing from the Ministry; a junior officer had visited regularly to deal with any official papers that came in his absence. He sent a servant to seek the man out, as he had some work for him.

He walked to the window and looked over the river. Upstream, beyond the bridge, near the fortress, he could make out the bare spars of the *Virtuous*. Turning back to his desk, he picked up his pen and absently tapped the nib on the metal sand tray.

What was it young Belkin had said? Something about making a mark on the world, making a difference… something like that. Perhaps he could help him to fulfil his wish, broaden his horizons a little. He would never have guessed that the amiable, rather unguarded, young man was the nephew of that dry old operator Alexander Petrovich. It would be amusing to ruffle the officious bureaucrat's feathers and take some small revenge for sins of the past.

For several minutes, the Colonel closed his eyes as if in meditation, then, drawing a sheet of paper towards him and frowning a little, he dipped his pen and started to make notes.

When the officer from the Ministry arrived, Kalinin relieved him of some paperwork and told him to look out for the dispatches that had been conveyed from the ship. He then picked up his jottings. 'I want you to arrange some surveillance. Here are the details. The man in question has just returned home from abroad. He lives at the Bogolyubov Palace, close to St Isaac's. I'd like him followed for the next couple of weeks. That should be enough. I want daily reports, possibly more frequent. Have the agent come to me today for full instructions. That will be all for now.'

Kalinin picked up his pen once again.

The English Embankment
From Colonel Pavel Kalinin to Thomas Maltby Esq.
15 July 1825

My dear Maltby,

I hope that my letter finds you well and that you are continuing to be profitably employed here in Russia. I am mindful that it is a little while since we had news from you in London and hope that you are not in any way indisposed. I arrived in Petersburg this morning, having taken ship from England. I expect to be in Russia for several months.

The reason for my immediate approach is that I have found a potential student for you. He is the young Count Vasily Nikolayevich Belkin, a member of a respectable, but now somewhat reduced, old Moscow family. His uncle, Alexander Petrovich, is a senior officer in the Interior Ministry holding the rank of State Councillor. The family appears to be under the protection of Prince Bogolyubov, a man of substance, known to be without close family and a former Senator. Vasily Nikolayevich has prospects of a post in the diplomatic service (which I think can only have been secured through the influence of the Prince).

When we met on the boat, the Count told me that it has been suggested to him that he should improve his English prior to taking up his position.

I do not know how you are placed at present, but I would be very obliged if you could help in this matter. Belkin lives at the Bogolyubov Palace, and I suggest you call on him there. He seems to be of an open disposition, presentable, and, as far as I could tell on short acquaintance, well educated, but probably innocent of any political sensibility.

My sister Irina is here with me. We can always be contacted through the apartment on the English Embankment, although we shall be spending what

remains of the summer at a house we have taken on the
Okhta River. Perhaps you will be able to visit us there?
I remain as always, Thomas... etc.
Pavel.

Two days later, Vasily woke with a powerful headache. Opening his eyes, he took in the angular form of his manservant, blinked, and then closed them again. He had been disturbed by the sound of Yakov opening the curtains. Now, it seemed he was rearranging items on the washstand to make room for his hot water. The clatter of shaving equipment was unbearable.

He groaned. 'Go away, Yakov.'

'It's ten o'clock, Vasily Nikolayevich, sir, and there's someone downstairs asking for you.'

'Who?'

'I don't rightly know, sir. Some foreigner.'

'Didn't he give his name?'

'The doorman couldn't catch it. Like I say, he's a foreigner.'

'A card? Did he leave a card?'

'Oh yes, sir!'

Vasily rolled over, sat up, took the card and squinted at it. 'Thomas Maltby Esq.' he read, and, turning it over, read the same name in Roman script.

'Don't know him. Tell him to go away.'

'Are you sure?'

It occurred to Vasily that the name was English. Oh, God! It was the English tutor. The Colonel had been as good as his word. He couldn't meet him in his current state. He needed to make a good impression.

'Ask the butler to present my compliments to Mr Maltby, Yakov. And to tell him that I regret that I am currently unavailable, but if he could return at say, at say…'

'Tomorrow?'

'No, no, I must meet him today. Ask him to come back at two. I should be able to pull myself together by then. Have someone bring up breakfast in an hour or so, and some kvass too.'

'Very good, sir.'

'And close the curtains!'

Vasily slumped back onto the pillow. His head was spinning. Perhaps he should have ordered his breakfast now? He dozed. Too hot, he threw back his sheet. Later, too cold, he pulled it back again.

Last night had been almost worth the current misery. The day after his arrival, he had sent out cards to find friends who might still be in town. He had only received a couple of replies but both were from men who promised to be good company. One of them, Mikhail Stenovsky, the older brother of a former schoolfriend, had suggested they visit an eating house that they had patronised in the past.

Vasily, in a tailcoat recently purchased in Paris, felt outshone when Mikhail Alexandrovich appeared, tall and glowing in the white, red and gold uniform of a cornet of the Chevalier Guard. They embraced warmly and admired one another, and then, having strolled for a while among the reduced crowds on Nevsky Prospekt, they sat down in an eating house. Wine was ordered.

'I'm surprised to find you in town, Mikhail,' said Vasily. 'I thought you all had to be present and correct at summer camp at Krasnoye Selo.'

'I'm long overdue some leave. I'm staying with my mother. She's decided to stay in town this summer.'

'And the rest of your family?'

'All well, as far as I can tell. My older brother Nikita is

now a captain on the General Staff, but he's on our estates at present, dealing with an issue with the serfs. Ivan's fighting in the Caucasus, which seems to suit him. It wouldn't suit me.'

'So how is army life?'

Mikhail shrugged. 'Much as I was told to expect in peacetime. Drill or riding school in the morning, dinner with the Colonel on Thursdays. It can get a bit tedious if I'm honest. I'm not a great enthusiast for gambling or uproarious drinking bouts, and I'm not really looking for a wife. Alek, who's joining us, wants me to broaden my horizons by joining some literary group. But what about you, Vasya? What are your plans now?'

'I'm hoping to join the foreign service. Dmitry Vladimirovich and my uncle think that would be the best course for me.'

'So you'll be going abroad again?'

'Yes, in time, although probably not until next year.'

Mikhail tipped his chair back; his smile was sardonic. 'Well, you'll certainly make a charming diplomat, but how will you feel about representing the official face of Russia? Won't it embarrass you?'

'Embarrass me?'

'Can you really stomach championing a country that enslaves the majority of its own people or whose ruler can practically do what he pleases?'

Vasily was taken aback. He'd thought he was coming out to enjoy himself, not to defend his choice of career. 'I'm not sure it's much different from being a soldier, and at least diplomats aren't generally required to slaughter people.' He realised that he sounded irritated and defensive.

Mikhail leant forwards and, shaking his head, took his arm. 'I'm sorry, Vasya. I didn't mean to put you on the spot. I'm not in the best of moods, actually. I'm distracted by this problem on the estate.'

'Where, in the south?' The Stenovsky family had extensive land holdings across Russia.

'No, on the estate near Moscow. As I said, Nikita has gone to deal with it. I don't think he can achieve much, however.' Mikhail reached for his glass. 'I won't bore you with the detail, but one of our girls recently agreed to marry a house serf from a neighbouring estate. We gave our permission reluctantly. Her family are good people, they seemed pleased enough with the match, but my mother was concerned. Our neighbour has a reputation for taking advantage of his female serfs… you know the sort of thing I mean… but we didn't think that would extend to claiming the right to enjoy a bride prior to her wedding. Our girl put up fierce resistance. The prospective husband was whipped for objecting. He was badly hurt; it's possible he won't survive.'

'Surely the police… surely they should act?'

'You know, or should know, that the police rarely intervene. A landowner can deal with serfs more or less as he likes. It was arguable that our neighbour didn't intend to kill the man. In any event, the incident hasn't been deemed sufficiently important to warrant investigation.'

'So, what can be done?'

'Not much. Nikita is aiming to get the dowry, such as it was, returned to the girl's family, if that proves necessary. We'll probably end up compensating both families ourselves. My brother will report the matter to the Governor's office, complain to the Marshal of Nobility. It's possible, given our neighbour's reputation, the authorities may intervene if there's danger of a public scandal, but that's not expected.' Mikhail paused. 'But don't you see, Vasya: there must be something wrong with a government – with a society – that tolerates such things. We're in the nineteenth century, not the Dark Ages.'

Mikhail poured another glass of wine. He leant back and ran his fingers through his light brown hair. 'Anyway, enough of that. I'm very pleased to see you and really don't want to burden you with our problems. Tell me something of your travels.'

Vasily spoke for a while about his tour of Europe, his German classes in Leipzig, the art he had seen in Paris, and the music in Vienna. Then, quite suddenly, Mikhail interrupted him.

'I envy you your trip, Vasya. You must have met interesting people, enjoyed some fascinating debate – learned a good deal.' He glanced about the room as if concerned about being overheard, and continued with urgency: 'Tell me quickly, before we're disturbed: what do foreigners think about Russia these days? What do they say about us?'

Vasily took a few moments to reply.

'I think that we're still respected abroad, due mainly to admiration for our army. I'm not sure how much people are exercised about other matters.' Vasily didn't know what more to say. In truth, while on his travels, political issues hadn't troubled him.

Mikhail was silent for a moment. Draining his glass, he pushed it forward for more. He was setting a good pace for a man who claimed to drink moderately. He was about to speak again, but then Alek arrived, followed almost immediately by two of his friends.

More wine was ordered. One bottle led to another. The current state of Russia was set aside.

The following afternoon, Vasily finally had his interview with Thomas Maltby, the English tutor. Afterwards, he went to look for Yakov. Mikhail's story about the serf girl had disturbed him. Unlike the estates belonging to the Stenovskys, the Belkin lands were no longer extensive. The birth of too many sons in previous generations had diluted Peter the Great's original generosity, and Vasily's family now owned a few hundred rather than thousands of serfs. He had always believed them to be fairly treated, but was he mistaken?

He found Yakov hunched on an upturned bucket in the hallway, the knees of his long legs sticking up past his ears. He was examining pairs of boots, setting some aside for cleaning, others for the cobbler, the rest for the use of the servants.

'I want to talk to you, Yakov. Come into the breakfast room.'

Yakov struggled to his feet. 'Is something wrong, Vasily Nikolayevich, sir? Do you still have a headache?'

'As it happens, yes, but that's not why I want to talk to you. Are you pleased to be home?'

Yakov blew out his cheeks. 'Well, I'm glad to get off that ship...'

Vasily paused. He had failed to reprimand Yakov for disturbing Colonel Kalinin, but it was too late now. 'What's it like coming back to your old duties? You've done pretty much what you pleased over the last year.'

'Don't you worry about me, sir. I'm happy enough. No disrespect, but you're no trouble, and it's just you I have to worry about. It's not a hard job.'

It was true that Yakov seemed to spend a good deal of his time asleep.

'What about your family on the estate? Do you think they're happy?'

'Well, why shouldn't they be, sir? It's where they live. It's where we've always lived. They're better off than many: Father being a woodworker, having a trade. Some of the cousins are happy for me, of course, pleased that I've seen the world, so to speak. But few want to follow me. The only thing they worry about is being taken for the army, unwilling like. That's a worry for most. But when the levy comes, they generally sort things out alright with the help of your uncle, or the steward. So, the few as want to go, go, and them who don't, stay.'

'But don't they care that they're not free to go where they want? Work where they like? Indeed, wouldn't *you* like to be free?'

'What for, sir? I gets my bed and board and generally do what I want: going to the tavern, having a bit of fun with the girls, that sort of thing.'

Vasily felt that he wasn't getting anywhere. He told Yakov Mikhail's story about the serf girl. His servant scratched his head. 'Of course, you do hear of such things. There were stories of a landowner who kept a regular harem near Ryazan, and there was a nasty incident at the Golitsyns a year or so ago, but there would never be anything like that at Dubovnoye… your grandmother wouldn't stand for it, nor Alexander Petrovich. I'm not saying there aren't beatings from time to time, although, when I think about it, I never heard of your father ordering one. He was a good master, kind; people said too kind.'

Yes, his father had been kind. As always, when his name was mentioned, Vasily felt a pang of loss. But Yakov was continuing: 'These days, the manager does send men to the stables, of course, but generally, those who get the whip at Dubovnoye deserve it. Although…'

'Although?'

'Your grandfather wasn't averse to severity when your grandmother was looking the other way, and your great-grandfather was a cruel man, at times. He owned a lot more land, of course. They say he barely visited Dubovnoye. He mainly lived in Moscow. There were tales of some savage punishments in his time, very heavy-handed, if you take my meaning.'

'Oh.'

'But you can't blame yourself for the sins of your forebears, sir.'

'No, I suppose not.' But was that really right? *Should* he feel guilty?

'Don't fret about it, sir. It was a long time ago.'

———

From Thomas Maltby to Colonel Pavel Pavlovich
Kalinin
15 July 1825

My dear Pavel Pavlovich,
Thank you for your note concerning the young Count Belkin.

It took me a little time to catch up with Vasily Nikolayevich, who was unavailable when I first presented my card, but we met two days ago. I have delayed reporting on my visit until I received confirmation of my engagement from the Prince. Lessons will take place on three mornings a week, at least until the New Year.

What are my impressions of the young man? It has to be said that when we met, the Count appeared to be somewhat the worse for wear and, indeed, admitted having taken excessive drink on the preceding evening. I have no way of knowing if his assurance that this was an unusual occurrence was true. Of more interest to you will be the fact that one of his drinking companions was Nikita Stenovsky's brother, Mikhail, with whom I know you are acquainted.

Setting aside the issue of his sobriety, on the whole, I was favourably impressed. Vasily Nikolayevich seems well favoured, courteous, intelligent, and has a sense of humour. He has been well educated, initially at home, and in recent years at the gymnasium. His French is fluent, his German good, and, happily, he does not seem to have any problems speaking or writing his mother tongue. As far as his English is concerned, he appears to have some vocabulary, but his usage and grammar are chaotic. His principal interests seem to lie in music, literature of a romantic rather than polemic nature, and fine art. (As an aside, he is quite an accomplished artist. He showed me some sketches and watercolours produced on his recent travels in Western Europe which were well executed.)

You are right to suggest that the Count is a political innocent. His knowledge of current affairs, national or international, is commensurate with being raised in a household where discussion of such subjects is not encouraged. He does, however, seem to have a lively curiosity, and it may be that he could be persuaded to take a broader interest in matters of a social nature.

But I must warn you, Pavel, and I hope that this will

not offend you, I do not wish to encourage any scheme you may be contemplating to try to instil radical ideas in the young man's head. I have been engaged to teach him English and nothing more. Nonetheless, I have suggested that our lessons, in addition to a return to grammatical foundations, include a little Locke and Byron, and also perhaps some history of the British Constitution. It would be beneficial for the Count to learn something of alternative systems of government.

Although I have made discreet enquiries, I have found it impossible, thus far, to discover any particular reason for the favour shown to the Belkin family by the Prince other than his longstanding and close friendship with his former junior officer at the Ministry, Alexander Petrovich, Vasily's uncle.

At the risk of writing an overlong report, I should add that the Prince's palace is quite extraordinary. It is almost completely unchanged from the time of its construction in the last century. Although somewhat shabby, it is, in its way, magnificent. Moreover, the place is alive with serfs. On my arrival I was greeted by a crowd of flunkeys wishing to relieve me of my hat and stick. The Count and I conducted our meeting in the garden, which lies between the wings of the house and is exceptionally well tended. As we sat down to converse, a fountain set in the middle of the lawn started to play, as if spontaneously. Clearly, the Prince maintains a slave whose sole role is to operate the mechanism on demand. (Doubtless, another slave irons the daily newspaper, and there is another whose only aim in life is to supervise the ice house.)

Finally, Pavel Pavlovich, I should like to thank you

for the introduction to the Count. Business cannot be said to be flourishing at the moment, and the stipend for my services that has been suggested by the Prince is both generous and welcome.

I, too, hope that we can meet in the not too distant future.

I remain, Pavel Pavlovich... etc.

Thomas Maltby

CHAPTER THREE

THE SUMMER DAYS passed slowly in the ochre-painted corridors of the Ministry of the Interior. Those unlucky clerks who found themselves working in July paced the hard floors mopping their sweating brows. In the hallway, a fine longcase clock struck each reluctant hour.

Count Leonid Fedulov, Collegiate Assessor, stood by the window at the top of the main staircase contemplating the greenish surface of the water outside. Some rotting cabbages, debris from the nearby street market, bobbed in the stream, their green heads gently rolling towards the Neva. The corpse of a cat added to the mix.

The Count covered his nose and walked towards his temporary office. It belonged to his superior, Alexander Petrovich Belkin, who, like many of his fellow officers, was away. As he strode through the clerks' room, the few men present stood up, avoiding his eye. Reaching the State Councillor's spacious chamber, he sat down, took off his jacket, and put his feet up on the desk.

He had little work to do. Even subversives, if they had had any sense, had left Petersburg. The files related to his other responsibility, approving the issuance of internal passports, had dwindled to a small pile. He barked for a clerk. An elderly man shuffled to respond. A straggle of grey hair clung to his head, and the cuffs of his uniform were starting to fray.

'You called, Your Honour, sir.'

'Get me the latest police report on the Kolomna matter. And then I'll have tea.'

Reading the report, Fedulov could see that no progress had been made since the beginning of the holiday period. The owners of the illegal printing press and store of uncensored foreign books discovered in a crowded district of the city were, like everyone else, out of town. He marked up the report: the police were to inform him when the men returned, and the operation must be closed down swiftly and the criminals incarcerated. It had been allowed to drag on for too long.

He moved on to his private papers. He paused over one of them, studying the note written in an ill-formed hand.

Leonid Sergeyevich,
I write to inform you that the merchant Muller, despite your assurances that he would be stopped, continues to trade his wares at the port to the detriment of my own business. You have been more than well rewarded to ensure that his activities cease. If this does not happen as we agreed, I will be forced to apply to you for a return of the not inconsiderable funds advanced to you last year.
I remain etc....

Fedulov set the letter to one side and considered it. He had been taking inducements from both parties in the case, a happy situation that had lasted longer than expected. Now, it seemed, he would have to choose between them – decide which of the two men to ruin.

The only other correspondence of interest was a letter written on fine paper. He fingered it, hesitating, and then broke the seal. The contents did not please him. He had been pursuing a young heiress for some time, had believed the courtship to be going well, and had begun to hope that he could put his financial difficulties behind him. But her father now wrote that the match was out of the question. Although he was titled, his substance was not adequate, his rank in the Service not sufficiently elevated, and so on, and so on.

He frowned, and as he did so his eyes involuntarily shifted to contemplate another failed matrimonial endeavour. The sweet features and black curls of Katya, the niece of State Councillor Alexander Petrovich Belkin, taunted him from her portrait on the wall. In frustration, he slapped his hand down hard on his desk, terrifying the elderly clerk, who had crept unnoticed into the room with his tea. Amber liquid sank into the fine grain of the desk.

'Damn you, you idiot,' Fedulov rose to his feet. 'You're not too old to feel my cane!'

The bureaucrat fled.

Fedulov threw back his chair and shrugged on his jacket. He'd had enough for one day. Problems that seemed to be resolved at one moment unravelled the next. Sometimes, it really was too much to bear. Picking up his papers, he walked out of the office, throwing the police report at the head clerk as he passed.

'I'll be back tomorrow,' he said, making for the staircase.

CHAPTER FOUR

A FEW DAYS later, Vasily and Mikhail were sitting in the ruins of the Summer Garden. Last year's flood had destroyed the flower beds, torn up trees by the roots, and felled many of the statues. Nine months later, the wreckage had been cleared. Fine new iron gates were being installed and the paths and fountains reinstated. Nonetheless, the once-decorous park was still a wilderness where shaded spots offered respite from the stale summer air of the streets.

The garden's strict dress code had been relaxed during the restoration, so Vasily wore a loose Russian smock which, he believed, gave him an artistic aura. Mikhail wore civilian clothes, prepared to risk the opprobrium of any passing martinet who expected to see guards officers in uniform at all times. The marble torso of a Greek goddess lay broken in the grass. Vasily, who had sketched the curves of her body, was now adding the stone tracery of her robe. Mikhail lay back, propped on one elbow, and watched the image take shape.

'Mr Maltby seems quite a reasonable sort,' said Vasily, setting his chalk aside. 'He wants us to go beyond transitive verbs and the like. He's suggested reading poetry and studying some history. At the moment, it feels too hot, but I need to make a start. My English is pretty poor.'

'The language is a complete mystery to me,' said Mikhail. He looked more closely at Vasily's sketch. 'That's not at all bad, Vasya. When did you learn to draw? You clearly didn't teach yourself.'

'Any skill I have I owe to Boris Abramovich. He's a serf owned by the Laptevs, my mother's cousins from Oryol. The father of the present Count Laptev discovered that Boris was a talented child and sent him to an art school in Azarmas that admitted serf children. I think he spent six years there.'

'I didn't know such places existed.'

'Not many do. Boris taught me the basics when we visited our cousins for a family wedding. I was about ten at the time. Later, the Prince hired a tutor for me. For a while, I hoped to go to the Academy, but my mother and uncle were set against it.' Vasily looked up and sighed. 'I think that's why the Prince sent me abroad. Although my uncle didn't let me go to Italy.'

'I expect he was worried you wouldn't return,' said Mikhail.

'You're probably right. Anyway, I hope to hear news of Boris soon. Some of our cousins are shortly coming to town.'

'Oh, which ones?'

'The elder daughter of the house, Elizaveta Gavrilovna, and her Aunt Darya. They'll be staying with my sister, Katya. I think the aim is to find the girl a husband. She's quite a catch; the Laptev estates are substantial, and she and her sister can expect decent settlements.'

This caught Mikhail's interest. He sat up. 'Perhaps she'll take to you, Vasya.'

'I don't think so. We were at daggers drawn when we were children.'

A penetrating voice interrupted their conversation. 'Count Belkin! Not just a democrat but a dilettante as well!' The solid figure of Colonel Kalinin was approaching along the shingle path. His companion, a woman, walked among the trees a little way beyond. Mikhail scrambled to his feet, and Vasily followed him. How strange to meet the Colonel again so soon.

'And Cornet Stenovsky, too, I see,' the Colonel continued. 'I won't ask you why you're not in uniform, Mikhail. Well, what a romantic scene!' Kalinin appeared to be in good spirits. He swept his arm out to encompass the destroyed garden as he declaimed, in English:

'Dull is the eye that will not weep to see
Thy walls defaced, thy mouldering shrines removed!'

He leant forward and took Vasily's sketch. He examined it for some time. 'Very good, Vasily Nikolayevich!' he said at last. 'But I wouldn't let the police see it. Life drawing in the Emperor's garden? Mustn't offend public morality, you know!' He laughed and turned to the woman who had caught up with him. 'Look, Irina, a naked goddess!'

The woman reached for the sketchbook.

'How is your respected brother, the Captain?' the Colonel asked Mikhail.

Vasily didn't hear Mikhail's reply, or indeed the ensuing conversation. He looked at the woman as she considered his work. He took in her light muslin dress, old-fashioned, simple and free-flowing; her shoulders covered with a sheer shawl of emerald green; her hair, gold-brown, piled up and falling forward in curls onto her brow; and her skin, her pale, pale skin! Lustrous as the marble goddess that now lay forgotten at his feet. Under the shifting shadows of the trees, she seemed like a water spirit.

She raised her head. Green-grey behind dark lashes, her eyes appraised his face as steadily as they had his sketch. He found he could not speak, and she did not choose to. Why hadn't he dressed more conventionally? He must look like a serf.

But the Colonel was addressing him: 'Vasily Nikolayevich!

Forgive me! How rude. You don't know my sister, of course. Allow me to present Baroness von Steiner. Irina, this is Vasily Nikolayevich, Count Belkin. Met him on the ship. Can't remember now if I told you…terrible manservant…'

'No, I don't think you did.' The Baroness acknowledged Vasily's bow. She smiled briefly, returned his picture, and turned to Mikhail. 'Misha! How good to see you again. Your mother, brothers, all well, I hope? It has been a little while.'

She extended her hand. Mikhail brushed it with his lips. 'Yes, all are well. My mother's in town and intends to remain at least until I rejoin the regiment in a couple of weeks.'

'You must come to our dacha before you return to duty. It's not so far out of town. We'll be going this week and have taken it until the end of the summer.'

'Perhaps you'll bring Count Belkin with you?' the Colonel added.

Vasily glanced at his new friend. How would Mikhail reply?

'I'm sure we'd both like that, wouldn't we, Vasya? Vasily's stuck here in town, needs some country air!'

'Good. We shall send a note to arrange it,' the Colonel said, and then, as an afterthought: 'Has Thomas Maltby been in contact with you, Count?'

'Yes, he has. We'll be meeting shortly to start work.'

'That's excellent! I am sure you'll find him an illuminating guide to the spirit of Britannia! Well, good day to you both. We shall send to you.' The Colonel offered the Baroness his arm, and they walked away towards the river.

'Shut your mouth, Vasya! Something will fly in,' said Mikhail. 'She's perhaps a little mature for you, my friend.'

'Why, isn't she married?'

Mikhail laughed and put his arm around Vasily's shoulder.

'She is married – or has been. She lives apart from her husband now. Come on, finish your drawing, and we'll go for dinner.'

Vasily looked down at his sketchbook, flicking at the paper. 'No, it will do. I'll finish it later.'

Later, at home, Vasily went directly to his room. Taking out his sketchbook, he turned over his half-finished drawing and started a sketch on a fresh sheet. No, he couldn't quite catch her likeness. He threw his chalk down and, tearing out the page, crumpled it and threw it at the wall. He stretched, yawned, and then lay down on the bed. No, he couldn't quite catch her now, but he would, in time.

———

The note from Kalinin came a few days later. Vasily was helping the Prince to rearrange his books. He jumped down from the library steps and broke the seal.

'I'm invited to go out of town for a couple of nights,' he said, failing to hide his excitement.

'That's good,' said the Prince. 'Who invites you?'

'Colonel Pavel Kalinin. The man I met on the boat. You said that you know him.' The Prince seemed to know everybody.

'Yes, that's right, but not well.' The Prince frowned, collecting his thoughts. 'He's in the foreign service so has been abroad a good deal since he left the army. He had a good war record and comes from a decent family, but he has liberal views, I think. And there's something odd about his sister… But you don't have to ask my permission; I don't fret like your uncle. Just don't come back singing *Ça Ira*. By the way, have you commenced your sessions with Mr. Maltby?'

'He came yesterday. We made a start on grammar revision. Well, at least he was polite enough to call it revision, and then we discussed what we might read together. He suggested we start with some Byron.'

The Prince snorted. 'I'd have preferred something more astringent, but it's entertaining enough stuff, and I would guess not too dense. I think we have one or two volumes over there.' The Prince waved towards the bookshelves. 'Where is this summer rental of Kalinin's?'

'Somewhere on the Okhta River. Pavel Pavlovich says the journey will take under two hours and that servants are optional. I may give Yakov a couple of days off. He's worked hard since we got home.'

'You're too soft on him, Vasily, but you know that. If you're going unattended, Grigory will take you in the gig.'

'There's no need. I'm invited with Mikhail Alexandrovich. I can drive us both. No doubt, on the way, he'll give me another lecture on the state of Russia.'

'Oh, yes?'

Vasily picked up another pile of books and started to sort them. 'He's particularly critical of the Emperor,' he said. 'He feels that when Alexander came to the throne, he made a lot of promises to bring about social reform and political change, but that none have been fulfilled.'

'What else does he say about him?'

'That he's allowed his military and diplomatic success to go to his head. Alexander now sees himself as the "Holy Saviour of Europe", and spends too much time abroad, leaving Count Arakcheyev, who, of course, isn't popular, to rule here in Russia.'

'I see.'

Vasily glanced at the Prince. Surely the old conservative would support the cause of the Tsar? But he was mistaken.

'I think much of what Stenovsky says is justified,' the Prince said. 'Alexander, despite appearances, isn't a strong ruler. In fact, I'd say he's something of a waverer. He finds it hard to stand up to his advisers, who, on the whole, benefit from the status quo. And, although in his youth he meant well, his autocratic approach never really changed. Although a wolf moults every year, it still remains grey, as the saying goes.'

The Prince picked up a book and contemplated the gilded characters on the spine. As he found a place for it, he continued: 'Mikhail's views are probably influenced by those of his older brother. For years, Nikita has been rumoured to be involved in various…what should one call them?…discrete informal discussion groups that aspire to bring about social change.' The Prince turned back into the room and frowned. 'But you do know, Vasya, that it would be wise to steer clear of such associations. Membership is, of course, quite illegal, and punishment for those found to be involved invariably harsh. Just be careful not to be sucked into apparently harmless discussion that turns into something else. It can be all too easy to find oneself in trouble.'

'Don't worry, sir. The plan isn't to talk politics. I'll be taking my sketchbook and intend to enjoy the country air.' Vasily flushed; some politics would be unavoidable.

'That's good! The river there is very attractive. You'll find plenty to occupy you.' The Prince smiled.

When they had finished sorting the books, they walked out into the garden. The terriers pursued them. The dogs tore around the lawn, spinning with excitement. The fountain started to play.

CHAPTER FIVE

August 1825 – A House on the Okhta River

VASILY ENJOYED DRIVING the horses. Weary of standing in their stable, the matched pair were fresh and keen to go. In the cool morning air, the open carriage rolled through the empty streets of St Petersburg, their hoofs echoing in the shadows between the sleeping palaces. The surface of the canals glittered under the bridges and light flashed through the gaps between regimented balusters.

Vasily turned into the yard behind the Stenovsky mansion. Mikhail was waiting, leaning against a mounting block in shirtsleeves and strapped trousers, his coat over his shoulder, a wide-brimmed hat on his head. He climbed up into the gig as a servant roped on his box.

They soon left behind the scattered homesteads on the edge of the city. The road became a broad track running between the trees. From time to time, they passed a village, a wooden church, or a large house standing back from the road. Dust flew up behind them. Vasily hoped that Yakov had remembered to pack his clothes brush.

They talked for a while as they travelled and then fell silent. Vasily was content. He and Mikhail had met almost every day since his return home, and he valued this new friendship. At school, Mikhail had been a rather remote figure; now, the difference of two years or so in their ages seemed unimportant.

Mikhail's voice cut across his thoughts. 'This is where we turn off, I think.'

They could soon see the gleam of the river in the distance. A little later, they pulled up behind a substantial wooden house surrounded by outbuildings. Dogs came bounding from all directions; chickens fled.

The Colonel strode out to greet them. 'How was the journey?' he asked. Not waiting for a reply, he led them inside.

The bright hallway rose to a glass-domed ceiling; a white-railed gallery ran round the walls. They walked through to an extended living room that, in turn, gave onto a veranda. The river was visible beyond. A fortepiano stood in the corner with a music stand beside it. The furniture was sparse but comfortable.

'Well, this is a fine place!' Mikhail said.

'Yes, we were lucky to secure it,' the Colonel said. 'In the past, we've taken a house on Kamenny Island, but last year's flood ruled that out. I think most of what wasn't tied down there was swept away. This house is almost new. The only drawback is that we're somewhat further from town.'

Vasily looked around. Where was Irina Pavlovna? He scanned the garden. A woman was walking up from the river, a sheaf of greenery in her arms and a little dog at her heels. It must be her. Yes, he could see her bright hair. Now she was climbing the stairs, rising from the grass like Venus from the sea. More substantial than the woman he remembered and imagined, she was captivating all the same.

Setting the foliage aside, she stretched out her hands and took theirs. 'Misha! Vasily Nikolayevich! Welcome, welcome. I'm so pleased that you could both come. You must be hungry, thirsty.' She walked to a small table and rang a bell. 'What would you like? We have cordial, lemonade, kvass, vodka, champagne… It's possibly a little early for champagne, but there's to be no formality. You're here to enjoy yourselves; you must come and go as you please. The river is safe for swimming, there are plenty of books. Do either of you play an instrument?'

'I'm afraid not,' Mikhail said, 'but Vasily will sing.'

Vasily was not at all sure that he would sing. He felt awkward and tongue-tied as Mikhail kept up a steady flow of chatter: his family, the regiment, the weather.

He escaped and found his room. It was large and looked over the back of the house. The Kalinin's summer rental was like a child's toy. He could see a cow and some goats in the paddock, stables to the right, and what seemed to be a dairy and kitchen block to the left. The gig had disappeared, but a horse's head nodded above a stable door. A groom was carrying a net of hay.

He turned to unpack his box, but it had already been emptied by invisible hands. The clothes brush was on a chest. Yakov had, after all, remembered to pack it. As he swept away the dust of travel, he realised that he missed his servant. It was strange and lonely without his constant presence. What should he do now? Perhaps he should read, lose himself in a book. But he certainly wouldn't attract the interest of Irina Pavlovna by loitering in his room. He looked around for his sketchbook and, sliding it into his satchel, set off to explore.

The house seemed deserted. He walked down the grass to the riverbank where he wandered for a while and then sat down to draw. Later, with more determined steps, he returned to the bottom of the garden but halted among the shady fronds of a willow.

Irina Pavlovna sat on a swing that hung from the branch of a tree. She was humming a tune as she swayed back and forth, her skirts billowing out, then settling around her legs.

He watched, transfixed, as she moved through the air, her breasts rising and falling. How perfect she was, and how he longed for her! Should he approach? But perhaps he should be cautious. Why wasn't she living with her husband, the Baron? What had happened to him? Perhaps she wouldn't welcome being disturbed by a man she barely knew.

At last, he overcame his scruples and stepped forward, but he was too late. Pavel Kalinin was walking down the steps from the terrace. Irina allowed the swing to slow, and Kalinin, catching one of the ropes, bent and spoke to her. She rose and took his arm. They walked together towards the house, and, when they reached the terrace, her brother turned to face her. As he spoke again, she laughed, reached up to stroke his cheek, and slipped away into the shadows. Kalinin called something after her, then followed.

What had they said to one another? What joke had they shared? He lingered a while longer in the leaf-patterned shade and then stirred himself. There were signs of activity up at the house. It would soon be time for dinner. Company was expected. He would probably be required to sing.

———

The following day, the small party gathered on the veranda in the late afternoon. Champagne was served. Pavel Kalinin was in an expansive mood. 'How have you all occupied yourselves today?' he asked. 'The house has been very quiet.'

'I went to visit our neighbours,' said Irina. They made me very welcome.'

'I don't know why you spend your time making calls, Irène,' Kalinin said. 'The whole point of being here is to get away from society. You may as well have stayed in town. For

God's sake, don't invite them here.'

The Colonel turned to Mikhail and Vasily. 'And what did you get up to? Something more productive than social calls, I hope!'

'It depends on what you mean by productive,' Vasily said. 'We walked a good way up and down the river. We swam where it widens upstream. The water was chill though, even though it's nearly the end of summer.'

'Yes, the river here always retains the breath of the ice, I think.'

'When we got back, I took out my chalks while Misha buried himself in some political tract. He's too bookish to be a soldier.' Mikhail said that he agreed.

Kalinin refilled their glasses. 'At least you have plenty of time on your hands for study, Misha. It's good to know that at least some of our guards officers can read. Now let's eat.'

After dinner, it was cool on the veranda and the Colonel ordered that a brazier be lit. They sat drinking tea and talking as they watched the evening light fade over the grass.

'You took part in the final assault on Paris during the war, Colonel?' Vasily hoped to stimulate some old war stories and was curious to know more about his host, who, while genial, seemed reticent about himself.

'Yes, yes indeed, Vasily.' Kalinin leant forward and, resting his elbows on his knees, continued: 'I was a lieutenant colonel in the Horse Artillery when we invaded France in the winter of 13/14. I was twenty-eight or so. Paris was taken in March. I joined up after Austerlitz, and, once the French invaded Russia, we saw a lot of action. Promotion was rapid in those days, for obvious reasons.'

'Unlike now,' Mikhail said, swirling the dregs of tea around his cup.

'Yes Misha, but you do have to avoid being killed while you're waiting. I was lucky. A few bullet holes in my coat, an occasional singed trouser leg, but something, or someone, in heaven protected me. I was with Andrey Nikitin's brigade in the later years of the war, and we had a hot time of it, at Borodino in particular. The Commander, Kutuzov, gave orders not to abandon the guns until the enemy was sitting on them. At Borodino, they very nearly were.

'People today think that after the great victory at Leipzig, the advance on Paris was easy, but that wasn't so. We crossed the border in January. I shall never forget the great 'Hurrah!' that went up when Russian feet touched French soil. The men were jubilant. The enemy was getting a dose of its own medicine, you see.'

Vasily's eyes were drawn to Irina. She was looking down at her skirts, smoothing a tassel on her gown. She had obviously heard Pavel Pavlovich's war stories before.

'We were surprised to encounter no resistance at all for a while, but Napoleon always showed great resilience. He soon pulled his army together and the fighting, when it came, was tough, casualties high.

'Take La Rothière, Napoleon's first defeat on French soil. That really was a struggle! We engaged in a snowstorm. I'll never forget it. The gunners' beards were stiff with frost. My men were blue with cold. At times, we couldn't see the enemy at all, despite the fact that we were placed virtually in the lap of their front line. Towards the end of the day, we were fighting in a blizzard. It was quite extraordinary to see great snowflakes mingling with the thick grey smoke. We fought on beyond sunset and all degenerated into chaos. In the end, though, the battle was reckoned a victory for the allies. We captured a large number of French guns, which they could ill afford to lose by that stage.

'Napoleon had his successes, too, of course, and, given the size of the army opposing him, they really were among the most brilliant of his career. As in the past, he seemed to be everywhere at once! The Prussians and Austrians were ready to give up. It was only the determination of our Emperor, Alexander, that kept us pressing on to the capital.'

'I didn't realise that,' said Vasily.

'Yes, it really was Alexander's victory. It wasn't surprising that, later, he believed he had saved the civilised world. The French National Guard lined the streets as we rode into Paris. The people had had enough of war. They were exhausted by it. The crowds cheered when we entered the city. 'Long live Alexander! Long live the Bourbons!'

As Vasily sat on the edge of his chair, willing Kalinin to continue, he looked across at Mikhail, illuminated by the flicker of the fire. He was absorbed by the story, a slight frown of concentration on his lean face. His long legs were thrust out before him, his arms resting on them loosely. The Colonel reached for a bottle of wine. He called for more fuel for the brazier and some glasses. Vasily's attention was drawn back to Irina. Her eyes were fixed in apparent fascination on the spot where his carelessly tied cravat revealed the skin of his throat. Catching his breath, his hand lifted involuntarily. She looked up, and as they held one another's gaze, she smiled and pushed back a curl. When he returned her smile, she seemed to shiver a little. She rose from her seat and went inside. When she returned with a shawl, Pavel Pavlovich was speaking once again.

'Like many young officers, I thought Paris the centre of

the world. For us at that time, everything worthwhile seemed to come from there: ideas, fashion, the language we spoke every day. And it fulfilled our expectations: the wonderful shops, the Louvre, Notre Dame, theatres, the opera. Mind you, it wasn't all pleasure. We spent hours drilling for the inevitable series of parades. I suppose the idea was to keep us out of trouble and impress the French.'

The Colonel rose and stirred the brazier; the logs glowed, and sparks flew away over the dark grass.

'People say that it was their time in Paris that inspired many young officers to embrace ideas of equality and fraternity, of republicanism and democracy; all those notions that hardly sit comfortably with our Russian system. But it wasn't just breathing the magical air of France that instilled these notions in us. Many of us had already been introduced to them by our foreign tutors at home, and we knew about the forbidden books.

'Also, although France seemed magnificent, it was in many ways no better, and in some ways worse, than what we knew at home. The poverty and begging in the streets and the overcrowding in the slums of the city were shameful. I expect you saw that when you were in Paris recently, Vasily?'

'Yes, it was surprisingly squalid in places. Our peasants' living conditions in many ways seem better than theirs,' he said.

'No, to my mind attitudes changed for another reason,' the Colonel continued. 'Army officers during those years of the war were often young, and most were from relatively well-to-do families. Here, at home, we lived in the artificial world that we enjoy today. Not much has changed. We still send our children to elite schools or employ foreign tutors at home. The vast majority of us depend on the service of bonded slaves: hundreds, sometimes thousands, of souls on the larger estates. I own plenty myself, of course, and I doubt if you know how many serve your family, Mikhail.'

Mikhail shook his head and looked at his feet.

'In peacetime, we live alongside these people every day,' Kalinin continued. 'But apart from the occasional conversation with our house serfs, our coachmen and huntsmen, we rarely get close to them or understand them. During the war, we experienced something entirely different. The common soldiers, with whom we now lived cheek by jowl, were suddenly transformed into human beings and became ends in themselves rather than a means to an end. And there was something else. We were fighting together for a common cause. We were all Russians, and all, whether nobleman or serf, were prepared to fight and die for our motherland.'

Kalinin fell silent.

'But the soldiers got no recognition for their sacrifice,' said Mikhail. 'It was shameful. Our Russian veterans were either sent to join the Internal Guard, often in distant garrisons, or just returned to their villages. They often weren't fit to work on the land. Or worse, they were expected to suffer the cruelties of the military settlements.'

'Yes, that's true,' said the Colonel. 'Instead of granting them their freedom, as many of them had expected, Alexander told the men that God would thank them for their services to Russia. They received nothing or, indeed, less than nothing from him.

'The end of the war was hard for us officers, too. Many of us felt that for two years or more, we had been part of the unfolding of history. Now we had to come back to Petersburg and kick our heels while old men advocated repression and censorship to reinforce the status quo. Many of us felt ashamed and unhappy when we realised that nothing would change. I was lucky to be in a position to leave the army, join the diplomatic service and go abroad.'

'But leaving is no answer,' said Vasily, heat rising to his cheeks. 'People know that the way we live here needs to change. I think even the Prince, my benefactor, knows that, and there are few more conservative than he. But what can actually be done? I know from Misha that...' He stopped, not sure how much it was wise to disclose. The Colonel was, after all, despite his liberal views, an officer of the state.

'What is to be done?' the Colonel asked. 'That's a complex question and probably one for another day. It's getting late, and we've already been to Paris and back. Yes, Vasily, we shall certainly consider the possible solutions to the problem, but not tonight.'

Kalinin yawned and rose to his feet. As he raked over the burnt embers, he asked: 'At what time do you two plan to leave tomorrow?'

'Dmitry Vladimirovich expects me home for dinner,' said Vasily. 'So around two o'clock, I think.'

'Yes, that's good. I'll make sure your gig is ready. I need to speak with you in the morning, Misha, about that business of your brother's.'

'Well, goodnight to you, Vasily Nikolayevich.' Irina was extending her hand. 'Perhaps I may look at your sketches in the morning?'

Here was progress! 'I should be honoured!' He bent to kiss her hand.

A servant was called to dim the lights, and the house soon fell silent.

CHAPTER SIX

A BOATHOUSE STOOD on the riverbank. The next morning, Vasily sat on the grass beside it trying to recreate the view downstream. Irina's white dog had accompanied him and was rootling nearby in some foliage. The sketch was not turning out well; he couldn't make the image live. He set down his chalk and frowned, trying to see the view afresh. Silver-green leaves of willow disconsolately traced the surface of the river. A water rat emerged from a hole in the sandy bank and, whiskers gleaming, plunged into the slow stir of the stream.

He had deliberately placed himself in full view of the veranda, but she hadn't appeared. Where was she? Had she really intended to come this morning? A bird carped among the thin reeds. He sat by the river for a little longer and then packed away his chalks and sketchpad. As he walked up to the house, he could hear the voices of Mikhail and the Colonel, who had disappeared after breakfast and were still deep in conversation.

The living room was cool. A pile of periodicals lay on the table. Vasily picked up the *Polar Star*; it was last year's edition. Taking the journal outside into the warmth of the terrace, he scanned the contents page but then set it down. Something moved behind him and he turned. Irina stood in the shaded doorway. She wore a loose pale-green gown, sheer, not quite translucent.

'I'm sorry that I missed you at breakfast,' she said. 'I find that I sleep a good deal here. It's either ennui, the country air, or a combination of the two.'

She yawned and settled in one of the low round-backed chairs.

'You get bored here?' he asked, sitting down opposite her. 'I find that hard to believe.'

'Sometimes, although usually I can find enough to divert me. I'm particularly solitary at present because my companion is visiting her family in Austria. We don't entertain a great deal here or in town, however. My brother is rather particular about the society that he keeps. Those invited to our home are generally connected with his work.'

'But you go into society yourself?'

'Sometimes, but there are those who won't receive me because of my ambiguous status. I thought Misha might have told you...'

'No. At least, he didn't go into detail. He's not a gossip.'

'Yes, I know that. He's a kind friend, as is his brother Nikita. Their mother can be less kind. But the truth is, Vasily, that the title of Baroness may be a necessary, but not a sufficient, condition for acceptance in the best circles. There's a general expectation that some sort of baron, dead or alive, plays a part in the story. When it comes to my particular fairy tale, the absence of that baron generally leads people to the worst kind of speculation.'

Vasily remained silent. He had been looking out towards the river, but now he turned towards her. She had spoken lightly, but her delicate features were tight; she seemed close to tears. Could he, should he, try to comfort her? What could he say? But now she sat upright and attempted a smile.

'Oh dear! What a poor hostess I am. You don't want to listen to my problems. Taking all into account, they're quite trivial. Now tell me something about yourself, and then I'd like to see what you've drawn while you've been here. When we met in the Summer Garden, I much admired your stone goddess.'

'I managed to produce a couple of decent pictures yesterday, but this morning's work was a washout, I'm afraid. I do have one or two other things upstairs.'

'Yes, I'd like to look at them, but I'm curious to know why my brother invited you here. He does nothing without good reason. Trying to discover his motives is always one of my keenest challenges.'

'I thought he'd invited me to keep Mikhail company, but, of course, we did meet on the boat from Stettin.'

'You're going into the foreign service, I think,' she said. 'I expect that's the reason for his interest. You're lucky to have the chance of a position. After an army commission, work in an embassy abroad would probably be the first choice for the flock of under-occupied young men around town.'

Vasily shrugged. 'Well I'm fortunate that I have a benefactor with some influence,' he said. 'My family has a long record of public service. I suppose between them they know how to manage these things.'

Vasily recounted as much of his life story as he thought likely to amuse her. She seemed to have recovered from her despondency. 'So you were only a child when your father died,' she said. 'That must have been hard for you and your sister.'

'It was. My uncle and the Prince have done everything possible over the years to make up for our loss, but I still miss him. I remember him very clearly. He always had time for me.' Vasily rubbed the back of his neck and looked down.

'Yes. It is hard to lose a loved one,' she said.

'Our Moscow house was completely destroyed in the great fire,' he continued. 'Although we received some compensation, my uncle couldn't afford to rebuild it. I suppose we're lucky to still have Dubovnoye, the estate outside Moscow. The compensation payments paid off most of the debts there, which was something.'

'Do you go there often?'

'Usually every summer, although not this year, of course, or last, since I was abroad. My uncle and mother are there now, and my grandmother lives there permanently. I'd like to settle there, too, eventually. Life in the country would suit me, I think. I could paint, of course, and there's plenty that could be done to improve the estate and the lives of the people who live there.'

'But you must make your mark in the world first, I suppose?'

'Yes, of course. At least, a period of service to the state is what's expected.'

A servant brought tea. The murmur of voices from above continued.

'Time's getting on,' she said. 'It seems that Pavel and Misha have a lot to discuss. Go and get your work. We'll put the sketches on the dining table.'

Vasily had several pictures to show. She sat at the long table, while he stood behind her setting each down one by one, She claimed to admire them, but was she just being polite?

She lingered over the final drawing, fingering its edge, saying nothing. He breathed in her fragrance, sweet lemons and delicate soap. A single curl of red-gold hair clung to the back of her neck. Dare he touch it? He stretched out his hand, then hesitated. She turned her head and looked up. Should he lean forward and kiss her? But now she rose, pushing his arm to one side, then laughed and carelessly ruffled his hair. He felt a twist of irritation, felt his cheeks flush. She thought he was a child! Swivelling round, he briskly collected up his drawings. Behind him, her shoes tapped in retreat over the wooden floor. She had gone.

He stared down at the polished tabletop. The house seemed very still. But then the silence was broken. Mikhail and Kalinin were clattering down the stairs into the hall.

He heard Irina's voice: 'It must be past noon. You will both need some food before you leave.' She reentered the living room and rang the bell.

Will you be able to visit us again, Misha? Vasily?' Kalinin asked. 'We'll be here for a week or two yet, and I have an interesting guest coming next Friday.'

'I regret I must return to my company on Tuesday,' Mikhail replied. 'But I expect Vasya would be pleased to come if you'll have him. Who's your guest?'

'I've invited Kondraty Ryleev to dine; the literary man, the poet. He and his wife are staying nearby with an acquaintance of ours. Some say the man embodies the spirit of the age. I should like to find out.'

Did he want to return? Just at that moment, Vasily wished the ground would open up and swallow him. He forced himself to smile and said nothing. Kalinin continued: 'I'll be sending the carriage to town to pick up Gretchen, Irina's companion, later next week, and you'd be very welcome to accompany her, Vasily. In fact, it would be kind if you would do so.'

'I can't commit myself at present, Colonel. My uncle and mother are expected back from the country at any time.'

'I'll send a note to you. Please join us if it suits you.'

'Yes, I'm sorry I can't give a definite answer.'

Vasily looked for Irina, but she had disappeared. Would he come back? He really didn't know.

The gig headed towards the city. Mikhail had taken the reins. In his wide-brimmed hat, he resembled the driver of a post carriage. While he drove, he catalogued the charms of Kalinin's summer house.

'I'm pleased that the Colonel and Irina Pavlova took to you, Vasya,' he said. 'And I envy you the chance to return before the autumn sets in. You should try to go if you can. I'm sure that you'll find Ryleev good value. I know him well. I don't think much of his versifying, but he has other interests in business and, of course, in politics. I wonder if his wife will be with him? That's an interesting story…'

Vasily was barely listening. 'How old is Irina, do you think?'

Mikhail brought the horses to a walk and turned to look at him. 'Vasya! Surely you're not seriously contemplating… I mean Irina Pavlovna is more than appealing, but I would think she'd be quite a handful. Has she given you reason to think…?'

'How old do you think she is, Misha?' Vasily repeated. 'You must know. I find it hard to guess.'

Mikhail thought for a moment. 'I'd say she's around twenty-six or seven, not more. Kalinin's much older than her, but he was the first son. There was another brother killed in the war. I know she was very young when she married the Baron.' He brought the gig to a halt, turned and rested his hand on Vasily's arm. 'But, Vasya, my dear friend, do be careful. You do know that she's not free to marry, don't you? And I have no idea how the Colonel would react. He can be difficult, unpredictable. He could call you out if he was minded to.'

'You think so?' He hadn't considered that possibility.

'Yes, I do think so, and given his background in the artillery, I doubt if it would end well. Please, Vasily, pause and consider. I don't want to find myself getting up in the middle of the night to assist a good man through the gates of heaven.'

'I'm flattered you'd agree to be my second,' Vasily said and attempted a smile. 'I don't think you need worry too much; I'm not sure I made much impression on Irina Pavlovna. She's rather out of my reach.'

'I wouldn't say that. I wouldn't say that at all, but just step warily.'

Mikhail shook his head and picked up the reins. He flicked the whip.

'Will you come in to dinner?' Vasily was content to change the subject. 'The Prince would be pleased. He keeps open house and likes to see new faces.'

'Yes, I should like to meet Dmitry Vladimirovich. I don't know him well.'

They were approaching the edge of the city. The carriage picked up speed.

Mikhail took his leave after dinner. 'I'll be returning to barracks here in town in a couple of weeks,' he said. 'We must meet again then.'

'I hope you'll be back for my birthday reception,' Vasily said.

'I'll be sure to come. But look, Vasya, do look out for yourself. Don't get too involved with... well, you know what I mean.' Mikhail shrugged. He took off his wide-brimmed hat. 'Here, take this. I won't be needing it again this summer. At least it'll protect you from the sun.'

Vasily stood on the steps of the palace, clutching the hat, and watched with regret as his friend disappeared.

CHAPTER SEVEN

St Petersburg

THE FOLLOWING DAY, Vasily soon became tired of his own company. He lingered in the garden, sat listlessly in the library and spent time in his room, hoping to start work on his English.

He winced as he recalled how Irina had laughed at his advances. He had been in too much of a hurry; he should have pressed Mikhail to reveal more of her story. Perhaps she still loved the Baron and regretted that they had parted? Perhaps she had a lover, although, for some reason, he doubted that.

Should he go to the country next weekend and risk further disappointment? His excuse had been genuine: his family could be back at any time. Although it would be fascinating to meet a man who was supposed to embody 'the spirit of the age', wouldn't it be better to stay here and study? He shot a guilty glance at his unopened book, then set it aside and pulled out his sketches of Paris.

Yakov, clearly irritated by his restlessness, suggested that they might go out together to a tavern that he knew a little way from the centre.

'Oh, I don't think so, Yakov,' Vasily said. 'Now we're at home...'

'No, of course not, sir.'

He knew he should refuse. During their travels, Yakov and he had sometimes gone out together in the evenings, but here in Petersburg such familiarity with one's body servant wasn't acceptable. Later, however, when a long empty evening stretched out before him, the temptation became overwhelming.

In the company of Yakov and his two other servants, Vasily left the palace wearing his artist's smock and Mikhail's hat. They went out through the stable yard to avoid the Prince's sharp eyes.

The square wooden tavern stood within sight of the town gates on the road to Pavlovsk. The open yard was crammed with wagons and carts owned by the merchants and traders who visited the inn on their way home. With some difficulty, they found a table inside the large parlour. The air was thick with smoke, sweat, and the savour of hot pies. Beer arrived, and Vasily drank deeply, leaning against the wall, his legs outstretched, content to listen to the banter of his companions. He laughed at their jokes and even ventured a few himself.

As the group settled in for the evening, a shrill cry split the air. 'Oy! Yako! You left me behind!' A young lad of singular appearance was hurrying towards their corner. He wore a tattered jacket that was too large for him, and tight trousers with holes at the knees. His face was so smeared with grime that it was impossible to make out his features, but the pink 'O' of his mouth worked energetically, as he continued to berate Yakov.

'Who's this?'

'It's Matvey, the boy from the kitchens.'

Vasily watched Matvey drink deeply from a flagon that Yakov placed before him, then lick the foam from his upper lip. A couple of coins lay on the table. The boy reached out towards them, but, realising that he was being observed, pulled his hand back. He then surveyed the room, unperturbed.

'Oy, oy!' he cried. 'Here's trouble.'

And here, indeed, was trouble. A group of men stood in the doorway. The landlord hurried to intercept them and seemed to be insisting that they take a table at the other end of the room.

Vasily recognised them as serfs from the mansion next door to the Prince's palace. Their owner was Kuprin, a nobleman originally of merchant stock. For years, there had been acrimony between the men of both households. The Prince's servants treated those of the parvenu with disdain. Their neighbours, regarding the Prince's servants as pampered toffs, missed no opportunity to insult them. The rivalry represented great sport for Yakov, and, over the years, he had done what he could to fan the flames of mutual hatred. Vasily, finding it amusing, had done nothing to discourage him.

'Oh, that's a pity,' said Yakov, eyeing the figure of the hefty man carrying a cudgel whom they knew to be Kuprin's doorman.

'Yes,' said Vasily. 'The landlord would have done better to turn them away if he knows there's been trouble before.'

'He doesn't want to lose trade, I suppose.'

Vasily pulled himself upright. Would there be trouble? Perhaps he should insist they all leave. But the merchant's men didn't seem to have noticed them and now sat peacefully some distance away. More beer arrived, then some pies and more beer.

As the evening progressed, snatches of song and raucous shouts increasingly disrupted the low throb of conversation in the parlour. A scuffle erupted in a far corner. As Vasily leant forward to suggest that it was time to depart, one of the merchant's men, passing their table deliberately slopped his drink over Yakov. One of the Prince's servants leapt to his feet, seized the offender and started to wrestle him to the floor. The lad Matvey dipped down out of sight.

The landlord gave a shout. 'Outside! None of that in here!'

One of his tapsters hurried to hustle the grappling men towards the door. Vasily and Yakov followed them into the street.

'You must go now, sir!' Yakov pulled Vasily to one side as a tide of people tumbled out of the tavern. Some formed a ring, laughing and jeering as they watched Kuprin's men fall on the Prince's servants. Others, seeking weapons to join in the fight, seized sticks and broke up chairs. A few started to throw punches. A pewter tankard sailed through the air and clipped Vasily's shoulder.

'Ouch!'

Yakov pushed him hard. 'Go, sir! Get away from here! I must find the boy, and then I'll follow you...'

'Yakov...it's dangerous. Come home now...'

But Yakov had already gone. Kicking up dust behind him, he skirted the crowd and made for the huddle of merchants' carts. More missiles were flying. Smoke started to rise from a covered wagon; a group of women were plundering another. Above the hubbub, Vasily heard the faint sound of whistles and bells. The police! He couldn't be arrested! Yakov would have to fend for himself. Slouching beneath his hat, he slunk away. Once out of sight, he started to run. He looked behind him. No one, but he could still hear crashes, roaring and shouts. He hurried on, and as he approached the centre of the city, fell onto a droshky that took him home.

He lay awake most of the night, fully dressed. His shoulder was bruised and sore. He strained his ears, hoping to hear Yakov and the other servants return. At dawn, hearing the squeak of wheels in the yard, he leapt up and looked out. A loaded handcart was being hauled towards the stables. He ran down the back stairs and found the boy, Matvey, assisted by Grigory, trying to help Yakov out of the handcart and onto his feet. Stark naked under a wrap of loose sacking, his man collapsed to the ground. His face was bloody.

Vasily turned to the boy. 'What on earth happened?'

'I had hid when the trouble started, sir. I was under a wagon. Yako came looking for me, see, but that doorman from next door got hold of him. I saw him pick him up high in the air and, as he was dangling, he gave him a fistful, and threw him down the steps of the cellar. I waited behind the barrels until the police and all had gone. One of the tapsters helped me pick Yako up and bring him back, but his clothes had been snitched.'

'Where are our other men?'

'Probably at the police house, sir. They took a lot of people away.'

Grigory was shaking his head, his face a study of disapproval. Vasily's heart sank. Yakov would need a doctor; his servants were in jail and must be extracted. Confrontation and confession couldn't be long delayed.

Vasily descended to the Prince's study after breakfast. Dmitry Vladimirovich stood behind his desk, his arms crossed and his face like stone. 'The merchant Kuprin has been here. He claims there's been another fight and that Yakov and our men were responsible. What do you know of this, Vasya?'

There was no point in lying. 'It wasn't our men who started it, sir.'

'Oh? Surely you weren't there?'

Vasily looked at his feet. His face was burning. 'I know it

was a mistake to go along, Dmitry Vladimirovich, but I did leave as soon as things got difficult.'

The Prince sighed. 'Oh, Vasily! I don't know. I just hope your uncle doesn't come to hear of this. My two men are still at the police house, as are Kuprin's. The authorities have closed the inn for a month, apparently.'

'This is my responsibility, Dmitry Vladimirovich. The men are in my service at present, and I'll sort it out.' Vasily sounded more confident than he felt. 'Please don't trouble yourself further. I'll go down and arrange to have them released.'

'You don't need to do that. I've sent a purse, and the men will be freed later, but they won't be in a fit state to work for a while, I fear. If they were uninjured when they arrived at the police house, they won't be by the time they get out. I think you might go to see Kuprin. He is talking about seeking compensation, though why he thinks that's appropriate, I can't think.'

'I'll call on him later today. I really am deeply sorry, sir.'

The Prince shook his head. 'It's time to grow up, Vasya. When you join the Service, you can't go off hobnobbing with the servants, and you shouldn't do it now. You must consider your reputation and that of the family. And you should take Yakov in hand before your uncle, Alexander, returns and decides to deal with him. You sometimes forget that he is a serf. I know it's difficult when you've grown up with your man. My valet and I were born on the same day, as you know, and as boys we were like brothers. But there comes a time when you have to insist that servants have their sphere and you have yours. You do understand that?'

Vasily nodded.

'I suppose we must thank the Lord that you're not in prison yourself. That would have been very difficult. Well, you can redeem yourself by sorting this out with the merchant next door. I suppose Yakov needs a doctor?'

'Yes, sir. And some new clothes.'

'Well, you should make him sort those out for himself, but you can call out the doctor.' The Prince spoke more gently as he waved Vasily away.

As he climbed the long flight of stairs, Vasily's legs and head ached. He had, of course, been foolish and had a lucky escape. He should be grateful, and yet he felt nothing but gloom. His happy days of freedom had slipped away. New obligations, different rules, now applied. He must distance himself from his childhood companion, live up to his position in society, and become an obsequious servant of the state. As he reached the upper hallway, he stopped for a moment and stood at the door of the garden. He stared at the fountain. It wasn't playing today.

Within a couple of hours, the two missing house serfs were tossed out of a police wagon onto the cobbles of the stable yard. The pair were able to walk, but they had been badly beaten. Vasily sent them away to recover and then asked an old servant, Venyamin, to find Matvey, the kitchen boy.

'Get him cleaned up, and bring him to the garden in half an hour,' he said. 'I have to take him with me on a call this morning.'

Vasily changed into his Paris tailcoat. He took a book of English grammar down to the garden and sat on a bench in the shade.

There was soon movement beyond the fountain, which

had started to play. Venyamin, his arms outstretched, was driving the kitchen boy Matvey before him like a goose. The boy came to a halt before Vasily, his cap in his hand, swaying from foot to foot, his features rigid with apprehension. He seemed ready to flee, but Venyamin stood close behind him.

'You can leave Matvey with me. He'll be quite safe.'

Matvey's round head twisted to watch the old servant leave. Last night, in the dark of the inn, the lad had seemed older. Now, in daylight, it was plain that, although tall for his age, he was a mere child, ten years old at the most. His dark eyes were bright. He had a slightly eastern look: Indian, perhaps, or Romany? His limbs seemed wiry and strong, but where they were free of grime, or not marked with bruises, they were as white as lard. His clothes were little better than rags.

Vasily knew that the child spent most of his time in the kitchens, a place that he had hardly ever visited. He realised that he knew nothing of the conditions in which most of the house serfs lived and worked. Kalinin's words came back to him: *We rarely get close to them or understand them. We just take their existence for granted.*

'Now, Matvey, do you know who I am?' He spoke as kindly as he could.

The boy looked at him with suspicion. 'No, sir, but you was with us last night. Are you going to beat me?'

'Beat you? Whatever for?'

The boy shrugged.

'I need you to come next door with me, Matvey. I want you to help me tell them what happened at the inn yesterday. I'll do most of the talking, but you may have to answer some questions.'

Matvey took a step backwards and started to tremble,

clearly unwilling to venture into the despised establishment next door. Vasily rose and put his hand firmly on his thin shoulder. He called a servant. 'Bring a flask of vodka and two glasses.'

Setting aside his concerns about the child's general welfare, he poured two shots. He gave one to Matvey and downed the other himself. With a practiced hand, the boy swallowed the spirit in one gulp. He stopped trembling and seemed altogether better. Vasily put on his gloves, took the child's clammy hand, and walked him towards the stairs.

The giant doorman, who could usually be seen prowling around the front steps of the merchant's house, was, of course, currently indisposed. The door was opened by another servant. Vasily sent up his card. They were shown into a room that served as an office. There was a sharp note of ink, an undertone of dog.

Some minutes later, Kuprin arrived. He thrust his black brows and blue chin close to Vasily's face. 'Who the devil are you? And what's this filthy brat doing in my house?' The merchant's head was as square as his squat body. His teeth were bad.

Vasily felt Matvey start to tremble again. As he opened his mouth to reply, he heard a rumbling behind him. A sturdy black mastiff with a continuous growl rolled into the room and took up his position alongside his master.

'You have my card, sir.'

'The only Count Belkin I know is that big-nosed pen-pusher from next door.'

'My uncle, Alexander Petrovich. I am Vasily Nikolayevich, his late brother's son.'

'I see. Well, what's your business?'

'I've come to discuss the incident at the inn on Friday

evening. My servants were involved, and I think some facts need clarification.'

'Not in my book. I'm preparing my bill for compensation and the Prince will get it shortly. If your servants were to blame, then you can pay it. There's nothing to discuss. I'm told you saw for yourself what happened, and I've lost three good serfs thanks to your men!'

'I think you'll find that you're mistaken, sir. The situation is indeed clear, but it was your servants who attacked mine. I have an eyewitness here. I am sure, if necessary, we can find others.'

'That's right!' Matvey said in a high-pitched shout. 'We was sitting quietly, and one of yours came and poured his drink right over us! Your boys was out for trouble. One of them had a cudgel. I picked it up. It's next door!'

'And, what's more,' said Vasily, 'Your doorman, in full view of everyone, assaulted my body servant for no reason and left him for dead in the cellar. The boy witnessed that as well.'

'That's right!'

Kuprin was silent. The snarling of the dog continued.

'I really would suggest, sir, that we let the matter rest,' Vasily said. 'I'll pay no compensation under the circumstances; indeed, it's I who should be looking to you for recompense. The innkeeper would have a good claim as well, I'd suggest.'

The merchant scowled. 'All I know is that I've lost three serfs, whoever was to blame.'

'How so, sir? They're not in good shape now, I suspect, but they'll recover.'

'You think that I'd keep them with me after this?'

'Well...'

'No. They'll go back to the country as soon as they can

75

travel, and it's off to the army with them. There's plenty willing to take their place here, and it's a good example to other troublemakers.'

'Isn't that rather harsh, sir? The brawl was unfortunate, but these things happen, and my man, while injured, is expected to recover. I have no doubt that your men have already received adequate punishment at the hands of the police.'

Surely the merchant wouldn't be so cruel? Sending the men to the army would be regarded by their families as a death sentence. Even if they survived the experience, they wouldn't be seen again for twenty-five years. Vasily felt a stir of anger as he looked at Kuprin. The merchant, his eyes, empty and blank, stared back as he pulled himself up to his full height.

'Don't you presume to tell me how to treat my serfs you young puppy!',

The dog started to bark. Kuprin took its collar. The barking continued. Matvey shook with fear. Glancing down, Vasily saw that a small pool had appeared on the tiled floor. The child had wet himself. Time to leave.

The merchant had also noticed the puddle, but it seemed he did not dare to let the dog loose. 'Get out of here!' he shouted. 'Take that disgusting child with you, and don't come back.'

Vasily took his hat and bowed. 'I won't expect to hear more from you, sir,' he said, edging Matvey towards the door. As they left, he heard Kuprin shouting for a servant. The barking continued.

'Did you really bring back the cudgel?' asked Vasily as they walked home.

The boy grinned up at him. 'Nah…but it was the right thing to say, sir!'

Vasily took Matvey up to the apartment. The child stank.

'Give this boy a bath, Venyamin,' he said. 'And find him some decent clothes; these rags should be burnt.'

Venyamin took the boy by what remained of his collar.

'Perhaps you'd like him to help you round the house for the next day or two? He's not to go back to the kitchens.'

———

On the following day, Vasily received a letter.

Tuesday
Okhta River

Vasily Nikolayevich,

I hope that it will suit you to join us here at the end of the week?

If you are able to come on Thursday rather than on Friday, I would ask a favour of you. As I think I mentioned, the Baroness's companion, Frau Geyer, who has been visiting family in Austria, has arrived back in Saint Petersburg and will be ready to join us on that day. I shall be sending my carriage for her, and it would much oblige me if you would agree to accompany her on her journey.

Please let me know if this arrangement would be convenient. I would propose that you be collected from your home at around 10 a.m. on Thursday morning.
I remain etc.
Pavel Kalinin

Postscript: I know that you are probably engaged for English lessons with Mr. Maltby at some stage this week,

but you need not miss a session with him. He will be
coming here on Friday to meet Mr Ryleev, and will, I am
sure, be delighted to spend time studying with you here.

Vasily frowned. Did he want to return to the dacha? If he did go, did he want to busy himself addressing the finer points of English grammar when he might be entertaining himself in other ways? He was still wondering how to reply when there was a knock on the door. Matvey was much improved. He was clean and wore a set of ill-fitting but respectable clothes.

'Yako is awake, sir, and he wants something to eat. Shall I go to find him something?'

'No Matvey, I'll ask Venyamin to go down. Tell me, do you like your work in the kitchen?'

'It's alright, sir. Don't know how to do much else. They says it's a good place to be because one day I might learn to become a cook and, when the Tsar lets us all go free, maybe have my own cook shop.'

'And you'd like that?'

'Not really, sir. There seems to me to be a lot of dirty pots to wash, and beatings to take between here and there, if you take my meaning.'

'If you want to stay up here and help Venyamin for the time being, I'll see if it can be arranged. I can't make any promises, though.'

'I'm not sure, sir. How often must I have a bath?'

'At least once a week, but it won't be like yesterday. You'll be cleaner, so next time you can go to the bathhouse.'

Matvey scowled. Clearly, the child had not enjoyed his experience in the Western-style tub. His screeches had been audible in the stable yard, as Venyamin had scrubbed the child's skin raw, removing months of encrusted grime. How had he been allowed to get into such a state? Vasily knew that he couldn't contemplate sending the boy back to resume his previous life sleeping on the kitchen floor, nosing in discarded bottles, being plied with drink or otherwise abused by the older servants. He must speak to the Prince.

'I've got a job for you, Matvey. I have to write a letter. When it's finished, I'd like you to take it to the hall downstairs for delivery. If anyone sees you, tell them you are running an errand for me.'

The boy stood by the desk. Vasily looked at Kalinin's letter again and picked up his pen. What should he write? Matvey's presence did nothing to concentrate his mind. Now the child was retrieving something from the floor. It seemed that a second sheet, previously unnoticed, had floated there.

There were just three words and a signature, written in a clear, upright hand:

'Please come, Vasily, Irina.'

CHAPTER EIGHT
A House on the Okhta River

ON THURSDAY MORNING, a highly polished carriage rolled up at the front door of the Bogolyubov Palace. A coachman, in subdued grey livery, climbed down and lowered the step. A small woman with an unremarkable face but a warm smile was seated inside. She clasped a cylindrical lacquered travelling case on her lap and wore a sparsely dressed bonnet and a plain travelling pelisse. She introduced herself, in French, as Madame Geyer.

As they drew away, Vasily noticed Matvey. He was sitting on the low steps of the palace watching the carriage depart. Vasily raised his hand, and the boy waved with enthusiasm. He must find something to occupy the boy, to keep him out of the kitchens. Dmitry Vladimirovich had been surprised, and not altogether pleased, that he hadn't been sent back to his work. But he had been persuaded that Venyamin couldn't cope alone in the apartment.

Vasily hadn't felt able to speak of other matters: that the child had been neglected; that he was scarred and bruised; and that he had developed an enthusiasm for drink. In general, the Prince cared for the welfare of his serfs, but he had been blind to the boy's condition. Perhaps he had simply not known.

Madame Geyer proved to be easy company. The journey passed quickly, and soon they were drawing up at the dacha. Irina's dog rushed out to greet them and then, barking, circled Vasily as he handed out his travelling companion.

The Colonel and Irina approached. Pavel Pavlovich went

directly to his sister's companion, and, taking both her hands, kissed them. He then embraced her. Vasily was surprised at this transparent display of affection.

Irina presented her hand to Vasily, and then drew close to him and caught his arm. 'Vasily Nikolayevich, I'm very pleased to see you again. I feared…' Speaking quietly and rapidly, she continued: 'Please don't take it amiss if I can't immediately entertain you. I must spend this afternoon with Gretchen… Madame Geyer. She's been gone for some months, and when she's away, I realise how much I depend on her. It would be very wrong to neglect her today. We'll all meet at dinner, of course. Shall we agree to walk out together tomorrow morning? Perhaps you can help me improve my drawing?'

She looked up at him. There was the hover of a smile about her lips, a sly green flicker in her eyes. His throat constricted. He swallowed. 'It will be an honour to help you, Baroness. I think that Thomas Maltby will be here tomorrow. I'll spend this afternoon working on the subtleties of English auxiliary verbs.'

Irina laughed. 'You may want to take a bath. The banya is hot.'

'Perhaps I'll do both. In any event, don't be concerned on my account. I won't be unoccupied.'

———

Pavel Kalinin and Vasily sat in silence in the bathhouse, sweating generously. Mint, thyme and branches of pine perfumed the steam-filled air. Vasily rolled onto his back and lay supine on the high wooden bench. When he could bear the heat no longer, he moved down to where the air was cooler. The Colonel, clearly more resilient, continued to occupy the upper level. After a while, Vasily stood up. Kalinin roused himself and, climbing down, reached for a bunch of leafy birch twigs.

'Want me to thrash you?'

Vasily shook his head; he had already noticed his host's muscular arms. Now seemed a good time to head outside and plunge into the river for a second time.

The Colonel shrugged and started to beat himself noisily.

Having enjoyed the shock of cold water, Vasily returned to the steam room. Kalinin was stretched out once more. He had added more water to the coals. It was searingly hot. Having raised a sweat, Vasily went into the adjacent room to soap and then douse himself with water from the wooden tub. He called for a towel and, wrapping himself in it, poured himself a beaker of cool kvass from a large jug. As he stood drinking, the Colonel emerged, his flesh scarlet.

'You should use the birch,' he said. 'It's good for the circulation.'

'Not today.'

Vasily hoped Kalinin wouldn't take offence, but an element of trust was necessary before voluntarily submitting to a beating, however restorative the intent, and he didn't trust the Colonel. Kalinin volunteered so little information about himself that he was almost impossible to read. Mikhail had said that the man could be difficult. Vasily wished now that he had asked him what he had meant.

Later, as they sat together on the veranda, Vasily felt more at ease. Kalinin was speaking about Kondraty Ryleev. 'When I heard that Ryleev was staying nearby with his wife, I thought it would be diverting to invite him here. I know something about him. *Polar Star*, the periodical that he publishes with

Alexander Bestuzhev, has been very successful. He's made some money out of it, which is unusual in the publishing game. We have a copy around somewhere.'

'Yes, I took a look at it last week.'

'At the moment, he works at the Russian American Company. I'm not really sure what he does there, but it seems to be a well-paid post, and that, with the income from the periodical, seems to have, in part, solved his financial problems. His family have an estate somewhere outside Petersburg, but it's nothing but a pile of debt.'

'And Madame Ryleev?'

'Yes, she'll be with him. He met his wife when he was serving in the army near Voronezh. He wasn't much of an officer, by all accounts. The girl must still be very young, but it's said that she's devoted to him. When he met her, she was quite illiterate, the daughter of a landowner who didn't believe in educating his daughters. Ryleev taught her to read and then offered for her. There was some resistance, I think, but they married in the end.'

'And he's a poet, too?'

'Yes, but, I fear, not a great one... he's no Pushkin, no Zhukovsky... it's generally polemical stuff. He's been in trouble in the past for writing satires that insulted various dignitaries. Now he writes so-called "meditations" on historical characters. It's transparently liberal and, as a result, not liked on principle in some quarters. Taken altogether, he's a strange chap; one can't help feeling that he's on a quest to become part of his own mythology.'

'I look forward to meeting him,' said Vasily. 'I've not met many literary men.'

'That's not such a bad thing, in my experience,' said Kalinin. 'So, is all well at the Palace?'

Vasily told Pavel Pavlovich about the events of the week, feeling a twinge of conscience as he omitted his participation in the excursion to the tavern.

'I knew that man of yours was trouble!' said the Colonel. 'And now it seems you're planning to take on another liability in the shape of some urchin. You're too soft, Vasily.'

'So what would you do, Colonel?'

'Pack the child off to the army!' he said.

Vasily looked at him. Was this a joke? It was hard to tell. Kalinin was rising to his feet, saying he had business to complete before dinner. Vasily stretched and yawned. As usual, after bathing he felt at ease, hollowed out and pure. The little white spitz was trotting across the grass. There was no sign of Irina, but they would meet at dinner and walk out tomorrow. Perhaps he would learn something of her story. He felt more certain of her now.

When Vasily emerged the following morning, Irina was already standing on the grass throwing a ball for her dog. He stood watching for a few moments from the shade of the veranda as she tried to control her wide-brimmed hat with her hand each time she stooped for the ball. The dog ran back and forth in a state of rapture. It seemed unlikely that she would exhaust the animal. He descended the steps, and, as the dog dropped the ball at her feet once more, he stooped to pick it up. The dog span around and barked, springing high into the air to try to reach it.

'Good morning, Irina Pavlovna,' he said, raising his voice above the hubbub. He threw the ball, and the dog streaked away. 'I think we'd better get started. Once we're walking, she'll forget about the game. Shall I bring some paper and crayons?'

Irina smiled. Her cheeks, already pink, took on a deeper blush. 'Yes, perhaps, but you'll find me a poor pupil.'

'Well, we'll see.'

He found his leather bag and a woollen blanket and then took her arm. He led her away from the house, towards the plumes of mist that hung above the river. The dew had not yet dried on the grass, and a few yellow leaves lay on the ground. The dog ran before them, tail quivering.

They took the path downstream to a spot where a fallen tree had created a natural seat. Vasily spread out the blanket. As Irina sat down and removed her hat, he pulled grey drawing paper and some black and white chalks from his bag. He pointed to an old willow that leaned across the stream nearby.

'Have a go at that.'

The result was not good. He sat down beside her and explained how to assess and measure the outline of the trunk and create an impression of the drift of leaves.

'Have another try.'

He looked away down the river. Its surface was smooth and oily. Fragments of branches drifting downstream fractured its glossy veneer. The hollow rattle of a woodpecker sounded from the other bank. He sensed that Irina had stopped drawing. He risked a look. The result was a little better.

Her face was flushed with the effort of concentration. He took the chalk from her, set the drawing aside, and then he took her hand and examined it. She didn't pull it away. The back was slightly freckled; her nails were oval pearls. He turned it over, kissed the palm and enclosed her fingers within his own. Leaning forward, he fleetingly kissed her mouth, then again with more resolution. He sensed her catch her breath, to seem to respond, but as he embraced her, she turned her head away.

'Vasya, my dear. We can't do this... at least...'

'What can't we do... I thought...' Had he completely misread her?

She escaped his arms and rose to her feet. 'I wanted to come out with you this morning to talk to you.'

'Well, if you insist, but I suggest we move from here. People will walk by. We'll go back to the boathouse.'

They walked back along the riverbank in silence. He kept her hand clasped in his. The boathouse steps were warm in the morning sunlight.

'Now say what you have to say, and then I can kiss you again.'

'We have to speak about my past, and my present situation, too.'

'I hope it won't take too long.'

'You're not taking this seriously!'

'I am, Irina, I am. But I find it hard to think of anything that you can tell me that will divert me from my intention to make love to you.'

She looked at him sharply, and then away towards the far bank of the river.

'So?'

'How much do you know about me, about our family, Vasily?'

'Not a great deal, although since the Prince made no objections to me coming here, I have to assume you're quite respectable.'

'I suppose we're generally considered to be. We have an ancient name, a long record of military service. We own numerous serfs on extensive estates mainly in the south, and a house in Moscow.'

'Your parents are dead?'

'Yes, Pavel is the head of the family, as I am sure you guessed. We had a younger brother, Yury, who was killed in the war in 1812… the same year as your father.'

'I suspect the circumstances were different.'

'Yes, it was during the autumn campaign. There was some sort of misunderstanding; he was shot by our own side. Our father, who was a widower, never got over it. He was still grieving terribly when he died two years later. I was fifteen.' She spoke in a monotone, as if she had rehearsed the story many times. Vasily recognised it as a ploy he used himself to dispel the bitterness of his own family's tragedy.

'My father's death was not at all convenient for Pavel. He was then on the staff of a general in the suite of the Emperor at the Congress of Vienna. The sessions started in the autumn of that year. I could, of course, have stayed on the estate, but that didn't prove practical. In any event, I wanted to come out into the world. My education, such as it was, was considered complete.

'A cousin of my mother's was married to an officer at the embassy in Vienna. Pavel intended to lodge with them during the conference. Hotel rooms were hard to come by, so it suited him well. It was they who suggested that the easiest solution was for me to go to them, too. It wasn't intended to be a long-term arrangement. The Congress wasn't expected to last for more than a month or so, but, in fact, the negotiations dragged on until the following summer.

'I'm sure that Pavel would never have taken me to Vienna had he realised what it would be like. Everyone who was anyone was there, and that attracted all sorts of adventurers, hangers-on, mistresses and courtesans. It was certainly an education for me! I was very young, headstrong, reputed to be wealthy, and, as it happened, not well supervised. It wasn't long before I met the Baron. He was, still is, superficially a fine man... rich, handsome, a member of an old Austrian family. Pavel much approved of him. It was a rare occasion on which he failed to get the measure of a person.'

'How old is the Baron?'

'He's fifteen years older than me, so would now be just over forty. He had been married before, but his wife had died. He had no children. He courted me for a very short time, and I imagined myself in love. Maybe I was. In any event, I agreed to marry him. I was so pleased with myself. I felt that I had made a brilliant match! Almost immediately after the wedding, Napoleon surprised us all by escaping from Elba, and Pavel had to return to his regiment, leaving me behind.

'The problems started after I had my first child in 1817. When I gave birth to Frederick, my husband seemed to resent the time I spent with the child. Although, you know, he doted on him. We started to argue, but I still loved him, and when we made up our quarrels he was always very tender. The result of one night of "forgiveness" was another child, a second boy, Manfred, born a little over two years after Frederick.'

She stopped. Tears spilt onto her cheeks, and she brushed them away.

Vasily tried to hide his shock. Two children! Where were they now?

'After Manfred's birth, the nightmare began. The Baron set up a strict daily regime. When his rules were broken, he would fly into terrible rages. He would tell me that I was a failure as a mother, that I was a slovenly Russian bitch. But much of the time, he would behave completely normally. When we went out in society, he treated me like a queen. To this day, I don't think anyone outside the house or, indeed, his mother who lived at his country estate knew how he behaved in private.'

She was pulling repeatedly at the skin between the thumb and forefinger of her left hand. He caught the hand between his own and held it as she continued.

'It was at around that time that Gretchen was employed as our housekeeper. She quickly realised that something was wrong. I thought she would leave. In fact, she almost did, but she became fond of the children and of me. I had stopped apologising to him for my imagined shortcomings. That made his rages worse, and he started to beat me. I feared for my life. I began to imagine that perhaps he had murdered his first wife. Perhaps he had.'

'Why didn't you seek help, go to the police?' Vasily asked.

'I had no proof, and the police, I was told, weren't interested in domestic altercations. At one stage, I approached the wife of the Russian Ambassador, but she discouraged me from making a fuss. It would all be far too embarrassing, she said; husbands did sometimes beat their wives; the Baron was a delightful man; she could hardly believe what I was saying; in any event, she would be eternally obliged if I didn't create a scandal.

'Finally, I decided to leave him. Gretchen and I planned it together. We were aiming to go to England with the children, to take refuge with Pavel. We didn't get very far. Gretchen was instantly dismissed. The children were sent away to the country.'

'The Baron told me that if I wanted to leave I could, but that divorce would be impossible, and I would never see the children again. Predictably, when I was getting ready to go, he came to my bedroom and begged me to stay. He wept, he promised to change. But we had been through this performance so many times before. The truth is I don't think that he could help himself, and I certainly couldn't help him by that time. Even after I'd gone, he sent me letters pleading with me to return.'

'But your children?'

'I haven't seen them since the day I tried to flee. Pavel has returned to Vienna, has tried to reason with the Baron to persuade him to let us see them but has got nowhere. The law is not on my side.' Her tears were now flowing down her cheeks.

'I know it was a terrible thing to leave them, but I had no choice. I honestly feared for my life. Besides, in Austria, my boys enjoy status, the promise of high office in the future, and, of course, their inheritance. We are not poor, of course, but we could promise them nothing comparable here in Russia. Pavel tells me that I must be realistic, understand I did the only thing I could in the face of a terrible mistake. But Vasily, even though I know he's probably right, the guilt I feel is unbearable at times. Perhaps I should have stayed.'

Vasily could think of nothing to say. He pulled out his kerchief and wiped her face. She seemed to recover herself, to be determined to tell the story to its end.

'I lived in England for a year or more. Gretchen followed. She's been with me ever since. I never felt comfortable in London, even though my grandmother was English, and we have relatives there. I know I was something of an embarrassment to Pavel, although he was kind enough never to say so. And he has always felt culpable; he believes he failed me in Vienna. He suggested that Gretchen and I come back to Russia, and he took the apartment on the English

Embankment. We've been there ever since. It's not a bad life, but lonely at times.'

Vasily looked out over the river. He couldn't find it in him to judge her. How could anyone mistreat someone so beautiful, so transparently good?

She seemed to read his thoughts. 'Don't think that I'm an angel, Vasya. I can be difficult at times, stubborn, and I have a short temper. I can be terribly indolent, and, of course, my own life hasn't been entirely blameless since I left Vienna.'

Her face coloured; it was fascinating how changes in her skin tone betrayed her.

'You don't have to confess everything, Irina.'

' You're different from the others. I don't want there to be any secrets between us.'

The others? Vasily wanted to smile. He resisted the temptation.

'You should know I've taken lovers since I left my husband.' Her colour deepened. 'But neither of them were free, like you, or particularly young.'

'I don't see why age should matter.'

'Don't you? Then let me explain. They were men who were established in life, and, of course, they were married. I was fond of them. They were, I think, fond of me, but ours could never be anything other than a casual affair. It could do their careers little harm. You're just twenty, Vasya.'

'I'm twenty-one next week.'

'But you have everything before you. You should be casting about for an heiress to secure the future of your estate; not wasting your time and reputation with a married woman of doubtful provenance.'

'That's for me to decide, Irina. I'm really not a child.'

'No, I do know that. But I also know that I ought to resist you. It's possible that I'll never be free, and even if I were, I'll always be tainted as a woman who abandoned her husband and children. You do understand?'

He was silent for a moment. 'I'm grateful to you for your honesty, but nothing that you've said changes my feelings. I want you, and, if you're willing, I will have you. You'll have to allow me to take my own chances.'

He dropped her hand and held her close against him. He felt her tears, warm through his shirt, and as he kissed her, her response aroused him.

But now they heard voices. There were people on the terrace. Breaking apart, they left the seclusion of the steps and emerged from behind the boathouse. The elongated form of his English tutor, Thomas Maltby, was advancing at speed down the grass.

'What nightmare is this? 'Vasily said quietly. He raised his hand to his mouth, coughed, and bowed. The Englishman stopped short and looked first at Vasily and then at Irina, who had turned her face aside. He hesitated, muttering something under his breath. Then, with a forced smile, he returned Vasily's bow and came on once more.

CHAPTER NINE

'AND HAVE you visited America yourself, Mr Ryleev?' inquired Thomas Maltby.

'No, not personally, although, since I've worked for the company, I've learned a good deal more about the country. I'd very much like to go, but I'm kept busy by affairs here. In any event, it would be hard to justify. We have at least one American representative on our board of governors.'

Vasily looked up from the dining table. It was growing dark outside; dinner seemed to have continued for a long time.

When Ryleev had arrived accompanied by his wife, Vasily had thought him unremarkable. His build was slight, his hair artistically disordered, and his heavy brow hung above unexceptional features. When the man spoke, his manner had been nervous and hesitant, but he seemed to have a good deal to say for himself. Much of the conversation thus far had concerned his literary activities and his work on the *Polar Star*. Now he was speaking of his hopes and fears for the Russian American Company, where he worked as office manager. Vasily knew the company's building well. It stood on the embankment of the Moyka River, only a few minutes' walk from his home, its façade dignified by a prominent double-headed eagle.

Servants came in to light the lamps and lower the netting at the open windows. Vasily's attention drifted. He had tried to resist the impulse, but now he looked at Irina. She sat at the end of the table, between Maltby and Ryleev, apparently paying close attention to the economic future of Russia's

American possessions. Her hair glowed in the lamplight, and a slight flush touched her cheeks. As she listened, her eyes shone, perhaps with interest, perhaps with happiness. Had he really kissed her, held her in his arms? Had he imagined it?

Could he risk going to her tonight? He glanced at her brother. Their eyes met. He ventured a smile that the Colonel acknowledged but did not return. Vasily turned his attention back to their guest. What was it that Mikhail had said about a duel? Perhaps he would keep to his room tonight, after all.

Now it seemed that the Englishman had another question. 'Do you think we can learn from the American way of government, sir? You must have received some impressions.'

Ryleev paused for a moment. 'I think, quite honestly, Mr Maltby, that the federal republican system is the best arrangement possible. All citizens have a stake in their country and have equal rights before the law. Power is shared and divided, local differences respected.'

As Ryleev warmed to his subject, it seemed to Vasily that he underwent a transformation. His dark eyes, which a moment before had seemed commonplace, glittered; his whole face came alive – became remarkable. It was astonishing. Vasily began to listen more carefully. 'Anyone who loves and cares about Russia would want to see such a system introduced here eventually,' Ryleev said. 'What's more, given Russia's vast geography and its plethora of different nations, a federal constitution would work well here, without doubt.'

'But what of the Tsar?' asked Maltby. His bony fingers reached for his glass. 'Surely you wouldn't dispense with him? I would have thought that a limited monarchy, like that in Britain, would be more appropriate, given Russia's current arrangements?'

Ryleev now had Vasily's full attention. Surely he wasn't going to suggest the removal of the Tsar? This was dangerous talk.

'Pah! Britain!' Ryleev said, his voice full of scorn. 'The constitution, or whatever you want to call the arrangement they have over there, seems to me to be obsolete, full of defects. There, as here, there are too many heartless grandees. The rich and influential have their fingers firmly on the levers of power and their sticks on the backs of the people. There remain slaves and paupers in England, as everywhere else. Britain will be the last place to change their government because the British think, complacently, that it's already been changed.'

It seemed that Maltby wasn't going to let the fate of the Emperor lie. 'But I ask you again, Ryleev, how would you deal with the Emperor? An imperial family doesn't sit well with the idea of a republic. Cut off the ruler's head, as we did in England? Send him into exile? We've been known to do that, too. And then how would you deal with the rest of the family?'

Maltby appeared to be enjoying himself. Vasily held his breath. How would the poet reply? Ryleev hesitated. It seemed that he was backing away from an open recommendation of regicide. What a pity! That would have been something!

'Well, I said that, in my opinion, the creation of a republic would be best for Russia eventually, but I'm not sure that it would be right to introduce it without what one might call an interim period. The people could then decide what arrangements they'd prefer.' Ryleev hurried on: 'A role could be found for the Emperor if he were willing to accept it, although he should have no more power than that of the President of the United States. But it isn't really up to me, one man, to dictate what should happen after successful revolutionary struggle. What I *am* convinced of is that the current situation in Russia, where all are subject to the whim of an autocratic despot, cannot and should not continue!'

'Your ideas seem to be rather out of step with most of Europe at present,' Kalinin said. 'All that Napoleon seems to have achieved is the firm establishment of autocrats across the continent.'

'Yes,' agreed Ryleev. 'Napoleon proved to be the greatest monster of all. He presented himself as representing the spirit of the age but actually was no better than the rest of them.' He fell silent.

Irina rose to her feet.

'The samovar is hot,' she said. 'Would anyone like some tea? Natalya Mikhailovna?' she turned to Madame Ryleev, who had remained silent throughout the evening. She looked to her husband for guidance.

'I think it's time to go, my dear,' Ryleev said. 'It is getting late. We're staying with friends, remember. We should be considerate and not keep them up.'

'I'll call the gig round,' said the Colonel.

When Ryleev and his wife had left, the room felt emptied, as if oxygen had been removed from the air. Those who remained were subdued while they drank their tea.

'Well!' said Maltby rubbing his hands along his thin shanks. 'That character will either end up in the Senate or on the scaffold, I'd say.'

'Probably the latter,' replied Kalinin. 'I'd put money on it, in fact.'

Vasily lingered downstairs for a while, hoping to find Irina, but she did not reappear.

It was warm in his room. He blew the candle out, opened the window and lay naked on his bed. It would be hard to sleep, but a book would not hold his attention.

Irina's presence had distracted him at dinner, but he had been absorbed by Ryleev's comments about republicanism and the future of the Tsar. He had never heard such matters spoken about so openly. At home, they were certainly not discussed. Surely the poet could have had no idea whether or not he was among friends? He was either very brave or very naive.

Perhaps he could raise these matters with Maltby? The Englishman had seemed to comprehend everything well enough this evening. In fact, he had seemed to be deliberately leading Ryleev on. Mikhail knew the poet well. Perhaps he could arrange for them to meet again? He would like to prove to his friend that he was developing an interest in his political and social concerns. What might Ryleev say about the issue of the serfs, about the lack of a functioning legal system, the economic problems of the country, the military settlements?

The house was very quiet. Cooler now, Vasily pulled up his sheet. He thought he heard footsteps in the hallway. Was it Irina? Was she coming to him? The footsteps stopped. He watched the door, willing it to open. But then the steps resumed, fading away towards the front of the house. He heard the click of a latch and all fell silent again. He tossed himself onto his side; she wouldn't come, he was sure of it.

He was drifting into sleep when she came. In the glow of her candle, he saw her hair, a veil of red gold falling over her shoulders. A breath of air touched his skin as her robe slipped to the floor.

He sat up and she came into his arms. Drawing her down beside him, he held her to his heart. He kissed the top of her head, her brow and her lips. She smelt of warm oranges and strange exotic spice. He smoothed back the fragrant mass of her hair and starting with the hollow of her throat, embarked on a prolonged voyage of discovery.

Irina had left him at dawn. He rolled into the hollow of sweet citrus warmth where she had lain and immediately slept again. A little later, he woke, entangled in the sheets. Freeing himself and pulling on some clothes, he went downstairs and made for the river. Early sunlight was streaking the grass, and daisies like snowflakes were silvered with dew. When he got to the bathing place, he stripped and, oblivious to the chill, pitched himself into the cold water and swam a long way upstream. He drifted back slowly, turning at times onto his back beneath the dense massed crowns of the trees.

She hadn't been as he had expected. He had expected an encounter with something smooth and cool, an avatar of the marble statue in the Summer Garden; he had expected distance and restraint, a politely sophisticated encounter. But it had been nothing like that, nothing at all. She had been warm and generous, passionate and all-embracing.

He swam back towards the bank. To his surprise, a house serf was standing by the river bearing a towel and a robe. A rigid figure on the grass, the lackey pretended not to notice his nakedness as he struggled out of the water. He took the towel, dried himself, and put on the robe gratefully. Then he made his way up to the house, the servant following with his discarded clothes.

Irina was waiting for him on the veranda, She must have seen him go down to the river and had sent the man after him. He could hear the samovar hissing inside. He could smell coffee and warm pastries.

'I didn't want you to catch cold,' she said. 'Or go hungry. Now I have found you, I don't want to lose you.'

'Well, I'm glad about that.' He embraced her.

'You weren't what I expected,' she said as she drew him to the table.

'What did you expect?' Clearly, they had surprised one another. 'Did you think I wouldn't know... I hadn't...?'

She shrugged, her face flushed.

'I didn't learn much on my recent travels, I admit,' he said. 'But I did learn something.'

'Yes, yes, you did.' She smiled and pulled her robe closer about her.' Come and eat,' she said. 'And then we can plan our day. I wonder what else you can teach me while you're here?'

———

Pavel Kalinin looked down from his bedroom window. That young fool Vasily was wandering down to the river, barefoot in the cold morning air. It was obvious that he had been with Irina and was now enjoying the exhausted delirium of spent passion. He rubbed his head and sighed. It seemed the man was less naive than he had thought.

Did it matter? Should he worry about his sister's honour? It was really a little late. He had failed her when their father died. He should have arranged for her to stay safely in Russia, or at least have prevented her hasty marriage to the Baron. He had been careless, and she had suffered as a result. Now it seemed he had been careless again. He shouldn't have suggested that she be kind to Vasily and encourage him to visit them for a second time. He knew she had found him appealing, but he hadn't expected them to become lovers. And now he could hardly play the heavy-handed brother. In any event, she would certainly take no notice.

And Vasily Nikolayevich? It might be good for him to live a little, shed his last vestiges of boyish guilelessness, and, more importantly, lose the air of unthinking complacency that was the curse of their class. In the end, it would probably do him no harm to be associated with a touch of scandal. And, of course, if he were close to Irina for a while, he could keep an eye on him and further his own plans; although, in truth, he felt less comfortable about that now.

Gretchen was stirring in the bed. She woke up and smiled at him. He growled back. She laughed.

On Sunday after dinner, Vasily and Thomas Maltby travelled back to the city. Vasily dozed in his corner as the carriage rolled along, a jolt occasionally arousing him. He was profoundly content. Irina had come to him again last night and had promised to send to him as soon as she and the Colonel returned to St Petersburg. Kalinin had been reserved, but It seemed unlikely that a challenge would be forthcoming.

He opened his eyes and shut them again. Thomas Maltby was scrutinising him. It seemed that his tutor didn't entirely approve of him and believed he was wedded to pleasure and self-indulgence. Well, the Englishman had some reason to think that. He hadn't been an assiduous student thus far.

A particularly deep pothole almost threw Vasily from his

seat. He blinked and shook his head. Now wide awake, he smiled at Maltby. What should he say? 'Weather seems to be changing,' he ventured. It was true: for the first time in many weeks, they had awoken to grey skies and a chill wind.

'Yes, it will be September soon. I confess I rather dread the coming of winter. I've never really become accustomed to your climate.'

Vasily nodded. 'An envoy was sent here from Italy about fifty years ago; I think he was his city's first representative to Russia. He begged to go home after a fortnight. He couldn't take the weather. But at least we heat our houses. I was told by an Englishman I met on my travels that you keep your rooms damnably cold.'

'Yes, that can be the case. Particularly in the country.'

'What did you think of our guest on Friday night? I found him remarkably outspoken. But I suppose in England that's normal enough.'

'Up to a point, Count. But it's unusual, even in England, to hear the assassination of the monarch being discussed over dinner.'

'Yes. After all, Ryleev doesn't know me from Adam. I could be a government agent.'

Maltby laughed. 'I don't think that's likely, but there's no doubt that Ryleev allows his enthusiasm to run away with him. He's the sort of man who, when he hears a man uttering mild disapproval of the Emperor, immediately assumes he's a committed revolutionary. It's an optimistic and endearing approach, but not an altogether safe one, I think. But it must be said that Ryleev isn't just full of poetry and rhetoric. He puts his ideals into practice. He served as an elected magistrate in the St Petersburg District Criminal Court, quite a role to undertake at a young age. They say he did the job with great integrity and also with courage. He wasn't afraid to stand up to the grandees. Ordinary people queued up to have their cases heard by him. He still goes down to the courts when he can to offer free help to the needy.'

'That's very admirable!' said Vasily. 'You know, Mr Maltby, I'm not blind to the condition of the poor and the peasants, although I'm ashamed to admit that I've only recently woken up to it. I'm aware of the privilege that we, the gentry, enjoy. But what one can do as an individual seems so trivial in the overall scheme of things that, in the end, it barely seems worth doing anything. Something more fundamental is needed, but I'm not certain I'm up for dramatic action.'

When Maltby smiled, his gaunt features were transformed. 'Small things are important, Vasily Nikolayevich, if only for the sake of your own integrity, your own soul. Greater change might take time but, when enough people understand that it's actually in their interest, and, of course, the time is right, it'll come.'

Vasily paused for a moment. 'Thomas... you don't mind if I call you Thomas? There is one small thing that you might be able to help me with.' Vasily told him about the child, Matvey. 'He's a bright boy, and if we can resolve his immediate problems, I would like to see him learn his numbers and be able to read. Would you take him on? I'll pay you, of course.'

Maltby looked doubtful. 'Children aren't really my specialty, and I've no experience in teaching Russian at any level. However, I confess that I'm not overburdened with work at present. I wouldn't mind making the attempt. You don't need to pay me... Let's see how we go on.'

'That would be good of you.'

They fell silent. The carriage rocked gently on the smoother surface. Vasily's head began to nod again. But when they reached the Prince's palace, he sat up, suddenly alert. There was an unusual amount of activity in the yard. A large coach stood by the stables, laden with luggage; servants nearby were emptying a wagon.

'My family have returned from the country! I can't invite you in now, Thomas; all will be in disorder. We'll meet, in any event, on Tuesday, I think.'

Once Vasily's box had been unloaded, the driver, with some difficulty, turned the horses in the restricted space and Kalinin's carriage disappeared out into the street.

CHAPTER TEN
St Petersburg

THE APARTMENT WAS entirely changed. Boxes and bundles cluttered the rooms; furniture that had been transported temporarily to the country stood in the corridor; jars of preserves and baskets of produce from the estate blocked the top of the stairs to the kitchens. Serfs ran around carrying luggage and shouting instructions to one another. Once he had carried in Vasily's box, Yakov sloped off, and there was no sign of Venyamin or Matvey.

Vasily's mother, Maria, emerged from her room. 'Vasenka! Let me look at you! It's been such a long time… over a year!'

He found himself enveloped in a soft rush of muslin and velvet, a cloud of May Rose. The familiar scent recalled his childhood, and he blinked back unbidden tears. His mother would certainly be weeping; he didn't want to encourage more emotion. As he escaped from her embrace, she held his arms tightly.

'You're even more like your poor Papa!' she said, finally releasing him as she dabbed at her eyes with the kerchief that he was quick to extract from his pocket.

His mother was now over forty, but she hadn't changed while he had been away. There were some grey hairs among her dark curls, but her face was almost unlined and her brown eyes clear. She was a fine-looking woman, but he knew that, despite no shortage of admirers, she would never remarry.

'I'm so looking forward to hearing about your travels! We got your letters, of course, but not as many as we would have liked. I expect you were busy with your classes.'

'Yes, Mama.'

'I'm surprised you didn't go to visit Katya at Tsarskoe Selo when you got home. You must make use of our new connections, Vasya, and you know you're to be an uncle, don't you?'

'Yes, Mama.'

His mother was still rejoicing in the match that she had managed to secure for his sister Katya with Prince Polunin, a nobleman with close ties to the court. The Prince was, of course, not in the first flush of youth, but, nonetheless, the marriage had been a great triumph for a family in reduced circumstances.

'I've been quite busy. I've spent some time out of town,' he said.

'Oh, with whom?'

'I went with Mikhail Stenovsky to visit the Kalinins. They've taken a place on the Okhta River this summer.'

'Oh, that's your schoolfriend Ivan's brother, isn't it? I didn't think you knew him.'

'Well, I do now.'

'He's of very good family, of course, but I'm not sure I'm acquainted with the Kalinins.'

'Possibly not, Mama. The Prince judged them to be respectable enough. But where's my uncle?'

'He's gone down to see Dmitry. I expect they'll have a lot to say to one another. He'll be up before too long.'

———

Vasily did not meet Alexander Petrovich until the family gathered in the drawing room before descending to the Prince's for dinner. He felt a small twist of apprehension as his uncle bore down on him. Alexander was a tall man, his features dominated by a remarkable nose, which, as he aged, made him appear increasingly intimidating.

'Well, Vasily,' he said, his face impassive. 'Dmitry tells me that you've largely been loafing around over the summer and have made little progress with your English.'

'Very good to see you too, Uncle,' He hoped he had gauged his uncle's mood correctly.

Alexander yelped sharply. Vasily, recognising this as laughter, was relieved. His uncle briefly clasped him to his bony chest, and then drew him over to the fireplace. 'It's good to see you back, boy. Dmitry tells me you have proved a good companion while I've been away. He seemed very pleased with the purchases you made on his behalf. And he tells me that I'm now obliged to stare at your portrait when I'm writing letters… I'm not sure that will stimulate any profound thoughts, but we'll see.'

'How did you find my grandmother, sir?'

'She's pretty fit. Not much looking forward to the winter. I wonder sometimes if she shouldn't come to live here, where we can keep a better eye on her. She won't hear of it at present, though.'

'And the estate?'

'Oh, things improve slowly. Karl Feodorovich has done a fine job since your father died. Let's hope the new manager can keep it up. The piece of land we bought last year is under cultivation, but it's been the devil's own job to persuade the serfs to work it. They're always loath to attempt anything new.'

Alexander paused, and then said, 'I gather you've been running about with Mikhail Stenovsky?'

'Yes; he happened to be on leave when I got home. I've seen quite a lot of him.'

'And his brother, Nikita?'

'No. He's been on his estates.'

His uncle fell silent. He seemed to want to pursue the matter further but thought better of it.

'And you've been to the country?' he said finally.

'Yes. I think you know Colonel Kalinin? He invited Mikhail and me to stay at his dacha. As it happened, I'd already met Pavel Pavlovich on the boat from Stettin. he was returning from England, from the embassy.'

'I wonder why he's back in Petersburg. Did he say?'

'I've no idea, but he mentioned that you and he know one another.'

'Yes, we are acquainted. We met during the war. I think it was after the battle of Maloyaroslavets. I seem to remember that there was some unpleasantness about prisoners. Kalinin made some protest or other; there was something of a row. But it was years ago. I don't really recollect.'

A small crease had appeared between his uncle's eyes. Vasily knew he was being evasive. Alexander had an excellent memory and was unlikely to have forgotten the incident. But he must change the subject. His uncle wouldn't be pleased to learn that the Colonel had introduced him to Ryleev, or that he had been party to discussions about the fate of the Tsar and the advantages of republicanism, or, indeed, that he had commenced a love affair with the Colonel's sister.

Vasily wondered if he should bring up the matter of Matvey. There was still no sign of the boy. But now a lackey had come up to say that the Prince was waiting for them. Vasily ran to fetch his mother a shawl, and they made their way towards the stone staircase.

———

'What's this I hear about you removing a young serf from the kitchens?'

Vasily, summoned to his uncle's study the following morning, knew he must hold firm. 'I needed him when Yakov was indisposed...The Prince couldn't spare anyone else...' This was partially true.

'But you don't need him now, so I suggest you return him to his normal duties.'

'I really don't want to do that, sir.'

Why not? I can't see why you need another servant, but if you do, your mother has at least one who, in my opinion, is surplus to requirements.'

'The boy's very bright. He's wasted in the kitchens, and besides...' Should he describe the conditions in which the boy had been living? Why not? As he spoke, his uncle's face darkened.

'Well that's very unfortunate, and we'll have to look into it, but it's no reason for you to take him under your wing. You should return him to Dmitry. I suppose, if he thinks fit, he may find some other position for him.'

'I'm sorry, sir, I'm not prepared to do that. If he's given a role where he can't use his brains, he will inevitably become a reprobate. He needs to be cared for, occupied. I believe he would prove very useful in time, could become a steward or a secretary, at least.'

Alexander hesitated but then shook his head. 'That's all very well... but if every clever serf were taken up, encouraged to expect something better, where would we be?'

'Perhaps I might buy him?'

'Buy him? Don't be ridiculous. You have no money, and besides, in theory at least, such a transaction would be illegal.'

'But it's regularly done all the same. I'm sure I can find the money.' Would Mikhail lend it to him? Probably. 'Let me speak to the Prince.'

'No, Vasily. He's to go back to his master, and that's final.'

Vasily took a deep breath. He had rarely defied his uncle in the past, but he remembered Matvey's bruises, the filth on his body, his eyes bright with lively intelligence.

'I'm sorry, sir. I cannot agree.' As Alexander watched him, open-mouthed, Vasily rose to his feet and left the room.

———

Two days later, an hour before dinner, Vasily descended to the Prince's rooms. His mother was in the hallway, bidding farewell to his sister, Katya, who was returning home to the Polunin Palace. She patted him on the back as he passed.

The last couple of days had been uncomfortable. When it became obvious that Vasily was not going to comply with his uncle's wishes, Alexander had ignored him. His mother had overcompensated with suffocating solicitousness. Matvey had lain low. The only course of action was to appeal to the Prince. He found him in his drawing room.

'Ah, Vasily! I wondered when I would be seeing you. You've not been down to dinner!'

'No, sir.'

'You've come to return my kitchen boy, I suppose.'

'No sir.'

'No?' Dmitry's bushy brows rose.

'No, sir. I think you should sell him to me.'

'Sell him to you? I don't think that's possible.' The Prince turned away. He said nothing for several minutes. 'Look Vasya. I know that the boy was neglected. I slipped up, should have

taken more care. I promise his life will be better in future…
Perhaps he could become a page…'

'That's not good enough, sir. Matvey's uncommonly bright,
but left uneducated will certainly come to nothing, worse than
nothing. He already drinks regularly and is only passing honest.'

'And do you really think you can change that?'

'Yes sir, I do. He has been badly treated and needs care, but
most importantly, he needs stimulation.'

The Prince nodded his head and frowned. 'But your uncle
won't like it… I don't know… perhaps…'

While they continued to wrangle, Vasily's mother came
in from the hallway. She sat down and, having listened for a
while, remarked: 'May I suggest a compromise?' She paused.
'As it happens, I might have use for the boy. If we run him up
some livery, he could attend me on my visits to Katya. That
would be very appropriate! Perhaps, at the same time, he
could start learning his letters. It will soon be clear if he's as
promising as you think, Vasya.'

The Prince scratched his head. Vasily knew he must press
his advantage. 'And I will work harder on my English, Dmitry
Vladimirovich,' he said. 'And speak to Yakov about his
indolence.'

The Prince brightened visibly. 'I suppose Alexander might
agree to those conditions. You must help me persuade him,
Maria.'

'Of course.'

Vasily sighed with relief. Matvey was safe for now.

CHAPTER ELEVEN
September – St Petersburg

VASILY STOOD, GLASS in hand, and surveyed the brightly lit saloon. More people than he had expected had come to his birthday reception and now they were reflected, multiplied a hundred times, in the tarnished mirrors around the walls. A group of musicians was tuning up in the corner. Soon he would be obliged to dance. It was a pity that Irina could not be here, but she and her brother had not yet returned from the country.

Katya's new husband, Prince Polunin, joined him. He was a wispy streak of a man, with thinning hair and a face that shone pink above his receding chin. 'We were sorry you didn't visit us this summer, Vasily Nikolayevich,' he said.

'Yes, I felt obliged to spend the last few weeks studying.' Vasily hoped the Prince wouldn't enquire about his progress.

'Of course, of course, but you missed a fine spectacle.' Polunin proceeded to describe the military review that he and Katya had attended at the Tsar's summer residence. Although he displayed the tastes and prejudices of a loyal servant of the Emperor, the Prince seemed amiable enough. Katya appeared content with him despite the difference in their ages.

Alexander Petrovich was approaching, accompanied by an unknown guest: a tall well-formed man in a black frock coat. His face was remarkable. His lips were narrow, his pale eyes deep-set, and his fine-boned nose sat thin and straight between the shaded hollows of his cheeks.

'Count Fedulov, allow me to present my nephew, Vasily Nikolayevich,' Alexander said.

Vasily bowed. 'It's a great pleasure to meet you, sir.' He signalled for a glass of champagne as Count Fedulov returned his bow.

'Leonid Sergeyevich serves with me at the Ministry,' said Alexander. 'He was obliged to call in with some documents. I was sure that you'd be happy for him to join our celebration.' After some further pleasantries, his uncle walked briskly away.

Vasily tried to recall what he knew of this man. There was certainly something. Of course: Fedulov was the suitor that Katya had been persuaded to refuse some time ago. The Count's marriage proposal had been greeted with excitement, but his mother's diligent inquiries into his true worth had been revealing. Katya had been disappointed, but she had taken Mama's advice and the man had been rejected.

Now, however, he must be entertained. 'Have you eaten, sir?' Fedulov indicated that he had.

'So, how do you find life at the Ministry? Is my uncle keeping you occupied?'

'There's always work to do, Count Belkin.' His tone was clipped. 'There's plenty to keep us busy. We're always alert, I assure you, always on guard seeking out the Tsar's enemies, keeping our ears close to the ground.'

'Oh! How very commendable.' Vasily hoped he sounded enthusiastic.

Fedulov leant forward a little. 'No doubt you have heard about our successful mission in Kolomna last week? The Police closed down an unlicenced printing press and arrested all the criminals implicated.'

'No, sir, I wasn't aware of it.' His uncle rarely spoke of his work at the Ministry and generally deflected attempts to discuss it. 'Was the output of the press worth reading?'

'I have no idea.' Fedulov stared at him briefly, his brows raised, his stone-coloured eyes devoid of life. 'The enterprise was, of course, illegal. Its publications were examined and, where appropriate, conserved or destroyed, as is required by the regulations.' The Count seemed to take himself very seriously. Silence fell.

'I'll be starting work soon,' Vasily said finally. 'But I won't be going into publishing. I'm hoping to join the Foreign Ministry after Christmas, and I'm currently trying to improve my language skills.'

'How pleasant to be under no pressure. To have time to travel abroad and then to have everything so neatly arranged on your return, Count.'

'Yes, I suppose it is…'

Vasily glanced around. How could he escape this humourless bureaucrat? Could he introduce him to somebody? There was no one obvious to hand. Katya appeared to have noticed Fedulov. Perhaps, despite the awkwardness of the past, she might come to his rescue? Vasily caught her eye. She turned to Polunin and, having whispered something in his ear, crossed the room and joined them.

'Ah! Leonid Sergeyevich, how good to see you here!' she said, extending her hand. She seemed genuinely pleased to see him. 'How have you been keeping? You're looking well. We, the Prince and I that is, have been at Tsarskoe Selo. It's been something of an ordeal for me, all quite new, but Prince Polunin has been a great support.'

'I'm indeed well, Ekaterina Nikolayevna. Life is looking up. I've received a small legacy and hope to receive a promotion at the Ministry in the not-too-distant future.'

Vasily wondered if this was true but then reproached himself. The man had dissembled in the past, but that didn't mean he was generally untrustworthy.

'Oh, that's excellent news. And how are your sisters?' Katya asked.

'All were well when I last saw them. They generally remain on the estate these days.'

'You know, Leonid,' Katya said, risking the familiarity of his given name, 'You must come to my reception next week. There will be many young ladies present, and there is one you may find particularly appealing. Elizaveta Gavrilovna, daughter of my mother's cousin, the Countess Laptev. She's shortly arriving in town with her aunt to enter society. Hers is a very good family, and quite a small one!'

'I should be delighted,' said Fedulov.

'Oh… that's good.' Katya stroked her fan and looked at the floor. Vasily realised that his sister already regretted being carried away in a moment of nostalgia, but she had committed herself and would be obliged to send a card. Mama wouldn't be pleased. The musicians started to play, and desultory dancing began. A servant dropped a glass somewhere behind a screen.

As Katya began to speak once again, a footman approached with a letter. Perhaps here was hope of relief. Fedulov eyed the note with interest as Vasily took it up from the tray. It was Irina's hand. He needed to find somewhere quiet to read it. Making his excuses, he left his sister with her former admirer.

On the way to the door, he stopped to greet Mikhail. His friend had returned with his regiment from summer camp and was once again occupied by drill, riding school, and dinner with the Colonel on Thursdays.

'That's Leonid Fedulov, isn't it?' Mikhail said. 'Nikita warned me to be wary of him. He's a particularly energetic sniffer-out of dissent, I understand, but it's said he isn't beyond taking the odd inducement to keep quiet.'

Vasily wondered if his uncle knew that. 'I've not met him before,' he said. 'He's not the easiest company, and he does seem very keen on his work.'

As they watched, Fedulov took his leave of Katya and, scanning the room, picked up another glass of champagne and drained it. Then, apparently finding nothing further to interest him, he took his leave, bowing deeply to Maria Vasilyevna as he went.

Mikhail noticed Vasily's letter and laughed. 'Is that from Irène? So, you're still in hot pursuit!'

'I've progressed a little way beyond the chase, my friend,' Vasily replied, and, smiling at Mikhail's obvious surprise, withdrew to a corner. As he opened Irina's note he was conscious of a faint hint of lemons.

My dear Vasya,
First of all I send you greetings and many kisses for your birthday. I hope that your party is going well.

We returned from the country today and are now back in the apartment on the English Embankment. I was sorry to leave the summer house and the happiest of memories behind, but the weather has now changed and it seems that the season is ending.

Will you come to me here tomorrow at five and we shall see if we can breathe some life into its last days?
Your,
Irina

He folded the letter, tucked it into his breast, and went in search of the means to reply. Count Fedulov was forgotten.

———

'I'm sure he's seeing a woman,' said Alexander, rubbing the back of his thin neck. The guests had departed, and he was drinking brandy with Dmitry in the Prince's study. The night was chill, and the reflected flames of the fire shimmered on the gilded clock and ormolu desk trappings.

'Who is?'

'Vasily, of course. He received a note halfway through the evening.'

'How do you know it was from a woman?'

'Well, it was pretty obvious. First of all, he visibly cheered up, then he sniffed at it... that's a sure sign you know... and then he ran off to read it as soon as he was able. Since our return from the country, I've had my suspicions. Where did he disappear to that day last week? Why is he always too distracted, or tired, to study? And he's become more secretive.'

'I thought he went out to see some of his friends, or his sister and Polunin. Anyway, if he has found a girl, it's only natural, you know, Sasha. You've got to let go a little. He's a man now...'

Alexander grunted and stared into the flames. He mourned the passing of his nephew's youth. It was inevitable that his trip abroad would have changed him, but the extent of that change was striking.

'He looks more like his father every day,' Alexander said. 'Thank God he seems to be more reliable, more balanced, but he's developed a streak of determination that Kolya never had.'

'Well, that's probably not a bad thing. By all accounts, Nikolay Petrovich should have taken more of a grip, been more tenacious.'

'Yes, you're right. I was surprised at the strength of Vasily's resistance when I told him to return your young lad to the kitchens. Being honest, the dispute took away much of the pleasure of our return home. Vasya and I never used to have such differences.'

'Well, we've a compromise now,' said Dmitry. 'As you know, I was not entirely without blame.'

'That is all nonsense, Dima. The lad will never return to the kitchens. Yakov is incorrigible, and on present showing, Vasily is unlikely to apply himself to his English. He and that tutor of his spend too much time chattering in French and reading poetry. But if there's peace in the house, I suppose I'm content. At least I can enjoy Vasily's company again for the short time he'll be here. If the Foreign Ministry send him straight out to an embassy, he could be gone soon after Christmas… I don't know what he will do with that boy then.'

'Stop fretting, Sasha. Vasily will be alright. I know he appreciates all you do for him.' Dmitry called for a log to be put on the fire. 'Anyway, how did you find the Ministry on your return?'

'Much the same as when I went. Apart from some specific

operations, we're still wasting our time following up on false leads, harassing innocent foreigners and looking for non-existent secret societies. There have been rumours of dissent, particularly in the South, but the Emperor hasn't been minded to make much of them. No doubt, he's right, although that old woman Benkendorf sees conspirators behind every tree. On the whole, Dima, I'd say there's not much of a threat from radicals and republicans in Russia at present.'

CHAPTER TWELVE

ON THE DAY of Katya's reception for the heiress from the south, Vasily was strolling with Mikhail along Nevsky Prospekt. Matvey dawdled behind in his new blue livery, carrying their parcels.

The street was busy. The elite of St Petersburg were visiting the shops and eating places or taking a drive along the broad highway. Coaches, carriages and wagons filled the road; flower sellers and hawkers cried their wares; the drivers of droshkies sought potential customers. Cavalry officers, mounted on long-limbed horses, bowed to right and left, removing their hats as they recognised acquaintances. On the pavement, well-dressed women ambled along, followed by servants loaded with bags and boxes.

Vasily lost Matvey several times as the boy lingered in front of shop windows, deciphering the signs, and he watched in horror as he was almost flattened by a carriage that sped by. The coachman shouted some choice words of abuse, and Vasily felt obliged to give Matvey a sharp cuff round the ear, which he instantly regretted.

They were entering a jewellery shop, seeking a gift for Irina, when a bugle call sounded from the direction of the Admiralty.

'A grandee from the palace is on the move,' said Mikhail. 'They'll be clearing the street. We'll have to move if you need to get home quickly.' Mikhail smoothed down his uniform and checked his helmet.

'Let's see them pass', said Vasily. 'We've plenty of time.' He felt a flutter of excitement. He had never quite lost his childhood enthusiasm for military spectacle.

Carriages and horsemen prepared to depart. Pedestrians hurried to finish their business, and, by the time Vasily had made his purchase, the street was almost empty. A troop of policemen had ranged themselves along the edges of the broad pavements to hold back gathering onlookers. Minutes later, Vasily could hear the sound of horses' hooves approaching from the direction of the palace. Which elite regiment of mounted Guards would be accompanying the royal personage today? He soon recognised the Lifeguards, their dark plumed helmets and metal breastplates burnished to a dull grey gleam beneath the red collars of their white uniforms.

A small advance guard led the small procession. Mikhail Pavlovich, the Tsar's younger brother, rode a short distance behind. The Grand Duke's flushed face flaunted curly sideburns; his tall body was rendered taller by his bicorne hat. His grey horse danced obliquely as he progressed along the highway, flanked by his staff and followed by a further detachment of guards.

As the leading horses passed, Vasily noticed a disturbance on the pavement opposite. A dog had run out across the street and was being pursued by a young workman who had forced his way through the line of policemen and now crossed the road directly in front of the Duke's horse. The beast reared up, almost unseating its rider. Matvey cried out and dropped his parcels; Vasily felt a small hand thrust into his. The workman plunged into the crowd a few yards away. Two policemen caught and restrained him and then, joined by some of their fellows, started to beat him energetically with their fists and cudgels.

The Grand Duke, now in control of his mount, uttered

a clipped command and drew his sword. The order was repeated. The column came to a halt, and the police drew back. All fell silent. The young man lay on the ground, shaking with terror. Vasily looked at the Duke. Surely he must call a halt to this barbarity? But the Tsar's brother advanced his horse and, with a face filled with malevolence, rose in his stirrups and indicated that the policemen should continue their work. The pitiful shrieks were renewed.

This was unbelievable – intolerable! They would kill him. Surely the Duke would call them off? Vasily dropped Matvey's hand and threw himself towards the melee of swinging batons. Matvey tried to grasp the edge of his coat.

'Vasya, for God's sake!' Mikhail caught him firmly from behind and wrestled him back between the silent onlookers. 'What the hell do you think you're doing! Leave it, leave it, you must leave them be!'

'Let me go, damn you, Misha!' Vasily struggled to free himself, but Mikhail's hold was too strong.

The Duke sat, immobile, his sword still raised. The young man lay in a bloodied heap on the pavement. The sound of blows continued, but his cries had ceased. Someone had caught the dog and kicked her; she whined, shivering beside what remained of her master and unable to run away.

Vasily's heart surged. He must at least save the dog, but Mikhail's heavy hands still gripped his shoulders. He cursed and struggled once again but, restrained as he was, could do nothing. He sank down onto the stone of the pavement with his head on his knees and with blood pounding in his ears. Looking up, through gaps in the crowd he watched the Grand Duke turn his horse, drive his spurs into its sweat-darkened flanks, and give a signal that the detachment could proceed.

As the troop of Lifeguards moved off, a lieutenant peeled off from the rear and rode towards them. 'Is that man with you, Stenovsky?' he barked.

Mikhail released Vasily, came to attention, and saluted. 'Yes, sir, I have him under control, sir.'

'Well, get him away from here before someone decides to arrest him.' The Lifeguard wheeled his horse and trotted back to the column, which was fast disappearing on its way out of town.

Half an hour later, Vasily was recovering his composure on a bench in the garden of his home. Matvey, his teeth chattering with shock, had been hurried upstairs by Yakov. Mikhail was taking turns around the fountain staring at the ground. They had returned in a droshky from Nevsky Prospekt and had not spoken since the incident. Vasily didn't know what to say. His actions had not only been pointless but they had also been foolhardy and dangerous. His sudden fury had been justified, but now he could hardly believe what he had done.

'That's the true face of autocracy, Vasya,' Mikhail said finally. 'Such incidents remind me what slaves we all are. They make me ashamed to be Russian. No one, whoever they are, should be able to destroy an innocent man with impunity! And in broad daylight, too!' He fell silent again and then continued: 'But you know, my dear friend, that lunging at a group of baton-wielding policemen in full view of the Tsar's brother wasn't the wisest response.'

''I know... but really! What a spectacle. It was the behaviour of a man with no sense of proportion, or of compassion.'

'It was the response of a man who's afraid. And he's right to be afraid. The days of his kind are certainly numbered. The clock is ticking.'

'You sound like Ryleev'

'Yes, I suppose I do, and he's completely right. The day of reckoning can't be that far off.' Mikhail sat on the edge of the fountain and pulled his sword from the scabbard that he had unstrapped and rested against the wall. He squinted down the blade. Silence fell between them once again. Water from the fountain plashed onto the surface of the pool.

'I was impressed by Ryleev when I met him at the Colonel's,' Vasily said. 'He certainly doesn't keep his opinions to himself, and his views have been fully justified today. It would be good to meet him again.'

'Nikita will be coming back from our estates shortly. He's known Ryleev for years, and, although they don't always see eye to eye, their views are close enough. He'd be pleased to arrange a meeting, a dinner perhaps. You're obviously developing a taste for politics, Vasya.'

'Yes, perhaps I am. You remember I told you about the fight that took place at the inn on the Pavlovsk Road? It forced me to reflect on Kalinin's words about the plight of the serfs here in Russia. One has to be blind not to see that things need to change.' He told Mikhail about the Prince's ignorance of Matvey's condition and the dismal fate of the serfs belonging to the merchant Kuprin. 'Both events brought home to me the cruelty of the entire system,' he said. 'It's been something of a revelation. I was barely aware of it, but that isn't really an excuse. I recently learned from Yakov, that years ago my grandfather and great-grandfather treated our own people badly. I had no idea, none at all. But I think they're dealt with more fairly now.'

'In the case of Yakov, I'd say more than fairly!' Mikhail said.

'That's possibly the case, but serfs should be treated as human beings.'

'Yes, there must be change. Many serf owners are good

enough, but a few are certainly not. Female servants are often particularly vulnerable as I now know to our cost, and even in the best-regulated households, there are sometimes one or two individuals, like your lad Matvey, that fall through the net.'

As time passed, Vasily's mood improved, although the incident on Nevsky Prospekt continued alternately to arouse his anger and depress his spirits. Finally, he pulled out his watch and rose to his feet. 'I suppose we must go to Katya's reception. I have to say, I don't much feel like it. Let's stop somewhere on the way, and I'll tell you about my plans for Matvey. I met with some resistance from my uncle at first, but we've now reached an agreement.'

'I was surprised to see that the boy's still with you. I thought he'd be sent back to the kitchens.'

'I think he's safe from that now. Maltby's prepared to help him to read, learn his numbers.'

Mikhail frowned slightly. 'I hope it's wise to encourage him.'

'I think that it is. Matvey's such a bright spark, it seems wrong to leave him in a state of ignorance. Serfs sometimes do take jobs that require education after all. And if change does come, as we hope it will, then he'll be well prepared.'

Mikhail looked as though he was going to argue, but then he shrugged, and his arm encircled Vasily's shoulders. 'You're a surprising fellow, Vasya.'

'Yes, I surprise myself these days.'

Mikhail waited in the garden while Vasily went upstairs to change, and then they set off for the Polunin Palace, calling in at the English Tavern on Galernaya Street on the way.

They arrived at the reception late and slightly inebriated. Vasily found it an effort to put the morning's events behind him, but he greeted his acquaintance and paid the necessary respects to his sister's new protégé, Elizaveta Gavrilovna. His second cousin was a striking girl with thick black curls, clear eyes and a slightly overlong nose. She didn't yet seem completely at ease in society. He left as soon as he could politely get away.

Walking the short distance to Kalinin's apartment, he paused for a few minutes and looked out over the dark river. An occasional flare of light reflected on the water, and ripples slapped the stone-clad banks. He needed to see Irina, to be distracted, to banish the vision of the young workman lying lifeless beside his whimpering dog.

She was reading in the drawing room, her legs curled beneath her on the sofa. Soft lamps lit the velvet drapes and the dusty pink and sage green cushions. She rose as Vasily entered the room. Moving swiftly to her, he caught her in his arms and kissed her. Then he raised his hand to her face, pushed back a wisp of her bright hair, and clutching it, held her close against him for some minutes. His spirits lightened, but then, at the sound of Pavel Pavlovich's footsteps, they drew apart.

'I understand there was a small contretemps on Nevsky this morning,' Kalinin said. 'I'd like to hear what happened.' He turned to his sister. 'Can you spare Vasily for a few minutes, Irène?' Irina turned, gave a small shrug, and sought her discarded book.

Vasily followed Kalinin to his study. Perhaps, at last, Kalinin would open up a little. He accepted a glass of brandy. As he described the morning's incident, he didn't try to hide his feelings or his continuing sense of outrage. Kalinin made no comment, nor did he ask any questions, and when Vasily had finished and he had still said nothing, Vasily broke the silence. 'You said when we spoke of Russia's problems in the summer we would discuss what could be done about them at another time. We never have, you know.'

'No, we haven't... although we did hear Ryleev's solution, which was quite radical, I think you'll agree.' Kalinin was sidestepping the issue.

'Yes, I hope to meet Kondraty Feodorovich again; he knows Mikhail's brother well.'

'Well, that would do no harm,' said Kalinin. 'But I'm sure I don't have to tell you to be more discreet. I can see that what you witnessed today may well have enraged you and reinforced your views about the character of our government. I can also understand your desire to meet others who share your opinions, and, in principle, I don't discourage you. But you must realise that opposition to the establishment is dangerous; punishment for open dissent can be heavy – fatal, even. There are spies and informers everywhere. If you want to live to see the revolution succeed, you must be prudent, be cautious about what you do and with whom you share your thoughts.' He leant forward. 'Don't even think about discussing such matters with your uncle, and you must take care about what you say to my sister. It's hard to keep secrets from people one cares for, but it's all too easy to compromise them, put them in jeopardy.'

'Of course, I've said nothing to anyone,' said Vasily. 'I would never compromise Irina.'

'I'm pleased to hear it. But, Vasily, it must be clear to you that quixotic exhibitions of protest, such as the one that Mikhail averted today are not only pointless, but also dangerous. You do understand that?'

'Yes, Pavel, I do, of course, but—'

Kalinin cut across him: 'That's good. Well, you mustn't keep your woman waiting, Vasya. I'd write today's foolish behaviour off to experience if I were you, but I urge you to reflect, and to try not to repeat it.'

The Colonel drained his glass and rose to his feet. 'I suppose you'll be here for a good while longer. Can you remember to tell the man to lock the door when you finally leave?'

CHAPTER THIRTEEN

ELIZAVETA GAVRILOVNA WATCHED her father's carriage roll out of the stable yard of the Polunin Palace and turn into Galernaya Street. It was returning to her family's estate in the south.

'I do hope he goes carefully, Lisa,' her aunt, Darya Stepanovna, was saying. 'There were moments on the journey when I thought we would be overturned! He drove as fast as the Post, at times!'

Aunt Darya had not enjoyed the long carriage ride from Oryol to St Petersburg, despite the fact that they had broken the journey in Moscow and had only been forced to spend one night at a post house. Lisa wondered if she could escape her chaperone's incessant chatter. But now she had moved on to the dressmaker's bill.

'And I do hope that Gavril Ivanovich is not annoyed about the expense, but Katya was quite insistent that you have some new gowns...'

'I'm sure that Papa won't mind. He's expecting this visit to be costly. But, Aunt, I think that now the carriage is gone, I'll go up to my room for a while. I have letters to write.'

'More letters! Goodness me, Lisa, you have only just sent some... Well, I suppose if you must.'

Released at last, Lisa made her way to the suite of rooms that she shared with her aunt. They faced south, looking out towards the canal, and enjoyed such sun as could be found in this grey northern city. She did want to write more letters; there had been little time in recent days. She had, of course, written to her parents and her sister Nadezhda, but she must take time to compose a letter to her old nanny and Miss Roberts, the English governess. She knew they'd be thinking about her and would be wanting to receive her first impressions. St Petersburg was as wonderful and extraordinary as she had hoped, its dignified buildings and open-spaced elegance such a contrast to the jumbled buildings and unpaved streets of the town and villages close to her home. But it wouldn't be easy to describe this city that had sprung up, apparently from nowhere, in the middle of a bleak marshy wilderness.

She sat down at her desk. How should she start? It was, of course, not possible to send the news they were aching to hear, that she had found an eligible suitor at last.

But would she find him? At home in Oryol, the few local men worthy of consideration had, for one reason or another, not come up to scratch. Her expectations were perhaps high, but surely she shouldn't need to compromise. She and her sister were heiresses to a considerable estate, she was not without intelligence and had been led to believe that her looks were better than average. It shouldn't be impossible to find a partner of standing with wealth equal to her own.

The family's annual visits to Moscow for the Christmas season had not proved fruitful. It had been wounding when a well-meaning friend had confided in her that potential suitors considered her – in no particular order – too bookish, too tall, too pious, too proud and, worst of all, too provincial. This spring, following her twenty-first birthday, her mother had started to express concern that she would never find a man worthy of consideration. But Nanya had remained sure that God was looking out for the right husband for her and that all would be well. Lisa's faith in God was strong, but even she had begun to question the old woman's conviction.

It was Aunt Darya, her mother's widowed sister, who had hit on the idea of an extended visit to their cousins, the Belkins, in St Petersburg. Her aunt had remembered receiving news of Ekaterina Nikolayevna's fortunate marriage to Prince Polunin. Surely, she had said, this excellent connection must yield results. Lisa's mother had been too busy to accompany her, so Darya Stepanova had offered to be her chaperone.

Katya had risen to the challenge with enthusiasm and had started to introduce her unmarried cousin into society. On her arrival in the capital, Lisa had been taken to Court and, in the absence of the Empress, had been presented to the Empress Dowager, Maria Feodorovna. That hurdle having been cleared, the day before yesterday, a reception had been organised 'to launch' her, like a ship stuffed with merchandise, into society.

She had not much enjoyed the first part of the evening. It had been embarrassing to stand with Aunt Maria and Katya while men and women alike had scanned her face and attire with inquisitive stares. Some had rudely raised their lorgnettes to study her features; others openly discussed her looks in a manner that she couldn't fail to overhear. On the whole, the comments had been favourable, but it was offensive nonetheless. At last, she had been rescued by the arrival of Katya's brother, Vasily Nikolayevich. Since her arrival in St Petersburg, he had been strangely elusive, and when they finally met, she didn't recognise him. It had been ten years or more since his family had visited their home in Oryol.

When he had arrived, she had been trying to conceal her discomfort. He had entered the saloon, a compact man with dense dark hair, dressed in a fashionable tailcoat and an extravagant cravat. He had been with a guards officer: tall, in a crisp white uniform. The contrast in the men's appearance had amused her, and she had wondered who they were. The lofty guardsman had stepped aside to greet an acquaintance, so it was Vasily alone who, having introduced himself, had taken her by the arm and led her to the window under the pretext of admiring the view of the river.

'You can't stand over there with your aunt, Katya and my mother all evening, Elizaveta Gavrilovna, You'll never meet anyone and be bored to death.'

Her cousin's dark eyes had sparked with interest and amusement as he tried to recall his family's visit to Oryol many years before. She started to feel more comfortable. In time, Vasily's tall friend joined them and was introduced as Cornet Mikhail Stenovsky of the Chevalier Guards. The soldier had barely spoken; he had simply fixed his blue eyes on her and observed her carefully. He was attractive in a quiet way, particularly when his long, rather serious face had brightened in a smile. They had promised to drive out with her to show her the sights and then made sure that she was reunited with a family that she had met in Moscow. After that, her evening had improved, although when she looked around later she was disappointed to see that both Vasily and his friend had disappeared.

On the whole, the reception had been a success. Her acquaintance from Moscow had promised to call. She had stimulated some interest, particularly from an older man, good-looking and very elegantly attired in a dark frock coat. He wore a civil service order of some sort and introduced himself as Count Leonid Fedulov. He explained that he worked at the Interior Ministry with Katya's uncle. They spoke for some time, and he had made a point of seeking an introduction to Aunt Darya, who had found him quite charming.

And now, as Lisa picked up her pen and started recording her first impressions of the capital for her friends at home, her maid Vera hurried into the room in a state of agitation. 'Elizaveta Gavrilovna, Miss, you must put that away! The Princess has said you must tidy yourself and come down to the drawing room at once. Madame Stenovsky, Cornet Stenovsky's mother, has sent up her card and will shortly be taking refreshment.'

———

The open carriage circumnavigated the boulevard that surrounded the Admiralty Building. From here it was possible to see many of the city sights: the Neva river with the broad view upstream to the walls of the Peter and Paul Fortress, the statue-topped façade of the Winter Palace; the arc of Palace Square; the muscular classical columns of the Lifeguards' Riding Hall.

It was almost two weeks after the reception held for Elizaveta Gavrilovna, and Vasily and Mikhail were fulfilling their promise to drive out with her. They were accompanied by Katya, who had been keen to chaperone her guest. Mikhail asked the coachmen to pause from time to time as he pointed out the places he thought worth seeing.

The sky was grey, and the weather had become cooler in recent days. Vasily rode next to Mikhail, their backs to the horses. The two women opposite sat in their stylish bonnets, Katya's plum-purple cloak and Lisa's cherry-red cloak glowing against the black leather seats. Lisa's face was full of interest as she absorbed Mikhail's commentary.

Vasily knew that Mikhail's courtship was going well, although, clearly, Lisa had been wise enough to maintain a friendly distance from her suitor. At present, this was spurring the young officer to produce a flow of more or less accurate information. He was sound on the sights they were passing, less so on their history: his dates were erratic.

Mikhail paid close attention to Quarengi's great Riding Hall. He spoke at some length about the hours that he was obliged to spend at the manège on several mornings each week. He, however, failed to point out the muscular naked statues of Castor and Pollux restraining their rearing horses that flanked the portico. Vasily smiled when Lisa turned her head and observed the controversial statues with unconcealed curiosity.

The carriage then started its drive up Nevsky Prospekt. They aimed to reach the Alexander Nevsky Monastery some six versts or so to the east.

Mikhail commented on various buildings that flanked the street. They passed the newly finished Mikhailovsky Palace, the arches of the expanding Merchants Court and the Kazan Cathedral, whose winged colonnades were, he said, designed to reflect those of St Peter's in Rome. As they drove on, the way became less developed. In some places, the road was edged by green spaces and wooden buildings of the past. At one point, a chicken crossed the road. When they arrived at the monastery, they looked into the churches, and then, before they returned home, wandered for a while in the Lavareskoye Cemetery.

At the end of the excursion, they drew up at the corner of the embankment, intending to walk the short distance to the front doors of the Polunin Palace. Vasily remained seated and looked about.

Irina and her companion Margarethe were approaching along the riverside walk. They were looking out, watching a small boat with red sails that was tacking along the broad reach to the east. Irina turned and saw the carriage. She raised her hand to Vasily for a moment, but then let it drop. Vasily rose to his feet. He hadn't expected to see her today. He would jump down to greet her. But, as if she guessed his intention, she firmly shook her head. She took Gretchen's arm, turned, and walked back towards Kalinin's apartment.

Vasily was surprised. Why didn't she want to acknowledge him? Surely there was no harm in it. Mikhail, for one, would be pleased to see her. He turned to him for support, but he was busy, handing Lisa to the pavement.

'Who's that woman?' Katya asked. She must have observed the brief moment.

Mikhail looked up and, seeing Irina's retreating figure, said, 'That's the Baroness von Steiner with her companion, I believe.' His tone did not invite further inquiry.

'I don't think I know her; do I, Vasya?' Katya asked. 'But she is very striking! I've noticed her from time to time walking here with her friend. She's sometimes with a man, her husband, the Baron, I suppose. They must live nearby. Should I call on her?'

'I think not,' said Mikhail. 'I understand that the Baroness is particular whom she receives and doesn't go out in society a great deal.'

'Oh, I see.' Katya sounded affronted.

'You can't call on all your neighbours, Ekaterina Nikolayevna!'

'No, I suppose you're right, one's diary is already much too full!' She gathered her cloak and led the way into the palace.

Vasily sighed and looked back along the embankment. He wanted to follow Irina, to speak to her, if only for a moment, but she had gone. Today, the entire family was to dine at Katya's. A number of other guests were expected, including

Mikhail's formidable mother. Later, there would be music and cards. No doubt, he would be called upon to sing. It was all part of a ritual dance that would propel the golden couple, Mikhail and Lisa, towards their inevitable betrothal. There they were now, standing with their heads close together. Mikhail seemed to be pointing out yet another highlight of the townscape. Vasily knew he should be happy for them, but his heart was gripped with undignified envy.

———

It was late when they left the palace. As Vasily accompanied his uncle and mother home, he remained despondent. Irina had warned him that their relationship would be difficult and that it must remain concealed. He knew that, but he refused to be ashamed; there was no reason to be. His love for her was something unique and special. He felt transformed when he was with her, completely alive, and when they made love, completely content. He could hardly believe that this wonderful woman not only returned his affection but took his views seriously and even laughed at his jokes. She complained about her lack of formal education, but to him, she seemed very wise. He had told her almost everything about himself, his childhood, his hopes and his evolving view of the world.

Was there a way in which their love could flourish openly? As things stood, that seemed unlikely. But he wouldn't allow her to hide away entirely. If they didn't give their friendship the opportunity to breathe, it would die from a lack of air. There would be no harm in some innocent excursions. He knew that the Prince would lend him the brougham. They could repeat today's drive; Gretchen would accompany them. With some persuasion, Irina would surely agree to that.

CHAPTER FOURTEEN

THE HONEYED REEK of cigar smoke melded with an aroma of roast meats and fine wines. As Vasily climbed the steep stairs of Andrieux's Restaurant, he could hear men laughing and low voices in debate. On the threshold of the private dining room, he was greeted by a waiter with a glass of champagne. Gulping the chill yeasty bubbles, he struggled to suppress his excitement and curiosity.

The group was larger than he had expected. In addition to Mikhail and his brother Nikita, Ryleev was accompanied by two other men. The soldier was Mikhail Bestuzhev, a staff captain in the Moscow Guards Regiment and the younger brother of Ryleev's co-editor of the *Polar Star*. The other man was an employee of the Russian American Company.

At the far end of the room, Nikita was speaking to Ryleev with quiet intensity. The poet stood frowning, staring at the floor. As Vasily and Mikhail approached, the two men drew apart. 'Vasily Nikolayevich!' Ryleev welcomed him. 'It's good to see you again. I'm pleased that you found our last conversation engaging enough to seek more of the same.'

Mikhail introduced Vasily to his brother. Nikita's voice and manner were similar, but he was shorter, darker and altogether more substantial.

'You were at school with Ivan, our younger brother, I think,' Nikita said. 'I'm afraid I don't really remember you at all. I'm glad you've made a friend of Mikhail, though. He needs all the friends he can get!' Mikhail did not respond to his brother's joke.

As they sat down to eat, the waiter circled the table with more wine.

Nikita opened the conversation: 'Have you heard the news about that vampire, Arakcheyev?' No one, it seemed, had heard the latest story about Tsar Alexander's right-hand man. 'While he was busying himself in Petersburg in the absence of the Emperor, the serfs on his estate at Gruzino rose in revolt. It seems that Minkina, the woman who purports to be his wife, was murdered.'

'I'm not in the least surprised,' said Bestuzhev. 'They say she was as savage as the Count – that the serfs there are subject to a constant reign of terror.'

Nikita took a sip from his glass and continued: 'Apparently, earlier this month, the woman took it into her head to discipline three of her maids. One was beaten and tortured with pincers, the others thrown into the jail they see fit to maintain there. This it seems, was the last straw. The serfs rose up, and during the uproar and confusion, the brother of the maid who had been beaten broke into Minkina's bedroom at night and cut her throat.'

'How macabre!' said the official from the Russian America Company.

Nikita laughed without amusement. 'Not half as macabre as it will be when the Count arrives home to wreak vengeance. When Arakcheyev put down the revolt near Kharkov in '19, he sentenced more than 50 men to run the gauntlet. Only half survived. It's said that, afterwards, many of the bodies weren't recognizably human. I'd predict a similar outcome this time.'

Bestuzhev rose to his feet, and declaimed: '*Proud favourite! Both vile and insidious, The ruler's cunning flatterer and thankless friend.*'

Vasily recognised Ryleev's satirical ode of a few years earlier, in which the identity of the Emperor's favourite had been barely concealed.

'Did that one really get past the censor?' said Ryleev, grinning as he passed round the bottle. 'But seriously, when the time comes, I think the revolution will be fully supported, maybe even led, by some of these oppressed serfs and, of course, the soldiers and veterans now suffering in Arakcheyev's miserable military settlements.'

'We don't want to see a repeat of the Terror in France,' Nikita said. 'That can't – must not – happen in Russia. In the end, it would be self-defeating, as it proved to be there.'

'If the people choose to rise up and wreak vengeance, no one should be surprised,' Ryleev said. 'And, personally, I shouldn't try to stop them. You can't cut down a wood without a few splinters flying.'

They fell silent as Andrieux, the proprietor, came up to check that all was well. When he had left, the conversation moved on. Bestuzhev spoke with feeling about the savagery with which some of his fellow officers treated the common soldiers. Ryleev spoke of a cousin whose sister had been seduced and abandoned by a scion of the aristocratic Orlov family. Nikita discussed at some length the probability of a liberal-minded senator joining the movement when the time was right.

Vasily listened, completely absorbed. Of course, at school, boys had passed round odes and pamphlets of a subversive kind, often childishly rude. Some had been penned by Ryleev. It had all seemed daring and exciting, even dangerous, when some boy got caught. But there had never been much substance behind it. It had seemed quite remote. These men, in contrast, might speak lightly and sound humorous, but there was nothing frivolous about their intentions.

Eventually, some of the company stood up to leave. Vasily rose from the table, too. His head spun a little. Perhaps he would walk around for a while outside. As he made for the door, Ryleev called him back.

'Vasily Nikolayevich,' he said. 'Could I detain you a little longer? And you, too, Mikhail.' As they sat down again, Ryleev reached for more champagne. The lamplight illuminated his pale face. His strange eyes were glittering. He placed his hands on the table in front of him. 'Why did you come along this evening, Count?'

Vasily looked up, tempted to give voice to his growing convictions, but how far could he, should he, commit himself? He spoke slowly, considering his words. 'I'm here because in recent weeks I've come to understand, to believe, that Russia needs to change. And it seems that the only way to bring about that change is to reform our way of government, end the absolute power of the Tsar. Mikhail has played his part in bringing me to that conclusion. He doesn't let these matters rest, as you know.'

Mikhail studied the tablecloth.

'Since I returned from Europe,' Vasily continued. 'I've found it increasingly hard to ignore the evidence of my own eyes. You know, I suppose, that we witnessed that young workman being beaten insensible on Nevsky? I found that barely believable. And there have been other incidents since my return home, trivial in the overall scheme of things, I suppose, but crucial to those whose lives were affected.'

Ryleev was nodding his head.

'I had already begun to develop an interest in social and

political theory,' Vasily said, 'but now I've moved beyond that. If you recognise that there is something rotten in our way of government, then I feel it's shameful to do nothing about it. But I'm not an extremist, Ryleev; I agree with Nikita. I'm not sure violence achieves anything but more violence.'

'But you do realise,' Ryleev said, 'what you've just said would in some circles be regarded as treason? Some would already consider you a confirmed revolutionary! What is revolutionary to an autocrat, of course, is to most right-thinking people merely a response to the spirit of the age. It's an impulse to force our beloved country to swim with, rather than against, the tide of progress.'

Ryleev leant across the table. 'Look, Vasily. You're plainly a man of conscience and a lively thinker. You owe it to yourself to develop your recently aroused interests. You already understand, you have already seen, that despotism drains politics of all morality, that it's an affront to the country you love, and, therefore, as a moral being, you have no option but to fight for change.

'At the very least you should come along to our meetings. We have what you might call a discussion group. It meets privately here in the city from time to time. We are not alone; we are not unique; there are similar societies elsewhere, and of course, there are people in the government now, men of influence, who will certainly rise up and join the struggle when the time is right.

'I understand what you say about violence. There's no need, you know, to commit to more than supporting our cause. You must take an oath of secrecy, of course, but you won't have to take up arms. There are others who are better suited to that. They'll force the issue when the moment comes.'

Ryleev paused and leant back, rubbing his chin. He looked at Vasily and held his gaze. 'But you should have no illusions. Although I confess that, at present, the day of reckoning, of sacrifice, seems some way off. In the end, there will be resistance, violence, blood will be spilt. *Your* blood might be spilt. The danger is greatest for those who move first! But it will be worth it; it will be a price well worth paying. You must see it as a debt incurred for mankind's better future. You will think about the lives that will be saved, the generations of people who will be liberated.'

Ryleev took another sip of champagne. His unblinking eyes seemed to paralyse Vasily, his eloquence disarm him.

Twice he opened his mouth to reply, and twice he shut it again. The silence seemed to stretch across the table like something physical. He tried to weigh the poet's words. He had a choice, of course, but he knew his heart had already made it.

'Yes, Kondraty Feodorovich, I will join your cause. I feel I have no option.'

Ryleev gave the sweetest of smiles and swayed back on his chair. Mikhail rose to his feet and, embracing Vasily, said, 'Oh, Vasya. So you will join us! I hoped you would.'

Later, Vasily and Mikhail sat wrapped in furs in the chilly divan room in the Prince's palace and talked through the night. As he left just before dawn, Mikhail turned back and said: 'Well, Vasily my friend, together we shall be famous! We shall make history.' Pulling on his cap, he disappeared into the chill of the morning.

CHAPTER FIFTEEN

Two days later, Mikhail's orderly brought a message asking Vasily to join him at the Russian American House after dinner. As he read it, his heart beat faster. What did this mean? What did Ryleev want with him? Would he now have to take some sort of oath?

When he arrived, Ryleev, Mikhail and Captain Bestuzhev were already deep in conversation. The poet waved him to a window seat. Bright lamps lit up the poet's huge desk. Bookcases flanked a painted dresser, and on the walls were scenes of Alaska and a wooden Russian church perched on the Californian coast. Ryleev's small daughter warbled somewhere nearby, accompanied by the softer tones of his wife.

They had just lit cigars when a note was brought in. As Ryleev read it, his pale face came alive. 'So he's finally called him out!'

'Who's called who out, Kondraty?' Bestuzhev blew smoke into the air and smoothed the braid on his dark uniform.

'I told you the other evening, I think, about my cousin Konstantin Chernov, the young guardsman whose sister has been so vilely treated by that prig Novosiltsev? Well, Konstantin has challenged the scoundrel and asked me to be his second. I'll agree, of course.'

'Is there no hope of a compromise?' Vasily asked.

'Of course, I must try to arrange one, but I doubt I'll succeed. Konstantin is determined to fight. His sister's reputation is at stake; Maria is a great beauty, and Novosiltsev was very taken with her. The hussar led the girl to believe that he would marry her. They became very close; too close, if you take my meaning. But he simply disappeared when his distinguished family insisted that he abandon what seemed to them an entirely inappropriate connection. Chernov wrote to him seeking an explanation. The man played him along with excuses for a while, but it's clear that Novosiltsev has no intention of keeping his word. His arrogance and dishonesty are astounding, but of course that's only what one might expect from one of his sort.'

Ryleev set the note aside and perched on the edge of his desk. 'Well, I shall need some support, gentlemen. Can any of you accompany me? You'll have to leave town tomorrow to avoid attention.'

Vasily's stomach turned over. Were they expecting him to go?

'I'll come along,' said Bestuzhev, his thin boyish face bright beneath his unruly curls. He seemed young to be a captain. 'Chernov's a decent sort, deserves support.'

Mikhail shook his head. 'I'm sorry, Kondraty, I can't be there. We're on guard duty at the Palace this week. If it got out I'd dodged that to come fighting with you, my promotion prospects would be set back for years.'

Ryleev turned towards Vasily, his bright eyes narrow and a smile around his lips. 'What about you, Belkin? I think you're pretty free at present.'

Mikhail sat up. 'Oh, no, Vasily can't come…'

'Why not? Let him answer for himself. Do you fancy a drive out into the country?'

'No, really, Kondraty, he's too… and his uncle…'

'Let him answer for himself, Mikhail,' Ryleev repeated. 'Come on! Your brother Ivan, his classmate, has been fighting in the Caucasus for years.'

Mikhail shrugged and settled back. Vasily considered. Duelling was illegal, but participants rarely seemed to face punishment. It should be safe enough. Only Irina might miss him. His uncle was busy and distracted; the Prince had taken to his bed with a chill. Besides, if this was some sort of test of his courage, of his resolve, he knew he mustn't fail it. He stretched out his legs and tried to look unconcerned.

'Of course I'll come with you, Kondraty Feodorovich.'

The woods were flat and grey in the hour before sunrise. Pines, a few oaks, larches and groves of birch stretched in all directions. The track from the main road along which they had come wound back through the gloom. The duel was due to start in half an hour, but there was no sign yet of Ryleev and Chernov, or of the party supporting his opponent.

Vasily and Bestuzhev had driven out of town yesterday afternoon with Yakov and the Captain's orderly and had put up at an inn some versts away. These woods, to the east of the city, were a popular choice for the resolution of matters of honour, and, although they could have been travellers, or out hunting, the landlord had appraised them with knowing eyes.

Despite anxiety about the morrow, they spent a companionable evening. Bestuzhev told Vasily of his years in the navy: how he had joined as a cadet at the age of twelve and had been occupied after the war transporting troops from France. He had also served for two dull and chilly years with the northern fleet in Archangel. Later, the government's neglect of the fleet had prompted him to join the army. As a lieutenant in the Moscow Guards Regiment, he had rapidly come to the attention of his superiors, due, he said, to his skill in drilling troops effectively without recourse to brutality. He had recently been promoted to staff captain.

Now, in the chill September morning, Bestuzhev was pacing backwards and forwards, crunching over pine cones at the edge of the broad glade. His orderly sat on a fallen tree, surrounded by browning drifts of ferns, their spear-shaped leaves rimed with a razor edge of frozen dew.

They heard the carriage before they saw it. It came to a halt and stood, swaying, some distance away. A bright coat of arms shone on its glossy panels. Four men climbed out: Novosiltsev's party. An older man wore the uniform of a Captain of Hussars; the other three, like Vasily and Bestuzhev, wore frock coats and top hats. It was easy to identify Novosiltsev. Bulky and blond, he was the youngest of the four, and his forced cheerful laugh could be heard from some distance away.

Finally, a few minutes after the appointed time, Ryleev and Chernov arrived in an open gig. They passed Novosiltsev's supporters and, crossing the clearing, came to a halt within a few yards of Vasily and Bestuzhev. Ryleev leapt out and, clapping his hands together, stepped forward to greet them. Chernov remained seated in the gig for a moment, looking up at the trees and the sky.

Vasily, his throat tight, watched as the guardsman climbed down from the carriage. A slight figure who looked younger than his twenty years, he moved with the light step and lithe grace of a deer. His soft brown hair curled above a fine-boned face that could only be described as beautiful – as beautiful, perhaps, as that of his forsaken sister. He shook himself and squared his shoulders. 'Thank you for coming, gentlemen,' he said in a clear firm voice as he shook their hands. He didn't seem nervous. Perhaps all would be well. He turned towards Ryleev. 'Well let's get this job done, Kondraty, and then we can go for breakfast.'

The Captain of Hussars, Novosiltsev's second, stood on the grass in the centre of the clearing. Ryleev now moved to meet him. Formalities had apparently already concluded, as well as final attempts at reconciliation. A box was being carried from the carriage. As Ryleev weighed each pistol in his hands, Vasily could see the gleam of their fine silver fretwork.

'I'm told they've agreed eight paces...' Bestuzhev said. 'They seem to mean business.'

Vasily swallowed. Eight paces were close to the minimum permitted under the Code. The guns were loaded. Chernov and Novosiltsev moved to join their seconds and took their weapons. They stood back-to-back. The seconds withdrew, and the signal was given.

Vasily had to force himself not to look away. As the men walked forward, leaden time seemed to linger over each step. They turned. Less than a second divided the two shots that shattered the silence. Stinking smoke curled across the clearing and the grating calls of startled crows sounded in the sky. Both men were on the ground. It was over.

'I think Chernov's hit in the thigh,' Bestuzhev said. 'But we must stay here.' Vasily couldn't have stirred had he wished to: the Captain was holding his arm in a ferociously strong grip.

The hussar lay hunched on the ground, groaning with pain. One of Novosiltsev's party, clearly a doctor, hurried to examine him. The major removed his coat and held him while the doctor pressed a wad of white silk to his abdomen. A minute or so later, he was supported to his carriage. Then the doctor turned to Chernov. Shaking his head, he knelt and exposed the young man's pale shirt. Blood was pumping freely onto the sand. The bullet had found not the guardsman's thigh but the soft flesh of his stomach.

'It seems I was wrong.' Bestuzhev released Vasily and stared at the ground.

Ryleev stood by the gig, his pale face impassive. The doctor finished his work. There was little difficulty in lifting Chernov's light frame into the gig. Vasily drew out his kerchief and twisted it helplessly. The slender trunks of the pine trees seemed to blur. Nausea rose in his throat.

Bestuzhev took his arm again, more gently now. 'There's nothing more for us to do, Vasily Nikolayevich. We've given our support. We must just wait and pray.' He extracted a flask from his pocket, took a swig, and offered it to Vasily, who shook his head. The brief wave of sickness had passed, but his heart was heavy. What a meaningless waste of life! Why had he agreed to come?

The vehicles carrying the wounded men rolled away up the track. A sudden breeze caught the trees, troubling the yellowing leaves. Bestuzhev's man fetched their carriage, and, after some minutes, they followed the slow cavalcade back to St Peterburg.

———

Later, they sat, subdued and thoughtful, in Ryleev's rooms. The poet had taken his cousin to his quarters at the barracks of the Semenyovsky Guards a short distance away. Now he walked in briskly showing no sign of grief, or even of concern, and, going to his desk, started to pile up some papers.

'Well?' Bestuzhev finally asked.

'I'm afraid there's no hope for him… he'll linger for a day or so, perhaps, but…' Ryleev didn't look up.

'And Novosiltsev?'

'They've taken him home to his family. He's in much the same state. Two fatalities! An unusual outcome, I must say. But Konstantin, at least, has made his peace with God and seems resigned to his fate.'

Ryleev turned towards them, setting down his sheaf of papers. 'But the important point is this, gentlemen: my cousin should not – must not – die in vain! It's vital that his terrible fate delivers a strong message to the world.' He paced backwards and forwards across the room, waving his arms. 'His funeral will be an ideal time to express in boldest terms the contempt of all right-thinking people for the vile behaviour of the aristocratic elite. We have a perfect example in Novosiltsev's arrogant and shameless conduct! Yes, we must make sure that Chernov's funeral is an unanswerable protest on behalf of the weak against the strong!'

Vasily looked at Bestuzhev. He was nodding in agreement. Had both men forgotten that their friend was dying? Was a political gesture the only thing of importance? Had Ryleev sought a victim, a death, simply to make a point? Had Konstantin Chernov been deliberately goaded into fighting this duel? Surely that couldn't be so, but it was clear that the poet wasn't going to miss this opportunity to exploit his tragedy. What had Ryleev said at Andrieux's? *Blood will be spilt, perhaps* your *blood will be spilt.* In a war, casualties couldn't be avoided. Chernov's death must be seen as a sad but necessary sacrifice, evidence of commitment to the cause they had all chosen to embrace. Vasily's heart seemed to swell within him, whether from exhilaration or fear he couldn't tell.

———

On the day of Chernov's funeral at the Smolensky Cemetery, a great throng converged on the burial place of the young officer. A cortege of some two hundred carriages blocked the city streets, while a looping procession of mourners followed the coffin on foot.

As Vasily stood with Mikhail by the freshly dug grave, waiting for the ceremony to begin, he recognised a tall figure standing some way distant.

'Look, there's Fedulov.' The officer from the Ministry was scanning the crowd, his face displaying its customary expression of disdain. His lips were moving; he seemed to be talking to himself. Vasily realised that he was, in fact, making observations to two clerks who flanked him with paper and small pencils.

'Has he seen you?'

'No, I don't think so. I don't know. He's taking names, I think.'

'Well, don't look at him. Look the other way.'

Vasily lowered his head.

They could hear the steady beat of approaching drums. Chernov's coffin was arriving, carried by his comrades from the Semenyovsky Guards. At the graveside, a man started to read a poem written by Ryleev. It contained, among other inflammatory phrases, a pledge of honour to fight tyranny on behalf of the 'trembling slaves of the Tsar'. The enthusiast was, however, prevented from completing this polemic by his companions who had noticed the large number of spies and representatives of the police who stood with sullen eyes, scanning the faces of the crowd.

Vasily and Mikhail listened as a more moderate eulogy was delivered. An excerpt from Chernov's last letter was read aloud. He had chosen to die, he wrote, 'to show depraved snobs that gold and noble birth could not overcome innocence and gentility of the soul'. Once the body was interred and the priest had withdrawn, a seditious verse, which had been circulated privately, was sung to the tune of a popular folk song. Vasily felt a glorious sense of optimism as hundreds of men's voices echoed in the pure September air. He had been right to commit himself to the cause of freedom.

That evening, he went with Mikhail to Ryleev's apartment. There, in the presence of a small group of men, he swore a solemn oath. He was now a member of the Northern Society, a clandestine group devoted to fundamental change, to freedom for the serfs and the destruction of autocracy in Russia.

CHAPTER SIXTEEN

October 1825 – St Petersburg

LISA BARELY NOTICED the dancers as they fluttered and swayed across the stage. Sitting with Mikhail at the front of the Stenovsky family box, she knew that she was an object of interest, that her new diamonds sparkled so convincingly they could not fail to be admired. She smiled. Everything had fallen into place; Mama and Papa would be so proud of her.

True, the events surrounding Mikhail's proposal of marriage had not gone entirely smoothly. When the time had come, he had very properly approached Prince Polunin, who had referred him to Aunt Darya. When he asked Lisa's aunt to write to seek permission from Count Laptev in Oryol, a process that might have taken at least three weeks, he had learned, to his surprise and Lisa's mortification, that her father's consent had already been sought 'just in case'. All that remained was to settle the question of the dowry. Her father's agent was already in touch with the Stenovskys' representative in Moscow.

Without the need to wait for her parents' approval, they had already enjoyed the greater liberty afforded a betrothed couple and had been only lightly chaperoned. Mikhail was everything that she had prayed for. He seemed to share her views on many issues and always treated her with respect. Of course, he had some minor shortcomings. It turned out that he was less interested in spiritual matters than she, and sometimes he smelt of the cigars to which so many officers seemed to be addicted.

Soon after their betrothal, he had taken her to a small

reception given for them by Colonel Kalinin and his sister, the exotic Baroness von Steiner. Irina Pavlovna, it seemed, was not just a friend of Mikhail's, but also an acquaintance of her cousin, Vasily. At this first meeting, Irina had politely declined Lisa's invitation to call at the Palace and so, emboldened by her new status, Lisa accompanied by her maid, had called on Irina. To her surprise, the Baroness had at first seemed reluctant to receive her, but she soon relented and now they were close to becoming friends. They had much to discuss. Irina's experience in the management of her brother's estates was of interest, since, in time, she expected to fulfil a similar role. They had a shared enthusiasm for the latest publications and romances, but, disappointingly, Irina had told her nothing of her husband, Baron von Steiner.

Tonight, at the theatre, the Baroness, her companion Gretchen, and Vasily were seated in the dark recesses of the box. Lisa could smell her distinctive perfume and wondered where she'd bought it. How graceful Irina Pavlovna was! She felt solid and ungainly in comparison. Irina had unerring taste. It would be good to seek her advice about dress. Somehow, the gowns that her aunt and Katya had helped her to buy never felt quite right.

After the performance, they were invited to supper at the Kalinins' apartment. Irina's brother, Pavel Pavlovich, was at home. The Colonel was almost as beguiling as his sister. On the rare occasions that he became animated, his striking claret-coloured hair and pale, sharp-featured face seemed very attractive.

As they drank a glass of champagne, Lisa felt elated. Among these new friends she felt truly independent, a whole person at last. She looked around the comfortably elegant room, content to listen to the light-hearted conversation about the merits of two dancers who had made their solo debuts that evening.

'I felt that there was little to choose between them,' Mikhail was saying.

'I agree,' Irina replied. 'But I wish that their supporters had made less noise. I could hardly hear the music.'

'Oh, were you listening to the music?' Vasily said, his face straight. 'I hadn't realised that. I thought you were too busy looking around, trying to attract your admirers in the audience.'

The comment seemed rather rude. Was Vasily serious, or was it meant as a joke? Irina laughed as she hit her cousin smartly on the head with her closed fan.

'I wouldn't put up with that, Vasya!' Kalinin exclaimed.

Vasily set down his glass with deliberation and, with a slight smile, caught the Baroness round the waist. Then pulling her towards him, he kissed her hard on the lips. She struggled, emitting a chirrup of protest followed by a sigh of pleasure as their kiss softened and deepened. Vasily finally released her, put his arm around her shoulders, and drew her close to his side. The Colonel and Mikhail laughed, and Gretchen clapped her hands.

Lisa's breath caught in her throat, and her eyes widened. How very surprising! Indeed, how inappropriate! Surely Irina was married? From somewhere, she heard the tinkle of broken glass. Her champagne had fallen from her hands. Liquid was trickling down her skirt and into her shoe.

'Oh, I'm so sorry!' She felt herself flush crimson.

Irina was regarding her with concern. Another glass of champagne appeared and the Colonel, declaring that Lisa must be faint with hunger, said that all must sit down to eat. He took the head of the table and, pulling out a chair for her, engaged her in conversation about her home near Oryol. It seemed he knew the town quite well; it was only a day's ride from his estates in the south. From time to time, she glanced at Irina and Vasily who were listening to Mikhail hold forth on a topic she couldn't quite hear.

Now Vasily looked towards her and attempted a tentative smile. She found herself smiling in return. She had become fond of her cousin; he had been kind to her since they had met and more than once had helped her escape from moments of embarrassment or boredom. But he had startled her tonight. It seemed that his relationship with Irina was quite improper, although no one here, including Mikhail, seemed to think much of it.

Later, as she and Mikhail were leaving, Irina drew her aside. 'I'm sorry if you were shocked, Elizaveta Gavrilovna. Vasily and I should have behaved better, and Mikhail should have told you of our situation before he brought you here. I do hope you'll continue to call on me.'

'Of course, I shall call again.' Lisa was reluctant to give up this interesting new friend. But what would Aunt Darya or, indeed, Mama, think if they knew?

Mikhail accompanied her on the short walk along the Embankment to the Polunin Palace. A lackey lit the way with a flaming torch; Vera, her maid, trailed along behind, yawning.

'I'm sorry, my love,' he said. 'That shouldn't have happened. I should have warned you in advance.'

'I was taken aback, I admit.'

Mikhail briefly described Irina's situation, and then, sensing Lisa's continuing disquiet, added: 'But she's entirely blameless, you must see that. You shouldn't judge her harshly. Many of the better sort won't receive her, but they don't know the whole truth. And, of course, it's plain that Vasily is devoted to her. I find their predicament heartbreaking. Unless her husband dies, there's not much hope that they can marry. It's probably as well that Vasya's likely to go abroad next year.'

'I wondered why Vasily doesn't seem interested in his family's attempts to encourage him into society. I thought he was focused on his studies.'

Mikhail seemed amused. 'No, I don't think so,' he said. 'Life isn't as simple as it's made out, Lisenka.'

'I suppose not. In any event, I like Irina Pavlovna a good deal. Her brother is charming, too.'

'Yes, when he chooses to be. But Pavel is a different creature. He's no victim of fate; in fact, he operates very much on his own terms.'

When they reached the steps of the palace, Mikhail took his leave, promising to call on the morrow after manège.

She watched his tall figure walk away towards Palace Square and the barracks beyond. He was right; life was not simple. Her narrow education and experience to date seemed hardly to have prepared her for it. She hoped Mikhail understood that. She had felt so confident earlier, but now she wondered how many more surprises and pitfalls lay in wait.

———

'This one is good,' said Vasily, picking up the sketch of a Neapolitan peasant woman drawn in red chalk.

The Prince looked at the work over his shoulder. 'Yes, this young man has talent, I think.'

A few days after the trip to the theatre, Dmitry Vladimirovich asked Vasily to help him to consider a batch of artworks on offer from a dealer. The pictures had been spread across the dining table. The aroma of coffee, one of the Prince's weaknesses, pervaded the warm comfort of the room.

They had already looked at a folio of botanical drawings and had moved on to the work of a young artist, a student at the Imperial Academy recently returned from Rome. The vivid Italian scenes, filled with southern sunshine and trailing vines, were a welcome distraction from the needling wind and steady drizzle of autumn rain in the street outside.

The Prince moved the works around and pulled out the final offering. 'She may not be by Greuze,' he said. 'But I rather like her.'

The girl's head was thrown back in a wanton manner that seemed to fall on the wrong side of good taste.

'Do you, sir?'

Vasily was saved from having to offer his opinion by the arrival of Alexander. Clearly, his uncle, having considered the weather, had decided to postpone his journey to the Ministry. He picked up the picture. 'That's awful, Dima,' he said. 'I hope you're not going to give it houseroom.'

The Prince put his head on one side and considered the image again. 'You don't like it? Oh well, never mind. I suppose you're after some coffee?'

As he spoke, they heard an insistent hammering on the front door. Vasily went to the window. A carriage had drawn up on the pavement. Two policemen stood beside it, but he couldn't see who was seeking entrance.

The butler addressed Alexander. 'Collegiate Assessor Fedulov is here, Sir.'

'Show him into the study.' Alexander turned to the Prince.

'I don't know what he wants. I expect he's following up on matters connected with that young guards officer's interment a couple of weeks ago.'

Vasily felt a flutter of unease. His uncle must be speaking of Chernov's funeral. He knew from Ryleev that a few arrests had been made after the event and that there might be more.

A closed police wagon now pulled up behind the carriage and loomed, a dark square, outside the window. Vasily watched a policeman lift the bar at the rear and reach inside. He heard a metallic clank as the officer pulled out a length of chain and, examining it, started to straighten and smooth out its rings. Sweat broke out on Vasily's brow. My God! Supposing they were coming for him? His stomach seemed to have detached itself and churned alarmingly. He turned away and stared at the pictures on the table.

'Are you alright, Vasya?' the Prince said.

He was unable to answer. The tranquil waters of the Bay of Naples did nothing to ease his disquiet.

'Too many late nights?' The Prince persisted.

'Yes, I suppose so.'

Dmitry Vladimirovich's obvious indifference to the sight outside calmed him a little. He took a deep breath. His reaction had been irrational. There had been hundreds of people at the funeral; why come for him? He reached for his coffee, but his hand was shaking. He pulled it back. Fedulov was taking his leave. They heard his carriage draw away and the wagon door slam shut. Vasily closed his eyes and tried to breathe normally.

Alexander returned. 'I'm sorry, I have to go out,' he said. 'I had rather hoped to work here today, but I have to deal with some young idiot who breached his internal exile to attend that farce of a funeral. They're going to bring him in now.'

'He obviously found it harder to get out of Petersburg than to get in,' said the Prince.

'So it seems. They'll probably lock him up for the rest of his term, in rather less comfortable conditions than those he enjoys on his family's estate near Tver. I can't understand how he thought he'd get away with it...'

When his uncle had departed, Vasily sat down. He felt limp and rather foolish. The Prince was shaking his head. 'It's their families I feel sorry for, Vasya. Of course, the offender himself only has himself to blame, but his mother, sisters, and brothers, they'll suffer, too. I can understand that young men feel frustrated, that they want to kick over the traces. But they should stop and think what damage they might do to those who love them.'

Vasily's fear had turned into a keen-edged sense of guilt. He didn't want to get drawn into this conversation.

'It was plain that that funeral was nothing but a political demonstration,' Dmitry continued. 'Most of the people there didn't even know the unfortunate young man. So why do they do it? Why agitate? Why foment unrest? All it does is lead to disaster. Look at France! That got no one anywhere. I hear there are even riots and strikes in England now. That's even more unlikely to change anything.'

The Prince looked at him intently. 'I know you think I'm an old fool, Vasily, but believe me, you can do far more good in the world by serving your country faithfully and, most importantly, with honesty. That's the way to help your fellow countrymen. Better far than empty political gestures, sitting in darkened rooms plotting pointless upheaval.'

The Prince turned back to the table and contemplated the pictures.

'Your uncle's probably right about the French girl,' he said with a sigh. 'But I'll take some of the rest. Sort out the ones we both liked, and then I'd be grateful if you'd drop a line to the dealer?'

'Of course, sir.'

Left alone, Vasily shifted the works around and sought a pen. What did the Prince know? Did he suspect that he, too, had gone to Chernov's funeral? Was he trying to steer him away from trouble? He looked at the window and ran his fingers through his hair. The rain had stopped but the street was still grey and damp.

The thought of distressing the Prince, his uncle, or, indeed, any of his family, was painful – far worse than painful – but it was too late now for regret. He had made his decision; he had given his word. He couldn't be moved by sentiment, mustn't waver at the first sign of danger, real or imagined. He recalled Mikhail's commitment to the cause and Ryleev's burning passion for justice. Chernov's sacrifice. He couldn't, wouldn't, let them down. Ryleev had already suggested some practical ways he could be useful, both now and if he went abroad next year.

Besides, what could any one person achieve on his own? He could sit in his room reading books about the benefits of democracy until his brain ached; he could try to redeem more boys like Matvey; he could make sure his own serfs were treated well. But those small gestures would do little to relieve the country's ills. No, although conservatives like his uncle and the Prince had mocked the event, Chernov's funeral had shown what combined action might achieve. No one could doubt its impact on public opinion. There were signs that the tide was turning; he must strive to rise on the flood.

CHAPTER SEVENTEEN
26 November 1825 – St Petersburg

THE FRENCH AMBASSADOR, in recognition of the cordial relations between his country and Russia, was holding a ball at the embassy.

Alexander Petrovich had taken up a position behind a column at the far end of the ballroom. He was not in the best of moods. Although his dancing days were, in his view, well past, he had been obliged to suffer for half an hour, partnering his sister-in-law, Maria, in the opening polonaise. Now, many older guests were making their way to the card room or settling down to watch the dancing continue.

He flinched at the noisy melee surging around the edge of the floor as young men hastened to find any well-favoured young women with empty spaces in their *carnets de bal*. Violins shrieked as they were retuned. Chandeliers shone with unbearable intensity, their light reflecting on the expanse of intermeshed geometry inlaid on the wooden floor. The scent of hothouse flowers, mixed with French perfume, was insupportable. He was already too hot. His hands itched in his gloves, and his cravat felt tight around his neck.

He was not just physically uncomfortable. On entering the embassy, he had met his niece's husband, Prince Polunin. Stopping to converse briefly, Polunin had imparted a worrying rumour: the Tsar, who was, of course, travelling, had fallen ill. He was suffering from a fever that was proving hard to shake off. The story had not been substantiated; Polunin hoped that there was no truth in it.

Alexander was considering whether this alarming news might have substance when he noticed the Stenovsky family descending the stairs to the ballroom. Nikita was accompanying his mother and Mikhail followed, a vision in white, red and gold, with his future bride, Lisa, on his arm. She was certainly appealing in a gown of deep pink and with a cream rose set among her black curls. Behind them, Lisa's Aunt Darya, Madame Svetlov, wore crushed violet.

And here, at last, was Vasily. He was very late; it was just as well this was not a State ball. He seemed to be accompanying the diplomat, Pavel Kalinin. Alexander knew, of course, that Vasily was acquainted with the man and had visited him in the country, but he had not realised that they had maintained their connection. He was not sure that it pleased him.

The Colonel's sister, the Baroness, was on Vasily's arm. Alexander scrutinised the couple. Vasily had turned to the woman and was whispering something into her ear. Now he reached across her and touched her left arm seeking, it seemed, to reassure her. The Baroness smiled at him, and he briefly stroked the skin below her white puffed sleeve before turning from her to greet Mikhail Stenovsky.

The woman was undeniably arresting, and it was clear that his nephew was more to her than an escort for the evening. But it wouldn't do; it was not a suitable connection. Irina Pavlovna was not free. If their intimacy was obvious to him, surely it must be clear to the world at large. Vasily's departure abroad must be accelerated. He knew there were some suitable openings. Officers were urgently needed in Washington. He would call on the Minister on Monday.

The master of ceremonies was announcing the waltz. Vasily bowed with a flourish to the Baroness. They were going to dance. Was the money spent on years of dancing lessons now about to pay dividends? Alexander observed the pair with apprehension as they took the floor. They linked their right hands and started to waltz in a mannered old-fashioned style. Irina supported her train with her free hand while Vasily held his left arm rigid across his back. They moved across the ballroom, their eyes never straying from one another, their bodies hardly connected but effortlessly as one. A lump came to Alexander's throat. He had to acknowledge that they were an affecting sight. They must have spent hours practising and had obviously spent a good deal of time together.

He blew his nose and then departed to find the Prince. No doubt Dmitry had saved him a place at the card table.

After an hour or so of whist, Alexander resumed his vigil. He had left the gaming room in frustration when Dmitry Vladimirovich had trumped his partner's ace for the second time. Dima shouldn't play cards in company. He didn't concentrate and was always too busy listening to what was happening at other tables, and gossiping with casual passers-by.

The mazurka was now in full flow. The intricacies of the dance had always been beyond him, but he appreciated its passion and fervour. It did seem to go on for a very long time, however, and it was noisy. His head was ringing from the sound of stamping feet and his eyes were confused by the brilliance of the jewels and the billowing of feathers. He should retire. He scanned the room's upper levels; there were some quieter spots to be found there.

A few guests, some older couples, some solitary observers, were in the galleries surveying the scene below. Two men, in particular, caught his eye: his junior at the ministry, Leonid Fedulov, and the diplomat Pavel Kalinin. They stood at the balustrade opposite one another, both in dark evening dress, their faces impassive. As they looked down, contemplating the endlessly shifting pattern of the dance, they resembled two buzzards hovering in the air, seeking out their prey among the pretty creatures who, innocent and oblivious to danger, darted and swooped across the floor.

Alexander dismissed the fancy; it was, of course, ridiculous. But he should try to catch Pavel Kalinin. He may have some intelligence about the Emperor and might also be prepared to discuss his thoughts with regard to Vasily and his sister. Suppressing a persistent premonition of misfortune, Alexander embarked on the climb to the upper level. But when he finally reached the gallery, he found that both Kalinin and Fedulov had gone.

The mazurka was coming to an end. Alexander took up a position high above the ballroom. The music grew ever louder and then finally stopped. Amidst a roar of renewed conversation, the assembly surged in a wave towards the supper rooms. Just four people remained in the centre of the floor. Vasily, Irina, Mikhail and Lisa stood together, illuminated by the radiance of the central chandelier. Their hands were joined, and the light of a thousand candles shone on their hair. They were talking and laughing, animated by the spirit of the dance. They seemed to glow with joy, with the euphoria of love, each one of them enraptured by the rest – a living tableau briefly suspended in time. Mikhail put his arm around Vasily's shoulder; the two women kissed.

But then the image disintegrated; the spell was broken. Mikhail's mother and brother had emerged from the card room and were walking across the ballroom. The musicians were setting aside their instruments. Alexander decided to go home.

The next morning, Vasily woke in Irina's bed. She was curled in his arms, her body cupped against his. He lifted his head. It was still dark outside; the sun would not rise until after nine o'clock. His sleep had been broken by the sound of a servant feeding the stove in the corridor. It must still be early.

He nuzzled her neck and pressed his nose into the spiced warmth of her hair. She moved towards him slightly but did not wake. He closed his eyes and, drifting back into sleep, was lost in the images of the room's Chinese wallpaper: a waterfall, a pagoda, a lotus blossom, a bird, the scent of oranges, the rustle of silk.

Later, waking once more, he saw a line of grey light at the window. He should think about rising, but he had few commitments today.

Irina still slept. Over the past two months, he had found ways to prise her away from her books and the sofa. They had driven out and sometimes gone walking but were always accompanied by Gretchen. Mikhail had sometimes secured his family's box at the theatre, where she had been happy to join the party and sit close to Vasily in the darkness. There had been other private gatherings, but she had resisted any attempt to encourage her into wider society. Although she enjoyed company, the threat of social embarrassment was abhorrent to her. Moreover, he knew that she hoped one day to be reunited with her children, whom she keenly missed. She would do nothing that might jeopardise that possibility. Staying at home was preferable to the risk of any hint of scandal.

She had been reluctant to attend last night's ball, despite

the fact that, as the sister of a senior diplomat, she had every reason to accept the invitation. Pavel Pavlovich had finally told her that he would be obliged if she would go for his sake, so, with some misgiving, she had made an appointment with the dressmaker. And all had been well.

But, of course, the problem remained: they couldn't marry. Surely there must be a solution? Vasily imagined going to Vienna, calling out von Steiner, winning the inevitable duel with honour, burying the Baron, rescuing her children and coming back to Russia in triumph. More realistically, he dreamed of taking her away to Italy, or to America, where he imagined no one would care about their status. He could find employment, develop his political ideas, and work on his art. He reflected that poverty and starvation would inevitably follow.

Irina stirred and opened her eyes. Stretching and smiling at him, she pushed back the covers. He kissed her and, rising from the bed, put on his robe and opened the curtains. The morning light was grey. He lit a lamp. Her body was pearl-bright, her hair on the pillow polished copper. He took a sketchbook and chalk from the drawer which contained essentials that had migrated from his room to hers. Then he sat on the edge of the bed, scrutinised her carefully and caught her likeness.

When the drawing was finished, he set it aside. He removed his robe and captured her once again.

CHAPTER EIGHTEEN

27 November 1825

WHEN VASILY FINALLY left the apartment, there was no sign of Kalinin. He must have been called out on business. Mist sharded with ice curled through the city, driven by a bitter breeze that penetrated all but the thickest of coats. Aiming to avoid the direct chill of the frozen river, he used the back entrance, hoping to find a droshky on Galernaya to take him the short distance home. But the street was deserted.

As he emerged into Senate Square, he was startled to see a procession of carriages drawing up outside the palace that housed the Senate. He stopped and looked about him. More traffic was heading towards the Winter Palace, followed by what looked like several companies of foot guards. A troop of cavalry was drawn up beneath the statue of Peter the Great, high on his rearing horse. Towards the river, a number of coaches stood empty, their drivers motionless and bulked up like bears against the cold air.

A small group of onlookers huddled around the steps of the Senate, surveying the grandees and officials as they came and went.

'What's going on?' he asked a young tradesman.

'It's the Emperor, sir.'

'What about the Emperor?' He knew that Alexander Pavlovich was travelling in the South.

Despite the cold, the man crossed himself, took off his hat, and bowed his head. 'It's said he's gone, sir.'

'Gone? What do you mean?'

'He's gone, sir... He's dead.'

'Dead?' Was that really possible? The Emperor can't yet have reached fifty, and as far as he knew, there had been no concerns about his health.

'Yes, sir. That's right,' a female house serf added. 'The courier arrived this morning from the Azov Sea. They say it were a fever picked up on his travels. All the lords and officers are coming here or going to the Palace, to swear the oath to his brother, Constantine. It's a terrible thing! Isn't that so, sir? Our little father Alexander's gone!'

Vasily walked slowly away. Would this sudden death make any difference to the autocratic system, to these people's lives? Probably not. It was hard to believe that Constantine, now serving in Poland, would be an improvement on his brother. Like Alexander, he had treated his first wife badly, and he suffered from the same obsession with parades and the minutiae of military life. The Imperial Family must want this matter settled quickly; they had wasted no time in organising the oath-taking. For anyone wanting to take advantage of an interregnum, it could already be too late.

When Vasily arrived home, he found the Prince and his uncle preparing to leave to take the oath. He stood with them as the carriage was brought round.

'Polunin did speak last night of rumours that the Emperor was unwell,' Alexander said, 'but I hoped he was mistaken. Apparently, he died in a modest bedroom at the Governor's house in Taganrog, surrounded by his entourage. What a sad end!'

'What sort of man is Constantine?'

'I barely know him. He's been in Poland for some years, heading up the army there. He showed personal bravery in the war, I seem to remember, but was said to be something of a hindrance to the generals. I'm not sure he has much imagination. But we shall have to see.'

The carriage pulled away and Vasily went inside, grateful to retreat from the winter chill. What should he do now? Would he hear from Ryleev? Would there, after all, be some call to arms? His spirits lifted when the doorman handed him a scribbled note from Mikhail suggesting they dine together on the morrow.

———

28 November 1825

Vasily had not been able to meet Mikhail alone for a couple of weeks. As he walked through the streets, the stinging air crept into his bones. Despite his hat and thick boots, he couldn't feel his ears or feet. The city was as silent as a sepulchre. Frost rimed the iron railings that flanked the crystal surface of the Moyka. In the late afternoon dusk, lamplight glowed in the windows, casting trembling rectangles of gold onto the glazed streets.

Pictures of Constantine, the new Emperor and autocrat of Russia, were already appearing in the shop windows on Nevsky Prospekt. He wasn't appealing. He had the ugly snub-nosed features of his ill-fated father, Paul, which probably didn't augur well.

The tavern, some ten minutes from the centre of town, was almost empty. Mikhail sat at a corner table, his face drained of colour. He had been on duty for hours on city squares and frigid parade grounds. 'I had to take the damn oath of allegiance to Constantine,' he said, his voice hoarse. 'It was sprung upon us so quickly, there was no chance to urge the men to refuse. So, one autocrat dies and another pops up; it's like trying to sever the Hydra's head.'

'You're right about that,' said Vasily, rubbing his ears that ached in the warmth of the room. 'And there are at least two more heads to cut off after this one.'

'Yes, if Constantine fails to come up to scratch, the Imperial Family still have two in reserve. Ach! It seems the chance has come and gone, and we've been caught napping. Everything happened too fast.'

Mikhail drained his beer and banged the glass down on the table. He called for another and ordered one for Vasily.

'But surely there's no need to act at once,' Vasily said. 'In the past, the victims of coups had been in power for some time. In the case of Peter, it was a year or so, and Paul was Emperor for four years before he met his end. In any event, you know that we're not really ready to move.'

'But one has to take one's chances when one can. It's hard not to see this as a missed opportunity.' Mikhail gulped down his second beer. His colour gradually returned, and he became more lively. When their food arrived, he fell on it with enthusiasm. 'What have you been up to, Vasya?'

Vasily looked about him. No one was within earshot.

'I have to say that the Society hasn't taken up much of my time. I've attended a couple of meetings, but they've not really been what I'd expected. They're more like literary soirées than political gatherings.'

'Yes, I'm afraid that for some, particularly the older men, the whole thing has become like a game. I suppose that the room was full of smoke, and there was plenty of champagne, cries of 'Death to the Tsar!' and the opportunity to listen to more of Ryleev's doggerel?'

'That's a little unfair, Misha. I find some of his verse quite inspiring, and I've been entertained by some of the discussions. There was one about the virtues of Brutus, compared with the shortcomings of Julius Caesar and Nero. It was like being back at school.'

Mikhail snorted.

'But I've spent some fruitful time with Kondraty and with one or two others,' Vasily continued. 'His commitment is beyond question. He told me that there are differences of opinion within the group that need to be resolved... the form a post-revolutionary government should take, for example. He and your brother have resolved to meet Pestel and his associates from the south in the spring to thrash things out.'

'Yes, well it seems that now there will be time for that, at least.'

'I've put in a bit of legwork myself, too. Delivered a few messages around the town, that sort of thing.'

Mikhail looked up from his plate. 'Have you? for Ryleev? I'm surprised he asked you.'

'I told him I was happy to do it. Why make a commitment if you're not going to do something? It's a pretty cold exercise I can tell you, waiting around outside barracks and gatehouses. But I keep well wrapped up. Last week, I took a sled over the causeway with a note for a man at the naval barracks at Kronstadt.'

'Did you?' Mikhail looked at him and frowned. You must be careful. You ensure you're not recognised?'

'Yes, of course. Kondraty has provided me with some convincing papers naming me as a clerk from the Russian American Company. Only one guard has ever asked to see them. They seemed to serve their purpose.'

'Well make sure we don't lose you before the revolution. That would be a pity.' Before he could speak further, there was a gust of cold air as the door flew open and a group of merchants arrived. They threw their coats at the waiter and, stamping their boots on the wooden floor, shouted for beer, bread and onions. It was time to change the subject.

'Will your wedding be put off because of Alexander's death?'

'I hope not,' Mikhail said. 'Although it may be a small affair, which to my mind is no bad thing. I should like to have it settled before Lent. There's talk of promotion, too, at last.'

'Misha! Congratulations.'

'Well, it's not before time. I've been a cornet too long. I'd prefer Lisenka to be a lieutenant's wife.'

'I don't think she'll mind too much either way... It's you yourself she wants, she loves.'

'I just want the best for her, the best of everything.'

Later, as they left, Mikhail said, 'I suppose that the excitement's over now. Life will go on as before except the theatres will be closed for a while and there won't be any more balls this year. If there is any change, I'll send to you. We have at least one informer who is privy to the inner workings of the Palace, but I think that the game is postponed.'

CHAPTER NINETEEN
9 December 1825

ON BRIGHTER DAYS in winter, the ice-covered Neva cast strong northern light into Katya's small drawing room. Today, instead of reading, Lisa was obliged to sew; a trousseau had to be produced at speed. She sat, brow furrowed, attaching fine lace to a sheer white chemise, while Katya, now showing her pregnancy, reprised the nuptial arrangements for what must have been the twentieth time.

'I always think a winter wedding is best. Bells seem to sound different, better, in the cold, and there will be flaming torches, hot punch... I must remember to arrange that.' Katya looked out of the window. 'I do hope there will be snow on the ground. There's only been the odd flurry this year, even though the river has frozen.'

She yawned and stretched. Setting aside her own sewing, she rose to her feet. 'I must go to check today's menu, Lisa. Do you want to come down?'

'I need to get this done. I'll be there presently.' Lisa finished her piece of work, knotted the thread, and stabbed her needle into its cushion. Needlework was tiresome, but she couldn't leave everything to Vera.

Out on the river, a thickly padded fisherman was trudging towards his fishing holes. A bonfire burned on the ice, and smoke drifted across the river. Upstream, a few skaters glided in front of the Palace. It would be wonderful to go skating. Perhaps Mikhail might be persuaded to take her, although he was currently much occupied with duties, parades and oath-takings.

She allowed herself a sigh of contentment. Nanya had been right after all; God had found her a husband. She hadn't been obliged to compromise like her cousin Katya. Mikhail was, without doubt, the right person to whom to entrust her future. He wanted to pursue his career in the army, but they had decided that they would, in time, settle onone of their estates where they could live very comfortably while devoting themselves to the education of their children and the welfare of their serfs. What could be more satisfactory?

She could hear footsteps and voices in the larger drawing room. A lackey appeared at the door. 'You have a visitor, Miss. The Princess asks you to come through.'

Katya and Mikhail stood together by the fireplace.

'Misha! I didn't expect to see you! You're not at the manège? On duty?'

'I had some business to do this morning, and it's been some days since I called.'

'Well it's a lovely surprise, but you're looking worn out.' Mikhail had dark smudges under his eyes, and his face was almost as pale as his tunic. 'Everything's still in disarray due to the Emperor's death,' he said. 'No one knows what's happening from one day to the next.'

Moving into Katya's smaller room, they settled in the comfortable chairs to drink tea. Lisa looked into her cup. She felt unprepared; she hadn't expected to see Mikhail, and he, unusually, was saying very little. Katya, however, managed to keep up a steady flow of talk until, remembering some essential business, she left them alone.

As soon as her footsteps faded, Mikhail rose to his feet. 'I've missed you, Lisenka. There's been too much to do, too many late nights.'

What duties could be keeping him up at night? Should she ask? But before she could speak, he startled her by taking her into his arms. He held her close against him, almost too close. His lips ran over her hair, down her neck, and then when they rose again to find her mouth at last, he kissed her with a disturbing depth of passion.

When he released her, they moved towards the window seat, where he sat in silence, playing with her fingers. He didn't meet her eyes but looked upriver towards the fortress.

'Are you sure that everything… You don't seem…' She hesitated. As she spoke, he seemed to return to himself. Dropping her hand, he smiled, shook his head, and straightened his uniform.

'No, I'm fine. Just tired and overworked. But it won't be long until this business of the succession is settled and everything gets back to normal. We'll then be together more often, Lisenka. This wasn't the best time to become betrothed.' He seemed about to say more, but the clock in the corner struck twelve. The roar of the noon gun rolled over the ice from the fortress. She shivered. He picked up her hand again and kissed it.

'I'm so very glad we found one another. Your love has changed everything.' He paused. 'But I regret, much regret, that I now have to leave you. I must call in on Vasily today and shouldn't neglect my duties entirely.'

They walked together towards the door. Under the cherub-carved lintel, he turned her towards him and studied her face. He raised his hand to her cheek and stroked it. His eyes seemed very bright. 'God bless you, Lisa. I'll return when I can.'

His lips were gentle, and the kiss was brief. Then he was gone.

She picked up her work, a pale froth of bridal lace on white fabric. She breathed in its crisp scent, then held the cloth against her face where his hand had rested. Surely nothing could be wrong. Surely he was just overwhelmed with fatigue; this hectic time would soon pass.

The ice-bound river beyond the window gave her no answer; the fisherman had vanished and wisps of smoke, drifting away downstream, marbled the opaline surface.

———

'Really, Thomas?' Vasily said in Russian. 'You suggested this book! At least help me to read it. I can't understand why you wanted me to dig about in this dry stuff. Let's go back to Byron. It's much more entertaining and, just now, more closely suits my mood.'

Vasily was struggling through his translation of a passage from Locke's *Second Treatise of Civil Government*, and Thomas Maltby was much amused by his attempt.

'Do try to speak in English, Vasily Nikolayevich! You said you wanted to read some English political thought. Locke was the inspiration for all the books you young men find it easy enough to read in French: Diderot, Constant, and the like.'

The English lessons were not going well. It was not Thomas's fault. He was an excellent teacher and, now that they had become accustomed to one another, good company, too.

Vasily sighed. 'Would you like to take tea, Mister Maltby?' he said in English.

'Does that mean you've had enough of the Locke?'

'During today, at least.'

'For,' corrected Maltby.

'What about "for"?'

'*For* today, at least.'

'Vasily shrugged and then asked in French: 'Well, would you like tea or wouldn't you?'

'Yes please, that would be very kind,' said Maltby, persisting in English.

Vasily thought that he had been rescued from further embarrassment when there was a knock on the door. It was Matvey.

'You're early for your lessons, Matthew,' Maltby said to the child in English.

'Yes I am, Mister Maltby, sir.' Matvey grinned. His English intonation was excellent.

'For God's sake, his English is better than mine! I give up, I really do,' Vasily said, again in French.

Maltby winked at Matvey. He and Matvey proceeded to demonstrate some other expressions that they had clearly been practising. Vasily picked up the Locke and, resisting the temptation to throw it into the waste bin, set it aside.

'What do you actually want, Matvey? Sadly, there's another half an hour of this lesson to go.'

'Please, sir!' Matvey continued in English, 'Mikhail Alexandrovich is here and asks to see you.'

'Thank you, ask him to come up.' This was some relief.

Matvey ran off.

'That boy is like a sponge, you know.' Thomas reverted to French. 'This was just a little joke. We haven't been studying English seriously, of course, but he's very bright. We always start with a few English pleasantries. I have told him it makes me feel at home. He is an amiable child.'

'He's amiable with you, Thomas, but he can be naughty. I think it's the threat of that thing. He knows I won't use it, but you might, I suppose.'

He waved towards the cane that he had found three months earlier in the long-unused schoolroom and had hung on the wall. At the time, he had said that it was a reminder that Alexander Petrovich expected exemplary behaviour from all of them. It had gathered dust ever since.

'He knows I won't use it. You can't beat knowledge into a child,' said Maltby. 'But in any case, I find him a very good boy altogether.'

Mikhail arrived, followed by Matvey, who was examining the Cornet's uniform with great interest.

Mikhail acknowledged Thomas Maltby with a short bow. 'Mr Maltby. Good morning, sir.' Turning to Vasily, he said, 'I'm sorry, Vasya, but I need to speak to you urgently. I regret interrupting your classes.'

'You're not interrupting anything. 'It's almost time for Matvey's lesson. We'll go into the drawing room.'

When they were settled, Vasily said, 'You're not at the riding school this morning?'

'No. I made my excuses. I wanted to see Lisa. I've been neglecting her, and I've come to see you because there have been developments.'

Vasily knew that Constantine's accession to the throne of Russia was not going as expected. Unknown to anyone but members of the Royal Family, some years before, on the occasion of his marriage, Grand Duke Constantine had written a formal memorandum. The document declared that although he was next in line to the throne, he was giving up the right to become Emperor. In the event of the death of his childless elder brother, Alexander, his younger brother, Grand Duke Nicholas, should become Tsar while Constantine continued to occupy himself in Poland as Commander in Chief of the Polish Army, and effective Viceroy.

Grand Duke Nicholas, unhappy about this agreement,

had urged Constantine to come to the capital to formally renounce his claim to the throne. Constantine had thus far refused to leave Poland. Imperial couriers had been galloping back and forth between Warsaw and St Petersburg for almost two weeks, carrying urgent but sometimes contradictory messages between the two brothers.

'We've just heard that Nicholas has finally accepted Constantine's refusal of the crown, and Constantine won't be coming to Petersburg.' Mikhail said. 'Nicholas will now demand that an oath of allegiance be sworn to him to supersede the one already sworn to Constantine.'

'So what does that mean for the cause?' asked Vasily.

'We can't let this opportunity slip. We really can't. An oath already given to Constantine is the perfect excuse for resistance to Nicholas who, as you know, is much disliked by the army. He is as odious a martinet as his father was. A plan of action is close to being decided. A temporary leader of the provisional government has been chosen and I'd expect to see armed rebellion within days. The most likely moment would be when the Guards are asked to pledge their oath to Nicholas.'

'I see.' Vasily felt his chest tighten. He was committed to supporting a revolution, but he hadn't expected it so soon. He looked at his friend. Although Mikhail spoke with confidence, his face was pallid, and his hands trembled slightly.

'Who's been chosen to lead the revolt?' Vasily asked.

'Prince Trubetskoy.'

The name gave Vasily some comfort. Trubetskoy was a member of one of the oldest and most distinguished families in Russia.

'What does Kondraty say?'

'He's totally committed to action. He says that to miss this opportunity would be craven; that fate has offered us this chance and even if we fail, we must take it.'

Vasily rested his elbows on the table, put his hands up to his cheeks, and then rubbed the back of his neck. 'God save us all from failure…'

'Don't think about it. I feel sure that we won't fail, but there is always a chance.'

Mikhail pushed back his chair and walked to the window. Vasily joined him. The fountain in the garden was an arc of weeping ice; scant flakes of snow were falling.

Michael placed his hand on Vasily's shoulder and looked at him directly. 'But, you must be aware that Kondraty and the Prince are determined that this must remain a military undertaking. Civilians, and that means you, Vasya, must keep clear of any fighting, avoid bloodshed. You shouldn't go to any more meetings, and you won't be asked to carry more messages. You and I can't meet again until the business is over. If action takes place somewhere in the capital, as is likely, you should join the crowd there and lend support. Otherwise, please preserve yourself and the Society by being disciplined, saying nothing, and keeping out of trouble. You do understand me?'

'Yes, of course; but I would like to do more!'

'Your time will come after the revolution. We will need men like you to build our new state. But I beg you, my dearest of friends, do as I ask you now.'

Mikhail's eyes were glistening. He wiped his nose. 'Seem to be getting a cold,' he said. He swallowed hard. 'Well, I must leave you.'

They clasped one another briefly.

'To freedom!' Vasily said.

'To victory!' Mikhail turned abruptly from him. Vasily heard his steps retreating down the hall, his spurs clinking on the wooden floor. He felt hollow with foreboding. They were not ready. He knew they were not ready, and Mikhail knew it, too.

CHAPTER TWENTY
12 December 1825

IT WAS TWO o'clock in the morning, and Colonel Kalinin was in bed. He stared into the darkness. It would soon be time to leave. His paperwork was prepared, and his carriage would come at four. There was no need to rise yet, but he knew he would not sleep. Anticipation of a long journey always disturbed him.

It was irritating that he must depart before he had planned, but there was no help for it. The Emperor's premature death had spoilt his project. He felt like a chess player who, having developed his pieces well, could sense victory; but then, as he was moving in to checkmate, someone had kicked over the table, scattering his pieces on the floor.

The uprising must be imminent, but events were moving against the conspirators. He knew that related revolutionary activities in the south of Russia had been compromised; just yesterday, a young officer recently recruited to the Society had lost his nerve and would today warn Grand Duke Nicholas that something was also planned here. The security forces would be grinding slowly into action. The Ministry of the Interior, the Police, and the City Governor's spies and detectives would wake from their slumber. Files would be dusted down, lists of names compiled, and the usual suspects tracked to squalid attics, Guards' quarters and literary drawing rooms. Yes, it was definitely time to go.

He heard footsteps in the hallway, and then the click of the front door. Vasily Nikolayevich was leaving. He sighed. How he regretted involving Vasily in his schemes! It had been a lazy and somewhat mischievous decision to take advantage of their chance meeting on the ship. His long-held grudge against the young man's uncle was no good reason to have chosen him. He should have found someone else, one of his usual contacts. Of course, Stenovsky had unwittingly done much of the legwork, but the plan had gone all too well. Vasily, now firmly committed to the liberal cause, had just reached the point where he might have been useful.

The failure of the coup seemed almost inevitable. The conspirators had had little time to prepare, they had no real plan and their objectives were unclear. When the uprising was quashed and investigations started in earnest, Vasily would be unlikely to escape. His uncle's influence would not save him. If he remained in the capital, someone would remember seeing him; his name would be on some compromising list. Arrest would mean his imprisonment, torture, a trial, exile, or perhaps worse. He must attempt to save him from destruction, if only for Irina's sake. He knew he shouldn't have involved her, but he had not expected that she would fall in love. He could never do the right thing by his sister.

He rose and lit a candle. The room was cold. He roused a servant and told him to work on the stove.

He picked up his pen.

My dearest sister,
I have had to leave St Petersburg for a while. I shall contact you and Gretchen when I am settled. I am returning to the London Embassy.
I know that what I have to reveal to you will cause you great hurt, and I deeply regret that. However you

should know that Vasily Nikolayevich is in great danger. He has become entangled in an imminent conspiracy against the Emperor that, in my judgement, will end in ruin for all concerned.

It is essential that you go to him and warn him to leave the city at once. If this is impossible (although he should be able to arrange the necessary permits) then he should go into hiding. I think that to avoid any possible unpleasantness you and Gretchen should consider leaving too. Our cousins in Moscow would be pleased to see you, or you could travel direct to Bryansk.

I am unable to express to you how much I regret encouraging Vasily to participate in affairs that he would have best avoided, although in my defence there were others who brought much greater influence to bear on him. I am also deeply sorry to have asked you to look kindly on him, to encourage him. I did not anticipate that your feelings would become so much engaged. Forgive me my dearest Irène. I shall do my best to make amends.

Destroy this letter.

Your brother, Pavel.

He blotted the ink. Would this save Belkin? There was some chance, provided the man left in advance of any trouble. Afterwards, the city would be sealed, and few would get away. But would he be persuaded to desert his friends and betray the principles he had so recently embraced? And, if he did manage to escape, he might have to lie low for months, perhaps years.

There was little more that he could do. He himself must live to fight another day. Vasily must take his own chances.

Alexander generally avoided working on a Saturday morning, but, following news of unrest in the south, now there was evidence of conspiracy here in the capital. If a revolt was indeed imminent, he had not made much progress in uncovering it. Two of his more useful informers had been brought in, but their replies to his questions revealed that they knew nothing but did not want to admit it. He was contemplating what further action to take when he was told that the Baroness von Steiner and her companion were here and wished to see him.

He cracked his knuckles, trying to relieve his irritation. What was this about? Now was emphatically not the time to become embroiled in issues concerning Vasily's personal life. He knew his nephew had been with the woman last night and had returned home before dawn. He sent word that he would receive the Baroness but only had limited time.

He rose as the two women were admitted and ordered that the door be shut. He did not invite them to sit. They stood a little way apart, both dressed in shades of black and grey. In the clear winter light, they seemed diminished and shrunken on the expanse of parquet flooring. The Baroness pushed back her dark veil and he could see that her face was flushed, her eyes pink-rimmed. He thought it the effect of the cold, but when Irina began to speak he realised the extent of her distress.

Irina Pavlovna's message was brief and simple: his nephew, Vasily, was involved in the expected uprising. If the plot failed, as seemed likely, he would be ruined. As she spoke, Alexander felt the blood drain from his face. Surely it couldn't be true?

'How do you know this?'

'I can't reveal that. Vasily himself, of course, said nothing to me, but I assure you I have it on good authority.'

'Does your brother know of it?'

'Pavel Pavlovich is no longer in town.'

This was evasive; her brother almost certainly did know and may well have been the source of her information. But it was unthinkable; it must be untrue. Vasily was a rather indolent, good-hearted dilettante who had only ever expressed a passing interest in politics. It was inconceivable that he had become embroiled in plots – in revolution.

'Why have you come to me, Baroness? Even if what you say is correct, I'm not sure that there is much that I can do.'

'But there is, Alexander Petrovich, there is! Vasily must leave the city at once and you must make him go. I can do nothing for him. Vasily is fond of me, but I don't have the power to persuade him to leave. I know that he won't easily abandon his friends or a cause he believes in.'

Alexander stared down at his desk. Was this really the Vasily he knew? Had Stenovsky been more to Vasily than a drinking companion? Was it no coincidence that Kalinin was this woman's brother? Had he fooled himself, been blind to the truth? How could he have been so mistaken?

'I can't imagine why you thought it right to come to me. Vasily may be my nephew, but, if this story has any substance, in my position I should immediately have him arrested and questioned, as well you know.'

'But you won't do that. You're devoted to Vasily. You won't throw him to the wolves.'

The woman's green eyes met his own. He couldn't hold their gaze. As he sought to control his rising sense of panic, he began to understand what she was asking of him. Perhaps he had been wrong about his nephew; perhaps he was indeed involved in the plot, but there may be a way out. He reflected for a moment. 'That rather depends, Irina Pavlovna,' he said. 'Depends on how deeply he has become engaged in the matter. You have no idea?'

'No, but I can't believe that he has done so very much. He has only been home from abroad for a few months. Please, sir, I beg you. I know that you love your nephew…'

Irina seemed close to tears. Margarethe moved to comfort her.

What should he do? The woman was right. He did indeed love his nephew, would go a long way to save him from catastrophe. He could arrange for him to leave the city quietly; it was the sort of operation at which he excelled, but it would be risky. If too much was known, if there was too much evidence against him, there could be no safe hiding place for Vasily in Russia, and it was too late to spirit him away abroad.

'I will do what I can, Irina Pavlovna, but I can make no promises.'

'He must go at once. There's no time to waste. My brother left town today, and you must tell Vasily that I have left with him. He mustn't think of staying here on my account.' Irina paused. She seemed calmer now. 'I fear that Pavel's part in all this has not been entirely blameless. He took up Vasily, encouraged him to take an interest in politics, but I really don't know what his motive was. He asked me to be kind to him, invite him to our home, but not of course to… and I never realised… never intended…'

'No.'

'Vasily will not understand why I have left without a word. He may well think the worst, that I have deceived him, that

I never truly loved him. That's not the case, but it seems it is how it must appear. Really, it's for the best. Our affair could not last much longer, Vasily would probably have gone abroad after New Year as you know, and I am not free to marry, could not have gone with him.'

Alexander nodded. That might be true, but, nonetheless, Irina Pavlovna clearly did love his nephew and was certainly making a selfless sacrifice. It would be far from easy to salvage the situation, but he would try. Damn Kalinin! He had been playing games with Vasily and with his own sister. How could he have thought it right to do that?

When the women had left, he sat for some time with his head in his hands. He must pull himself together. His assistant knocked on his door seeking orders. He took a deep breath. 'I have nothing further for you at the moment. Ask Count Fedulov to question some more agents, continue to bring in obvious suspects. Oh, and can you have my carriage brought round? I need to make one or two calls. I won't need an escort.'

If he was to do anything, time was very short.

CHAPTER TWENTY-ONE

SINCE MIKHAIL HAD left him three days ago, Vasily had been troubled by a constant ache of anxiety. He had tried to hide this from Irina, blaming his subdued mood on the threat of imminent transfer to the Russian Embassy in Washington. He wasn't too distressed, however, to receive a note from her saying that she was not able to receive him this evening.

He decided to take up his open invitation to dine with Thomas Maltby. On the way to the Englishman's home, he was obliged to pass beneath the double-headed eagle that hung above the door of the Russian American Company. It was already dark, and he did not see the approaching figure of Kondraty Ryleev until he was almost upon him. The poet wore a bright red muffler beneath his dark overcoat.

'Vasily Nikolayevich! Good to see you! Were you coming in to us?' he croaked. It seemed that he could hardly speak.

'No, I'm on my way to Maltby's. You remember him, I'm sure.'

'Oh yes, the Englishman who seemed determined that I should condemn myself to hang. Otherwise, he seemed a good fellow. Anyway, now you're here, have you time for some tea, or something stronger?'

'That would be kind, but I can't stay long.'

The Ryleevs' apartment smelt strongly of cigars. There were signs of recent company. Madame Ryleev was playing with their little daughter, but as they entered she took the child from the room. Vasily accepted some tea from the samovar that seemed to be in perpetual use.

'You've been unwell?'

Ryleev had not removed the muffler, and his voice was barely audible.

'Yes, I have had a throat problem, a cold, or something like, but I am a lot better now.' He coughed.

'And is all prepared?'

'As far as it can be. We still don't know when the oath-taking is planned. It seems it's a state secret, but I would guess that it must be imminent. On Monday, the day after tomorrow, or soon after that.'

'And you're confident?'

'It's too late to worry about success or failure, Vasily Nikolayevich,' Ryleev whispered. 'It's the determination to make the attempt that matters. Some who oppose us are aware of our intentions, and that might make one lose faith, give up. But conspiracies are regularly betrayed, one cannot mind that. We must act! It's better to be arrested on the streets than dragged from our beds like criminals. You will show your support on the day?'

'Of course.'

'Good man! Well, our fate is sealed. In the worst case, we must sacrifice ourselves for the future freedom of our country!' Ryleev coughed several times, then fell silent.

Vasily was astonished at the man's calm confidence, alarmed at his apparent indifference to failure. Ryleev offered him more tea, and, as he refused it, he heard men's voices in the hallway. Several army officers were removing their hats, caps, and greatcoats. One or two had been at the meetings that he had attended here; another had been the recipient of one of his messages. He bowed briefly to them as he left.

He walked out into the frozen street with a lighter step. Ryleev was right. Their fate was sealed.

He paused under a street lantern. As he straightened his hat and pulled up his muffler, he realised that he was being observed. A tall man, warmly wrapped, his face obscured, was standing on the corner beside the watchman's brazier. As Vasily looked at him, his attention seemed to shift towards the ornate ironwork that graced the brightly lit windows of Ryleev's ground-floor apartment.

Was the man keeping watch, noting who came and went? Had he been recognised? Had he covered his face in time? Perhaps not. The bulky figure turned towards the hot coals. He removed his gloves, extended one hand towards the warmth, and, pulling out a flask with the other, started a conversation with the watchman. It seemed, after all, that he was just keeping warm and seeking some company. Reassured, Vasily walked away.

⸺

Thomas Maltby's book-lined apartment was small and enjoyed the luxury of an open fire. Vasily knew he had taken the place because it reminded him of home. The dinner was good; he had procured some excellent fish. Vasily relaxed, his fears forgotten.

If his tutor was aware of the rumours that surrounded the Imperial succession, he did not expand on them tonight. He merely commented that it seemed strange to an Englishman that so vital a matter could be settled by a private arrangement between members of the Imperial Family without any consultation at all with the Senate or the Council of State. They agreed that it was another example of the shortcomings of autocracy and moved on to other matters.

'My uncle's latest plan is to send me to America,' said Vasily.

'I don't really wish to leave Petersburg at present, and certainly don't want to travel so far from home.'

'I would have thought that a post in the Foreign Ministry here might be found in the short term,' said Maltby. 'But, surely, a position abroad must be the ultimate goal?'

Vasily said nothing and, stretching his feet towards the fire, stared into the flames. If all went to plan, if the coup succeeded, shortly he might be representing a quite different government in a quite different capacity. Who knew what his future might be?

'I think we should take some Madeira,' said Maltby. 'It's a gift from Kalinin and promises to drink very well.'

As he rose to fetch the decanter, his servant came in.

'Your coachman's at the door, Count. He says you're needed urgently at home.'

Vasily rose and pulled on his coat with reluctance.

'We'll meet next week, Thomas. I'll try harder with the English.' He embraced his tutor with affection as he left.

———

Grigory was waiting for Vasily in the street. He sat high on the box of the Prince's carriage wrapped in thick furs. He seemed unusually taciturn, angry perhaps, at having to turn out on a cold night. As they drove home through the frost-skimmed streets, Vasily shivered. His sense of foreboding returned. What could his uncle want? Perhaps his mother had sent for him? That seemed more likely.

The Yard was in shadow, but a light burned in the stables. He could make out a box-like wagon standing close to the entrance, but there was no time to ask what it was; one of the Prince's men had emerged from the house with a flaming torch.

'You're to go straight up, sir.'

There was no sign of his mother or any of their servants. Light from his uncle's study streamed out into the corridor; otherwise, the silent rooms were dark.

'Can you step in here, please, Vasily?' Alexander looked up from his desk. 'I'm sorry to have interrupted your evening with Maltby, but I urgently need to speak with you.' Setting his papers aside, he steepled his hands under his chin and scrutinised Vasily for a moment.

Vasily attempted to hold Alexander's gaze but failed. His uncle seemed to be trying to read his thoughts. His sense of apprehension deepened. What could be so urgent that his uncle had forced him to come home?

'Sit down, please,' Alexander said. 'I'll come straight to the point. I received a visitor today at the Ministry. That visitor informed me that you have become involved in the activities of a secret society, an organisation conspiring to foment an insurrection against the new Emperor. I hope that isn't true?'

'I'm not at liberty to say, sir.' Vasily licked his dry lips. He realised he should have taken his time and given a better answer. A refusal to comment was almost a confession. He should have lied, denied his involvement, and hoped to be believed. But the words were spoken now.

His uncle frowned. 'I had hoped that my informant was mistaken. I very much hoped that, but my instinct and your reaction confirm that the facts as told to me are correct. The ultimate source of my intelligence is, sadly, reliable. I am aware that a conspiracy has come to light, and now I think it very likely that you are indeed involved in it.' Alexander paused. 'I have to say, Vasily, that I find your behaviour beyond comprehension. To kick against a system that has afforded you so much privilege shows terrible ingratitude. What's more, it's reprehensible to betray your monarch, endanger the peace of your country.' Alexander spoke harshly, but his face expressed grief and disappointment. He cleared his throat and leant forward.

'Now I need you to tell the truth, Vasya. If you aren't too deeply compromised, I can help you to avoid the consequences of your perverse stupidity.'

Vasily remained silent.

'Well? We really don't have a lot of time.' Alexander glanced at the German clock on the bookshelf. It was past ten o'clock.

'I have nothing to say, sir.'

'You should know that the plot has already been betrayed. One of your number has today turned informer. I'm told that the rebels are disorganised; they don't have sufficient support among the troops. If a coup is attempted, failure is very probable. The new Tsar, Nicholas, is not known for his forgiving nature. His revenge will be rapid and pitiless.' A flush was creeping up Alexander's neck, but his face was now unreadable.

Vasily sighed and bowed his head. The revolution, for him at least, seemed to be over before it had begun. But he must say nothing, hold his nerve, keep his oath, be true to the cause he had embraced. Otherwise, what had been the point of it all?

As Alexander continued to reason with him, Vasily resisted the temptation to justify himself. When the clock struck the half-hour, Alexander rose to his feet. His tone became sharper: 'You need to hear some hard truths, Vasily, and then perhaps you'll see sense and accept my help.'

'I don't want your help.'

'You know you've been played for a complete fool, don't you? Your new friend Kalinin is not what he seems. Although he poses as a liberal, since he left the army he has worked for the Government, picking up innocent young people, manipulating them, involving them in various unsavoury affairs, and then using them in one way or another to get the information he needs. He's a past master at the game. He usually works abroad, but recently he's been engaged in operations here. The last Emperor suspected the existence of an organised plot to dethrone him. Kalinin was called back to try to penetrate it. His activities have now been overtaken by events.'

Vasily looked up. What was his uncle saying? Could this be true?

'When Kalinin met you on coming back from England, his interest in you was probably opportunistic. I expect he saw you as an easy target, a promising dupe, and no doubt he also thought it would be amusing to hit back at me. As you know, we've had our disagreements in the past.

'And Kalinin's sister's no better. She's just a promiscuous harpy. He uses her to seduce susceptible innocents in order to haul them into his net. I suppose she told you some story about her unhappy marriage? I happen to know that Kalinin has now left St Petersburg, possibly leaving a report and a list of suspects behind him. She's gone with him or won't be far behind. In any event, you won't see her again.'

Vasily was on his feet. 'That's not possible!'

'Why should I lie to you?'

'Because you want me to leave her. You clearly don't approve of her.'

'Do you really think I would invent such a story just to separate you from a mistress of whom you'll certainly tire in due course… unless of course you had the wit to see through her lies first.'

'But she didn't know anything. I never told her anything. It's impossible. She's not…'

'She may indeed have known nothing of the conspiracy. I've no idea what Kalinin tells his sister about his work, but she was certainly encouraged to reel you in like a fish on a line.'

Vasily sank down, his head in his hands. A trickle of sweat ran down his spine. Surely he hadn't been a complete fool?

Alexander's tone became more conciliatory: 'Please, Vasily, take advice from me. Don't get involved in any more secret societies. You make an improbable conspirator. Believe me, I've dealt with enough in my time. Now, tell me what you know, the extent of your involvement, and I'll decide what's to be done.'

Vasily looked at his uncle. Should he throw himself on his mercy and accept the help he seemed to be offering? It was tempting. But could he trust him? Surely Alexander's loyalty lay with the establishment. Besides, he couldn't reveal what he knew and inform against Mikhail, Kondraty Ryleev, and the others.

'I'll not betray my friends.'

'Vasya, you still don't understand, do you? The men you believe to be friends have already been betrayed and you, if you stay here, will inevitably be arrested. I won't be able to prevent it. Under interrogation, the truth will rapidly come to light. You may not think that you've done very much, that your part has been small, but believe me, when this revolt fails – and fail it will – punishment will be indiscriminate.'

Silence fell between them. Alexander looked once more at the clock. Shaking his head, he rose to his feet.

'I'm sorry. I can't argue with you all night.'

He walked to the door and shouted: 'Antonov!'

Within seconds, a heavy-shouldered man stood on the threshold. He was dressed in black. His face was expressionless, his arms swayed and his fists hung, heavy pendula at his sides. Vasily's head spun. Who was this? Was he here to take him away? To arrest him? Or worse?

Alexander walked to the window and raised his hand. A full-throated howl echoed round the stable yard below. Vasily jumped to his feet. 'What the devil's that?' Antonov moved towards him.

'That, my dear, is your manservant, Yakov, receiving the beating that I've frequently wanted to administer during the course of the past thirteen years.'

'Leave him alone! Stop! You must stop this! What's he done to deserve it?'

'Well, he's clearly failed to look after you as he should, that's for sure.'

More blows followed, and further cries. As if indifferent, Alexander sat down, picked up his pen, and turned to his papers. Vasily advanced towards the desk, but Antonov restrained him, taking his arms and forcing him back into the chair.

Alexander looked up. 'Vasily Nikolayevich, you must help yourself by helping me.'

This was unbearable. He couldn't put Yakov through more pain. And where was Matvey? Would he be next? What point was there in resistance? It seemed there was little left to reveal.

'For God's sake, stop that torture. I'll tell you what you want to know.'

'Good.' Alexander returned to the window. Yakov's howls fell away. Vasily struggled but could not move. Antonov continued to restrain him.

'Let him go,' Alexander said. 'I can't imagine why you're making life so difficult for us both, Vasily.'

Vasily rubbed his arms. His uncle now seemed completely at ease. He had often wondered how Alexander spent his days at the Ministry, what his work entailed. Now he knew. He hung his head.

'Fetch him a drink,' said Alexander. 'Then leave us.'

Beer was brought. As he took the glass, liquid splashed onto his lap; he set it aside. He looked beyond the motionless figure of his uncle to the portrait that had been painted in Paris. There he stood In his new tailcoat, looking down complacently with a half-smile on his lips, wondering how soon he could escape from the studio and continue his pleasure-seeking. It seemed centuries ago.

'Now, I really do need some facts from you, Vasily. First of all, when did Kalinin start filling your head with ideas? Or was it Mikhail Stenovsky? You met up with him very soon after coming back from Prussia.'

Vasily nodded. Mikhail had indeed opened the door; Kalinin had merely helped to push him through it.

'Look, Vasily. You have my word. You can safely tell me the truth. I can do nothing now to help or to harm Mikhail Alexandrovich, or anyone else you mention. They have already sealed their own fates. Mikhail's brother is a known radical. If the rebellion fails, both brothers will be taken, for sure. But I promise I'll not make life worse for them, or anyone else you mention.'

Vasily started to speak: 'Until recently, I've hidden little from you or from Dmitry Vladimirovich. You know that I've visited Kalinin in the country. There was some talk there of the war, of politics. I met Kondraty Ryleev.'

'Did you indeed?' His uncle frowned. 'How often did you meet Ryleev?'

'How often have you visited his apartment at the Russian American Company?

'What about Mikhail's brother, Nikita. How well do you know him?

'Have you been to other political meetings? With whom?

'Have you run errands? Delivered messages? Used passwords? What about ciphers? False papers? Think carefully. List all the occasions that you can remember that you have been seen out and about in society, particularly since the death of the Tsar.'

The questioning continued for some time. Vasily found he had drained his beer. He was not offered more.

Alexander sat for several minutes, deep in thought. Muffled moans could be heard, coming from the servants' rooms. Yakov had been delivered back to his quarters. Vasily wondered again about Matvey. What would happen to him now? He felt tears welling up and blinked them back.

Alexander stood to deliver his verdict. 'I think that we can try to save you, but the situation is by no means without risk. It's possible that you'll bring ruin on me, as well as on yourself, but from what you have told me, your part in all this, while imprudent, has not been significant. I would guess that some questions might be asked, but a plausible story can be concocted. I'm afraid the next few days and months will not be comfortable. You will leave here tonight under guard. Your box has already been packed and is in the vehicle downstairs.'

Vasily remembered the odd conveyance that he had seen in the yard. Of course, it was some sort of prison wagon.

'You will be taken to the Moscow estate, and you will

stay there under supervision until I deem it safe for you to leave. You may be there for some considerable time. When you arrive at Dubovnoye, you will go to your bedroom, and you will stay there. It will be put about that you are ill, that you have been ill for some time. You will leave your room when you hear from me and not before. If any stranger comes to the house, you will make sure that you are in bed. If you disobey me in any particular, I shall not hesitate to arrange for you to be arrested and brought back to St Petersburg to share the fate of your friends. Do you understand?'

'Yes, sir.' He looked around. Should he try to escape, make a run for it? He could hear Antonov pacing back and forth in the corridor and now he made out the low voice of another man. Could he get past them? And, if he did break free, where could he go without compromising others? There seemed no choice but to fall in with his uncle's plan.

Alexander opened the drawer of his desk and pulled out a sheaf of papers. 'I have prepared passes for you. You will be travelling in what will appear to be a prison vehicle and will receive government priority for horses. You will absolutely obey the instructions of your guards. I also have letters here for your grandmother and for Karl Feodorovich. Your guards will destroy them if you are intercepted on the journey. Initially, you will communicate only with them and whoever is assigned to be your body servant.'

'And Yakov?'

'Well, I don't think he's fit to travel, do you? And, in any event, he has played games with us all for long enough. The Prince will take him on for the time being, and he'll learn what it means to do some work.'

'But he's done nothing wrong.'

His uncle didn't respond. He gave Antonov the papers and what looked like a bag of coins. Then he turned his back. It was clear the interview was over.

Vasily's whole body ached. He staggered a little as Antonov, joined by a shorter man, each took an arm and led him into the hall. They helped him into a fur overcoat and hat and shepherded him like a child to the stairs. In the shadows of the yard, the black cave of the wagon's door gaped open. Antonov lit a lantern. 'Get in and lie down.' The floor was strewn with straw. Vasily heard a rasping clink as shackles bit his ankles; the weight of a blanket fell across his back. The door slammed, and a pall of darkness fell. It was very cold. As the wagon started to move, he was seized by terror. Could he trust his uncle? Was this some sort of trick? Were they taking him to the fortress?

Alexander watched the wagon roll out towards the street and then, wiping his brow, sat down at his desk. He picked up his pen, but his hand was shaking. It was several minutes before he was able to write.

St Petersburg
12 December 1825

Irina Pavlovna
Vasily Nikolayevich has today left town on government business. He is unlikely to be returning to St Petersburg for many months.

I know he would want me to express his regret that he was unable to bid you farewell personally.
I remain etc.

He signed the paper and then addressed and sealed it. The clock struck midnight. He felt very tired, but he knew he must take the note downstairs for delivery in the morning. The long stone stairway fell away into the darkness. As he reached the bottom, the Prince emerged from his rooms, his terriers at his feet.

'Come, my dear.' Dmitry reached out and took his arm. 'Come and sit with me for a while. I have a fire in here.'

Alexander followed him into the study and slumped into a chair. He covered his face with his hands. Tears trickled between his fingers.

The Prince gently closed the door.

PART TWO

'It is painful to be an ardent dreamer in a land of eternal frost'

Griboyedov

CHAPTER TWENTY-TWO

13 to 17 December 1825 –
The Road from St Petersburg to Moscow

THE PRISON WAGON rattled on into the night. The ride became rougher as the city streets gave way to a surface of sand, sunken logs and frozen mud. Vasily must have slept a little, for he was jolted awake as the carriage came to a halt. For a moment, he didn't know where he was. He felt numb and unable to collect his thoughts.

One of the drivers was climbing down from the box. The door of the wagon opened. It was the smaller man, whose name, it seemed, was Bortnik. He shut the door, set down his lantern, and, taking off his wide-cuffed coachman's gloves, drew keys out of the pocket of his shaggy coat. He knelt down and, rubbing his hands, unlocked Vasily's fetters.

'We guess you won't be wanting to escape. The chains are mainly for the benefit of the sentries at the barriers.'

Bortnik blew out the lantern and grunted as he lay down across the door. His snores soon filled the wagon. Vasily stared into the darkness. Alexander's words about Irina, interspersed with Yakov's cries of agony, echoed in his head. He rubbed his ankles where the shackles had bruised his flesh. The pain was a welcome distraction.

The wagon travelled on. When dawn finally broke, grey light filtered in through small mica-covered vents high in the sides. Vasily could just make out the hunched outline of his sleeping companion. He reached out to the pile of straw in the corner and took a handful to cover his feet. The heap seemed to shift a little. He shook his head and rubbed his eyes, but the straw was now completely still.

There was no sound; the wagon had stopped. Antonov stood in the doorway. Behind him, a line of forest stretched back along the roadside and feeble sunlight wavered on the track.

Antonov gave Bortnik a shove. He woke, scratched his head, and muttered, 'Damn cold!'

'We're a few versts from the post station,' Antonov said. 'Better shackle him up.'

'Surely people won't take much notice of him.'

'Better not take the risk. He'll have to get used to his chains.'

There was a slight rustle in the corner.

'A mouse!' said Bortnik. 'I cleaned this carriage out yesterday. It must have come in with the bedding.' He went to the corner, bent down, and reached into the pile. 'What have we got here? I think we've an extra passenger.' He pulled hard, and his hand emerged holding what appeared to be a small arm. He pulled again, and Matvey stood before them, revealed in a scatter of dust and chaff.

Antonov moved to hurl the child out of the wagon.

'No, stop!' Vasily tried to rise to his feet, but his legs wouldn't support him, and he fell with a crash against the rear wall and slowly slid back to the floor.

Matvey was wrapped in an old cloak. He wore a fur cap and, beneath the cloak, seemed to be dressed in several layers of rags even more disreputable than those that had been burnt by Venyamin some months before. His eyes were bright in his round face. He seemed unafraid.

'Who the hell is this?'

'He's one of our servants. His name is Matvey.'

'I'm one of the Prince's kitchen boys!' Matvey shrilled. 'I climbed into the wagon to have a sleep. I didn't know you were going to drive off! You'll have to take me back at once!'

The boy looked at Vasily, who took his cue. 'We can't take you back, you wicked boy! You'll have to come with us to Moscow, where you'll get the thrashing you deserve before we send you home.'

Antonov scowled at Matvey. He banged his hand in frustration against the side of the wagon, causing the horses to shift. He almost lost his footing.

'I'll give him the thrashing now, sir, if you like,' he said. 'And then we can throw him out and let him make his own way home.'

'I agree that would be convenient,' Vasily said. 'But he won't survive this cold weather. Even serfs as inadequate as Matvey have some value. I'm not sure my uncle would wish to see him casually discarded.'

Antonov scowled. 'This wasn't part of the plan,' he said.

'It's your call, Antonov. You'll have to face Alexander Petrovich and explain the loss of his patron's serf.'

'I'll need to go home, sir!' Matvey cried, thrusting out his thin chest. 'In the autumn, I'm to be sold for a good sum to a new master! I'm to be a chef!'

Bortnik shrugged. 'I don't see much risk in him coming along, Antonov. We can take him back to Petersburg ourselves. If there are questions at the barrier, we can say he's a runaway.'

Antonov shivered. 'We can't stay here too long. We'll all die of cold. He'll have to stay in the wagon, well hidden, until we get to the estate. Get back under that straw, boy, and stay there until I say you can come out again.'

'I need to pee, sir.'

'Off you go then, Matvey,' said Vasily, 'and be quick. No wandering off.'

Antonov sighed and turned away, stamping his feet.

Matvey climbed out of the back of the wagon. When he returned, Bortnik left to take his turn on the box. Antonov closed the door and, grumbling, lay down to rest. Matvey winked at Vasily and then, with a grin, disappeared into his nest in the straw. Vasily's spirits lifted a little. He was no longer entirely alone.

They reached the post house half an hour later. Fresh horses were quickly arranged. Once Vasily had managed to get his legs working, he had difficulty walking in his irons.

'You'll get used to them,' commented Bortnik. He sounded as if he knew.

'I hope I don't have to,' said Vasily, slowly making his way to the wooden buildings.

Antonov stood staring at the sky and then contemplated the striped verst post that was pitched at a crazy angle. 'The weather's settled enough,' he said. 'We'll likely make it to the estate without changing the wheels. If all goes to plan we'll make it in three or four days.'

The post house was not one of the grander establishments that were gradually springing up along the Petersburg to Moscow Road. It was, however, functional and relatively clean. The heat from the large square stove in the corner was welcome. They sat at a scrubbed table and were brought tea and rye bread, some cheese, dried fish and pickled vegetables. The woman serving the food peered at Vasily's fetters but gave no sign that she found them unusual.

Vasily's body gradually warmed, but as it did so, his heart seemed to lose its numbness and fill with molten lead. What had happened to Irina? Had he really been abandoned and deceived? He tried to thrust the thoughts aside. There would be plenty of time for bitter reflection. But he felt very tired. His throat was raw. He must be coming down with a cold. He remembered Ryleev's red muffler. He had probably caught it from him. First his politics, then his ailments; neither promised to do him much good.

Antonov stood up. 'We must press on,' he said. 'I'll order food to carry with us. We can't afford to stop for much longer than it takes to change the horses.'

They climbed back into the wagon. Bortnik returned to the box while Antonov removed the fetters. Vasily resumed his place on the straw. He was warmer than he had been and would probably sleep. They drew away. Once Antonov was safely snoring, Matvey emerged. He crawled under Vasily's furs and burrowed close to him.

'Where are we going, sir?' he whispered.

'To Dubovnoye, our estate near Moscow.'

'Is it far?'

'Yes. It will take another three days, at least, to get there.'

'Oh!' Matvey absorbed this information, and then asked, 'Are you pleased to see me, sir?'

Vasily hesitated. 'Did you really fall asleep in the wagon by accident, Matvey?'

'Well, I was scared, sir. Alexander Petrovich came home from his work in a bad mood. He was very stern and sent me downstairs. I don't like going to the Prince's, sir. He might think to take me back. So I hid in your room. I heard Alexander Petrovich shouting at Yako, and then he called Grigory and told him to take him down to the stables. Well, we all know what that means! I didn't want to get sent there, too, so I changed, to save my livery. Then I went and lay down in the wagon to… to have a think. I could have got out, you know. I had a good view of the door. But when I saw that they was bringing you out and that you were going with them, I decided to stay. I thought you might need me. I didn't think it would be such a long journey, though.'

'That story about being sold… becoming a chef!'

'Yes, that was a good one!'

'Yes, it was, Matvey, but…' This wasn't the moment to deliver another homily about lying. 'I'm more than glad you're here.' He pulled the boy closer to him for mutual warmth. 'When we get to the estate, you must make yourself scarce for a while. With luck, they'll forget that they agreed to take you back. Perhaps I'll ask Karl, our old tutor, to tell them that he'll make the arrangements to return you to St Petersburg.'

'But I don't want to go back!'

'Hush! You'll wake Antonov. No, you won't have to go back, Matvey. I promise you that.'

They travelled day and night, stopping only for fresh horses. Antonov and Bortnik took turns driving. When they reached Tver, the two drivers enjoyed a shave and a meal. They told Vasily to stay in the wagon, as it would be better if he were not seen. They brought hot food and tea for him and Matvey, but Vasily found it hard to eat.

They set off again, skirting around the northeast of Moscow, where, for a while, the roads became very rutted. They were all thrown around on the straw. By now, Vasily clearly had a fever. Antonov regarded him with concern. He had been told to look after him, he said. He didn't want to deliver a corpse.

At noon on the fourth day, the wagon swung up the drive of the Belkin estate. Several long dogs leaped out and, barking, surrounded the carriage. The doorman stepped out of the old wooden manor house onto the gravel of the carriage sweep. He looked at the police wagon and scratched his head.

Antonov went to meet him. It had started to snow. 'I've brought young Count Belkin home on the orders of his uncle, the State Councillor,' he said. 'But I'm afraid he isn't at all well.'

'I'll fetch the mistress,' said the doorman. 'Karl Feodorovich is also indoors.'

'I think the Count is able to walk. I'll bring in his box.'

The old Countess, Yevgenia Alexandrovna, stood with Karl in the wood-panelled hallway. It had been two years since they had seen Vasily, and it was clear that they barely recognised the whey-faced man with four days' growth of dark beard who stumbled into the house supported by Bortnik. He slumped onto a settle.

'I can't greet you properly now, Grandmother, Karl Feodorovich. I'm ill and don't want to infect you. I'm very pleased to be home.'

'But what are you doing here? You look terrible.'

'Antonov has a letter for you, I think. It should explain all.' Vasily leaned his head back, thrust out his damaged legs, and closed his eyes.

Both elderly people withdrew, needing a glass and better light to read. Antonov walked out and stood under the portico. He looked at the sky. 'It looks as though our luck has run out. It's started to snow. We may need to fix runners.'

'You can stay here tonight, go back tomorrow if you wish. Our wheelwright will sort you out,' Vasily wheezed. His chest was very sore.

'No, we'll make a start; it is not snowing hard. We can go

back through Moscow. We'll arrange things there. I'll go and fetch the boy.'

Within a few minutes, he returned. 'He's disappeared, the little shit.'

'He won't have gone far.'

'Well, we can't hang about…'

'Look, Antonov, Matvey is likely sickening, too… just leave him here, and we'll make sure he gets back to St Petersburg when he's fit. You get on.'

The Countess sent for provisions for the two men. As they left, they shook Vasily by the hand. He would have liked to have gone out to bid them farewell, but he felt too weak.

'Come, Vasenka, my dear,' said his grandmother. 'Alexander Petrovich has ordered that you go to bed, and I would suggest it's a good idea.'

CHAPTER TWENTY-THREE

January 1826
Dubovnoye Estate, Moscow Province

10 January 1826
Karl Feodorovich to Alexander Petrovich

Further to my letter of 17th of the last in which I confirmed the arrival of Vasily Nikolayevich here at the estate, I now write to you with further information which I hope will encourage you.

As I related, Vasily was unwell when he reached Dubovnoye. He had spent four days in the back of a police wagon, much of the time in freezing conditions, having contracted a cold before departure. There was no need to insist on following your instructions that he be confined to bed since it was the only possible course of action. I should reassure you that he is now somewhat recovered, but is still not in good health.

In the days after his arrival Vasily's cough became incessant and his condition deteriorated. Mindful of your orders that he see no-one and be seen by no-one, I was reluctant to call the doctor but finally, when his fever got worse, decided that I must do so. The doctor diagnosed a putrid congestion of the lungs. He recommended some proprietary potion of his own combined with bleeding.

Yevgenia Alexandrovna does not trust doctors as you are aware, and forbad any bleeding. Having received the diagnosis, she paid the doctor and dismissed him. Then, despite my protests, she called the priest from the village. He filled the room with incense which as far as I could see made Vasily's condition far worse, and then blessed the icons. The priest suggested that we call on a healer, an old woman, Agafya, in whom our serfs have considerable faith. I protested once again but was overruled.

The old crone came up to the house and immediately changed the way that Vasily was lying in his bed, putting a pillow beneath his legs. She said that he must try to sleep on his side, with his head raised. She then applied warm compresses to his body, and prepared a thick tea-like drink that seemed to comprise among other things, a quantity of dried mint and ginger. She returned twice every day, and repeated this procedure. She ordered the boy Matvey to fan Vasya's face and upper body several times a day, to change the sheets regularly, and to ensure that Vasily drank a good deal of clean water. Eventually he was able to keep the liquids down, and his fever abated.

Despite my objections, Agafya poured the doctor's brew away down the drain at the front of the house, saying that it only had any use as a killer of weeds.

The priest became a regular visitor. I much oppose, as you know, all this superstition. However, his malodorous, not to say irritating, presence turned out to be a blessing. As you had predicted, a day or so after New Year we were visited by two officers from the police house in Ramenskoye. They said it was a routine call. They were making checks for the police in St Petersburg. They wished to ascertain that Count Vasily Nikolayevich Belkin was on the estate, that he was ill, and that he had been here in that condition for some time.

As they arrived in the hallway they met the priest on his way out. This gave them the impression that Vasily was not just ill, but possibly close to death. This had the immediate effect of altering their officious attitude to one of respectful gravity. The priest confirmed to them that the Count was indeed very ill, and that he had been so for some time. He was not able, he said, to be precise as to dates, but nonetheless his testimony was very persuasive. This seemed to relieve the officers of the need to pursue the matter with excessive rigour. They asked me, Yevgenia Alexandrovna and the doorman similar questions, and received the same answers. They then went up to examine Vasily, and were clearly convinced by his pathetic appearance, and also the strong medicinal odour that pervaded the room, the multiplicity of religious images, candles etc. etc. The boy, Matvey, suggested that they not get too close since his disease was highly infectious. I did not feel that this intervention was necessary and punished the child later for lying.

This brings me to the question of the boy. I understand that he is in fact the property of Prince Bogolyubov, who was carried here, apparently by mistake, in the confusion and hurry of leaving St Petersburg. I am not sure whether the Prince wishes me to go to the expense and trouble of returning him to you? Now that Vasily is a little recovered he seems to find much comfort in the presence of the boy. I have to say that Matvey worked tirelessly to restore Vasily, whom he insists on calling his master, to better health. Vasily has asked me most urgently to request that the child be allowed to stay with us at least for now. I have to say that he is in general no trouble and his constant attention to Vasily has much relieved the few servants that we now keep in the house.

Apart from that above written, there is little news here. The winter is at last with us. We receive scant news of the outside world, which is probably a blessing. Has there been another edition of the Polar Star? If so we would welcome a copy.

My respects to Maria Vasilyevna, and to Princess Polunina.

I remain etc...

Karl

———

Dubovnoye Estate

15 March 1826

Alexander Petrovich,

Thank you for yours of the 8th inst. It was good news to read of the safe delivery of a son and heir to Prince Polunin. Please convey our best wishes to Ekaterina Nikolayevna. Vasily seemed to be pleased to hear that he has a nephew.

The two men that you mention arrived in early February and set themselves up as sentries in the hall. I suppose you know your business, but I have to remark that I do not believe that their presence is really necessary. Vasily Nikolayevich is mindful of your instructions and I am certain that in his current state of body and mind he will respect them. While certainly better, he is by no means fully restored and he shows little inclination to leave his room, let alone the estate.

He still has a cough, and is very weak. He sleeps a great deal. His spirits seem low and he can remain without speaking for days. I have tried to interest him in a little reading, and have put the drawing materials and paints that were in his box in full view, but as yet he has shown no interest in them. His grandmother, who spends much time with him, has had some success in cheering him, and once or twice has encouraged him to come down for dinner and even to play some whist. I suppose that whatever ails him, time will heal all.

I am grateful that you have not insisted that Matvey be returned to St Petersburg. He does seem to inspire some signs of life in his master, whom he serves very diligently. Vasily has asked me to spend some time helping him with his numbers and with reading. I was hesitant at first since the child is after all just a serf, but I wanted to humour Vasily and I have been most surprised by the child's aptitude. I have found his reading to be passable for what I suspect is his age, and he has made some progress with French and German. He has expressed an interest in learning some more English...he has a few phrases. However we have no English books here...just a copy of some political treatise which somehow found its way into Vasily's luggage and which is not suitable for a child. In any event it is beyond me! As you know my English is very poor.

The weather here has improved a little and some days there is a thaw. The roads I would imagine are not good at present so I hope that you receive this promptly. There is little news, either from here or from the wider world.

I trust that your health is well. Please convey my respects and congratulations to Maria Vasilyevna on the birth of her grandson.

I remain etc... Karl.

Alexander Petrovich,

I have not heard directly from you for a little while, but of course received your news through Yevgenia Alexandrovna. You have clearly ordered the withdrawal of our two 'sentries' since they have informed me that their work is done here and that they are leaving this week. Apart from occasionally chastising Matvey for irritating behaviour, they have had little to occupy them. I also understand from your mother that we are to expect the imminent arrival of Vasily Nikolayevich's body servant Yakov. This will please Yakov's family greatly as they have not seen him for two years.

Vasily is much recovered physically and has been out and about on the estate. He still has a cough, and is very thin despite being encouraged to eat a wholesome diet. His spirits are volatile however. Sometimes he appears to be quite back to his normal genial self; on other occasions he is uncommunicative and moody. He has been much helped I think by touring the estate with the new manager, with whom you are, I think, in regular communication. He has spent time shooting, both with a rifle and pistols, and has been hunting by the river with the manager. He also rides out alone on my horse, sometimes leading Matvey behind on one of the ponies. I am not sure that the child much enjoys it, preferring his books when he has free time.

I hope that you and Maria Vasilyevna will be able to visit us before the autumn. The garden is looking better, I think, than it ever has, and the new Manager is doing a fine job on the estate. He seems to be respected and liked by the serfs, and we have had no sign of the unrest here that, I understand, has occurred elsewhere.

My regards to Maria Vasilyevna. I was pleased to hear from Ekaterina Nikolayevna that the young Prince Polunin continues to delight!

I remain etc... Karl.

———

Alexander Petrovich,

I hope that this finds you well. I received your letter to me confirming the return of Yakov shortly after I last sent to you. The courier service is very poor at times.

I am writing for further instructions with regard to Vasily Nikolayevich. Is it still the case that he is to remain on the estate, or, now that his guardians are departed may he venture further afield?

I ask this because since the arrival here of Yakov, and the recent festivities etc. related to high summer and the harvest, Vasily's spirits and health have very much improved. I would not say that he is entirely back to normal but he seems in much better heart.

It has been a good season this year, and the yields are likely to have been high. Vasily himself went out to help to get the harvest in as he used to do in years gone by. This delighted Yevgenia Alexandrovna of course, and impressed the serfs.

He has not blatantly transgressed your instructions,

but I am aware that on occasion he has visited the inn in the village, and may have gone to Ramenskoye. I am not sure how to express this delicately, but I think that he may also have been seeking solace with a member of the gentler sex. This is of course quite normal for a young man, particularly at harvest time. It does however raise the question of what he is to do in the future. There is really no sensible role for him here, unless you wish to dispense with your Manager, and all the signs are that Vasily now needs to be found some useful work.

Matvey continues to work hard at his lessons with me, and also with Vasily who has been teaching him some history and geography. Matvey was excited when Yakov returned to the estate, although it must be said that Yakov takes advantage of the boy's willingness to undertake much of his work.

Summer has brought with it the arrival of the nobility to the countryside, and some have remembered to come to pay their respects to Yevgenia Alexandrovna. She has also returned some calls, and hosted some small dinners, but she now finds it tiring to go about too much in society.

We have heard from our neighbours of the terrible punishments recently imposed on the convicted men who were involved in the uprising in the Senate Square in December last year. I fear it does not bode well for the future. I know we do not see eye to eye on this, but I have always been the proponent of a more democratic approach in this country. This now looks even less likely I fear.

I will say nothing more about this save to say that it is a blessing that Vasily Nikolayevich, and others of our family, avoided any involvement.

I hope to see you here before the summer is entirely ended,
I remain etc... Karl.

Postscript: two letters have arrived for Vasily, one with the return address of Thomas Maltby Esq. inscribed on it. The other is I think in a female hand, and also comes from St Petersburg. You gave instructions that he is not to receive any mail. Do those instructions still pertain?

———

Bogolyubov Palace
St Petersburg
25 August 1826

Karl Feodorovich,
You can expect me at the estate shortly. I shall be alone and my visit will be brief. Maria Vasilyevna has been at Tsarskoe Selo with Katya and the baby, Nikolay Konstantinovich, who is now the centre of her life.

Please do not inform Vasily of my imminent arrival. I shall give him the letters when I have examined them.

Until we meet,
Alexander.

CHAPTER TWENTY-FOUR

ALEXANDER WALKED TO the river through the cemetery, stopping only to pause for several minutes at the family graves. As he approached the high bank, he heard the crack of a pistol shot. Another shot followed twenty seconds later, then another, then the sound of breaking glass and a shout of celebration followed by laughter.

He stood looking downstream onto a small beach shaded by trees. The sharp stink of gun smoke drifted up to him. His nephew Vasily was sitting on the ground wearing a floppy hat. A pistol lay on the sand beside him. Yakov was lounging on the grass a little way distant, observing proceedings, his long legs crossed, with a grey-and-white deerhound at his feet. A collection of targets – upturned logs, tin boxes, glass bottles – were ranged along the trunk of a fallen tree. The boy, Matvey, was busy replacing a broken bottle and examining the other items for damage.

'Two out of three!' he warbled.

They look like a band of robbers, Alexander thought.

'They're all set!' Matvey stepped away from the targets.

Vasily was removing his hat and reloading his gun. It didn't take him long. How many hours had his nephew spent down here practising?

'Sit down, Matvey.' Vasily stood up to take aim. Another bottle shattered. Vasily reloaded. He was wearing a peasant's shirt over loose trousers, belted with what seemed to be string. His hair flopped, thick, too long, over his eyes. His face and the visible parts of his body were tanned straw-bronze.

He frowned as he raised the pistol again. The full sleeve of his shirt was rolled back, and Alexander could see the sinews in his arm. He was lean, balanced, and dangerous.

Vasily fired once more, and then, looking up the bank, he noticed his uncle standing above them. He muttered something inaudible to Yakov. Then, with deliberation, he reloaded the pistol for a third time, took aim, and sent a tin box clattering high into the air.

Yakov struggled to his feet and took the gun. He checked its heat and placed it on the ground beside a wooden box. Alexander recognised the case; the pistol was one of a French pair that had belonged to his brother Nikolay.

Vasily was now climbing up the bank towards him, the hound following behind. He stopped some six feet or so away and gave a short bow. Then he looked up and held his gaze. 'Good morning, and welcome, Uncle.'

So, there was to be no embrace. He had not really expected a warm welcome, but he felt an ache of disappointment. 'Has someone called you out, Vasily?' he said dryly, 'or is this exercise solely aimed at terrorising the local fauna?'

'The latter, sir. There's little necessity to defend one's honour here in the country, as you know.'

Silence fell between them. Alexander looked back to the beach. Yakov was stooped, clearing away the broken bottles and the boy seemed to have disappeared. He cleared his throat. 'I don't have a lot of time, Vasily. I have business to do in Moscow and must leave in the morning. I wonder if you'd be good enough to meet me, with Karl Feodorovich, in the estate office in half an hour?' He surveyed Vasily's smock and bast-sandaled feet. 'Perhaps we'd better say an hour, so you have time to change. We need to discuss your future.'

Vasily inclined his head and turned back to the river.

Alexander took the shorter route up to the estate house. As he walked across the shaded lawns, he noticed that the bushes were already shedding leaves. Summer was almost over. He absently lashed out at some lower branches with his stick. Vasily's aloofness saddened him, but he was also irritated. His nephew had become so proud, so distant. Did he understand nothing? Did he not know what he had escaped?

———

The day was hot. Vasily had felt obliged to dress formally for the first time in months. He felt uncomfortable in his frock coat; it seemed too tight about the arms and shoulders, and too loose elsewhere. As he walked across the yard to the estate office he couldn't fail to hear Karl speaking about him.

'The widow of the miller... you know she was a ladies' maid here, a sensible sort. The miller bought her freedom. Kolya gave him a generous deal, of course. She owns the mill now, and she's not short of suitors. I'm sure it was nothing serious, no more than a casual...'

Vasily coughed to warn them of his approach.

It was cool in the office. Vasily breathed in the room's familiar air: seasoned wood, the sour tang of ink. His uncle stood behind the desk, fingering the sandbox. Two chairs were drawn up. Karl was seated in one, so he took the other. Alexander cleared his throat and attempted a smile. 'I understand from Karl Feodorovich that you have been unwell, Vasily. You are fully recovered now?'

Vasily knew that he was a picture of good health. He said nothing. There was no reason to make this easy.

'You've had some months to think about it. Do you have

any idea of what you might do now?'

'I should like to travel abroad, sir. I'd like to visit Italy and take some painting lessons.' This, he knew, was a forlorn hope, but what was he expected to answer?

'That's completely out of the question. Neither you nor I have the means to support such an idea. In any case, the new Emperor has expressed the wish that all who can should now devote themselves to state service. Perhaps it may be possible to travel in a few years; I know that Dmitry would sponsor you once again, in time, but it's not long since you returned from your last foreign trip.'

Indeed, it was only a little over a year. It seemed like an eternity since he had stood on the deck of the *Virtuous* in the Kronstadt Roads.

'I could stay on the estate. I enjoy being here. I can make myself useful. I'd welcome more freedom to come and go, however.'

Alexander shook his head. 'The financial position of the estate is much better than it was, but it can't sustain both you and a manager.'

'I've learned a lot from Karl already. In time, we could do without the manager.'

'I'm sorry, Vasily, but that's not practical, and there's no guarantee that after a while you wouldn't find life tedious here. It's a good long-term plan, perhaps, but you're too young to bury yourself in the country at the age of twenty-two.'

What vile drudgery did his uncle have in mind for him? It certainly wouldn't mean a return to St Petersburg. Vasily contemplated a small icon of the Virgin in the corner. She regarded the prints of the Caucasus on the far wall with disappointed eyes. His uncle continued to speak.

'I think that there's no option but for you to maintain the family tradition and enter the Ministry of the Interior. I know that we had hopes of a diplomatic career for you, and in the longer term I suppose that may still be possible, but things have changed under the new regime. Much has changed, in fact. The Tsar is anxious that the Ministries should strengthen their presence in the provinces. It's now generally hoped that recruits who come into the service as junior officers should spend two years in a provincial capital before transferring, if they wish, to Petersburg or Moscow.'

Vasily looked out into the stable yard. A drake was chasing a duck towards the horse pond. It seemed his exile was going to continue for some time.

'I have been making some inquiries,' Alexander continued. 'There are quite a lot of openings at present. The Volga region is very attractive...'

Vasily shook his head. The Volga! It seemed like another world.

'Or, your mother has suggested that you might go to Oryol Province. It's not too far from civilisation. The provincial capital is a garrison town, so there is some social activity. And, of course, you won't be without acquaintance there. You'll remember that your mother's cousins, the Laptevs, Elizaveta Gavrilovna's family, own an estate nearby. The Governor's office would find you lodgings in the town.'

Vasily reflected. It would be heartening to see Lisa again and he would hear some news of Mikhail. He mourned the loss of his friend and was deeply concerned about him. And, of course, Boris, the serf artist, was certainly still living on the estate. Perhaps he might be inspired to pick up his chalks and pen once again.

His uncle was tapping impatiently on the sandbox. He must make some answer. 'Well, why not? It seems as good a place as any, although I should have preferred some other fate. I assume that Yakov and Matvey will come with me?'

'If you wish, but Matvey may well be a burden to you. We could think about sending him to learn a trade.' Alexander clearly thought this a great concession.

'That's good of you, sir, but he wouldn't tolerate that for long, I fear. He needs to have his mind stimulated, and, in general, he responds well to kindness. If we go to Oryol I'll make some arrangement to occupy him.'

Alexander frowned. 'The Prince has given up hope of setting eyes on his serf again. I hope that one day the boy will repay his generosity.'

'I am sure that he will. Matvey is uncommonly clever.'

'So Karl Feodorovich tells me.'

Alexander fell silent. It seemed that the discussion was over. Vasily considered. Should he unbend a little? He was desperate for news. He knew that the rebellion had failed, but could he ask his uncle what had happened to the rebels, to Mikhail, to Ryleev? Could he ask about Irina? But such questions might at best result in uncomfortable dialogue, at worst encourage one of his uncle's lengthy homilies.

'Well, if that's all, sir?'

'Yes, I suppose so. But, Vasily, I do hope that you won't see this as a punishment, but as a way to bring new purpose and meaning into your life. As an officer in the Service, you can achieve a great deal.'

'Yes, sir.' He doubted it was true.

'There is one other thing. Some letters have come for you. I think that there's one from Elizaveta Gavrilovna. It arrived a little time ago. Is that right, Karl?'

'Yes.' Karl shifted in his chair and wouldn't meet Vasily's eye. Clearly, the wretched German had been keeping back his mail. Karl muttered something about an engagement, rose, gave a short bow, and left.

Alexander pulled some papers from his breast, adding another sealed note, Vasily took them without looking at them.

'I think you'll find another of those letters is from Maltby. He often asks for news of you. And there's a note from Dmitry.'

Vasily nodded in acknowledgement. As he walked towards the door, he heard Alexander speaking behind him and half turned.

'I know you're not very excited about these arrangements, Vasily, but I don't see what else we can do at present. Things are much changed in Petersburg. The atmosphere is bracing, to say the least. The Emperor sees conspiracy everywhere. Some of your acquaintances are, as we speak, on their way to Siberia. In my judgement, you cannot safely return there yet.'

———

Vasily ordered a groom to saddle up Karl's brown mare. He ran up to his room and, shouting for Yakov to bring his boots, changed back into his loose shirt and pulled on riding breeches. He looked at his three letters. One was obviously the note from Dmitry Vladimirovich. He broke the seal.

The short message assured him of the Prince's continued affection. Vasily was going to have to make his own way in the world for a while, at least, so he had arranged for him to receive an allowance, commencing on his birthday in September. He hoped that this would make his life easier; it would not do if Count Belkin could not hold his own in society. To his relief, the Prince did not mention Matvey.

The sum promised wasn't trifling. Vasily recalled Dmitry Vladimirovich's gentle smile and unfailing generosity. He would give a good deal to be able to confide in his kindly benefactor, to explain all to him. But he was far away, and, somehow, Vasily knew that he wouldn't demand any explanations.

He looked at the other letters. It seemed the seals hadn't been broken, but his uncle was probably adept at concealment. One was indeed from Thomas Maltby. It seemed quite bulky. He set that aside. He took Lisa's letter. He resisted the urge to tear it open; he must read it away from prying eyes.

His horse cantered upstream along the riverbank and took the path into the woods beyond the cemetery. The deerhound loped along behind. When Vasily reached a small clearing, he dismounted, sat on the grass, and opened the letter with shaking hands. It had been written some months before.

Polunin Palace
The English Embankment, St Petersburg
18 May 1826

My dearest Vasya,
Your uncle has told us that you are now recovered and I hope that's true. Alexander Petrovich didn't encourage me to write, but I'm writing anyway trusting that you'll receive this safely and can find time to reply. It would be a great comfort to hear from you.

I am sorry that what I have to write will be painful, but I know you will want to know my news.

You may know by now, I suppose, that our dear Mikhail,

was, together with his brother Nikita, implicated in the uprising that took place here in December. The disturbances came as a complete surprise! We only learned of trouble in the city on the morning of the rising. Prince Polunin came home from the Senate shortly after swearing the oath to the Emperor. He was concerned and said we must not leave the Palace: some soldiers had occupied Senate Square and were refusing to swear allegiance. Later, he was greatly distressed by the news that his friend, the Governor of St Petersburg, Count Miloradovich, had been horribly killed as he tried to reason with the rebels. He said that if the soldiers continued to refuse to leave the square it was only a matter of time before the Emperor would lose patience and use force.

I was deeply frightened. Senate Square is, as you know, close by, and of course I knew that Mikhail was on duty there with his troop. From time to time we could hear crowds shouting outside, and then, at around three in the afternoon, when the light had begun to fade, we heard a great roar of heavy guns! From the windows we could see soldiers fleeing across the frozen river. Some were trying to form lines. Then we heard more gunfire, and the men scattered as the ice broke under the weight of cannon balls. The Prince told us to come away from the windows, but we know that many died. Soon after that, silence fell. The uprising had failed.

I had no idea what had happened to Mikhail, but I was comforted when the Prince told me that his company, although summoned to support the Tsar, had not been part of the action. That evening a note arrived saying that he was safe and that he would come to me when he could. You can imagine my relief!

However, five days later, when we were all dining at Madame Stenovsky's, to everyone's astonishment the Commander of the Chevalier Guards came to arrest Mikhail. It was terrible; he had hardly any time to bid us farewell. As he left he begged me for my forgiveness. I had no idea what I was supposed to forgive! He embraced me and then was gone. I was so shocked that I am ashamed to confess that I fell to the floor in a faint.

They put him in chains and led him directly to the Emperor's Palace with another officer who had also been taken. We are not sure exactly what happened there, but it's said that they were harangued for some time by Nicholas himself, while courtiers stood around and applauded. They were then left alone under guard. A short while later they were told by Count Apraksin that the Emperor was minded to be lenient with them, and they should kiss his hand and thank him. They would be imprisoned for six months and then released.

When they entered his presence it seems that Mikhail and his companion didn't show sufficient remorse. Nicholas became angry and declared that he was no longer interested in receiving their thanks. They were taken from the city and locked up in different fortresses. Until recently Mikhail was being held at Reval, in Estonia. His mother learned that he was fairly treated there. At that time she received a hand written note from the Dowager Empress, expressing sympathy and saying that she was sure that mercy would be shown to him.

This raised our hopes, but recently they were quite dashed. At the beginning of the month, Mikhail was moved to the fortress here in St Petersburg where his brother Nikita was already being held. The place is quite terrible. The cells are cold and dark. Since the flood they are also very damp. Few people survive there for long, particularly in winter. It seems he is to stand trial for his part in the conspiracy. It's probable that he will be sent into exile, but we have heard rumours that his punishment could be more severe. I pray to the Lord every day that he will be saved.

Of course, I am deeply unhappy, but poor Madame Stenovsky's suffering is terrible. Nikita, who it seems had been involved in the secret society for several years, was arrested at much the same time as Mikhail. He was nowhere near St Petersburg on the day, but was attending to estate business and visiting his wife. She had no more idea than I of the brothers' part in the conspiracy, and had little time to say goodbye to her husband. She told me that when they arrested him, Nikita fell to his knees and begged for her understanding. She told him that whether she lived as his wife here, or in Siberia, she would always be his wife. He must take courage, she would not desert him.

Madame Stenovsky constantly petitions the Tsar, his wife, the Dowager Empress, for better conditions for her sons, to be able to visit, and for other favours, but so far she has met with little success. She is bitter that she was deceived by the note from the Dowager Empress. It seems that when Maria Feodorovna wrote she was sincere but that, as more evidence has emerged about the extent of the conspiracy, the Tsar has become less forgiving.

So Vasya, my dear friend, this is the sad place in which I find myself. It breaks my heart to have to bring *you this news. I know how close you and Mikhail were. Dearest Katya has been like a sister to me, and I have become attached to Mikhail's family. We try to support one another. Aunt Darya has returned to Oryol, and it is my intention to travel home once Mikhail's fate is known.*

I often think of you, dear Vasya, and the happy times we enjoyed together last year. I have not seen Irina. I believe that she and her brother left St Petersburg at the time of the disturbances. I am sure that she has been in contact with you but I would like to know that all is well with her.

I kiss you, and hope to hear from you,
Your, Lisa

Vasily read and re-read the letter. Mikhail and his brother would by now have been tried and convicted. He knew that the sentences had been announced in July, and this letter, written in May, had, thanks to his uncle's restrictions, taken four months to reach him. Poor, poor, Lisa. By now she may have given up all hope of becoming Mikhail's wife.

Vasily lay back and looked up at the sky. The bleak walls of the fortress seemed to take shape among the drifting clouds. Please God, let Mikhail have survived his ordeal in prison and received a light sentence. He must have been alone and terrified, have suffered greatly... suffering that he himself had, of course, avoided. He sighed, emitting a quiet groan. He had been a coward; he should have shown more resolve and resisted his uncle. Wouldn't it have been nobler to accept punishment, however unjust, than to hide skulking in the government offices of a provincial backwater?

He scanned Lisa's letter again. She had assumed that he must have heard from Irina. God, how he wished he had! But there had been no word from her. How distressed and angry he had been when he realised that she had left him. Almost deranged, he had plotted crazy schemes of revenge against her and her brother. At other times, he had plunged into unfathomable depths of self-pity. Thankfully, that madness had passed and now all that remained was this dull ache of melancholy and bitter resignation. He had tried to forget her, but everyday distractions – hunting, shooting, drinking, trysts with the miller's widow – couldn't entirely erase his sense of loss. Was it really true, as his uncle had claimed, that Irina had been her brother's creature, a lure to attract him into a web of intrigue? Had he meant nothing to her? That might have been so at the start, but surely she had come to love him? Their few months together had seemed so intense, so sweet, so free of pretence.

But perhaps she had deceived him. She did, after all, reject his early advances, had laughed at him, but then, quite suddenly, had seemed to change towards him. Had that change been prompted by her brother? The night he had been forced from Petersburg, she had told him not to visit her. Why? Had she been busy packing her boxes, preparing to depart? To abandon him?

He sat up, picked up his whip and, with its fine tip, drew a snaking pattern through the soft springy turf. Why reenter this whirlpool of futile speculation? There was little point. His horse moved restlessly, and he dog rose and shook herself. It was almost time for dinner. He must return to the house.

CHAPTER TWENTY-FIVE

CONVERSATION AT DINNER did not flow easily. Vasily spoke when he was spoken to but was otherwise silent. He escaped when he could and went to his room, leaving Alexander, Karl and his grandmother drinking tea on the veranda.

When he had arrived at Dubovnoye in December, he had been given his late father's bedroom, a large west-facing chamber that looked out over the gravel driveway to the road and the valley beyond. Evening sunlight now drenched the room, brightening the pine-boarded walls and the great wooden bed. He sat in his armchair by the window and for some minutes fingered Thomas Maltby's letter. What wounds would it reopen? What new pain inflict?

He broke the seal.

20 July 1826

My Dear Vasily,

I had hoped to write to you some time ago but Alexander Petrovich asked me not to trouble you with correspondence. I thank the Good Lord that you are now recovered from your illness. I very much miss our mornings together and hope that they might be resumed in the not too distant future.

I thought that you would want to hear news from here. The events of 14th December last in Senate Square have been mentioned in the broadsheets, but in a confused manner, and many people remain in ignorance even in Petersburg. I witnessed some of the proceedings personally, and have done a little research.

As I expect you know, the rebels hoped to exploit the constitutional uncertainties that surrounded the death of the Tsar. They claimed to support Grand Duke Constantine, declaring that his brother Nicholas was a usurper. In reality of course many were not interested in installing either brother on the throne. Some wanted to send the Imperial family into exile and introduce a full blown republic. Others felt that a constitution that reduced the powers of the Emperor would be more realistic. There were a few moreover who wanted to go further and foment general public disorder and assassinate the Tsar. This lack of clarity in the rebels' objectives was sadly a feature of other aspects of their endeavours.

They were very short of time of course, but when the day came for swearing the oath to Nicholas on 14th December they had been unable to persuade as many officers and troops as they had hoped to stand up for Constantine and threaten the status quo. Nonetheless they managed to muster around three thousand men, principally members of the Moscow Regiment, but some others, the Finland Chasseurs and the Lifeguard Grenadiers, to name two. A group of naval cadets came from their college, wanting to join the rebels, but, in consideration of their age, they were sent away by the army officers.

It is estimated that there were around nine thousand men who, in appearance at least, remained loyal to the Tsar. Some of these included officers who were involved in the conspiracy, but who found themselves among both loyalist and rebel troops. That was the position of your friend Mikhail Stenovsky, although I suspect that he had not been able to persuade many of the Chevalier Guard to throw in their lot with him. He was after all just a junior officer in an elite regiment with close traditional ties to the throne.

It is thought that the Emperor already had evidence of a plot and he therefore arranged that the Senate swear the oath of allegiance very early in the morning. Thus, when later the Moscow Regiment marched onto the square and announced they would not take the oath, there was nobody there. The troops waited for something to happen, for some orders to advance on the palace, perhaps, but their chosen leader and commander, Trubetskoy, failed them. He simply did not appear, and was later discovered to have taken refuge in the Austrian Embassy, his nerve having failed him. The other conspirators were reluctant to take on the role of leader without the consent of the rest. It seems they took their democratic principles that far! In the end Prince Obolensky took charge, but he was not by nature suited to the job and effectively did nothing.

One of the young officers involved in the conspiracy, Baron Andrey Rosen, a Lieutenant of the Finland Guards Regiment, whose wife's family is known to me, came to a halt on St Isaac's bridge with his men. He waited in vain for an order to advance from the absent Trubetskoy, but of course it never came. In the end he was hemmed in by loyal troops and could neither move backwards nor forwards.

I myself went down to the square at around midday.

As a foreigner, I endeavoured not draw too much attention to myself, but I tried to make sense of what I was witnessing. The rebel troops had been standing for some hours in the square, supported by civilian well-wishers, including Ryleev and other members of the conspiracy. As the day wore on, troops loyal to the Tsar gradually surrounded them and the crowd of onlookers got bored and thinned out. The Emperor himself, who stood for a time in full view of the rebel troops with his young son, the Tsarevich, tried to address them but got nowhere. The crowds cried out 'For Constantine and Constitution!' (It is a measure of the woeful ignorance of some of Russia's people that some onlookers thought that 'Constitution' was the name of Constantine's wife!)

A succession of leading men tried to reason with the conspirators. A General, I think it was Sukhozanet, entreated them to leave before the Tsar ordered force to be used. The rebels mocked him, telling him to 'go away and bang away' if he chose. Then the Grand Duke Mikhail galloped onto the square and begged the men to withdraw. The civilian Kyukhel'beker attempted to shoot him, but his pistol misfired, and the Duke rapidly withdrew. Then Count Miloradovich, the Governor General of St Petersburg, and a most popular war hero, of course, also attempted to persuade the men to lay down their arms. Obolensky tried to get rid of him by sticking a bayonet into his horse's rump to make it bolt, but at the same time the conspirator Kakhovsky, another civilian, pulled out a pistol and shot him dead. Kakhovsky also killed the Commandant of the Grenadier Guards regiment. Finally, the Metropolitan of Moscow tried to propose a compromise, but the rebel troops shouted: 'This is no place for you! Go home and pray for us all!'

It was approaching three o'clock in the afternoon and, of course, was by that time getting dark. The patience of the Emperor was, apparently, wearing thin, and, concerned that other soldiers might come to the aid of the rebels as night fell, he ordered the cavalry, who had been drawn up, to charge. But they were hindered in their advance by the ice on the square, and stones and wood hurled at them by the civilians who remained. It was thought, in any event, that many of the Horseguards sympathised with the rebels and were reluctant to ride forward. The square was slippery with ice and, whatever the truth of it, all ended in disarray.

Next, Nicholas ordered that cannons be fired to disperse the ranks of soldiers. They initially fired blanks, but then real ordnance. Then grapeshot was used, which caused the rebels to scatter and to flee across the frozen river. Guns were hauled after them by loyalist troops, and they started to fire canister, which caused many casualties among rebels, loyal soldiers and innocent bystanders alike.

At this point I decided to go home, but I understand that Mikhail Bestuzhev, a Captain of the Moscow Regiment, succeeded in forming up his men on the frozen river. He led the troops out to try to capture the Peter and Paul Fortress, but guns were deployed on the river bank. Cannon balls could be seen bouncing across the ice, which in the end shattered and, in breaking, took many men to their deaths. Some thought that had Bestuzhev succeeded the day might yet have been won, for it was thought that further support was at hand, but it was not to be.

In one way or another the military ringleaders and civilian conspirators all left the square unharmed. Astonishingly, none had received worse than some holes in their clothing. It was generally felt that had Trubetskoy not deserted the troops but instead shown some leadership at an early stage, support was such that others would have participated and a coup would have had some chance of success. But as it was, all was lost. As he withdrew from the scene, the Emperor was ironically heard to remark: 'Voila un joli commencement de regne!'

It only remained for the blood to be sluiced from the square and the bodies of the dead removed. Great bonfires were lit to illuminate proceedings, and such was the hurry of the authorities to obliterate all memory of the day, that many of the corpses were simply pushed under the ice of the river. They have been washing up, stinking on the shores all summer. It is thought that, in all, over two thousand people died, although estimates vary.

And then of course the arrests started. Few, if any, of the ringleaders were actually taken on the Square. In all, over five hundred people were detained in the days that followed.

Mikhail Stenovsky was apprehended at his mother's house a few days after the event. They arrested his brother on his estates. Bestuzhev tried to escape from the city but the town was completely sealed off and the streets so filled with police and informers that he found it impossible. In the end he gave himself up. As for Ryleev, he was soon betrayed by one of the first rebels detained and it did not take long to find him. He had left the square and gone home. Apparently he took the opportunity to destroy many papers relevant to the activities of the Northern Society, including the names of members, before a police chief came to arrest him late at night. They woke him from his bed, allowed him to bless his little daughter and embrace his wife and they took him straight to the palace, where Nicholas interrogated him.

Nicholas personally questioned many of the newly arrested, and they say that he behaved like a chameleon, flattering, shaming or threatening his victims depending on how he thought he would best extract the evidence he craved. He is apparently fond of amateur dramatics.

A committee of investigation was set up before the year end. It did not have the form of a regular court and indeed many of those who appeared before it did not realise that they were being tried. The committee generally questioned the accused at night. They had been held in terrible conditions in heavy chains and under threat of torture, both physical and mental. It was not surprising that some admitted to more than they had done and others betrayed their friends. Nearly six hundred men were brought to 'trial' in this way.

The sentences were announced on 12th July. They were extremely arbitrary in nature. Some totally innocent men were convicted and others, plainly guilty, got off relatively lightly. Trubetskoy was exiled to Siberia, although as 'Supreme Leader' of the revolt, most thought he would hang. Apparently Nicholas could not bring himself to destroy a sprig of such a notable family.

Five men, including Ryleev, were sentenced to death. In theory, this was impossible since the death sentence had been effectively abolished in Russia, but this detail did not deter Nicholas. A special hangman had to be brought from Sweden to fulfil the task. Many right thinking people both here and abroad were shocked by this.

Of the others, around half were acquitted, although some of the soldiers amongst them were demoted and transferred from elite regiments to the line. Of the remainder, one hundred and sixteen of the 'most culpable' were divided into categories depending on the extent of their 'guilt'. Those deemed most to blame were to be exiled with hard labour to Siberia for life, the rest for shorter terms. Nikita and Mikhail Stenovsky were both exiled to Siberia, Nikita sentenced to life in prison, Mikhail to ten years, followed by exile for life. Bestuzhev was sentenced to twenty years in prison followed by exile for life.

In the early morning the following day the convicted men were gathered within sight of the gallows. The soldiers among them were told to remove their uniforms, and all were given hospital smocks. Then swords were broken over their heads and their clothes were burnt, along with their medals, stars and gold epaulettes, of which I understand there were a good number. The ceremony signified the death of their civil rights, the removal of their noble status, their property. Their wives could, if they wished, regard themselves as divorced and marry once again.

Those who were destined for Siberia were led away back

to their cells, while the five who had been judged to be ringleaders were immediately hanged. Many are already speaking of them as martyrs for the cause of freedom.

Poor Ryleev. Kalinin, as I am sure you remember, predicted he would meet his end on the gallows. Some of his poetry can be seen as prophetic; it so accurately seems to foretell his own fate. It is said that when the time came, he faced death with courage and stoicism. He went to the noose with a volume of Byron in his hand. I will not dwell here on the cruel proceedings on the scaffold, they have been well rehearsed elsewhere.

We are not certain if all the exiles have left for their long journey east but a number have already gone. Their relatives have petitioned to see them before departure, but not all have succeeded. All depends on the whim of the Emperor. The men have however been able to take some comforts for their journey. It is hard to believe that the so called crimes of these men merited their fate, except perhaps the man Kakhovsky who committed murder in plain sight on Senate Square.

I regularly thank our Saviour, my dear Vasily, that you were not implicated in these schemes, and that you have avoided the risk of what was in many cases quite arbitrary punishment. I know however that you were close to Mikhail Stenovsky, and that you will be grieved by his fate.

I should warn you that tolerance for liberal writings and speech is at an even lower level than it was under the former Tsar. Discretion in all things is advisable. Nicholas is haunted by fears of opposition and memories of those he calls his 'amis de quatorze'.

Life here in St Petersburg is now, it must be said, rather dull. Army drills and cannon fire continue unabated, although just at present we enjoy a reprieve since the Emperor is keen to observe his troops on manoeuvres outside the city. He left for the countryside immediately after celebrations that were, to my mind, most inappropriately held after the executions.

Many people are away at their country houses and the streets are quiet. I remember our happy weekend last summer by the Okhta river with pleasure, and think often of Ryleev and our discussion that evening. I do not know if you have any news of Pavel Pavlovich and his sister? Their apartment on the English Embankment appears to be deserted.

I hope when the autumn comes you might return to town? I should like to persevere with the Locke, and build on the great progress that I am sure has been made by Matvey. I trust he is well; remember me to him.

Well my dear Vasily. This has been a long letter. I do hope that you will be able to reply in due course.
Your sincere friend,
Thomas Maltby

Vasily set the letter aside and stared at the ceiling, trying to gather his thoughts. So nothing had been achieved, nothing had changed. Kondraty Ryleev was dead. He may never see Mikhail again. He uncurled from the chair, lay down on his bed, and for a few minutes allowed himself to weep without restraint. Finally, he rose, poured water from the jug on the washstand, and doused his face.

He stood for a long time at the window. The sun was setting

and the distant sky over Moscow seemed to be on fire, a gauze of scarlet silk shot with smoke-grey clouds. A shifting breeze had sprung up and the creeper that grew outside the window scratched insistently at the pane.

The muzzle of his dog nudged his hand. He stroked the hound's rough head and felt the flick of her warm tongue. The vision of damp cells receded; the broken swords; the ropes swaying beneath the scaffold. It was over. There was nothing he could do. And he was, after all, alive, and if not entirely free, perhaps did have a future. Given a little luck, he could move on, live his life, and still try to make something of it.

As night fell, he put on his coat and went downstairs. His grandmother and Alexander were in the drawing room, still deep in conversation. Moving to the samovar, he poured tea and silently offered a cup to his uncle.

PART THREE

'There is nothing more strange than the entirety of the internal administration of any province in Russia.'

Sergey Uvarov, 1827

CHAPTER TWENTY-SIX

February 1827 – Oryol, the Provincial Capital

VASILY CLIMBED THE steps of the offices of the Provincial Governor. Once inside the heavy doors, he stamped his feet, ridding his boots of shards of snow. A doorman took his hat and cloak and asked his business. He presented his letter of introduction.

To the left of the hallway, a clamorous crowd was crammed into a large antechamber. The paint was flaking, the windows clouded and last summer's flies lay on the windowsill. The smell of dust was overlaid with cabbage and human sweat.

He ran his finger round his collar. It had rubbed his neck. His new green uniform felt stiff and constricting, but he supposed he must get used to it. Looking through the window, he could make out a broad roadway. There were not many people in the street. A troop of soldiers, hussars, were marching across the snow towards the river.

He waited, heard footsteps, and now he was faced by a man in a uniform similar to his own but displaying more gold braid, and of an old-fashioned cut. Vasily bowed briefly. The officer did not return his bow but stood regarding him for a few moments. He was about thirty-five, of light build, with wiry hair above a flushed face.

'Well, Count, the first thing is to see the Governor.' His voice was weary.

'You have the advantage of me, sir,' Vasily said. 'May I know who you are?'

The man scratched his nose. He seemed ill at ease. 'I was right to think that you'd find manners here somewhat different to what you're used to in St Petersburg,' he said. 'For what it's worth, I am Sergey Ivanovich Chudov, Titular Councillor. I'm the head of your department, but we must go upstairs and complete the formalities.'

He turned abruptly. Vasily followed him up a stone staircase. Chudov ignored the clerks working at the top of the stairs and passed on into an office where a blue-uniformed man rose to his feet.

'Is this Count Belkin for the Governor?' he asked. 'Come this way...'

A large man was sitting at a desk, his coat arrayed with ribbons and stars. Vasily stood, waiting to be acknowledged. The man looked up at him and winked. Vasily was taken aback and almost forgot to bow. He recalled that the Governor's wink was an involuntary spasm, the result of wounds received at Austerlitz.

The Governor stood up. 'Ah yes! Count Belkin! Vasily Nikolayevich, isn't it?' He winked again.

'Yes, Your Excellency.'

'And how is your uncle, the new First State Councillor? I'm impressed that he's decided that you shouldn't dodge service in the provinces! Many young men in your position would have managed to find a way to avoid it. But it will be first-class experience for you now! First class!' He paused. He winked. Vasily resisted the temptation to wink back.

'I always say one thing to young men when they arrive here, although it has to be said we don't see many from the capital. Don't forget to call on me when you arrive in the province, as you very properly have today, and to call on me when you leave. That's the best advice I can give you, Nikolay Vasilyevich.'

'Vasily Nikolayevich, sir.'

'Oh yes... of course. Anyway, that will be all, Registrar. Make sure you enjoy your time here! All work and no play, no need to overdo it, you know!'

'Yes sir, thank you, sir.'

Vasily bowed and made for the door. The Governor spoke again: 'Oh, by the way, why did Alexander Petrovich choose Oryol? We're a long way from St Petersburg.'

'We have family here, Your Excellency. My mother is the cousin of Countess Antonina Laptev.'

'Oh yes, excellent family! Good! Good! Well, off you go. Don't forget I expect to see all my ranked officers at social events in the town, and at the theatre. Can't let the military dominate everything!' The Governor winked once more and Vasily, bemused, withdrew.

He followed Chudov down the stairs, along a corridor, and through a room containing yet more clerks. There were piles of paper and ledgers everywhere, on the desks, on the floor, and on shelves that lined the walls. The next office was quite large and seemed to be entirely free of paper, or indeed of any sign of activity. All the desks but one were empty. An older officer sat by the window. He rose immediately and crossed the room.

'Welcome to Oryol, Count Belkin!'

'This is Collegiate Secretary Komarov, my second in command,' Chudov said. 'You'll be working in here with him. Choose any desk you like; we're not overrun with officers, as you can see. You'll be increasing our little family by fifty percent. Come to see me next door when you're ready.' He disappeared.

'I'd sit by the window,' said Komarov. 'You can watch the

goings-on in the street when they clean the glass.'

Vasily took the desk indicated and, for want of anything better to do, pulled the drawers open. There were a few dried unsharpened quills in the top drawer, a rusting sand tray, and what looked like a metal ruler and protractor. The other drawers were filled with paper, yellow with age and thick with dust. He sneezed.

'Clerk!' shouted Komarov. An emaciated young man appeared at the door. 'Fetch Registrar Belkin some fresh equipment and then clean out his desk.' He turned to Vasily. 'I'd go in to see Chudov if I were you. He may have some plans for you... I don't know.' Komarov swung round in his chair, took a pinch of snuff, stretched his legs out in front of him, and gazed at the window. Light snow had started to fall.

The door to Chudov's office was closed. Vasily knocked; there was a faint invitation to enter. The Titular Councillor sat behind a desk. 'You need to sign this,' he said. He pushed a sheet of paper towards him. The seams on the sleeves of his uniform were shiny with wear. 'It's your oath of office. Loyalty to the Emperor, the Governor, and so on. But I have to say, Registrar Belkin, I'm really not sure why you're here. Have you come to spy on us all?'

'Of course not, sir, not at all...'

'Or, alternatively. are you hiding from something? Is there something I should know?' Chudov looked at him intently.

Vasily shrugged, hoping to seem at ease. Surely Chudov could know nothing of his past. 'I've been ill for some months, sir. I had intended going into the foreign service but that's proved impossible, so, since I can't afford to be idle, my uncle thought it best that I join the Interior Ministry. My grandfather, his father, was also in the service.'

'But he didn't have to send you out here. Your prospective salary can hardly have covered the cost of the journey! Anyway, it's really none of my business, although I don't know quite what we'll do with you.'

'Why not? You say that you're short-staffed.' Vasily was pleased to change the subject.

'Of course, there's plenty of work, but that's the problem. There's so much we can't make much impression on it. We deal with all Ministry affairs that affect Oryol town and the surrounding districts. We've a fleet of half-literate clerks, as you've seen. They deal with things like internal passports, public health, and road maintenance. They receive letters on all manner of other subjects, too, register them three times in various ledgers, prioritise them if they have the wit, and try, if they can spell, to respond in duplicate to the most important ones. Then, of course, they must register the replies three times in different ledgers, and so forth. We get many more inward communications than we can ever hope to deal with.

'Then there are petitions. Now we're responsible for the police force, what was a steady flow of complaints and appeals has become a flood. Inevitably they're mainly filed and ignored. Komarov does his best to deal with the most egregious cases, and I help, of course, but it's often a tricky business. We try to avoid anything to do with the serfs unless there's civil disturbance, or a member of the gentry is criminally implicated, and sometimes even then it's not appropriate, so that reduces the workload. But, in essence, the overall task is undoable, and since it can't be done, it isn't.'

As if to demonstrate, Chudov rose to his feet, picked up a pile of paper and threw it into what appeared to be a waste box.

'My main occupation is to write quarterly reports on our activities,' he continued. 'There are direct dispatches to the Ministry in the capital, and those that the Governor sends to the Tsar. Our man, the Governor, is under some pressure at present. He didn't manage to collect enough tax last year, and what he did collect was paid in late. He's feeling the heat, so we must present matters in as positive a light as possible, giving an impression of dedicated service and activity. You can probably help me with that, invent things to say, maybe even resolve a few real issues if you're so inclined.'

'Can't you change the way things are done?' Vasily asked. 'Try to make the process less onerous and find some better staff?'

'No. Process is dictated by the Ministry in the capital. They change the rules from time to time but never reduce the workload. As far as finding staff is concerned, given our status, and the level of our pay, it's difficult to find good people.

'The other thing that's required is that we go about in society. The Governor is keen that we maintain good relations with the military and the local gentry. I'm afraid that won't be a great deal of fun for you. The number of soldiers here means that the ratio of men to women isn't helpful if you're seeking a wife. I'm sorry that I can't paint a more positive picture of how you'll fill your time...' Chudov paused and then changed the subject. 'Are you well settled in? Are your lodgings comfortable?' Now he had relieved himself of the burden of describing the nature of his work, the bureaucrat became more animated.

'Yes sir,' said Vasily. 'They're a little compact, but very convenient and well appointed.'

'Well, I'm pleased to hear that. You're aware you're living in a part of my house?'

Vasily hadn't known who his landlord was. On arrival, they had been greeted at his appointed lodgings by a woman who was to organise food from the next-door kitchen. The adjoining house seemed to be full of children. Chudov clearly had a large family.

'I know the apartment is small,' said Chudov. 'We were not aware you'd be bringing more than one servant.'

'We're comfortable, sir, and if we find it too cramped, I'll move to larger accommodation. I only have one servant. The boy, Matvey, is just a child.'

Chudov looked at him. 'You're a little young to have a child.'

'He's not mine, of course; he's my ward. I hope to find a tutor for him. He is bookish and talented. Can you recommend anyone?'

'Well, I think you could do no better than approach Vladimir Golovkin. He's a journalist and a writer, and he educates a small group of boys on his estate at the edge of town. I'll write you an introduction. My oldest boy attends there.'

'That would be very kind, sir.'

'Anything else? If I were you, I'd go over to see Golovkin today. We'll try to find something for you to do when you're ready. You can take a sled with a driver from here; they're at your disposal.'

'One thing, sir. I have some cousins living locally, Count and Countess Laptev.'

'Oh, you're related to the Laptevs, are you? They have a very pretty daughter! As far as I know, they're out at their estate near Bashkatovo. It's on the road to Mtensk, about half an hour from here at this time of the year. In summer it takes longer, of course.'

'I hope to drive out there when I'm free,' said Vasily.

'Go whenever you like; you shouldn't allow obligations here to hinder you. No one else does. I'd take the next few days off. Come in again on Monday morning. I'll write that letter to Golovkin now.'

Chudov stood up, yawned, and stretched. 'There is just one other thing...' He looked down at his shoes. 'You may travel about freely within the province, of course, but you must apply to me if you want to go further afield.'

'Is that a normal restriction, sir?' Even here, it seemed he would not be entirely free. His uncle must have known that, and he should have guessed.

'Well, yes. You will have to apply to me for a passport. Don't worry. It won't be unreasonably refused.'

Chudov yawned again. Vasily had been dismissed.

———

Vladimir Golovkin's large stone house stood on the edge of the town, evergreen hedges and conifers edging its short gravel drive. The bell jangled behind a front door glossy with new paint.

It didn't feel like a school. A crimson and black turkey rug lay on the floor of the brightly painted hallway. Dried rose leaves in a Chinese bowl gave off a musky scent. Vasily remembered the hollow stone corridors of the Gymnasium, the constant echo of running feet, the shouts of masters and senior boys, and the unsavoury smells. All was different here.

A servant showed Vasily into an extensive library. He scanned the shelves. Golovkin's taste seemed eclectic; some of the books were controversial or forbidden. Several were in English. Perhaps their owner would lend him one or two. A cough interrupted his thoughts. A spare, fine-featured man with thinning grey hair was approaching, bowing as he walked across the carpet. He didn't look very robust. Vasily returned his bow.

'Count Belkin!' he said. 'I'm Vladimir Vladimirovich Golovkin. I've read the note from Sergey Ivanovich. I'm always happy to try to oblige a colleague of one of our parents. I understand you wish to arrange some schooling for your… Chudov does not quite describe him.'

Glass doors led to the garden. The lawn was covered with snow. In front of a small frozen lake stood a circular fountain, where a statue of Neptune, coated in frost, twisted in eternal pursuit of a panicking nymph. As they stood looking out, Vasily told Matvey's story in detail. He saw no point in hiding the truth. If Golovkin had objections to teaching a serf, it was best to find out.

'You say that the boy is about ten or eleven?'

'I believe so, but we'll never be absolutely sure.'

'And he has been tutored for over a year?'

'Yes, he's had two competent tutors, one English, one German. He's covered a good deal of ground.'

'And what are your plans for him?' Vasily thought for a moment. He had never really reached a firm intention.

'I suppose I would like him to have a profession of some sort, be able to make his own way.'

'But you will have to secure his freedom.'

'When the time comes, I hope that won't be a problem. The Prince is a fair man.'

Golovkin was silent for a moment. 'I can foresee one or two issues, but nothing insurmountable, provided the boy is keen to learn. A year's instruction is not much. There will be large gaps in his knowledge. He'll be one of the youngest here, so that is less of a problem. But there's the issue of his status. As far as I'm concerned, all are equal, but I'm unsure how our parents might view him and the other boys treat him. It may be easier to say that he's your distant relation. I don't like deceit, but I wouldn't wish to see him bullied or humiliated. I think the first thing is to meet the boy, and then if we all want to proceed, I'll carefully consider how to approach it. I have to say that I should regard his schooling as an interesting challenge.'

They turned to Golovkin's writing. The teacher produced pieces for periodicals, short stories about provincial life, and articles of more immediate interest. Ever stricter censorship was making his work more difficult. A recent article, which he had considered to be unexceptional, had been rejected outright. The events of 14 December had not helped, of course.

Finally, their conversation at an end, Vasily agreed to bring Matvey to meet Golovkin on the morrow. As he was driven away, he reflected on Golovkin's remarks about increased censorship and repression. His uncle, too, had remarked that under the new Tsar, the atmosphere in the capital had become oppressive. Perhaps, since he couldn't stay at Dubovnoye, Oryol might, for now, prove to be a better place to live.

CHAPTER TWENTY-SEVEN
The Laptev Estate – Province of Oryol

THE JOURNEY FROM town to the Laptev's estate near the village of Bashkatovo took more than half an hour. The road was rough in places, scattered with ice and deep craters, and the driver was forced to detour through the fields.

The day was clear and the light so brilliant that Vasily could barely see the expanse of snow and distant dark woods along the way. How good it would be to meet Lisa again, to share at least some of his thoughts with her. She, of course, knew nothing of his involvement in the failed uprising, and he couldn't tell her. Living a lie was unpleasant, but now, away from the comparative safety of Dubovnoye, he felt exposed and vulnerable to discovery.

He had insisted that Yakov and Matvey trim their hair and wear his blue family livery, and, as his carriage approached the house, he sensed that he had been right to come well attended. Although it seemed smaller than he remembered, the Laptev mansion stood solidly, a great temple dominating the snow-bleached landscape. The columns of the portico made a sturdy statement between its matched wings. The formal garden beside the carriage sweep was guarded by rows of statuary muffled against the frost. A church of an earlier date was set a little distance from the house, close to a scattering of outbuildings. The whole spoke of solidity and wealth.

The carriage came to a halt. The harness clinked and creaked. The Ministry coachman climbed down from the box.

'Stay in the carriage, Matvey,' Vasily said as the boy made

to leap out. 'Wait until the steps are down, then follow us out.'

As he spoke, the doors to the house opened and several lackeys in scarlet ran out, apparently oblivious to the cold. Yakov helped Vasily down with an unnecessarily conspicuous flourish. He waited for Matvey and reminded him in a whisper to walk with dignity behind them both. For a moment, it seemed that Matvey wasn't going to comply, but then the boy smirked, stood to attention, and marched in step behind them with military precision.

Vasily was only faintly aware of this brief pantomime. Lisa had come out onto the steps to greet him. She was much as he remembered, although her features seemed sharper, her face a little more drawn. He took both her hands, kissed them, and held them close to him.

'Come inside quickly, Vasya!' she said. 'It's warm indoors. I've looked forward to seeing you so much!'

Caryatids adorned the arches of the grey marbled hall; great porphyry urns were twinned along the flanks of the stone stairway. It was as cold as it had been on the driveway.

'We heat less than half of the house in winter,' Lisa said as they climbed. 'These places weren't designed for our climate.'

The doors in the upper vestibule were closed. A footman took Vasily's hat and fur-lined cloak and opened the heavy doors that led to the east wing. There was a rush of warm air. A succession of rooms stretched ahead, their polished wooden floors shining in the morning sunlight.

'Mama and Papa are in the drawing room,' said Lisa. 'They're much looking forward to meeting you again.'

'And Aunt Darya?'

'Yes, she's here, but, like me, she is rather in disgrace.'

And now here were Count and Countess Laptev. Formal

introductions were made. Aunt Darya approached with tentative steps. He kissed her extended hand and greeted her with a few words and as kind a smile as he could manage. It had not, after all, been her fault that her well-meant schemes had ended badly.

But what a fine woman the Countess was! Antonina Stepanova was tall, and she wore a heavy silk dress that caught the blue of her eyes. Her face was fine-featured, although her lips were slightly over-full. She spoke to him in a deliberate, modulated voice, leaning forward a little too far and standing a little too close. She asked after her cousin – his mother – and, of course, the Princess and little Prince Polunin. She expressed astonishment that it had been so long since they had last met. She was, she said, so looking forward to getting to know him very much better. Vasily felt like a rabbit in the sights of a hungry vixen, and Antonina Stepanova seemed well aware of this.

When Vasily withdrew to change for dinner, he realised that he had barely noticed Count Laptev at all.

As was usual in the country, the meal was taken early. Vasily, placed to the right of the Countess, looked down the table. The Count clearly took his role of local patriarch seriously. Twenty or so people were assembled: the local surgeon; a neighbouring landowner whose obsequious manner suggested he was down on his luck; a retired nanny; and some cousins of Count Laptev, who, living close by, ate at the house regularly. The Count sat, a solid figure at the far end of the table, eating his meal in silence; his fleshy face flushed beneath iron-grey curly hair that was thinning a little on top. An English governess now brought in an awkward child of, perhaps, thirteen. This must be Lisa's younger sister Nadezhda.

Ignoring her husband's cousin, who sat to her left, Antonina Stepanova engaged Vasily in conversation, inquiring at length about the Polunins. She said how enchanted Darya Stepanova had been with the palace, and how she was quite miserable back at home. She supposed that Polunin was less at court now that the Emperor Alexander was dead, and, remarking on the age difference between the Prince and Katya, wondered why he had not married before. Vasily was unable to satisfy her curiosity on most of these matters but was able to say with honesty that he thought that his sister was content with her lot. Antonina Stepanova then moved on to the subject of the Moscow estate. She knew, of course, that the Belkins' beautiful Moscow house had been destroyed by the French. Had it not been possible to rebuild it? Surely they had received compensation? Vasily told her that the money that had been received had been absorbed by putting their estate on a sounder footing, which opened up a new line of questioning about Dubovnoye.

Towards the end of the meal, when Vasily's head was beginning to ache, Antonina placed her tapering fingers on his sleeve and said in a low voice: 'You know, Vasily, we're relying on you to be a good friend to Lisa while you're here. She needs to forget about what happened in St Petersburg, think about going out into society once again. She was badly betrayed! Oh, I know that your mother and Katya were ignorant of Stenovsky's crimes, but I do feel that your uncle Alexander, given his position in the Ministry, might have been careful to steer her away from a family with known liberal views.'

Vasily did not know how to reply.

'Be a good friend to her, Vasily Nikolayevich,' the Countess repeated. 'Who knows? Perhaps you might become more than a friend. I know that your mother always hoped that the two of you might form an attachment.'

Vasily began to find what might have been suitable words, but Antonina Stepanova had abruptly turned away and was now speaking to the man to her left.

———

When the company dispersed, Lisa took Vasily to the intimate divan room that occupied a south-facing corner of the mansion. Vasily scanned the pictures on the walls and picked out some sketches in ink.

'Those are good,' he said. 'They really catch the essence of the house and park.'

'They're Boris Abramovich's work,' said Lisa. 'You remember him, of course? He's a real treasure! So talented! He's painting Mama's portrait at present. We should look at it later.'

'Yes, I do remember Boris. He gave me drawing lessons here years ago. I've been looking forward to meeting him, seeing what he's working on now.'

'Your interest would certainly please him. Papa doesn't much care for art. He rarely buys pictures and furniture, just English agricultural equipment, horses and dogs. He doesn't encourage Boris to paint here or to work for other landowners as he did when my grandfather was alive. He now spends his time doing carpentry, mending furniture.'

'That seems a pity.'

'Yes, it's sad to see his talent wasted.'

She sank into one of the soft-cushioned ottomans. 'But Vasya, I've been very remiss. I haven't asked after Irina. I should so like to write to her but don't know where she is.

When I tried to call on her after the rising, I was told that she had gone and not left a forwarding address.'

He sat down beside her. 'I'm sorry Lisa, I haven't seen Irina. I'm afraid we've parted; she has left me. I suppose it had to happen. She wasn't free.' He spoke the phrases mechanically, felt his face redden as his heart twisted with renewed pain. He couldn't, shouldn't, say more.

Lisa took his hand. 'Oh, I am so sorry. But I do know how impossible your situation was. It seems neither of us have been lucky in love, Vasya.'

'No.'

A servant came in to tend the stove. He should change the subject. 'But tell me, when did you come back from Petersburg?'

'I only returned at Christmas. I wanted to stay until Mikhail left for the east. You know, of course, about his sentence?'

'Yes, Thomas Maltby wrote to me. It must have been very hard for you.'

Lisa looked down at her hands. She still wore Mikhail's ring. 'The days after the revolt were terrible for the friends and relatives of those detained. It's devastating to discover that someone you love isn't the person you thought they were. It makes you question the truth of your own heart.'

Vasily nodded, knowing she was right.

'Once I had recovered from the shock of Mikhail's arrest,' she continued, 'I initially accepted everyone's assumption that all must be over between us.'

'Did you?'

'Yes, I'm ashamed to say I did. Aunt Darya insisted that I should put the whole "sorry incident" behind me and, when I felt ready, ease my way back into society. No one would blame me for turning my back on a criminal, she said. There were several potential suitors in the wings, one or two with equally good credentials. She even mentioned Count Fedulov!'

'Well, his credentials aren't up to much.'

'I know that, but he won Aunt Darya's heart, at least. I could never have accepted Leonid Sergeyevich, of course, but I was disappointed, confused, and inclined to follow her advice. I was angry with Mikhail. He had pretended to be something he wasn't, and I had been made to look a fool. I had believed Nanya's notion that God would find me the right husband, one who would make me happy and fulfil all my ambitions. I thought God had done his part, but I was deceived. I said as much to Madame Stenovsky; we had a very uncomfortable exchange.'

'He never wanted to deceive you, Lisa. Events just overtook him. He had been pledged to the cause for years.'

'Yes, I know that now. One afternoon in March last year, when the ice on the river was just starting to break and drift towards the sea, Alexandrine, Nikita's wife, called on me. I almost didn't admit her, but, to tell the truth, I was finding it hard to forget Mikhail and was anxious for news of him. She told me that he was imprisoned in Reval, that there was some hope he might be released and pardoned; his crimes had not, it seemed, been so serious. That hope was, of course, subsequently destroyed, as you know.

'But perhaps more to the point, she spoke about Nikita and Mikhail's convictions, the beliefs that had led them to act as they did. They had not, she said, joined the conspiracy due to some childish hope of adventure, some cheap romantic notions about revolution. They had acted from sincerely held beliefs, a true desire to change Russia for the better. She said she knew that I felt I had been cheated, but I should realise that secrecy was essential if such plans were to meet with success. He had also, of course, wanted to protect me from harm, from danger. Was I so naive that I didn't understand that? Did I think so little of the man I had intended to marry? I can't tell you how small I felt when she asked me that.

'I wish you'd been there, Vasya. I needed someone to talk to, but you had gone to your estates and didn't seem likely to return. Irène had gone too, and Katya was obliged to respect her husband's wish that she didn't discuss the revolt with anyone. I started to question myself. Had I really loved Mikhail at all? Had I simply been dazzled by a handsome soldier in a white uniform with an ancient pedigree and riches that more than matched my own? Finally having thought and prayed a good deal, I realised that what Mikhail had done, his selfless sacrifice, made him more rather than less worthy of love. It was my destiny to give up ideas of wealth and status. He was indeed God's chosen husband for me, and I should honour my vow to marry him. I felt as though a great weight had been lifted from my shoulders. I still feel that.'

Vasily felt alarmed. He hoped that she was right.

'After that, life became easier in one way, but harder in others. I was reconciled with Mikhail's family and became close to them. It was our obsession to follow every rumour about the brothers' fates, to try to find ways to help and comfort them.'

'And did you manage to see Mikhail?' Vasily asked.

'Yes, but only once. After Mikhail and Nikita were condemned and sentenced in July last year, nothing definite was heard for several months. As groups of exiles departed for Siberia, we tried to find out if they were among them. Madame

Stenovsky called every day at the fortress, taking food and clothing. At last, one day in December, the Governor told her to take her food away. Nikita and Mikhail would be leaving for the east within a few days.

'Like other relatives of the condemned men, we travelled to the post station on the road to Moscow where the convoys always change horses. Madam Stenovsky, Alexandrine, and I waited there for two days and nights in freezing weather. We were having breakfast on the third day when the manager of the post house burst in.

'There's a convoy coming, Ladies!'

'We walked out into the stable yard. I felt ill – sick with anticipation and nerves. The cold was bitter: our boots creaked on the untrodden snow and the air stung our cheeks and lips. Four separate sledges were coming from the direction of the capital, escorted by the Internal Guard.

'We watched the prisoners struggle out. I recognised Mikhail and Nikita from the clothes we had sent them. But, Vasya, it was shocking to see them! They looked half-starved. They were in chains so could hardly walk. We weren't sure if we would be allowed to speak to them. I prayed that God would soften the hearts of the guards, that they would show pity, or, failing that, they would take payment to look the other way.

'They'll bring the men inside while they change the horses. That'll be your chance,' the owner of the post house said to us. It was clear he'd often played out this scene in the past.

'When Nikita recognised his mother, he called out, hobbled towards her and, embracing her, wiped away her tears. Then Mikhail greeted her, holding her close to him, repeatedly stroking the pelt of her cloak, seeking comfort.

'We went into the post house together. It wasn't an easy meeting. Misha seemed stunned to see me, at first too stunned to speak. He looked terrible: so thin, his cheeks marked with sores, his eyes edged with bruises. When he took off his hat, his once-lovely soft hair stood in dry tufts; in places, he was bald. And how he smelt! A terrible sour stench. I felt quite sick, had to force myself not to step away. To this day, I don't know what suddenly brought the old Mikhail back to me. I think it was when he found his voice. That was the same, you see; and his eyes were still blue, clear, and when he embraced and kissed me, his lips were still sweet.

'He told me that he had constantly thought about me. That he knew how his actions must have hurt me. He begged me to forgive him. Then, unable to continue, he started to weep.'

Vasily's own tears threatened to blind him. 'Oh God, I'm so sorry Lisa...'

'I said that there was nothing to forgive, that it had taken time, but I now understood what he had done and why he felt he must do it. My main regret was that his endeavours had ended in failure and that I had lost him.

'And then he said, choking back his sobs: "If that's really so... I don't know if it's fair to ask you, but please, my love, if you do still care for me, try to follow me, come to me. It may be possible."

'I told him I would do all I could to fulfil my vow to marry him but warned him that the process could be a long one. As I spoke, the door of the post house crashed open; the convoy captain barked out: "That's enough now. Time to go. We must get on the road again. Stand back, Ladies, please."

Mikhail held me close, but the guards pulled us apart. He looked back at me as they hustled him to the door.'

Lisa faltered, and her voice became a strangled sob as she continued: 'I tried so hard to smile, Vasya, to hide my pain. The promise had been easy to make, but could I fulfil it? Would I ever see him again? Indeed, *will* I ever see him again?'

Vasily didn't trust himself to speak.

She paused, cleared her throat and continued. 'They left the post station at a gallop some minutes later, clouds of powdered snow flying up behind them. We shouted blessings to them as the convoy disappeared. A small crowd had gathered by the road: peasants, travellers, stable lads, a merchant or two. They called out words of encouragement as the sledges left. We learned later that people came out to see them all along the way.'

'Yes, I heard that, too,' said Vasily. 'It seems that many ordinary folk at least supported...them.'

Lisa was silent.

'But will you be able to go to him?' Vasily asked.

'My parents are angry, of course, and at present say they won't give their consent. My mother is unlikely to change her mind, but my father at least seems to understand the importance of a sacred vow, and, despite appearances, he cares about my happiness. I am of age. If I were really determined, they probably would find it hard to stop me. I have Madame Stenovsky's support, emotional and financial, but I would prefer to go with their blessing.

'The greater difficulty is to secure the permission of the Emperor. Until recently, Nicholas has only allowed the wives of convicted men to follow them into exile. Women merely promised in marriage were refused. But just a week ago, we heard that he has granted a request from a Frenchwoman who is affianced to former Count Annenkov. She will lose any claim to rank and property, but she will be allowed to go.

Like Mikhail, Annenkov was in the Guards and his sentence is actually longer than his. So there is some hope. Mikhail's mother has commenced the petitioning process.'

Lisa rose to her feet, shaking out her skirts. 'And now I should show you the rest of the house before it gets dark. You must wrap up, it'll be cold. I'll send for our cloaks. It was a great comfort to me when you wrote that you were coming, Vasya.'

She didn't seem to want to discuss Mikhail further. Was she concerned that Vasily would argue with her, take her parents' side? Indeed, he was conflicted. Lisa was admirably determined and had great courage, but she would lose everything: her inheritance, her title. To travel six thousand versts across Russia wasn't a trivial undertaking. And what would her life be like when she reached Siberia? Mikhail was a prisoner and, in the absence of imperial clemency, would be a prisoner for years and may not ever be allowed to come back to western Russia. Would a true friend advise her to embark on such an uncertain adventure? But if things had been different, if he had been imprisoned, exiled, wouldn't he have wanted Irina to follow him? Yes, of course, but that was all fantasy, and she would never have come.

Lisa pointed to a box that stood on a small round table in the corner. 'It's a gift for you. I should leave you on your own to open it. Come and find me when you're ready.'

The box was flat and quite large. A wooden case lay inside. It was heavy. Vasily turned the key in the small gold lock. A set of pistols lay before him, their handles inlaid with silver and their barrels gleaming. The maker's name confirmed that they were English. A crumpled piece of paper lay under one of the guns. He pulled it out and recognised Mikhail's hand.

Vasily, dearest friend,
I can think of no one better to take care of my pistols.
Please use them wisely! Our friendship, although brief,
meant a good deal to me. If God wills it we shall surely
meet again. By then perhaps the time of tyrants will be
over. We shall drink champagne and laugh together as
before. Cherish Irina, take care of Lisa, and help her to
take courage.
Yours ever,
Mikhail

Half an hour later, he found Lisa in the drawing room. As they left the heated part of the house, a lackey helped them into their outdoor clothes. It was indeed very cold, and the chill seemed to double the weight of the revived pain that filled him.

They wandered in silence along the grand state rooms: the gilded ballroom where gods and cherubs chased one another across the ceiling; a large saloon set with pre-revolutionary French furniture and the Italian pictures so unloved by the Count; a card room; a library with a sad paucity of books; and a dining room with a table so long that the far end was barely visible in the gathering gloom of the winter afternoon.

'Let's go to see the portrait of my mother,' Lisa said.

They walked along the length of the dining room. The next door was closed. As she opened it, there was a strong smell of paint and solvent. The room, arranged as a studio, was warmed by a stove. A covered canvas rested on an easel against the wall. A tall man stood outlined against the window.

'Oh!' Lisa exclaimed, 'Boris! I didn't expect to see you here on a Saturday.'

'I find it a challenge to find time for the painting during the week, Elizaveta Gavrilovna. There's too much other work to do, and your mother is anxious to see her picture completed.'

The evening light caught the artist's face as he turned from the window. Vasily remembered Boris at once. He was a well-favoured man, now in his late thirties, clean-shaven, with dark hair that curled over his collar. He wore a European shirt, a waistcoat and wool trousers. Vasily had forgotten how well he dressed; he didn't in any way resemble a serf.

'It's good to see you, Boris,' he said.

'And you, too, Vasily Nikolayevich, sir.' The artist smiled as he bowed. 'The Countess said that you were coming. It's been a long time!'

'Yes, eleven years. But, of course, we did meet in Petersburg. I've kept my drawing going.'

'I'm pleased to hear that, sir. I'd like to see what you're working on when you have time. But I'm sorry, I was just packing up to go home. I've promised my son a drawing lesson.'

'We won't hold you up,' Lisa said, 'but I thought Count Belkin would like to see the picture.'

Boris uncovered his portrait of Antonina Stepanova. It was unfinished, but it was clear that the result would impress. He had caught her bold lips and the keen gleam of her eyes.

'It's very fine, Boris. I've always wanted to try painting in oils but have never managed it.'

'I can give you some instruction if you like, sir, if you have no objection to painting on a Sunday. I understand you'll be coming here often? I'm not available tomorrow, but perhaps next time?'

Vasily's spirits lifted. Yes, he would visit his cousins regularly, and learning a new skill with Boris would certainly divert him. Perhaps life in Oryol would not be such misery after all.

CHAPTER TWENTY-EIGHT

March 1827 – The Ministry of the Interior, St Petersburg

LEONID FEDULOV, RECENTLY promoted to the rank of court councillor, sifted through the pile of letters on his desk. All were addressed to foreigners in the city, and all had been intercepted by his agents. At first glance, none seemed of much importance, but when he looked again, one caught his attention. It was addressed to the Englishman Maltby and had been penned by Alexander Petrovich's nephew, Vasily Nikolayevich. That was interesting! It had been put about that the condescending young prig had been conveniently absent from the city at the time of the failed rebellion fifteen months before. He was said to have been ill on his estates, and despite being acquainted with some of the rebels, Alexander Petrovich had affirmed that Vasily had not been involved in any way. But this story was not entirely true.

He picked up the letter.

Chudov's House, Sadovaya Street, Oryol
February 1827
From Vasily Nikolayevich Belkin to Thomas Maltby

Dear Thomas,
I hope that this letter finds you very well and that the St Petersburg winter is not proving too depressing.
We have been here in Oryol for a few days. We travelled from Dubovnoye by covered sledge, and the journey was

swift if cold. It's good to have the company of Yakov and Matvey, although I have concerns that Yakov will have too much time on his hands. I'm not sure that my own work will be very demanding either, but I hope to be able to make something of it.

We found our appointed lodgings without difficulty. We have a place close to the Government offices and the centre of town. The apartment is small, but warm and well enough appointed. There is a yard and garden at the back with stable and bath house. It forms a wing of a larger house, which, I discovered on reporting for work, is the home of my superior at the Ministry, Sergey Chudov.

Chudov seems a strange character. He was abrupt almost to the point of rudeness when I met him at the Ministry, but once he moves on from the subject of his work (which he clearly does not enjoy) he is amiable enough. He has four children and I think finds it hard to make ends meet. We spoke at some length when he called to check that all was well with the accommodation and he has been helpful in a number of respects. It seems that although the Ministry pays us very poorly we do benefit from the use of carriages and drivers, free theatre tickets, and invitations to social events in the town. At present however I do not have much enthusiasm for society.

It was just as well that we came to Oryol from the Moscow countryside and not directly from St Petersburg, for the contrast would have been a shock! The idea of spending two years here (how long that sounds!) is dispiriting. The town, which is much like many other provincial towns, stands on two rivers, the Oka and the Orlik, and the confluence lies in the very middle. I understand that in the summer this is a major trading port for grain from the black earth regions to the south, but at present all is frozen.

The most unexpected feature of the town is the theatre. It occupies an entire block to the west of the square. It is the personal project of Count Sergey Kamensky, who keeps several hundred serf artists. The place offers a good number of productions of opera, comedies, tragedies etc. each year, and opens on three evenings a week. I have not yet had the opportunity to visit it, but will report on its pleasures, or otherwise, in due course.

Oryol is overrun by the military. Hussars surge around the town, drill, ride to and from the manège, and spend their spare time in taverns by the Orlik, playing cards, and at the theatre, at balls etc. I am told that in general the young officers take every opportunity to escape to the more elevated society of Moscow, where, to the disappointment of Oryol's local beauties, they marry one another's sisters.

One sad fact about Oryol is that there are no bookshops, just a shabby stall that sells religious tracts outside the gates of the monastery. I may have to order some volumes from Moscow, although I am hoping to be able to borrow some from the teacher that Chudov has suggested for Matvey. Vladimir Vladimirovich Golovkin, whose name you may know from the periodicals, has a fine library at his estate which contains many of the works we have discussed in both French and English. He runs a small school on what seem to be liberal principles and has agreed to take Matvey on for a trial period. Time will tell if this arrangement will turn out well, but I am optimistic. Matvey seemed to take to his new teacher. (*I still have your copy of Locke, by the way.*)

Tomorrow we go out to the estate of Count and Countess Laptev, Lisa's parents. She has now returned home from St Petersburg and I much look forward to seeing her. I fear that she'll be distressed by the fate of Mikhail Stenovsky, of whom I hope to receive further news.

Well my dear Thomas, the hour is late. It is quieter here than ever this evening. Snow fell yesterday, it is very cold outside, and there are few people in the streets. I often think of ideas that I would like to discuss over the madeira that we failed to drink when we last met. Two years does, as I said, feel a long period of exile, but everything passes. I'm determined that once I've served out my sentence here I shall go to Italy. In the meanwhile, I am told that the nearby countryside is charming in summer and that there will be many opportunities for artistic endeavour.

I hope that you have been successful in finding some new students.

Your friend,

Vasily

Fedulov dropped the letter onto his desk. *Go to Italy… artistic endeavour!* His mouth twisted with distaste. Leaning back in his chair, he stared through the window and watched as snowflakes swarmed like flies through the grey-blue shadows between the Ministry buildings. After a few moments' reflection, he jotted down some notes and sent for his assistant. The registrar hurried into his office and stood before him, his brow pleated with anxiety.

Fedulov looked up.

'Do straighten your collar, Malenkov…'

'Sorry, sir!'

Fedulov compressed his lips and then continued: 'You are aware, Malenkov, that my many new responsibilities include the supervision of the inspection regime at our provincial offices. To get the measure of the work, I have it in mind to undertake some reviews personally in the summer months.

'I'd like you to pull out the latest reports on a few places, let's say Saratov, Voronezh and Bryansk for a start… Oh, yes, and possibly Oryol. And it would be helpful to know how many ranked officers there are at each office.'

The registrar departed, feeling his collar, smoothing his uniform and shaking his arms in his sleeves. Within an hour he returned. Fedulov waved him away and immediately turned to the report from Oryol.

The record told him that the office was understaffed. There seemed to be only a handful of officers, and apart from the Governor and his assistant, he now outranked them all. There was no mention of Vasily Belkin; the record was almost certainly out of date. The latest report from the provincial capital was flimsy and incomplete. He took up Belkin's letter to Maltby once more. He noted references to the use of carriages and tickets to the theatre. An inspection seemed overdue.

He summoned the registrar again. 'I want you to ensure that I see all reports coming in from these four provinces for the time being, Malenkov. Have this letter copied and the original delivered to the addressee. I need to have early sight of all letters to Maltby. It's a matter of importance, so make sure none slip through. Oh, and one last thing… Can you find our file on the man Golovkin, Vladimir Vladimirovich? I'm sure that there will be one. He's some sort of hack, publishes quite regularly in the periodicals. That will be all.'

Fedulov picked up his pen and wrote a note to the Minister, seeking permission to make some visits to offices in the south after his annual leave. He knew that General Lanskoy was keen to see operations at the Ministry tightened up and the provincial offices better regulated. He didn't expect his request to be refused.

CHAPTER TWENTY-NINE
Oryol

ON THE MONDAY morning after his visit to the Laptev estate, Vasily arrived at the Government offices a few minutes after ten o'clock. Komarov seemed surprised to see him. Chudov, who walked into the office about half an hour later, appeared irritated at having to find him something to do. He led him into the clerk-filled, paper-piled office.

'Now, Mr Registrar, you could start collecting the numbers for the next reports to the Governor and the Ministry. They need to be ready at the end of the month; at least that's the plan. This is Slepov, he'll assist you.'

The miserable clerk in a stained uniform seemed almost blind, but he hurried to bring a large pile of papers to Vasily's desk.

And so began Vasily's career as a provincial bureaucrat. The work was not hard; the hours were not long; and, if he chose, he could spend each short day (apart from Sundays, and the multiplicity of saint's days, of course) idly collecting statistics and compiling reports at his desk. There was also the opportunity, if he liked to take it, to attend various meetings at the Police House, with the Governor's staff, the Military Police, or army liaison officers on the frequent occasions when Chudov and Komarov were absent. These meetings were generally inconclusive. A report was rarely required.

In fact, Vasily, who had already exhausted the daytime pleasures of the town, found the work more engaging than expected. It was good to have employment after a year of idleness, and it satisfied his curiosity about a world previously unknown to him: the sphere of the merchant class, the police, the urban poor, the prison, the district hospital. The numbers he was given were transparently inaccurate and incomplete, but making sense of them interested him, and the meetings broadened the scope of his acquaintance. He didn't sit chafing at his desk in frustration as he had feared he might, although, as Chudov had warned much of what went on around him was frustrating, indeed.

He volunteered to take his turn with the scrum of petitioners that was admitted three times a week to the waiting room downstairs. After an hour or so, when the room, ripe with the smell of onions and unwashed bodies, could take no more supplicants, the front door would be closed and an officer summoned to 'sort matters out'. An attempt had been made to arrange the requests into some sort of priority, and the officer would select a small proportion for consideration. He would then order, with a ferocious bark, that the room be cleared.

On the first two occasions that he supervised this ritual, Vasily, having set aside the 'successful' petitions, looked briefly through the pile of those that had been rejected. There seemed to be little difference between them. The writing on many was poor, the spelling sometimes execrable, the requests ill-expressed, and the wrongs complained of repetitive. He noticed that some petitions were written by a small number of individual hands. He had learnt that more than a few of the petitioners were illiterate and that their scripts were written for them by professional scribes who plied their trade at the Merchants Court.

He noticed that one particular group of petitions, although written legibly, were more than usually nonsensical in content. The third time he undertook the task of sorting them, Vasily made a point of identifying a man who was proffering one of these incoherent scripts. The man, a bearded peasant of middle years, could hardly conceal his joy. The Lord had taken his paper up! He prostrated himself on the ground while the other supplicants looked on with envy. Vasily waited for the serf to get up.

'Where did you get this?'

'It's mine. I paid for it, Your Highness.'

'Yes, but who wrote it for you?'

'One of them scribes in the Court, Your Honour.'

'And how much did he charge you for it?'

'Fifty kopeks, sir.'

That was a good deal of money for providing something that was, of course, completely useless. Someone was making a good living on the backs of these unfortunates.

'What's your name?'

'Artemy Kluchov, Your Excellency.'

'I would like you to come with me now to the Court, Artemy, and point out to me the person who wrote your petition.'

'Aren't it no good?'

'Not as it stands, I'm afraid, but we'll get it done again.' This seemed to satisfy the peasant. 'By the way, what's it about?' asked Vasily.

'The Master's sent my son out of turn for the army, Lord. You can see that if you read it, I suppose.'

Vasily said nothing. It was not clear at all. But the man's cause was a real one. He wasn't giving him false hope by taking an interest. When young male serfs were included in the recruiting levy, generally they went according to age, the oldest first. It was common for landowners to try to change the order and keep the older, more experienced men on the land. The recruiting officer might be persuaded to sort the matter out.

When the morning ritual was completed and the crowd of petitioners had been cleared from the building, Vasily put on his hat and coat and accompanied Artemy to the Merchants Court. The weather was warmer. The streets were heavy with mud, and grubby, puddle-edged heaps of snow stood at every corner. Townsfolk gave way to him as he walked along the raised sidewalks, but these refuges did not extend the whole way, and his boots and the hem of his coat soon became rimmed with filth. Yakov would take him to task when he got home.

It took twenty minutes to walk to the Court. A relatively new building, its arches occupied an elongated site on the arrow of land formed by the confluence of the two rivers. Almost everything that passed for trade in the town took place here. The extensive galleries housed a profusion of booths, offices and chambers selling goods and services to merchants and townsfolk alike. Further stalls spilled into the streets outside. The place was very crowded. They passed counters offering all manner of goods, different kinds of wheat and flour, vegetables, vats of pickles, fish and meat, cloth, carpets and metalware. Foul smells battled with more pleasant aromas.

Artemy led Vasily up the stairs to the upper gallery. He pointed to a double desk at which two men were sitting face to face, leaning back on their chairs and talking to one another. One was taking snuff.

'Thank you, Artemy. I'd leave now if I were you.'

'But what about my request, Your Honour?'

'Wait for me at the stairs and I'll look at that for you when I've finished here. You are sure one of those is the man who wrote your script?'

'Yes, sir. It was the taller one who gave it me.'

The two scribes wore black suits spotted with rust. They had rough blankets thrown over their shoulders to keep out the cold. As they saw Vasily, they stopped leaning back in their seats, but they didn't rise.

Vasily laid the petition on the desk. 'Gentlemen,' he said. 'Did one of you write this?'

'Yes, it's in my hand,' the taller of the two replied.

'You have written complete rubbish.'

'We write what we're asked to write.'

'What are your names? Where do you come from?'

The two men initially avoided answering his questions. It was obvious from his uniform that he came from the government offices. Persevering, Vasily discovered that until last year, the pair had been working as clerks at the Ministry of Finance. It seemed that, for some reason, their services were no longer required there.

'How much do you charge for these?'

'Fifty kopeks, or more, depending.'

'Is it too much to ask you to write scripts that are fit for purpose?'

'That's all we can manage… We're not trained to write properly.'

'Well, gentlemen, I'd advise you either to improve your skills or to take up another profession. Your efforts are doing a good deal of harm to poorer folk.'

'We can't. There's nothing else we're able to do. We'll die of hunger if we stop. The law doesn't forbid the writing of petitions.'

'So it doesn't suit you to take my advice?'

'We're not doing anything illegal.'

'Nonetheless, I must report this.' The men were not

uneducated, but many poor people were paying for nothing and being given false hope. It shouldn't be too difficult to remedy the matter. The men must be given an official warning so that they took care to write sense in the future. He would ask Chudov how to proceed.

Artemy was waiting by the stairs. On arrival at the Governor's House, Vasily noticed his filthy boots and sent a clerk home to fetch a clean pair. He then took the serf into the small waiting room. His request was a simple one. Vasily wrote the petition himself and ordered the clerk to deal with it promptly. He then wrote a report on the issue and sent it up to Chudov. As he put down his pen, he felt surprisingly cheerful. He had achieved something useful.

———

A few days later, the mud in the streets had dried out a little. Vasily suggested to Yakov that they go down to one of the eating houses on the north bank of the Orlik. Yakov deserved a break. He had worked hard since their arrival, rearranging their accommodation and keeping a close eye on Matvey. Unconcerned about propriety in this remote backwater, Vasily was curious to sample the local amenities.

It was a sunny evening. He could sense the breath of spring. The inns hung on the high bank above the narrow river, each much like the next. The wooden buildings were ramshackle; the signs that hung outside each establishment were crude, and almost all were misspelt. They weighed up the attractions of the 'City of Kleef' as against the 'Town of Odesta', decided on the latter, and entered the noisy saloon, coughing in the smoky fug. Finding a table, they ordered soup and rissoles. There were soldiers in the tavern and merchants and other townsfolk. The food was very ordinary, but the beer was good. Vasily began to enjoy his freedom.

After they had eaten, Yakov fell into conversation with a group of servants at the next table. After a while, Vasily remembered Matvey. He had gone to the Chudovs and may have overstayed his welcome. He rose to leave.

Yakov made to follow him, somewhat reluctantly.

'Don't worry, Yakov. You stay and enjoy yourself here. I must go home, though.' Vasily walked out into the narrow street behind the eating houses. It was crowded with people enjoying the evening air and was well enough lit. However, as he walked northwards through a grid of yards and alleyways, the route became darker. Some of the wooden houses were occupied, but others were deserted and derelict.

He must avoid getting lost. He stopped at a corner to take his bearings, and, as he did so, he heard footsteps. Two figures bearing heavy sticks were advancing on him. It was the two scribes from the Court. Their purpose was plain, and there was no chance of escape. Should he have foreseen this?

The taller man ran at him, moving erratically, his weapon raised. Vasily jerked back. The stick missed the crown of his head and glanced off his cheekbone. Having expected to hit home, the scribe was unbalanced. As he swayed forwards, Vasily took him by the throat and punched him hard in the face. To his surprise, the man crumpled to the ground.

His companion hesitated before coming on. Vasily picked up the stick, feeling strangely calm. The road was slick with filth, and his attacker skidded a little as he approached. Vasily parried the man's first couple of feints in a noisy parody of swordplay. The man, undeterred, attacked again. As Vasily tried to ward off the third or fourth blow, his foot slipped, and he fell. His coat was bulky; he couldn't get up, but he still had the stick. His assailant stood above him, tapping his own weapon against his hand.

'This will teach you to come telling us our business, you little runt!' He raised his arm.

Vasily swept at his knees but missed and lost his grip. He shielded his head, waiting for the blows, but there was nothing, only a cry of pain, the thud of a body hitting the ground, a groan. He looked up. Yakov was standing over his assailant, a grin on his face, menacing him with the stick. He kicked him hard in the groin for what was clearly the second time, and then pulled Vasily to his feet.

'Can't leave you alone for a moment, can I, sir? Were they after your purse?'

'No,' said Vasily, 'I fear I may have just discovered one of the hazards of the job.'

'Can you walk?'

'I'm fine… He just caught my face.'

They made their way home. When they reached Sadovaya Street, Matvey was reading, sitting close to the stove. He looked up and, seeing Vasily, jumped to his feet. He was clearly impressed.

'You're going to have a nice shiner, sir! Have you been in a drunken brawl?'

Yakov chased the child to bed. Vasily sat down. His cheekbone was sore, and his head ached. When Yakov returned and started to prepare tea, Vasily said, 'What made you come after me? I thought I was in real trouble.'

'It was odd,' replied Yakov. 'I knew I shouldn't have let you go home alone, and then, the strangest thing.' he paused. 'That night they bundled you out of Petersburg, Alexander Petrovich was furious with me. I won't ever forget it. He said I had failed to look after you, that you were now in trouble. I felt terrible, although in fairness, Vasily, sir, I never quite understood what I had done, what I was supposed to have protected you from.' Yakov's voice faltered a little. 'I know it sounds mad, but I swear, this evening, while I was sitting in the tavern, I heard him saying those words again. That's why I came after you.'

———

Chudov was enraged. He took one look at Vasily's developing black eye, remembered the report about the fraudulent scribes, and, having barked out a few curt questions, exclaimed: 'For goodness sake, man! What are you trying to do? Kill yourself? Achieve instant promotion? Are you after my job? You're welcome to it! I didn't think you wanted to take the work so seriously! If you have to run around the town righting wrongs, don't try to do it alone. We have the pick of the police force, such as it is, and the military are so bored they're always pleased to provide an escort. Take some of them! And tell Komarov or me what you're up to! It's no good writing a report, particularly if serfs are involved. It's likely I won't read it until too late, if at all.' He paused for breath. 'Yes, sir,' said Vasily. 'I'm sorry, sir.'

'Anyway, I'm having the men picked up. Attacking one of my officers is a serious matter; they'll probably end up in the army. Alright, Mr Registrar, run along and get on with your numbers.'

As he spoke, a messenger came in bringing a note from the Governor. Chudov read it and groaned. 'It seems that we are to receive some sort of inspection.'

CHAPTER THIRTY
May 1827 – The Laptev Estate,
Province of Oryol

THE FLOODS AND foul roads of the spring thaw had passed. As the snow disappeared, the English park surrounding the mansion was created anew. The lake reappeared as a swatch of gleaming water. The stone bridge emerged from drifts of snow; the paths and drives, the way to the woods, the grotto, and the summer-house took on colour and shape. Gardeners left the hothouses and removed sacking from the statues that graced the parterres. House serfs were dispatched to sweep leaves from the stone floors of follies and temples. They applied fresh paint to the benches, the rowing boat, and the glasshouses; they sharpened hoes and scythes, and they greased the runners of sledges and stored them away.

On a Saturday afternoon in early May, Vasily was sitting on the curved steps of the Temple of Friendship. The sun was warm. White fluff, seeds from the poplars, floated in the air and edged the grass. Matvey lay by the lake, his face hanging over the water, looking for tadpoles and other creatures.

Among the temple's shaded columns, a hesitant nymph stood on a plinth, marble drapery embracing her chill body. Vasily took up his sketchpad and appraised the statue. He drew a few fine lines on the page, but then his hand faltered. The light seemed to dim, the lake to lose its lustre. He closed his eyes. He was back in the Summer Garden, hearing the echo of Mikhail's lost laughter and watching a woman in a pale flowing dress walking between the trees.

A few weeks ago, during the thaw, he had woken one morning convinced that Irina was close by, was in Bryansk on her estates just a day's ride away. He had gone to the office, determined to seek leave to go to her. But, confronted by Chudov's curiosity and obvious discomfort, he had wavered, concluding that the journey would be pointless. The doorman would turn him away; he would stand bereft in the forest as melted snow from sodden branches dripped from above. Surely, if she had wanted to see him again, she would have found him by now. He must accept that she was gone.

He heard a splash. Matvey had dropped a stone into the water. Ripples furrowed the surface, disturbing a moorhen and her chicks.

'Don't do that, Matvey!'

'Oh! Sorry, sir!' The boy wriggled on the grass.

Vasily sighed and started a new drawing. After a while, he noticed Boris Abramovich walking towards them on the path from the woods. As usual, the artist was neatly dressed, his neckcloth carefully arranged and his dark hair slicked back as if he had just doused his head in water.

'May I join you, sir?'

He squatted down and looked over Vasily's shoulder at the sketch of the lake, the bridge beyond, and in the foreground, an image of Matvey, skinny rump in the air, his legs bent beneath him. Boris laughed. 'It's good, but Matvey won't thank you for that view!'

'It's all he deserves. If I try to draw him from the front he won't stay still. Sit down, Boris. I'd welcome your company.'

'You're good to the boy,' Boris said, settling on the steps.

'I'm fond of him. He keeps me cheerful, and I like to see him develop.'

'Ah yes… develop… but develop to do what? He's just a serf, after all.'

'I hope to see him a free man in time, but, at present, that isn't an option. I only have him on loan.'

'But that situation could end at any time.'

'I suppose so, but the Prince, his owner, isn't unreasonable.'

Anything can happen to a serf. You need to realise that, sir, and be careful.' Boris's face was grave. He looked out over the lake.

'It can't be wrong to give a boy an education,' said Vasily.

Boris was silent for a good minute.

'There are times, Vasily Nikolayevich, when I wish that I'd never gone to school, never learned to read, never picked up a brush and been taught to paint. My life would have been much happier, I think, if I'd lived in ignorance and worked in the fields like my parents and grandparents. Anything can happen to a serf,' he repeated. 'One peasant I know was trained as an artist, but when his village was transferred to a new master as part of a dowry, he found himself owned by a man who was a complete philistine. He wanted to retrain him as a pastry cook! The serf had great talent. He had come to the attention of the Academy in St Petersburg. As a result, he was saved and, after a campaign, freed, but he was lucky. If a master, a serf owner, doesn't want to release you, no one can make him.

'I spend very little time painting now, as you know. Instead, I work in the carpenters' shop, making furniture, gilding and varnishing. So, you see, sir, life can change, and a serf can do nothing about it. Supposing you died tomorrow, would the Prince continue to educate Matvey?'

'Well, I would think so.' Vasily was not entirely sure. His uncle, after all, had been determined to return Matvey to the kitchens.

'The thing that pains me most is my son, Petya.' Boris said. 'He's more naturally talented than I, but I find it hard to teach him. A father generally doesn't make the most patient tutor. There's no hope of professional training for him. It seems he'll be condemned to varnish furniture all his life.'

Boris's son was ten or eleven years old. Vasily guessed that he was a little younger than Matvey.

'The new Emperor has decided to prevent serfs being educated beyond elementary level,' Boris continued. 'A law will be passed this year. Even if Petya were to be given leave, he couldn't go to a gymnasium or a university. The Academy is now out of the question unless your owner will guarantee your release from service at the end of the course. The President of the Academy, Olenin, once remarked that it was pointless to teach serfs about art since it encouraged thoughts of individuality and freedom that were inappropriate for a slave! I suppose when you put it like that, you can see some sense in it.'

Boris's face had darkened. He pulled out his kerchief and, mopping the sheen of sweat from his brow, rose to his feet. 'I must get off home now. We'll meet after dinner tomorrow, I hope. I'm sorry to have burdened you with my troubles.'

Vasily watched the artist walk away. Boris was sensitive and proud. Words of sympathy would feel empty and might well offend him. It would be good to help the man, but how to persuade Count Laptev to value and use his talents?

He looked at Matvey, now asleep by the lake. Boris was right; he could make no assumptions about the child's future. He must strive to secure his freedom. It was wicked and wasteful to prevent him from using his skills and from fulfilling his potential. If the revolt had succeeded, of course, everything would have changed; the serfs would have been freed. But under the current regime, there was no prospect of that.

He started to pack up his chalks. For his own safety, he must keep silent and continue to conceal the truth about his own small part in the plot. For probably the thousandth time, he wondered how Alexander had discovered his involvement. Perhaps he would never find out. He still couldn't forgive his uncle, whose main motive had surely been to preserve his own career and the family's reputation as blameless servants of the State. He certainly hadn't prevented Vasily's arrest out of sympathy for his liberal views.

Matvey was stirring. He sat up and blinked, and then rewarded Vasily with a smile of such guileless affection that it brought a lump to his throat. For the first time since he had snatched the child from the kitchens, he felt a stir of doubt. Was Boris right? Would it have been better to have let him be?

That evening, his mood dark, Vasily decided not to take part in the musical entertainment. He'd slip away to his room. But as he was leaving the drawing room, he encountered Count Laptev. 'Do you have a moment, Vasily? I should like a brief word.'

Vasily hesitated on the threshold of Gavril Ivanovich's study. The room was like a shrine. A prie-dieu stood in one corner before a collection of icons, religious pictures from Europe hung on the panelled walls. Although it was still light outside, the curtains were drawn, and candles were lit. There was a faint trace of incense in the air. To his relief, Gavril Ivanovich snuffed the candles, drew back the curtains, and opened a window. Dust flew in the evening sunlight.

'Sit down, sit down, Vasily. We much enjoy your visits here, you know.'

'You've been most hospitable, sir. And it's been wonderful to meet Lisa once again, to get to know her better.'

'It is Elizaveta that I wanted to discuss with you, that and one other small matter. You seem to be very fond of one another.'

'We are good friends. We didn't get on as children, but when she came to St Petersburg, we took to one another straight away. And my sister Katya is fond of her.'

'I don't know quite how to broach the subject,' said Laptev, 'so I will get straight to it. Is there any possibility that you might offer for her? I should very much like to call you 'son', Vasily, and the prospect of marriage with you would, I'm sure, divert her from this determination to follow Stenovsky into exile.'

Vasily shook his head. In other circumstances, perhaps he would have been more than happy to marry Lisa. She was attractive, and they were indeed good friends. The practical convenience of such an arrangement was undeniable; her fortune would certainly ease the situation at Dubovnoye. But he must disappoint Gavril Ivanovich.

'I'm sorry, sir, I can't do as you request. At present, I have no plans to marry; my future is too uncertain. And, you must know that were I to ask Elizaveta Gavrilovna for her hand, she would never accept. She would see the very request as a betrayal. She'll never marry anyone but Mikhail Alexandrovich. He loves her, and he is, of course, my dearest friend.'

'I didn't know that you were so close to him.'

'I wasn't acquainted with him long, sir, but it was long enough to form a warm and fixed attachment. He's the best of men.'

'I find that hard to believe. He's a convicted criminal. His brother has been imprisoned for life. They've forfeited their entire inheritance, all their rights.'

'I can't speak for Nikita, but I know that Mikhail is both brave and honest. If he sinned, it was to be too firm in his commitment to his beliefs, although I assure you, sir, his views aren't extreme. He was convinced of the need to act, not simply to sit talking in rooms filled with cigar smoke. Had the revolution succeeded, he would have been one of its heroes.'

'Well, it didn't, and he isn't, and it won't be a surprise to you to know that I'm content that the rebels failed.' Count Laptev ran his fingers through his scant curls and sighed.

'Gavril Ivanovich, I beg you. Allow Lisa to go to Mikhail,' Vasily waved his hand towards the icons. 'She believes that her promise to marry him is sacred and cannot be withdrawn. She'll never marry anyone else while he lives. She may even take the veil.' He allowed this idea to sink in. 'I know that the journey will be long and difficult and Lisa's life in Siberia uncertain, but she won't be alone. Several women have travelled there already, including Alexandrine, Nikita's wife, and Maria the wife of Prince Volonsky... former Prince Volonsky. It's said that the presence of the women does much to lessen the cruelty of the men's conditions. People describe them as saints, as angels. I'm in no way surprised that Lisenka wants to follow them. Such sacrifice inspired by love is surely the highest Christian aspiration.'

Count Laptev was listening to him carefully.

'And Madame Stenovsky, Mikhail's mother, has promised her full support. She'll provide the transport and men for the journey. Once Lisa is there, she won't want for anything that she is permitted. Any children she and Mikhail have won't be beggars.'

'If she were to go, I myself would make sure she wanted for nothing,' said Laptev. 'Her mother would be distressed and angry, however.' He spoke with indifference, careless, it seemed, of his wife's feelings on the matter.

'You have been very plain with me, Vasily Nikolayevich, and I am grateful, at least, for that. I can't say I'm not disappointed. Well, I shall now pray for guidance and make my decision. The good Lord will help me.'

Vasily felt he could do no more to nudge the good Lord along the way. Lisa had told him that the Count prayed long and hard whenever he needed to make up his mind. He even looked for divine guidance when considering whether to punish a serf, and he generally found his initial inclinations confirmed.

'There was something else, sir?'

'Yes, I wanted to mention your young servant, Matvey.' Count Laptev cleared his throat. 'He is a bright boy, I can see that, but you must be careful that he keeps to his place. I hope you don't mind my commenting on it but I firmly believe that God created society as it should be and that there are those who lead and those who must be led. Lords should remain lords and slaves, slaves. It doesn't do to give a serf too much hope of improvement in life. At best, it leads to disappointment, at worst, to audacious pretensions. I don't agree with everything the Emperor says, but I must agree with his recent remark that we should permit the serfs some education, but not too much.'

Vasily didn't trust himself to respond politely. Would the power of Lisa's sacred vow trump Laptev's innate conservatism? It was hard to know.

'I understand what you're saying, sir, and thank you for your advice,' he said, determining not to heed it. 'And now, perhaps, if you don't mind, I'll go and listen to the music.'

He stood up and bowed briefly as he left. He made his way towards the music room. Someone was playing the fortepiano.

CHAPTER THIRTY-ONE
June 1827 – Oryol

CHUDOV'S ASSUMPTION THAT the Department was to be inspected proved incorrect. More permanent change was coming to Oryol. The Titular Councillor summoned his staff.

'Gentlemen, I have news of a development that will to some degree affect us all. His Imperial Highness the Emperor was, as I think we are all too well aware, most dissatisfied with the performance of our Ministry before the revolt in December of 1825. In his great wisdom, the Tsar has therefore decided to form two new organs of state aimed at, let me see… I have it here…' Chudov shuffled his papers. 'Ah, yes, "the upholding of public security and morality."' He paused to allow his words to sink in.

Stifled laughter was heard, and a brief scuffle broke out among the ranks of the junior clerks. Chudov glowered at them and continued: 'It seems that both these institutions will be directly answerable to, and receive their orders from, the Emperor himself. They will be led by Count Benkendorf. I am sure that you will all remember that it was the Count who warned the Emperor's late brother, Alexander, of the dangers of secret societies in what, in the event, turned out to be a most timely manner.

'One of these organisations will be part of the current Imperial Chancellery. There are already First and Second Sections directly answerable to the Tsar, and now we have a third, the Third Section.' Chudov paused once again.

'At the same time, an associated uniformed force organised

on military lines has been formed, and detachments are now being sent to all parts of the Empire. Here in Oryol, it seems we shall shortly see the arrival of these gendarmes, who will be led by a Colonel Strogov. At present, I know no more than that. I have no idea what these new officers will do, or how we at the Ministry are supposed to work with them.'

Chudov did not invite questions. He gathered his papers together, scowled at the assembled bureaucrats, and retired to his office, slamming the door.

The town of Oryol greeted the new police force with excitement. The officers wore sharp mid-blue uniforms with bright white cross straps and gloves. They were armed with swords and pistols and equipped with carriages and horses. It was rumoured that they were very well paid, and that their powers were almost unlimited. Instructions came from the very apex of government that they should receive every sort of help and cooperation.

'I'm hoping that they will deflect some of those damned petitions!' Chudov remarked to Vasily on the day after the arrival of the troop. 'I was probably wrong to worry about a turf war. After all, there's plenty of work for all, and Strogov seems a decent enough fellow.'

'Now, Vasily Nikolayevich, I think I have a job that will suit you,' he continued. 'The presence of these special policemen might well help us, but neither Komarov nor I are keen to increase our workload. So I want you to become our contact with Strogov and his men. I admit I want to keep an eye on what they're up to. You can show them around, help them out. The Colonel has already complained that he's received no funding for administrative help, and I'm sure he'll be pleased if we offer him support. We'll need to include much of their activities in our own reports, in any event, so that's a good excuse.'

Vasily nodded. He had plenty of time on his hands.

Later, he presented himself at Colonel Strogov's office. Strogov didn't look like the sinister policeman that everyone supposed him to be. He was in his forties and prematurely grey, and his moustache gave his face a fatherly appearance. His manner was cordial and reserved, and he smoked a pipe. Vasily knew that he had been a captain in the Russian navy.

Strogov first told Vasily that it was the wish of the Emperor that his gendarmes should be not only be honourable ambassadors of the government' but also 'the moral physicians of the people'. Then he asked Vasily some questions about his background, and without hesitation accepted the Ministry's offer of his assistance. Strogov introduced his troop. His deputy was a stocky lieutenant who had previously worked in the Ministry of the Interior in St Petersburg. He seemed in a state of constant surprise that he was now both well paid and the object of fear and respect. Four regular gendarmes, well-favoured ex-cavalry troopers, made up the entire contingent.

'Our first priority is to identify all potential troublemakers and foreigners in the province,' Strogov said. 'Count Benkendorf believes that routinely intercepting such people's mail is a cost-effective way of nipping sedition in the bud. It seems regrettable to me that such measures are thought necessary, so I intend to ensure that our powers are exercised with discretion.

'It's also the Emperor's special desire that the large backlog of court cases across Russia be reduced at speed. I know that in some provinces this has been achieved by randomly deciding the cases by the toss of a coin. Understandably, this has led to more trouble than it has resolved. I shall be sending the Lieutenant to examine the matter. I suspect it may take him some time.

'Another priority will be the supervision of the army recruitment levies. I know that the Governor is under pressure in this area. Not enough men have been sourced from Oryol recently. It seems that some landowners are unwilling to allow able-bodied men to go to the army, and others are so keen to get rid of miscreants and weaklings that they offer the recruiting officers liberal bribes to take them off their hands.'

The intention to routinely intercept people's mail alarmed Vasily, particularly when he learnt that Vladimir Golovkin was to be an early addition to the Gendarmes' list. When he next met Golovkin, he quietly alerted him to the danger. Maltby had written that there was a need to be more prudent in communication. Was his English friend's post also subject to scrutiny? He must be careful what he wrote to him.

———

Vasily's first operation with the Gendarmes turned out to be both unusual and unsettling. A week after Strogov's arrival, he noticed a good deal of activity in the tranquil corridors of the Department. More messengers than usual cluttered the hallways. A high-ranking officer from the newly formed Third Section arrived and spent his time striding with purpose between the Governor's office and that of Colonel Strogov. Chudov, his face pink with anxiety, rushed between one man and the other with uncharacteristic vigour. Komarov was alarmed by the comings and goings but proved unable to shed light on what was happening.

Finally, the officer from St Petersburg departed, and on the following day, Strogov called Vasily into his office. They were joined by Chudov.

'Now, Registrar Belkin, tomorrow the Colonel is going to need your assistance with a small but sensitive operation,' Chudov said. 'There is a state criminal at large in the town, an arrest must be made, and we need someone with some sense to complete the necessary reports. You'll be expected to take names of any accomplices and witnesses and collect and record any papers found on the prisoner's person. One of the gendarmes will accompany you.'

'I think I can manage that, sir,' Vasily said, cheered by the prospect of some excitement.

'The outlaw in question is seeking, it seems, to travel down the River Oka by boat, attempting, we think, to join the Volga at Nizhny Novgorod and then sail on down to Astrakhan and so out of Russia. We have information that he's currently hiding down by the wharves, probably seeking to find employment on a vessel heading north.'

'May I ask what the man has done, sir?'

Chudov looked to Strogov for guidance.

'He's a Captain Alexey Krylov, a man wanted in connection with the failed rebellion in the South in the winter of 1825/6. He was a known associate of Pestel and Murav'ev-Apostol, who, of course, were hung for treason last July. He's not a big fish though; he'll probably be confined in a fortress somewhere for his trouble or be sent east, of course. He's managed to lie low up to now, but, recently, an NCO from his regiment spotted him at an inn close to his estates. Now, government agents have pursued him down here.'

As Strogov spoke, Vasily felt a twinge of anxiety. He didn't know the man but to help to catch him felt like a betrayal.

To show reluctance, however, would attract suspicion. He couldn't afford to lower his guard.

'I didn't think that there were many rebels still at large,' he said.

'There are a few, but most of them have managed to make it out of the country in one way or another. Krylov is the last of the most actively sought fugitives still on the run in Russia, I think.'

Vasily reflected; surely, his own case was different. He was hardly concealing his whereabouts and obviously wasn't being 'actively sought'. If any evidence had come to light, he would have been arrested by now. As long as he kept his own counsel and played his new role with conviction, he should be safe enough. Nonetheless, as he watched Colonel Strogov, today rather less amiable, making arrangements for the forthcoming mission, he couldn't suppress a pulse of fear.

They gathered early the next day at the steps of the Governor's House. Strogov and his four troopers were joined by two veteran soldiers, members of the Internal Guard, who, if he were caught, would accompany the prisoner on his journey to captivity. A police driver with a closed wagon had been dispatched to a street on the far bank of the Oka, close to the warehouse where Krylov was thought to be hiding.

It promised to be a fine June day. They rode across the bridge that spanned the river under a pink-washed dome of cloudless sky. A heron seeking breakfast beat its way upstream with heavy wings. One or two dark-hulled barges were already creeping from the town on the slow river drift. Other vessels were moored along the shore. There was little other sign of life: the busy harvest season, when mountains of grain would be shipped from here to the heart of Russia and beyond, had not yet started.

They approached a spot downstream where a huddle of timber warehouses, merchants' dwellings, and workshops stood back from the low riverbank. The ground between the buildings and the water's edge ran in a broad strand down to some upturned boats and a rough wooden landing stage. Strogov reined in his horse and considered the terrain.

'The land on the river side is too exposed,' he said. 'We shall approach the warehouse from the rear. I don't anticipate too much trouble.' He turned to Vasily. 'Stay close to the road, Registrar, and don't come forward until invited.'

They skirted the edge of the settlement and left their mounts by the wagon. The Colonel and his four gendarmes advanced, the tread of their boots muffled on the sandy track. Vasily followed them for a few yards then paused. After some seconds of silence, he heard a series of loud crashes and the splintering of wood. Shouts followed, the sharp snap of a pistol, further shouts, and then running feet heading towards the river. Things didn't seem to be going according to plan. Should he retreat, move back to the road?

As he hesitated, a tall man with a tangled beard and thick curly hair sprinted around the corner and came to a staggering halt in front of him. Breathing heavily, the fugitive saw at once that his way was blocked. He looked at Vasily, his eyes staring from his ash-pale face. He seemed to be groping for something. Vasily froze and raised his hands; if Krylov had a weapon, he would be an easy target. He should shout out and attract the attention of the gendarmes, but he was loath to see the man taken.

Krylov glanced at the guards further up the path and at the horses and the wagon.

'Try that way,' Vasily found himself saying, pointing away from the river towards some merchants' houses. It seemed the best chance. The fugitive swivelled round, kicking up a spray of fine sand. Vasily lost sight of him. Unable to resist the temptation to follow, he jogged towards the buildings, but he had only gone a few yards when he heard a shot, a crack of fist on flesh, and the crump of a body hitting the ground. Krylov had been caught, his flight cut off by one of the troopers. Strogov, it seemed, had left no escape route.

Almost at once, a gendarme appeared, unruffled in his bright uniform. 'Are you unharmed, sir? He was too quick for us, disappeared through the back while we broke down the door. Of course, he didn't get far, but we could have done a better job of trapping him!'

'He saw the wagon, I think, and ran the other way.' Vasily spoke more robustly than he felt. 'Is he dead?'

'No, just out cold.'

As he walked with the gendarme towards the riverbank, he could hear the grate and squeak of the police wagon as it rolled forwards. He reached the shore in time to see Krylov's insensate body being tipped onto the thin covering of fetid straw inside. A guard slammed the door and pulled down the iron crossbar. A rancid prison stink corrupted the air.

Vasily stepped back, gasping. He shut his eyes for a moment. He must collect himself, hide his fear, and concentrate on the task at hand. He glanced at the gendarmes. They were preparing to leave.

Strogov looked disgruntled and the troopers uncomfortable. It seemed the men had failed to notice a shuttered window through which Krylov had managed to take flight. Without a word, the Colonel handed Vasily the prisoner's pack. He then marched away at a good pace towards his horse with three of his men trailing behind him.

The fourth gendarme remained with Vasily, and they spent an hour or so tracking down the owner of the warehouse and taking statements from him and his foreman. They made inquiries among the boatmen. Had any agreed to take the fugitive on as crew for their long journey downstream? If one of them had, he was not admitting it.

His work complete, Vasily rode slowly back across the bridge. Where would they take poor Krylov now? What would his fate be? It wasn't easy, it seemed, to escape the Emperor's vengeance. He mustn't find himself caught in a similar trap.

Chudov immediately emerged from his office to inquire how the operation had gone.

'So, even the Gendarmes make mistakes!' he said, failing to conceal a smile.

'Well, the first pancake is often a failure, sir,' Vasily replied.

Chudov grunted.

'Do you want me to make your duties with Strogov permanent?' he asked.

Vasily paused for a moment. Today's situation was unlikely to be repeated. He should agree.

'It occurs to me If you're going to get involved in more business of this sort, Vasily, you'd better take some pistols out with you. The recruiting levies can get quite contentious at times, and there are other dangers on the road. We'll issue you a pair. I assume you can use them?'

'Yes, sir.'

'Well, that's more than I can. Komarov was quite a good shot once, but now he's as blind as a mole. No point arming him.'

The following week, Vasily started to accompany Strogov as he went about the province. The gendarme preferred a horse to a carriage, and Vasily rode out with him on the sleek bay mare that he now kept at livery in the town. He found little use for the pistols but was pleased to have them. Sometimes, as Chudov had anticipated, tempers ran high. Moreover, the further reaches of the province were troubled by bands of runaway serfs and robbers who were known to attack travellers on lonely roads. On occasion, Strogov had requested a small troop of hussars as an escort.

Vasily enjoyed his new role. It brought some sense of freedom and an opportunity to learn. As he became increasingly useful to Strogov, the shortcomings of the provinces were largely forgotten. He only sometimes recalled that he had something to hide.

CHAPTER THIRTY-TWO
July 1827 – St Petersburg

ALEXANDER PETROVICH SAT behind his desk at the Ministry and contemplated the summer clouds outside the window. He had been busy of late and was weary. These new gendarmes had disturbed the equanimity of the Minister who, concerned about comparisons with his own department, had ordered a number of inspections in the provinces. Alexander was now short of staff, more so since a number of the better officers had transferred to the Third Section, and some had even joined the new force.

He was not just fatigued; he was also lonely. Dmitry had not been well during the spring, but, once recovered, he had travelled to a spa to take the waters. Maria Vasilyevna was constantly at Katya's. Should he recall Vasily from Oryol? They had seemed on slightly better terms when he had left Dubovnoye in August last year. But perhaps it would not yet be safe, and besides, his nephew had not written since he had started work. He was obviously still resentful and felt he was being punished. Surely he realised that, at best, he had been saved from an unpleasant encounter with the police, at worst, from a slow death awaiting trial?

Now there was something more. A week or so ago, when looking in his safe, he had discovered that Vasily's records were missing. From a sense of prudence, he had extracted his file from the thousands of similar documents in the central registry and put it in what he had believed to be a safe place. When he found the papers gone, he had looked at home in case he had absently taken the file there, but there was no sign of it. Then, today, when he had opened the safe, it had been returned, apparently untouched.

He looked at the record again. It had been opened in late September 1825, after the funeral of Ryleev's cousin, the unfortunate guards officer, Konstantin Chernov. Count Belkin had been observed at the graveside with Mikhail Stenovsky and other men, some of whom had subsequently been arrested for treason. Alexander sighed. At the time, he had no notion that his nephew had been there. Of course, the funeral had been an excuse for every liberal and potential troublemaker to come out onto the streets and for every policeman, government agent and spy to come out, in turn, to observe them. The authorities had made lists and cross-checked names, and a large number of new records had been opened at the Ministry. However, although some arrests had been made, the assembly had not been illegal in and of itself, and there was nothing here to condemn Vasily.

The papers also contained a report of the short inquiry after 14 December into Vasily's whereabouts at the time of the revolt. This had been raised due to his known connection with the Stenovsky brothers. Alexander remembered how the police had come to their apartment. Vasily, he had said, had gone away shortly after the ball at the French Embassy, and was now ill at the estate. The officer's report was in the file, as was that of the visit by the Moscow Provincial police to Dubovnoye, where witnesses, thankfully, had corroborated the story.

It had been a blessing that neither of the Stenovsky brothers nor any other conspirator had mentioned Vasily's name in their depositions to the Special Commission. Mikhail had clearly not betrayed his friend. It seemed that Vasily had told him the truth when he had said that his association with the group had been brief and his contribution to the enterprise insignificant. Nonetheless, men less culpable than Vasily were now imprisoned or in exile. The thoroughness of the government's response to the rebellion had been remarkable, the sweep for suspects wide-ranging, and the number of men arrested staggering. Had he known when he had plucked Vasily from the city how difficult it might prove to escape the reach of the law, he doubted that he would have had the courage to take the steps he had. Both he and Vasily had been very lucky.

Why would anyone find the file of interest now? Some radical sympathisers were still being picked up here and there in the provinces, but they were, in the main, identified wanted men. And who had found a way into his safe? He was letting things slip, losing his grip. He must change the combination and be more careful in future. Should he write to Karl Feodorovich, or to the Baroness, to warn them that someone may come asking questions? No, they had both learned their scripts. A letter, even sent with caution, might be intercepted. Everyone seemed to be spying on everyone else these days. The atmosphere in the capital was becoming insupportable.

CHAPTER THIRTY-THREE
The Laptev Estate

Bashkatovo

Tuesday

My dear Vasya,

I write to warn you that we are expecting a visitor.

Aunt Darya has heard from Count Leonid Fedulov. He is visiting the south, and intends calling on us on Saturday. No doubt he will be seeking to stay for a few days.

I seem to remember that the Count was not much liked by Mikhail, or indeed by you. Aunt Darya, however, thinks he is 'one of the finest young(?) men in St Petersburg.' And of course she issued an open invitation to visit, which he has now taken up.

I hope you will not alter your plans to come!

Still no decision on Siberia; father still praying for guidance, mother still opposed.

Your,

Lisa

When Vasily arrived at the Laptev's estate, Fedulov had not yet appeared. While Yakov unpacked his box, he went to the studio to see what progress Boris had made on the portrait of Antonina Stepanova. It was close to completion. He turned aside and regarded his own feeble attempts at oil painting with a frown. He really needed to devote more time to it, but there was no room to set up a studio in town.

He heard Boris's voice behind him: 'Vasily Nikolayevich! Good to see you, sir. Sit down and tell me about your adventures with the Gendarmes!' He laughed, seeming to find Vasily's new employment a source of great amusement.

Vasily sank onto the long divan that ran along the wall. Boris climbed onto his high painting stool.

'I didn't go out with them this week, but shall next. The levies are continuing. It's good to be busy... time passes quickly. And what news with you?'

'Good, very good. The Countess has secured a commission for a group portrait. It will result in a decent fee, so the Count is not too unhappy. I'll be able to escape the carpenters' hut for a while. It has given me hope: one order can lead to another. If the Count would allow me to look for other work, life would become quite bearable. The Countess has hinted that it may be possible. She has also told me of a group in St Petersburg that supports the freeing of serf artists. That would certainly be something!'

Vasily remembered his conversation with Count Laptev about Matvey. Surely Antonina Stepanova must be raising false hopes. Would she be so cruel as to do that? He really hoped not.

'Who ordered the work?'

'Prince Kukarin. He has an estate about ten versts to the north of here. The family are here for the summer. I'll go over and make preliminary sketches once the Countess's picture is finished.'

'Will you paint here or at the Prince's?'

'Here, I think. Once I've made the sketches, the composition itself will take time, they want hounds, children and a view of their park.' Boris seemed younger. He smiled, stood straighter, and his eyes shone.

They heard the sound of dogs barking and wheels on the gravel. An elegant turnout swept onto the driveway: a glossy new carriage pulled by fine matched greys. It seemed that Fedulov had prospered. Could he really afford such an equipage on his Ministry salary?

And now Leonid Sergeyevich descended. He stood for a moment, erect in his dark green uniform, and surveyed the mansion. Two red-coated lackeys from the Laptev staff scuttled around him, picking up boxes, unstrapping his large trunk, and bearing all into the house. Vasily wondered how long Fedulov was intending to stay. He seemed to have enough luggage for a month at least.

'He's a fine-looking gentleman,' said Boris. 'Do you know him well, sir?'

'No, not very. He works in the Ministry with my uncle. He was keen to marry my sister at one time, but my mother was opposed to it. I wonder if he's come to try his hand with Elizaveta Gavrilovna? I'm afraid he'll be disappointed.' Vasily turned away from the window. 'Well, Boris, I must go to prepare for dinner. Shall we meet as usual tomorrow?'

'Of course, sir.'

Vasily left Boris with regret and some concern. It was hard to regard him as a servant. He was quite unlike the underemployed and obsequious house serfs who stood, their faces etched with boredom, in every room in the house. Or, indeed, the bearded field serfs whom he generally only glimpsed from afar.

Most of the family were already gathered in the drawing room. Aunt Darya seemed to expand with importance as she made the introductions. 'Ah! Vasily Nikolayevich! You are already acquainted with Leonid Sergeyevich, Count Fedulov?'

'Yes, of course,' Vasily bowed. Fedulov returned the bow, failing to meet his eyes. The Count showed no surprise at meeting him in Oryol. His uncle must have told him he was here.

'Did you leave Alexander Petrovich well?' Vasily asked.

'He seemed well enough, Vasily Nikolayevich. He has been promoted again as you, I expect, know. He is as a god to us now!'

'And should I congratulate you, too?'

Fedulov now looked directly at him. 'Yes, indeed. I am proud to have been recently honoured with the rank of Court Councillor.' Fedulov paused, and then continued: 'I hope you will forgive me for mentioning it, Count, but I wonder that you are not in uniform. In society, it is now mandated by the Emperor.'

There was no humour in Fedulov's grey eyes. It seemed he was in earnest. Lisa, who had entered the room, extended her hand. 'So good to see you here, Count Fedulov. But you know Vasily is at home here. We are his cousins. We wouldn't expect him to stand on any ceremony with us.'

'None the less, Elizaveta Gavrilovna—'

'We are very glad you called on us, sir,' Lisa cut across him, not altogether politely. 'Are you on an extended trip?'

Fedulov flushed and frowned a little. 'Yes, I'm travelling in the south for a couple of months. I have some business to undertake and then shall visit some relations.'

'And then you return to St Petersburg?'

'Probably not. I'll be making some inspections of our provincial offices on behalf of the Minister. I may, in fact, return to Oryol in due course to visit the Ministry office here and shall enjoy calling on you again.'

The hairs prickled on Vasily's neck. My God! He must warn Chudov! He looked again at the newly made Court Councillor. For all his impressive presence, there was something lacking in the man. He seemed to have no sense of humour or proportion. What was more, Fedulov made little attempt to hide his dislike for him. It seemed that the old family issue still rankled.

Lisa started to speak again but was silenced as the butler announced that dinner was served.

Fedulov's arrival meant that Vasily was displaced from his usual seat next to Antonina Stepanova and found himself in a happy spot in the middle of the table. Lisa sat on one side of him and Miss Roberts, the English governess, opposite, with Nadezhda.

'Most of the hussars are back in town now,' Vasily told them after grace. 'They all went off to some mass review, an inspection by the Emperor. I missed them when they were gone. The taverns and theatre have been deserted.'

'You'll have to start attending social gatherings again,' Lisa said.

'Yes that's true, I suppose. But speaking of hussars, an amusing thing happened to me last week. At least I thought it amusing.' He paused.

Nadezhda leant forward. 'Do go on, Vasya!'

'On Tuesday, on my way to work, I walked past the back of the theatre. Just as I reached the steps to the stage door, I heard tremendous shouting coming from above.' Vasily swung back on his chair, warming to his tale. 'Looking up, I saw a very young soldier, a yunker, I think, barely out of the cradle, being hurled down the stairs. He landed in the dust directly in front of me. His sabre and shako sailed through the air after him. He lay still for a moment. I thought he might be hurt. Then the owner of the theatre himself, Count Kamensky, emerged and shouted at the poor boy: he would ban him from the theatre! He would inform his commanding officer! He would even write to his father, with whom he claimed to be intimately acquainted. The door then slammed shut, and Kamensky disappeared.

'Once he had gone, the boy showed signs of life. I helped him up and dusted him down. Apparently he'd been trying to arrange an assignation with one of the dancers. I don't think anyone had told him that such a scheme was unthinkable. Kamensky keeps his artists on a tight leash; it's almost impossible to meet them unless he permits it. He really does treat them like the slaves they are. It rather puts one off going to the place. He's been known to give the leading man a black eye during the interval if his performance in the first act was deemed inadequate.'

'Is that really true?' asked Nadezhda, her eyes wide.

'Yes, I'm afraid so. Anyway, to get back to my story, the lad was dusty and bruised, but otherwise unhurt. Two officers from his regiment came along, and I was able to pass him over to them. When I left, they were ribbing the young man unmercifully. I noticed that his Russian was poor...'

Vasily's audience laughed as he told his story. Count Laptev glowered from his seat. Fedulov raised his eyebrows. The Countess looked pained. Vasily pulled his chair forward, dropped his head, and fell silent.

'You must bring him here, Vasya!' Lisa whispered, struggling to control her mirth. 'It seems that he needs some friends.'

'Well, under the circumstances, we weren't introduced. But I'll keep an eye out for him.'

'Will you come out on the lake this afternoon?' Lisa asked.

'I'm sorry, I've promised to take Matvey to the woods. He likes the birds and the wildlife. He works hard in the week these days, so I try to indulge him.

'Well, we'll meet this evening. I hope you'll sing with me!'

———

Vasily sat in the music room with the family and other guests listening to Nadezhda playing the fortepiano. She was almost, but not quite, accurate. The misplayed notes didn't worry him, however; he was preoccupied with his own thoughts.

He and Matvey had set out together on their walk and made for the extensive woods that skirted the estate. He had deliberately put on his loose cotton shirt and Mikhail's floppy hat. He hoped that Fedulov would spot him from the drawing room where he was engaged in conversation with the Countess and her sister.

They walked through the lime grove and on into the woods among the wilder thickets of aspen and birch. Grouse and partridge flew up from under their feet. Ten minutes or so along the path, they came to a clearing where a small house stood, a pastiche of a wooden peasant hut. Dog roses and honeysuckle climbed around its carved window frames, and pelargoniums brightened the tubs at the door. Vasily thought that he might sketch the scene, and he settled down with Matvey in an elevated position. Within half an hour, they heard the sound of voices coming from the path below them. They peered down through the trees. Boris Abramovich and the Countess were walking together. Their dark heads were inclined one towards the other, and her hand rested on his arm.

Vasily heard Matvey draw breath as if to call out. He kicked him gently and put his finger to his lips. They drew back as the couple passed along the path below them. Then, to Vasily's astonishment, Boris and the Countess stood on the threshold of the cottage, embracing one another and kissing before entering the shadowy interior. They heard the bar drop behind the door.

As soon as he felt they could safely leave, they walked back towards the house and then took another path. Matvey was brimming with questions, which Vasily tried to deflect. In the end he told him that none of it was their business and that they must not talk about it, which he knew was an inadequate response.

Vasily's attention briefly returned to the music room, where one of the impoverished cousins was now thrilling the company with his versatility on the violin. Vasily winced, then his mind drifted again.

What did Boris think he was doing? The risk he was taking was immense. The man would end up in the army, in Siberia, or even destroyed by the knout if the Count was seriously vindictive. Perhaps he thought the risk worth taking for the sake of his art, for the promise of freedom? Or perhaps he had found the Countess irresistible? Who knew? But this couldn't end well.

Now it was his turn to perform. Lisa had found a book of airs by Handel in St Petersburg, and they had been working through them together. 'Where'er you walk,' he sang in his poor English. He could see Miss Roberts laughing behind her fan. Fedulov was staring at him, unimpressed.

As he sang a second piece, Vasily noticed that Lisa's father was dabbing tears away with his lace kerchief. The applause died, and the Count rose to his feet, blew his nose, and cleared his throat. What could be coming? Vasily remained standing by the fortepiano. Lisa's knuckles were white as she gripped the top of the instrument.

'Ladies and gentlemen, I have come to a decision.' Laptev blinked his glistening eyes. 'I have prayed long and hard. It has not been easy. I have prayed long and hard,' he repeated, 'and God has told me that I should not prevent my darling daughter, Elizaveta, from keeping the solemn and holy vow that she has made to her betrothed, Mikhail Stenovsky. If the

Emperor allows it, she may go to him in exile.'

'No!' the Countess cried out and rose to her feet. She hurried from the room, followed by Darya Stepanova. Lisa's grip relaxed.

'I am resolved,' said the Count. 'I know it is the right thing to do. That it is God's will.'

Vasily watched as Lisa ran to her father and embraced him, then she turned back to the piano and fell into his arms. Finding it hard to hold back tears, he looked over her shoulder at the assembled guests. They were smiling, congratulating Gavril Ivanovich. The violin player was laughing as he banged his bow repeatedly against the strings.

Only Count Fedulov seemed not to share the general mood. He sat motionless in his pristine uniform, his frame too large for his fragile gilt chair, and he surveyed the room with a stare of undisguised derision. As he rose to his feet, he met Vasily's eyes and held his gaze for several moments. His expression was cold and hostile. With what appeared to be a slight smirk, he made Vasily a low bow, then turned on his heel and left. Vasily felt a nip of unease as he watched the Court Councillor, his body rigid, retreat briskly along the enfilade into the shadows.

———

They drove back to town the following evening. The harvest had started, and the serfs were returning from the fields. Vasily would have liked to be out working with them, but no doubt Count Laptev wouldn't approve. He recalled the season last year at Dubovnoye: the crisp late summer mornings; the languid heat at midday; the singing of the women as they walked home, restored by the evening breeze. Later, they had danced or sat on the steps of the church and continued their songs, their voices drifting up to the veranda of the estate house. It had been healing, invigorating, to work out in the open air, and, later, there had been the plashing beat of the waterwheel and the soft arms and breasts of the miller's widow.

The carriage rumbled on. Matvey and Yakov were both asleep. Vasily hummed a snatch of song. If fate and, more importantly, the Emperor, smiled on them, Lisa and Mikhail would soon be reunited. At least one hurdle had been overcome. Fedulov's chill reaction to Gavril Ivanovich's decision had been unnerving, but perhaps it was not so surprising. Few bureaucrats from the Interior Ministry would approve of indulging a convicted state criminal, and, of course, Fedulov had certainly harboured hopes of securing Lisa for himself. And what of Boris and the Countess? Vasily stirred in his seat and stretched. God, he too could do with a woman! On his arrival in Oryol, Chudov had helpfully supplied him with details of the only acceptable brothel in the town. He supposed he might go there again, but the thought didn't excite him.

They had not been home for more than a few minutes when he heard Matvey telling Yakov about the sighting of Boris and the Countess in the woods. His story was interspersed with a series of questions.

'Matvey! We were not going to discuss that!' He supposed the child knew the facts of life. He pushed the thought away. Yakov came into the living room. Vasily sent Matvey to bed and closed the door.

'Well?'

'Well, what?' said Yakov. He was being more than usually obtuse.

'What do you think?'

'If you're talking about the artist and Her Ladyship, it's all round the servants' hall. You can't keep things like that quiet. There are people, serfs, everywhere in that house. I'm sure the Countess knows it. If you want to keep a secret, you have to be sly, make arrangements.'

'But the Count? He must find out!'

'He probably already knows. I don't think he cares too much about the Countess, and he certainly doesn't like her sister! Despite all his prayers and piety, he's not averse to the odd serf girl himself. He has them delivered to his room at night. Then he prays doubly hard the next day to make his peace with God. Sometimes he makes the woman pray with him.'

'Really? Well, you certainly have your ear to the ground, Yakov!'

His servant smiled. 'People seem to like to talk to me, sir. It's my honest face.'

Vasily sniffed and looked down, reflecting on Laptev's hypocrisy. There was a noise outside the door. He got up quietly and opened it. Matvey fell into the room. Vasily took him by the collar, walked him into the servants' room and dropped him onto his bed.

'Go to sleep, you impossible boy,' he said. 'It's late now. I promise you we'll talk about this tomorrow. No, no more questions. Quite honestly, I don't know what to make of it myself.'

That night, Vasily dreamed about Irina. He woke at dawn and knew he wouldn't sleep again. Outside, the street was silent. He stared at the ceiling. Where was she now? What was she doing? Who was she with? Did she have another lover?

Could she have been reunited with her husband, her children? Of course, if what Alexander had said about her was true, they may have been a fiction and may never have existed. He rolled onto his side, pulling the bedclothes close, and tried to shut out the image of her soft body curled beside him. Despite his doubts and his sense of betrayal, he still ached for her. When out in society, he still caught himself seeking her face in crowded rooms. He couldn't put his memories completely behind him.

CHAPTER THIRTY-FOUR

August 1827 – The Province of Oryol

VASILY DEVELOPED A good relationship with Colonel Strogov. The Chief of Gendarmes was keen to enter society and relied on him to arrange invitations to receptions and to introduce him to appropriate local families. Strogov's early encounters were uncomfortable. There was certainly some social disadvantage attached to the leader of a special police force known to have direct access to the Tsar. It soon became clear, however, that the Colonel's intentions were, by and large, benign, and that he seemed honest and was uninterested in investigating family secrets. He became popular, particularly among the conservative gentry.

They were at a reception at the Nobles' Club when a message came from the Governor's office. There had been disturbances on an estate three hours' ride to the northeast. Vasily felt aggrieved. He had arranged to go on to a private party. There were likely to be some pretty girls, possibly even some dancers from the theatre.

As he rode along the darkening roads with Strogov, he forgot his disappointment. The trouble must be serious; they were riding out in force. As well as the Gendarmes and the town police, a troop of hussars accompanied them from the Pavlogradsky Regiment. Two sealed wagons rumbled and squeaked at the rear.

'The family owns some four or five hundred souls, so it's a good-sized estate,' Strogov told Vasily. 'It seems that the owner recently died without children. A rumour went around that his widow had agreed that the place be requisitioned as a military settlement.'

'That can't have gone down well,' said Vasily. Life was harsh in these artificial communities, where field serfs became part of the army and retired soldiers were forced to become unwilling farmers.

'There's not a word of truth in the story,' Strogov said. 'The coachman who raised the alarm said that trouble started when some serfs organised a deputation. There was an argument, blows were exchanged. The estate steward tried to stop the fighting and was killed in the resulting turmoil. Shot, I believe. The widow is held hostage in the manor with some of her servants. We need to release them, restore calm, and reassure the serfs that no change is intended. I'd like as few arrests as possible; many honest men will have been misled, but the ringleaders must be brought in and the murderer of the steward identified. Unfortunately, as things stand, there's little incentive for the culprits to surrender. We must prepare for a standoff.'

They arrived after midnight. The troops trotted through sleeping villages under a half moon, the sound of the horses' hoofs deadened by the thick dust of the road. The estate house was just visible in a sheltered hollow surrounded by dark trees. There was no sign of life. They came to a halt on level ground above a long slope that ran down to the carriage sweep and prepared to wait for dawn.

Vasily watched as the hussars tethered their horses and the troopers lay on the ground to sleep. Their officers, a captain and a lieutenant, squatted on the grass with a young yunker, deep in discussion, their sabres and shakos abandoned on the ground beside them. He was tempted to join them but was reluctant to intrude. He tethered his mare under a tree, detached his blanket, and laid it down. Using his satchel as a pillow, he tried to sleep.

At dawn, he heard voices and the chink of bridles as the soldiers saddled up. Strogov was somewhere close by, speaking to the leading police officer. He turned to Vasily as he approached.

'Vasily Nikolayevich, Mr Registrar, good morning to you. You're to stay up here out of trouble. If things get nasty you should ride for home. If you approach the house before I give you leave, I shall have you arrested. Is that clear? When it's all over you can take details for your report.'

'Yes, Colonel.'

Vasily took up a position towards the top of the slope. He had a clear view of the house. The place had no architectural pretensions. Irregularly extended over time, single-storey wings of different sizes clung to both sides of the central cube.

The gendarmes and troops lined up. Strogov and a police officer trotted their horses to within hailing distance of the front door.

'I stand here as the representative of the Emperor Nicholas,' Strogov shouted. 'You have my word that there is no intention to create a military establishment here. All rumours to that effect are false. I understand that hostages have been taken. If those responsible will release them, I can guarantee—'

A shot was fired from one of the windows on the upper floor. The sound of screams erupted from within. As if it were a signal, a body of men emerged from the trees, armed with a variety of agricultural implements. One or two held hunting rifles or muskets. Vasily tried to count them; there were probably more than one hundred serfs lining up on the driveway.

Strogov and the policeman turned and cantered back up

the slope. The soldiers on their matched brown horses started a slow trot towards the house. They halted on command within thirty yards of the serfs.

Strogov rode forward once again. His horse frisked on the spot. 'Let the women go. Tell me your complaints, and I'll see what can be done. On my word of honour, I repeat, there are no plans to establish a military settlement here.'

A bearded peasant stepped out. He swayed and stumbled a little. 'It's not like what it looks, sir. We just wanted to know that our homes, our way of life were safe. We don't want to become soldiers here. The mistress wouldn't discuss the matter, you see, so there was talk. There was no trouble, no fighting, but then some oafs broke into the wine cellar, and all got confused. It were an accident that the steward was killed.'

The peasant looked at the hussars, at their pale blue-green dolmans and dark green tunics, their scarlet braids and cords, their white plumes and their weapons. He knelt on the ground with his head bowed. 'We'll deliver you the murderer, sir. Let the rest go free and we'll let mistress go and return to our work.'

'I can't agree to that,' Strogov said. 'The Emperor does not tolerate revolt or hostage-taking. If you let the owner and her servants go and all submit to questioning, then we'll withdraw. But you must disperse now, go quietly back to your homes and wait under guard. I shall deal fairly with you; only those who have committed crimes will be punished.'

The bearded serf was silent. He clearly didn't know how to reply. Another shot rang out and he fell, wounded, to the ground. It was unclear whether the bullet was meant for him or for Strogov, but it had an immediate effect on the serfs, who, as a body, surged forward. As the peasants came on, Vasily could see smoke rising from a wing of the house. Cries, more urgent now, came from within.

The Captain of Hussars gave the order to attack. Vasily watched, his heart pitching. The forces were hardly equal. On the right and in the centre, the cavalrymen on their well-trained horses quickly overran the loosely knit line of inadequately armed men. Those few who resisted were felled by slashing sabres, a few by pistol shots. Most, however, fled unharmed. One or two hussars toppled from their horses, hit by shots fired from the house.

Immediately below Vasily, at the bottom of the slope on the extreme left of the line, two hussars were in trouble. One was the yunker. The men had been separated from their troop and pushed out to the flank as a horseman beside them was brought down. They now faced a group of ten or more men.

As the two soldiers confronted the serfs, one of the peasants ran forward and sliced at the yunker's horse with his great scythe. The horse screamed and went down in a tangle of straps and contortion of hooves. The young soldier kicked free from his stirrups and rolled from his saddle. He landed neatly on his feet and emptied both pistols. One man fell, This gave the others pause for a moment, but then they advanced. The other trooper, still mounted, laid about him with his sabre, felling two more men as he fought his way to safety. He wheeled his horse to attack again from the rear, but, winged by a rifle shot, he toppled to the ground. The serfs hacked at him with their scythes. He screamed and then lay still.

The yunker, now on foot and alone, was making a run for it. Self-sacrifice was pointless. He was outnumbered, and, behind him, the battle was almost over. A couple of serfs had decided to make their escape and veered off into the woods, but four men still pursued him.

Vasily walked down the slope, his pistols cocked. The young hussar was sprinting directly towards him. When he reached his side, they faced their assailants together. The yunker stood ready, sabre in hand, his breath rasping. The serfs still came on. Vasily fingered the trigger of his right-hand gun. He must steady himself, wait until he couldn't miss. He squeezed, and as he heard the explosion, the leading attacker crumpled onto the grass. His sickle fell to the ground with a dull clang, and a bloom of blood blotted his loose shirt. Three men, one with a cudgel and two with scythes, now stood just a few yards distant.

'Which of you shall I take next?' Vasily shouted. 'Who wants to die? Give it up lads… The fight's over… Do you want another murder on your hands?'

The men hesitated, glancing at one another. Vasily could see the Hussar Lieutenant, his sabre raised, galloping up the slope behind them. If he could just hold the men off… But he had only one shot left.

'I quite like the look of you!' He aimed at the man in the middle. 'But on the other hand…' He moved the gun to the left. The serfs froze, their eyes fixed on his pistol. Then, hearing hoofbeats approaching, they turned and fled. Vasily fired above their heads, then watched as the lieutenant, his help no longer needed, spun his mount around and rode back to the house. Flames were leaping from the windows and licking the roof. The widow, now freed, lay on the grass surrounded by her servants. Police were arriving. Many serfs were on their knees or prostrate on the ground, weeping and pleading for mercy.

Strogov sat on his horse a little to one side, his face expressionless. He had sent his men to arrest the marksman. A cacophony of shots came from within the house. The body of the gunman crashed through an upper window and fell onto the gravel like a sack of grain.

Strogov looked up the bank and, seeing Vasily standing on the grass, he frowned. Vasily knew that he should retreat to avoid the Colonel's wrath, but the yunker had dropped to the ground beside him and was sobbing and shaking like an aspen. His face was familiar; it was the young hussar he had encountered outside the theatre a few weeks previously. The lad had been the butt of his comrades' jokes then. He must pull himself together now or they'd laugh at him again.

Vasily crouched down and forced the soldier to look at him.

'I can't spend my life picking you up, you know.'

The yunker hiccoughed. Vasily pulled a kerchief from his pocket. The yunker wiped his face with it. He looked a little better, but he was still trembling. Vasily thought some social pleasantries might calm him, so he introduced himself. With an effort, the soldier replied: 'Uspensky, Yevgeny Filipovich. How do you do, Count? I am eternally obliged.'

Vasily laughed, rose to his feet, and pulled Uspensky up after him. 'Come on! You did well! Take some deep breaths, then go down to join your troop.'

He looked up. Strogov, his expression grim, was riding towards them. Vasily braced himself, preparing for the worst. The Colonel pulled up his horse and surveyed the damage: the bodies of the dead, the wounded horse struggling to rise, the discarded weapons.

'Well, you've been busy up here, Registrar,' he said. He turned to the yunker. 'You need to report to your company, soldier.' Uspensky set off down the slope. He was more or less steady on his feet. A loose horse galloped past him up the hill, reins flying and flanks flecked with foam.

The Captain trotted up. 'What's the damage?' Strogov asked him.

'Two dead troopers, a few wounded – one quite badly. Costly, given the situation.' The Captain looked down at Vasily. 'Still, I'd have lost the yunker if it hadn't been for you, sir. I'm very grateful to you. You shoot well, have a cool head. You're wasted as an ink-blot.' He turned to Strogov. 'You should take him on, Colonel. The loss of Prince Uspensky would have been an embarrassment. It was probably a mistake to bring him. This wasn't the tea party I expected.' He wheeled his charger and cantered back to the house.

Strogov looked at Vasily keenly and said with a faint smile, 'I'll allow your failure to follow orders to pass this time, Vasily Nikolayevich. But don't make a habit of it. Now you should come down to the house and earn your keep.'

'I need my papers. I'll fetch them now.'

Vasily walked back up the slope. His head was spinning, his legs weak. When he was out of sight, he collapsed onto the grass and threw up. He closed his eyes. He could see the dead serf, the blood on his pale smock, the surprise on his face as he fell to the ground. He could still hear the agonised shrieks of the wounded horse. This was what it meant to shed blood. This was the reality of the carnage he had carelessly planned to unleash two years before. He gagged.

'Here, sir, take this.' The driver of one of the prison wagons had hurried to bring water and a rough towel. Vasily wiped his face and hands and, breathing deeply, fought to calm himself. Killing the serf had filled him with revulsion and a bitter sense of guilt, but what else could he have done? He must take comfort from the Captain's words. He had managed to keep his head, save another's life, and possibly his own. But this was no time to dwell on it. He must start on his work.

The driver offered him a flask of vodka. He took a mouthful and passed it back. 'Take some more, sir.' He shook his head.

Some minutes later, he found his horse and his papers. He rubbed the mare's familiar neck, briefly buried his nose in her mane, and collected up the reins. The manor house was now fully ablaze. Black smoke curled above the treetops. Coughing in the fume-filled air, he rode down with as much dignity as he could muster to report to the Colonel.

Vasily did not return to Oryol for several days. Once the widow had departed with her servants and the surviving ringleaders of the revolt had been taken to prison, he agreed to take charge of the estate until the deceased landowner's brother arrived from Moscow. The Lieutenant of the Gendarmes and some of the Internal Guard stayed with him.

He was obliged to spend the first night on a padded bench in the estate office. In the morning, smoke was still rising from the ruins of the house. All but part of one wing had been destroyed; only the separate kitchen block, the bathhouse, and some outbuildings had survived.

He rode out with the lieutenant through the settlement that straggled along the edge of the highway. Unlike the sturdy wooden huts with steep planked roofs at Dubovnoye, here the izbas were small and roughly thatched with moss-encrusted straw. Wattle fences sagged around the open yards. All was silent and apparently deserted. When they reached the fields, it was plain that little work had been done for some time. The hay seemed to have been taken off but the winter wheat was still standing.

The lieutenant reined in his horse. 'What a mess! Some military discipline might not have been such a bad thing here, after all.'

Vasily laughed. 'Yes, we'll have to get that crop taken in. We may have to resort to some determined persuasion.'

When they returned to the house, an official carriage stood on the driveway. Outside the estate office, Vasily was greeted by the welcome sight of a clerk from the Ministry who had come to assist him and also Yakov, who had brought fresh clothes. They were looking in dismay at the rubble.

Vasily dispatched them to find accommodation. He then sent for the members of the mir, the village council run by the serfs that would normally have regulated daily work on the estate. Only a handful of men appeared. It seemed that several of the others had been among the instigators of the revolt. With the help of the local priest, appropriate men were found to take their place. He recognised some from yesterday's fight. They stood before him, peering with suspicious eyes from beneath their brows, their shoulders hunched and their caps clasped in front of them.

'Work in the fields must restart as soon as possible,' he told them. 'It's not only your duty; it's in your own interest. Your families will starve unless the crop is brought in and ploughing gets underway.'

To his relief, the men made no complaint. They knew he was right and seemed relieved to return to normality. Later, one of the Internal Guards came to tell him that workers were returning to the fields.

Once the matter of the harvest had been resolved, it was time to deal with the queue of supplicants that had gathered outside the door of the estate office. They would have a range of problems, many unrelated to the recent troubles. As the first man entered and knelt before him, a lump rose in Vasily's throat. Sometimes, as a child, he had stood by a similar desk, watching attentively as his father dealt with the peasants' problems. He couldn't be as indulgent as Nikolay Petrovich had been but, nonetheless, he must try to be fair.

Time passed quickly. On his last day at the estate, a young woman came to the office. Holding the hand of her young daughter, she stood straight-backed in her blue sarafan, with her head covered. She seemed close to tears.

'My husband's been taken to the prison, lord,' she said. 'Will he be coming back?'

He couldn't lie to her. The rebels would be harshly punished, and those who survived would either be sent to the army or into exile.

'No, I think not.'

'Then I ask you to allow me to go home to my village.' She named a place in the south of the province. 'I have no one to take me in here.'

He sighed. The wives and dependent children of the arrested ringleaders were a particular problem. Unless their own relations could take them back, without a breadwinner, they could be driven from the village into a life of prostitution or crime. Thankfully, most were now safely settled with their extended families, but this woman seemed to have no such support.

'I shall speak to your new master. Provided he agrees to let you go, and I see no reason why he shouldn't, we'll make sure that you get home. Do you have food?'

'For now, sir.'

The woman left, apparently more content. His clerk looked

outside. There seemed to be no further supplicants; peace and order had been restored. Vasily signed the ledger with relief. Only the memory of the serf he had killed continued to trouble him. The man had no wife or children, but there was a grieving mother and several brothers and sisters. He would have liked to visit them to offer compensation, but the lieutenant had advised against it. It would not be appropriate, he had said. Vasily was not to blame in any way and must not reward rebellion.

The widow's brother-in-law arrived the following day in an agitated state. He quickly agreed to grant the request of the rebel's wife. Having reviewed Vasily's other efforts on his behalf, they stood together, surveying the blackened timbers of the house.

'Will you rebuild it?' Vasily asked. The landowner shook his head. 'I doubt it. We'll hire a new steward. My sister-in-law is unlikely to return here, I think. But I must sincerely thank you, Count, for your work here… Everything seems in order; the harvest has resumed. Matters could be much worse.'

'It was nothing… Just a few small things…'

'Perhaps, but I am very grateful.'

Vasily lost no time in returning to Oryol. It would be good to sleep in a decent bed once again. As he rode away behind the Ministry carriage in the late August sunshine, all was quiet on the estate. The Internal Guard was preparing to leave. Men and women were out in the fields, wagons were bringing the wheat into the barns, and dogs, children, and chickens were chasing one another in the road. He felt satisfied. Perhaps there was more he should have done here, but he had done what he could.

CHAPTER THIRTY-FIVE

September 1827 – St Petersburg

From Irina Pavlovna, Baroness Von Steiner
Kalinin Estate, Bryansk Oblast
August 1827

My dear Alexander Petrovich,
I hope that this letter finds you in good health.

I write to tell you that in recent days we have received a visitor. Count Leonid Fedulov wrote to us from Bryansk that he was travelling in the region and would like to call. I do not recollect ever having met the count, but he referred to you specifically in his note, saying that in addition to being your fellow officer at the Ministry, he was a family friend.

He arrived, very richly equipped, two days ago and stayed to dine. While here he asked questions about Vasily. He was keen to know when I had last seen him and where.

As we had agreed, I told him that the last time we met was shortly after the ball at the French Embassy in November 1825. I said Vasily had gone to his estate at Dubovnoye where, as far as I knew, he still remains. He learnt nothing more from me. I have to say that, although Count Fedulov may have no malign intent, his curiosity concerns me and I feel that I should continue to have no communication with Vasily for the time being. You know in any event that, as I expected, he has not tried to contact me.

We live a quiet life here on the estate. My cousin is

currently away and as I enjoy running the establishment, I am moderately content. Pavel Pavlovich has been spending some of the summer with us, and we have gone out a little in society for his sake. My brother will shortly be leaving to go abroad once again, I think somewhere in Europe, although he is not specific.

The position with regard to Baron von Steiner remains unchanged.

Your great-niece Sophia gives us all great joy. She has had her first birthday now and babbles away constantly, making us laugh. Thank you for the gift you sent. I would ask you, Alexander, to maintain your silence concerning this matter for the time being. I know that at some stage Vasily must be told about his daughter, but I do not feel the time is yet right.

As ever, your

Irina

Alexander frowned and set the letter aside. Before reading it, he had examined it closely. It did not seem to have been opened. Matters had come to a sorry state when even he worried about the security of his post. Of course, it was Fedulov who had removed Vasily's file. That was obvious now. Ever since Katya had refused him, he had felt uncomfortable about the man, knowing that the Count held an understandable grudge against his family. Now Fedulov seemed to entertain a suspicion that Vasily was culpable of something, or at least would like to think so. But what had he been looking for? The file certainly contained little of interest. Alexander doubted that he had any real evidence.

Should he write to Vasya to warn him to be careful? But

careful of what? Fedulov was still away on leave. He knew that he was then scheduled to make an inspection in the Voronezh region, or further east. Some distance from Oryol. That would keep him busy until Christmas, after which he would be obliged to return to Petersburg. All in all, there did not seem to be much cause for concern.

And then there was the child. He couldn't find it in his heart to be angry about that, although Vasily might have realised that certain behaviour had consequences. It troubled him that his nephew was unaware of his daughter's existence. But he must respect Irina's wishes; they both owed her that, and more.

The late summer evening was hot, and he rose to open the window. The air was not entirely fragrant. The Prince's barouche was in the stable yard. He would go down to see him later. The apartment was very quiet. It seemed that all but one of the servants were out. Perhaps tomorrow he would go to Katya's for dinner, or to his club. He must get out more.

CHAPTER THIRTY-SIX
The Laptev Estate

ON THE SUNDAY before Lisa's departure for St Petersburg, the family had, as usual, attended church. The priest blessed Lisa as she started what she hoped would be the first stage of her long journey.

There was a large company at dinner in the state dining room. Vasily noticed that Antonina Stepanovna was making the best of the situation. She had placed young Prince Uspensky to her right. When not in a state of terror, Yevgeny Filipovich was a lively young man. Vasily watched as he charmed everyone with his pink cheeks, his curly blonde hair, and elegant French. Not for the first time, Vasily wondered why he had decided to volunteer for the Russian army. Yevgeny probably asked himself the same question.

The first of the food was brought in. Today Boris was required to wait at table. Stiff in red livery, he carried the plates, avoiding meeting Vasily's eye. Poor Boris! Why did Antonina Stepanovna see fit to humiliate him in this way? Surely it wasn't necessary? Once the food had been served, the artist was obliged to stand motionless behind a guest's seat before the fine murals of ancient Rome that he had created.

Dinner came to an end, at last. Lisa and Vasily took the rowing boat out onto the lake, an arrangement that had the advantage of affording privacy for conversation while being in full view of the house.

Vasily shipped the oars. The boat drifted slowly in circles. Lisa trailed her hand through the water. She seemed happy and serene, secure in the hope that she and Mikhail would soon be reunited. Today, he knew he must speak of his own part in the December uprising. Would she be hurt that he had kept the truth from her? Resent the fact that he had escaped Mikhail's fate?

'Will you send a letter with me for Mikhail?' she asked. 'I know that he'll want to hear from you. But be careful what you write. All messages to and from the prisoners are censored, although I suppose they can't stop me speaking to him freely.'

'Of course I'll write. I'll send all my news to you in St Petersburg before you leave. Securing an audience with the Emperor will take time, I suppose.'

'I don't expect to go until after New Year. Madame Stenovsky is very hopeful that the Emperor will give his consent. Nicholas knows that the harshness of the sentences has been criticised and he's now keen to be seen as compassionate. At times I confess I'm nervous about seeing Mikhail again. We knew one another for such a short time, and I know that his time in prison has changed him. Perhaps I have changed, too.'

'His heart will be the same, I'm sure of it, and he knows you'll make a great difference to his life.' Vasily took the oars and pulled on them. But, Lisa, there are things I need to tell you before you meet him. We should have no secrets from one another when we part.' He stared at the surface of the water and continued: 'You know that I share Mikhail's beliefs. That must be clear enough. But you should also know that just before the uprising I, too, joined the Northern Society, took an oath of secrecy. I only knew Ryleev and some of the other conspirators briefly, but for that short time I was wholly committed to the cause. I didn't have the opportunity to make much contribution. Nonetheless, judging by the fate of others, I would have been condemned had I been taken.'

Lisa listened to him, her gaze steady. If she was surprised, she didn't show it.

'Two days before the uprising, my uncle discovered my involvement. He didn't tell me how he came to find out. Initially, I assumed it was through his work at the Ministry, but, had his colleagues known, I don't see how he could have helped me. I would have been arrested and charged along with all the rest. No, someone else must have told him.'

'I'm sure Alexander Petrovich has many informal contacts, Vasya, and in any event, whoever it was did you no harm. You have, after all, escaped arrest.'

'Well, thus far at least.' He paused. 'But when confronted by my uncle, at first I refused to confess anything. In the course of what turned out to be a long evening, he told me that I'd been a foolish dupe, that I'd been befriended by Pavel Kalinin because he intended to use me to penetrate the circle of conspirators. That seems plausible because, despite his reputation, Pavel Pavlovich continues to work as a Russian diplomat, apparently a trusted servant of the Tsar. But what really crushed me was the claim that Irina was complicit in her brother's plans. My uncle said that she'd been part of such intrigues before and that her love for me had been a sham. This confused and distressed me beyond reason.'

'Surely not! That can't be right. I can't believe that of Irène!'

Vasily shrugged. 'That evening, my uncle tried to break down my resistance. Finally, he resorted to having poor Yakov beaten, tortured. By that time I was frightened for myself, for Yakov, of course, and for Matvey, too. I was in despair about Irina, desperate about the fate of Mikhail and the others. Finally, I told him everything. I feel so ashamed that

I broke my oath, but I found it impossible to resist. At one point, he told me that I would never be able to withstand a police interrogation, and, of course, he was right. I would have betrayed everyone.'

'You shouldn't be ashamed,' said Lisa. 'Many of the rebels confessed. As soon as they were locked up alone, felt the weight of the chains, the damp, the darkness, they threw themselves on the Tsar's mercy. A few kept silent, and they suffered for it, but most sang like birds.'

'It seems that Mikhail never named me during the investigations,' Vasily continued. 'No one did, but my part was, as I said, minor. My uncle forced me to leave the city that night, and I was confined at Dubovnoye. The police did come to the estate asking questions, but when they saw that I was genuinely ill, they seemed to accept Alexander's assurance that I had been there for some time.'

'Yes, I wondered where you had gone so suddenly,' Lisa said. 'Your uncle said you had been obliged to go to your estate due to some problems there and had taken ill on the journey.'

'Well, that's true in part. By September, I was fully recovered, was allowed to receive letters, and learned the whole story of the failed coup. I felt guilty that I'd escaped punishment. I still feel that guilt. I was worried that Mikhail and the others would think that I was a coward, that I had run away.'

'I'm sure Mikhail would never think you a coward. I don't think he was even aware you'd left town. But, Vasya, I really can't believe that Irina was capable of knowingly using you for her brother's purposes. She was devoted to you. It was obvious how happy you made her.'

'On good days I can almost think that. But, Lisa, there are reasons to believe my uncle. The whole encounter with

Kalinin was strange. Why did he take so much interest in me after a chance encounter? I can't believe our meeting in the Summer Garden was a coincidence, either. He invited me to his dacha that day, but he barely knew me. And then, at first, I don't think that Irina was much attracted to me. She laughed in my face when I approached her. But just a few days later she wrote to encourage me to return to their dacha on the Okhta River. Was that under pressure from her brother?

'It's also certainly true that both Kalinin and Irina left St Petersburg suddenly, without warning. I had no clue that they were intending to go; Irina never told me, and I was her lover. And why hasn't she written to me, contacted me? She could probably find me if she wanted to. She may have come to care for me for a while; indeed, I think she was fond of me, but her feelings can't have been very profound. And now I fear she's forgotten me.'

Lisa shook her head. 'I'm convinced that she loved you, Vasily, and I would judge she still does, but even if she does know where you are, she may not think it right to contact you. Who knows what she thought when you suddenly disappeared? Perhaps she believes *you* abandoned her.'

'Abandoned *her*? No! She would never have thought that!' But it wasn't impossible. He had, after all, left without a word.

'And there are other possibilities,' Lisa said. 'Perhaps her brother advised her to forget you, knowing you were involved with the rebels. Perhaps she actually discovered you were in danger and told your uncle in the hope that he might save you.'

'Do you think she'd have done that?'

'Well, she certainly loved you enough.'

Vasily shook his head. Could Irina have told Alexander? But how had she discovered his part in the conspiracy? If she had found out in some way, and told his uncle, it would have been a risky and high-handed act, even if her aim had been to save him.

'And, of course,' Lisa continued, 'it always worried her that your affair would ruin your reputation and your future. She may simply have decided that since you must part eventually, she should let you get on with your life.'

'I think, sadly, that's very likely,' Vasily said. He looked out over the lake. Reflected clouds moved across the water. Lisa was speaking again.

'And surely you can see how much you owe your uncle, how courageous he has been?' Vasily looked at her. 'He took a great risk in arranging your escape. It would have been much easier to have you arrested, to throw you to the wolves. Many of the rebels' families did just that. They walked away from their brothers, sons, husbands; sometimes they denounced them themselves. Princess Volonskaya danced all evening at the Palace to prove her loyalty, while her own son was lying in chains just across the river.'

The boat had drifted to the side of the lake and was now caught up in rushes. Vasily took an oar and pushed away from the shore. A swirl of muddy black water bubbled up to the surface.

Perhaps Lisa was right about his uncle. He had believed that Alexander, deploring his involvement in treason, had wanted to punish him, while, if possible, keeping the family name unsullied. He had never had the courage, or faith in his uncle's affection, to challenge that idea. Had he been stupid? Blind?

He couldn't speak. He swallowed hard and looked away. Lisa took both his hands. She raised them to her lips.

'Vasya, you must help yourself now. Contact your uncle,

make peace with him. Find Irina, stop torturing yourself about her motives, discover the truth for better or worse. And then if all is well between you, find a way to be together. If her situation remains the same, it won't be easy, of course, but living an honest life is often not easy.'

She fell silent. A pair of swans flew down, streaks of white careening onto the water. Eventually, Vasily spoke. 'I'm committed to serving here in Oryol for at least another year, but I shall write to Alexander Petrovich. He may know where she is. Perhaps I can get some leave to visit him, to look for her. If the truth proves painful, I'll try to move on. But what you've said rings true. I may have been too quick to believe the worst. I'll miss you greatly, you know, Lisenka.'

'I'll miss you too, very much. But now I think we must go in. We shouldn't leave Yevgeny alone too long with Nadya and Miss Roberts.'

Vasily took up the oars and rowed with a few strong strokes to the landing stage. He leapt from the boat and handed Lisa out. He regretted her departure, but his heart felt lighter. He had regained a sense of purpose, and now had some sort of plan.

CHAPTER THIRTY-SEVEN
Oryol

A FEW DAYS after Vasily and Lisa had parted, Vasily asked Chudov for leave of absence.

Chudov looked anxious. 'Leave? What for? I'm not sure we can spare you...'

'Oh come on, Sergey...'

'Where do you want to go? Back to Petersburg?'

'Perhaps.' This wasn't true, but how would Chudov react to the suggestion? Vasily had suspected for some time that his superior was, if not spying on him, certainly keeping him under supervision.

'Well I've heard nothing from the First State Councillor, and he...'

'And he?'

Chudov flushed and looked shifty. 'Look, Vasily, we were told that you'd be staying in Oryol for two years and wouldn't be leaving unless recalled to Petersburg. As far as I know, there's been no such request, so where do you want to go?'

'I have some friends in Bryansk. I want to go over there for a few days, just a social call. I'll need permission to leave the province, a passport.'

Chudov rubbed his chin. He turned and looked out of the window.

'Do you need to go now?'

'Well, I would like to.'

'You can't wait a week or two?'

'Look, I give you my word that I'll be back within five days.

I'd like to go before the weather breaks and the roads become difficult.'

'You won't go alone.' It was a statement, not a question.

'I'll take Yakov with me, of course, and take a carriage.'

'Oh, very well. Make sure that Strogov doesn't need you.'

'He won't. The levies are complete. He's going to Moscow himself next week.'

'Well, you can organise the paperwork for yourself, you have my reluctant permission. But Vasily, don't let me down. No more than five days.'

———

Bryansk

They set out two days later, expecting to reach Bryansk the next day. The road between the two towns was busy with wagon trains as merchants took advantage of continuing good weather. They took a room in an inn close to the river. The following morning, having barely slept, Vasily rode out. taking a local man to guide him through the forests. The Kalinin estate house was about ten versts to the east of the town.

On the previous day's journey, he had seen the woodlands that covered the region, but it was only when he rode amongst the trees that he absorbed their extent and beauty. The leaves had begun to turn, the air held the spiced taint of woodsmoke, and the warm autumn sunlight threw lively patterns on the grass. Perhaps he would see her today; perhaps all between them would be made well.

The house surprised him. He had expected a classical mansion or a rambling wooden grange like his own home at Dubovnoye, but the Kalinin estate house was of recent construction. There was no pediment, no columns, just a stone face presented to the world. The panes of the large windows on the ground floor reflected the sun and he was dazzled as he approached the front door. No dogs barked, and no flunkeys emerged to greet him and take his horse. A ginger cat lay on the doorstep in the sun, indifferent to the visitor.

He hauled on the bell pull. After some time, a doorman in dark grey livery with silver braid stood looking down on him from the step.

'Your business, sir?'

Vasily wished he had thought to bring his card, but he hadn't expected a formal reception. 'I am Count Belkin, Vasily Belkin. I'm calling on Pavel Pavlovich, and his sister, the Baroness.'

'I am afraid both are from home, sir.'

Hope seeped away. 'Is any of the family here?'

'Georgy Mikhailovich, the Colonel's cousin, is in residence, sir.' The doorman scrutinised Vasily, as if uncertain that he was whom he claimed. 'Come in, sir,' he said at last. 'I shall see if he is available.'

He ushered Vasily into a large square hallway and indicated a hard wooden bench. All the inner doors were shut. Vasily took off his hat and waited. Voices echoed in the depths of the house. A child was babbling upstairs. He sat for some time, his formerly bright spirits entirely faded. At last, a door opened. The man who entered wore an old-fashioned frock coat of good cloth. He was middle-aged, overweight and bald. He in no way resembled his cousins.

'I'm sorry, Count Belkin. You should have sent ahead.' Georgy Kalinin's orotund tones rang with exaggerated politeness. 'You've had a wasted journey, I'm afraid; neither

Pavel Pavlovich nor Irina Pavlovna is here. I take it your business is with one of them?'

'Yes. Can you tell me where they are?'

'No, not precisely. They departed for Italy a couple of weeks ago. They will be wintering there. Pavel has some business in Milan…'

'Oh, I see.'

Georgy Kalinin looked out of the window. 'You don't have a carriage?'

'No, I rode out from town this morning.'

'Oh, good.' Georgy Kalinin appeared to hope that he might ride straight back again, and his next words confirmed this: 'Would you like some refreshment before you return? I am sorry that I cannot invite you to stay. My wife is unwell and some of the servants have returned to their villages.'

Georgy Kalinin shifted from foot to foot as he spoke. He was sweating slightly. Vasily knew he should leave. 'No, I shall dine at the inn. Is there any way I can contact Pavel Pavlovich?'

'Well, I suppose you could write to our consul in Milan. That would reach him in time, I suppose, but he'll be back in Russia by next summer unless he goes on to Vienna or London. Perhaps a letter to the Ministry in St Petersburg would be most likely to catch up with him. Yes, that would probably be best.'

'If you send to Colonel Kalinin or the Baroness, please ask them to write to me. I can be reached at the Governor's House in Oryol.'

Georgy Kalinin briefly surveyed Vasily's uniform as if noticing it for the first time. 'Yes, yes, of course. No doubt one of them will contact you.'

The conversation was over. The doorman already stood by the front door. Vasily took his hat.

Back on the gravel drive, Vasily took the reins from his guide, who was dismayed not to have been invited to the kitchens.

'I'm sorry,' Vasily said. 'I'll make sure you get a good dinner.'

The man shrugged. 'Some folks is hospitable... others, well...'

As the man gave him a leg up, Vasily glanced at the house. The sun had gone behind clouds, and he could just make out a figure looking down from an upper window, but, by the time he had settled and adjusted his reins, the shape had drawn back. Someone was taking an interest in him. Georgy Mikhailovich's sick wife, perhaps?

As his horse moved away, Vasily slumped in the saddle. It hadn't been much of a welcome. Georgy Kalinin had barely seemed to know who he was. But then why should he know? As the shadowed edge of the forest approached. He tried to rekindle his former optimism. It had always been possible that she wouldn't be here; in fact, it had been very likely. He should have kept his hopes in check. At least he now knew where she was, and with whom. But it would not be easy to reach her.

He turned back to take a last look at the house. The outsized windows reflected the sky where dark corvids flew, their rasping cries breaking the silence. Uninvited, his uncle's words echoed like a mournful canticle: *she's nothing but a harpy... hauling innocents into her net...*

He straightened his back, shortened the reins, and kicked his horse on. Hadn't he decided that couldn't be true? He must wait for her return and have faith. He could not give up hope.

CHAPTER THIRTY-EIGHT
October 1827 – Oryol

THREE WEEKS LATER, Vasily arrived at the government offices on a blustery Monday morning. He had been at the courthouse. A wait of over a year for a preliminary hearing was not acceptable to the Emperor, nor indeed to Strogov. Something must be done. When he walked into his office, still pondering the problem, he was surprised to find Chudov, his face scarlet, sitting at the desk next to his own. He had a pile of papers in front of him. Komarov also appeared unusually busy.

'Good morning, gentlemen,' Vasily said and turned to Chudov. 'To what do we owe the pleasure of your company, sir?'

Chudov seemed to simultaneously speak and grind his teeth.

'I, Registrar Belkin, have been ejected from my office!'

'Ejected? Why, Sergey? Are they going to redecorate? It wouldn't be before time. Shall I send for some tea?'

The door to Chudov's office swung open. Vasily turned. Leonid Fedulov stood in the doorway, his finely shod feet apart, the vine leaves on his collar glinting, a brass topped stick in his hand. Vasily glanced at Chudov. He had warned him that the Court Councillor might arrive, but they had decided, wrongly it seemed, that he would turn his attention to a larger office elsewhere.

'You're very late, Belkin.' Fedulov shifted the stick from one hand to the other.

'Good morning, Leonid Sergeyevich. Welcome to Oryol.' He gave a short bow, determined not to show any discomfort.

'"Councillor" to you, Belkin, or "sir",' Fedulov said. Vasily bowed again. He didn't reply.

'You are late, Belkin, and you are improperly dressed, as usual.'

Vasily remembered Fedulov's obsession with uniforms. He did up the top button of his jacket. He noticed that Chudov, pretending to adjust his collar, was doing the same.

'Yes, that's better. I don't want to see you incorrectly attired again. I repeat, Belkin, you're late.'

'I've been out with Colonel Strogov.'

'What business do you have with him? There's plenty of work to be getting on with here.'

'I work with the Gendarmes on business of mutual interest.'

'Sir,' prompted Fedulov.

'Councillor,' Chudov snorted. Vasily suppressed a smile. Sergey was trying not to laugh. In truth, it was the best response.

A clerk entered. Would one of the officers come down to sort out the petitioners?

'It's your turn, Registrar, isn't it?' said Chudov. Vasily made his escape.

Later that day, Fedulov called them into what had been Chudov's office. He had, he said, made a preliminary inspection, and there were many areas that fell short. Vasily didn't find this conclusion surprising.

'As inspector, I intend to remind you all of some basic rules so that a full examination can proceed without delay,' he said. 'I should like to be away from Oryol before the year's end. Firstly, all staff must attend, properly dressed for work, on time. That means before the hour of ten in the morning, and they must not leave before five.'

Chudov looked horrified.

'There will be no wandering off into the town during the hours of work without good cause. The practice of routinely using government transport for private jaunts will cease. I intend ordering a preliminary review to ensure that all paperwork is being correctly recorded and processed. Tea will only be drunk once in the morning and once in the afternoon. At least one officer will be here on duty on a Saturday; it is, after all, supposed to be a working day.' Fedulov paused and turned to Vasily. 'You, Belkin, will stop running around all over the province with the Gendarmes. Uniforms will be worn correctly at all times, both in and out of the office, and the rota of attendance at balls and town events will be more rigorously adhered to.'

Komarov, who had not gone to a ball in any capacity for many years, blew out his cheeks.

At one minute past five, Chudov, Komarov and Vasily left the Governor's House and went to the Town of Odesta to complain about their lot. They resigned themselves to weeks of misery before normality was restored.

———

Two weeks later, on a Saturday morning, Vasily was eating his breakfast. Matvey was working on his homework and Yakov was still in bed. The smell of warm bread floated in from the kitchen next door.

Although Vasily continued to think of Irina and had written a conciliatory letter to his uncle, much of his time and attention had been absorbed by Fedulov's inspection. The work had prevented him from riding out to the Laptevs, but, in any event, visits there now seemed less amusing. Lisa had, of course, gone with her father to St Petersburg, and Fedulov was taking full advantage of his open invitation to call. It was hard to take the man seriously. He gave off an aura of self-importance and barely suppressed frustration that, in other circumstances, might have been comical. Most of Fedulov's new rules had swiftly been flouted, although he had remained adamant that Vasily's work with Strogov must cease.

After a week, the Colonel had sent a note to the Court Councillor suggesting they meet to discuss cooperation between his men and the Ministry, as mandated by the Emperor. Shouting had been heard from the other end of the corridor, after which Fedulov, his face set, had informed Vasily that his liaison role would be resumed.

He heard a knock on the door to the street. Matvey jumped to answer it. The boy was warbling at someone in the hallway.

'Mister Golovkin, sir!' Matvey couldn't conceal his pleasure at the arrival of his teacher.

'I regret the early hour, Count, but I have been much troubled and unable to sleep. I thought I should come to see you as soon as I could.'

Matvey hovered by the door. 'You can take your books into my room, Matvey. And could you wake Yakov?'

He turned to Golovkin. 'How can I help you, sir?'

'Well, the problem is this, Vasily Nikolayevich. You seem to have a new officer at the Governor's House, I think, a Councillor Fedulov. He has now come to visit my estate on three occasions, and I have to say I find his interest increasingly oppressive. The first time, he said it was a courtesy call, that he had read some of my journalism and wanted to meet me.

He was very polite. He asked questions about the school. He didn't stay long.

'The second time he came, the questions were more searching. He asked whether I had recently had any works refused or altered by the censor. Well, you are aware, Vasily Nikolayevich, that in the current oppressive climate very little gets through unchallenged. He pretended to discuss the question of censorship in general, but I felt that he was probing to find out what exactly had been excised from my work. I left him for a few moments to seek out an example. It was an article on provincial life, I think, from which some comments on illiteracy had been removed for some reason. Anyway, when I got back, he was peering with great interest at the books on my shelves. I have had most of the volumes for years. Some were left to me by my father. Of course, it would be illegal to buy or sell a number of them now. Foreign books, I believe, are now subject to the same censorship rules as our own. Anyway, he didn't say anything about them and left shortly afterwards.

'He came again yesterday. His manner was altogether less polite. He demanded to know with whom I am currently in correspondence.'

Vasily frowned. Surely Fedulov already knew the answer. The Gendarmes routinely shared information about intercepted mail with the Ministry. Certainly, Golovkin corresponded with some liberal-minded professors at the university and other journalists, but there had been nothing subversive in the contents of the letters. He had, after all, warned him that they may be opened.

'He wanted a list,' Golovkin continued. 'I suppose he has the right to ask for that?'

'I don't know.' The Gendarmes had the right to do almost

anything in the name of 'protecting public morality', but as far as the Ministry went, he didn't know.

'But then he started to ask about the school once again. Could he see the titles of the essays written by the older boys? What books were they studying, and the like. It was quite frightening, really. I hope he's not intending to close the school down. He also asked, and this affects you and Matvey, Vasily; he asked if I taught any serf children. He said that if I did, I would be in trouble if I taught any over the age of eleven since the recent change in the law. I gave a somewhat evasive answer. But what's the man doing, Vasily Nikolayevich?'

'I wish I knew. He's only here for a while. He's inspecting the department. We expect to see him gone... we very much hope to see him gone... in a month or so. I wouldn't say his interest in you falls within his remit. Subversion, if that's what he's looking for, is now mainly the responsibility of the Gendarmes. As far as Matvey is concerned, I'll take full responsibility if necessary. Besides, I have no idea how old he is. He may well be less than eleven.'

'I don't think so, Vasily. I would say that he is certainly eleven, possibly more.'

'I wouldn't concern yourself too much, sir. If Fedulov becomes really troublesome, I'll mention the matter to the Chief of Gendarmes. Strogov is a reasonable man and has considerably more power than Fedulov. I suggest you be 'unavailable' if Fedulov calls again.'

'That's easier said than done, but I'll try. My sister is talented at seeing off unwelcome guests.'

Golovkin changed the subject, and they spent a comfortable hour in conversation. He then took his hat and stick and left.

When he had gone, Vasily sat in thought for a while.

Fedulov's hounding of the writer seemed unwarranted. He would certainly talk to Strogov. He looked out of the window; it was a fine day. He would ride out into the countryside. The roads were still reasonable, and the autumn rains had barely started.

He rode between the wooden houses at the edge of town and, once reaching open fields, kicked his horse on. The fresh breeze was welcome, but he couldn't shake off a nagging sense of unease. Why had Fedulov come to this relatively unimportant town? Surely the Ministry office here didn't merit this extensive inspection? What game was he playing? What was he looking for? Perhaps he should stop regarding him as a figure of fun.

CHAPTER THIRTY-NINE
November 1828 – Oryol

VASILY STOOD WAITING for Yevgeny under the arches at the edge of the Merchants' Court. It had turned cold; the sky had a yellow cast that foreshadowed snow. As he turned back into the market hall, he noticed Boris Abramovich. The artist stood by a pillar, wrapped in a heavy cloak with his hat pulled down over his brow. He was staring at the ground.

'Boris!'

Boris looked up. He seemed quite changed. His eyes, usually so quick and alive, were bloodshot. His face was shadowed with stubble. He didn't respond at once to Vasily's greeting but gazed at him with indifferent vacancy. Then he seemed to come to himself. He removed his hat and bowed. His once glossy hair was matted and unkempt.

'Good day, Boris,' Vasily said. 'Do you have business in town?'

'I've come to pick up some goods ordered in from Moscow, sir. But, we've missed you recently at the estate.'

'We've been enduring a departmental inspection. By the time the weekend comes, I'm not good for much. With luck, the worst will be over by the end of next week. Count Fedulov, who ordered the exercise, has stated his intention to leave within the month. He's been a regular visitor, I think?'

'Yes.' Boris looked down once again.

'But how's the new picture going?'

'The preliminary sketches are finished, and I've outlined the whole. The Kukarins are leaving soon for the season in

Moscow, so I needed to complete them. I still have to draw the dogs, but they aren't going to Moscow, of course. And then there's the frame.'

Vasily remembered that Boris was to adapt a large frame which had originally come from Italy.

'Will that be difficult?'

'Not really, but the wood is old, already carved, not easy to handle. It's in the barn at the Kukarins and still needs some attention.' He fell silent and looked away.

What was wrong with Boris? He was usually so keen to talk about his work. Before he could ask, the artist said, 'I'm not sure there will be any more commissions after this one.'

'Whyever not? You had such high hopes.'

'The master should be back soon from St Petersburg. We expect him by Christmas. I had hoped that the Countess would, as she had promised, approach her acquaintance to promote my services while he was away. But she has been distracted entertaining Count Fedulov and has been busy with other matters. In any event, nothing has happened. Now there's talk of the family going to Moscow for the season.'

'You should allow me to approach some of our officers,' said Yevgeny. Vasily had been so preoccupied by the alteration in Boris that he had barely noticed the arrival of his friend.

'That would be kind, sir! If I could secure a commission without relying on the Countess's help...' Boris paused and fell silent.

'I'll ask around. We're expected at the estate this weekend as long as it doesn't snow too hard. Shall we talk about it then?'

'Yes, by all means.' Boris seemed to have regained some spirit. A merchant's boy approached, wheeling a cart. 'Here are my goods. I look forward to seeing you gentlemen on Saturday.'

He turned to Vasily. 'Will you take a painting lesson, sir?'

'I should like to, if you're not too busy.'

'No certainly. It would be my pleasure.' The artist counted his crates and sacks, then bowed, replaced his hat, and made his way out into the street.

'He looks rather seedy,' said Yevgeny. 'Perhaps he's sickening for something.'

'Perhaps,' said Vasily. It could be that Boris was ill. He feared, however, that the artist's malaise might have a different explanation.

———

A week later, Vasily was working late. The sooner these tasks could be completed, the sooner Fedulov would leave and the life of the office get back to normal. But the work was dull. He stretched, yawned, set his pen aside and tipped back his chair.

A letter had arrived today from his uncle. It had merely confirmed what he already knew: Irina Pavlovna was currently travelling in Europe with her brother. Alexander didn't know where. Vasily sighed. There was little more that he could do. He must be patient.

The recent visit to Bashkatovo hadn't been a success. He had missed Lisa's company. Boris had remained taciturn and morose. But worse than this, Yevgeny had developed an enthusiasm for Miss Roberts. This, combined with Fedulov's relentless attention to the Countess, had created an atmosphere of cloying romance which, in his present mood, he had found almost insupportable.

It seemed he would soon be losing his new friend. War between Russia and Turkey was increasingly likely. Yevgeny's captain had told the yunker that he must be prepared to depart for the front before spring. Yevgeny's mood lurched between anxiety and enthusiasm, but, true to his word, he had been successful in drumming up several commissions for Boris.

Vasily heard a step outside. To his surprise, Fedulov emerged from the shadowed stairway. On seeing Vasily, he seemed taken aback and slipped quickly into his office. The room was quiet and chill. Vasily wondered if the doorman downstairs could be persuaded to bring some tea. He called a clerk and then applied himself once more to his work.

Time passed. It was getting late. Fedulov had not emerged. He started to pile up his papers. As he did so, the Court Councillor opened his door.

'Come in, Belkin, will you?'

Vasily checked his buttons. Surely there was not to be another lecture on uniforms?

'Sit down.'

Two candles had been placed on the desk. Fedulov could scrutinise Vasily, but his own face remained in shadow. Vasily reached forward to move one.

'Leave that alone.' After a moment's silence, Fedulov said, 'Why are you here, Vasily Nikolayevich?'

'I'm trying to finish the checking.'

'I don't mean tonight. I mean in general.' Fedulov spoke sharply. 'You know, Belkin, I often ask myself why you, a member of an ancient and well-connected family, are working as a low-grade officer in a second-rate provincial capital. It doesn't make sense.'

'It's a requirement for everyone going into the Ministry to spend time in the provinces before taking up a post in St Petersburg or Moscow. There's nothing strange in that. And of course, we have cousins here.'

'Cousins whom you had rarely met until recently. You could have got a dispensation from provincial service; most of the gentry do. In fact, thinking about it, I can't recollect any who haven't. Even I, who, as your mother has been quick to point out, haven't really made the grade socially, didn't have to fester for years in the backwoods when I transferred from the army.'

'My uncle thought it would be good experience, and so it's proving.'

'That's nonsense, Belkin, and you know it.' Fedulov's right hand was flexing involuntarily. One of the candles was smoking a little. Vasily's eyes were watering. He leant forward again to move it.

'Leave that alone!'

Vasily pushed back his chair. What was this about? Surely Fedulov wasn't interested in a friendly chat about his career prospects. But now he was speaking again.

'The truth is you're here because you're hiding from something. Isn't that right?'

Vasily felt Fedulov's eyes resting on him. His heart beat faster; this line of questioning was dangerous, and he must try to deflect it.

'I have no idea what you mean,' he said.

'Don't you? Well, let me speak plainly. I know more about you than you imagine, Vasily Nikolayevich. I know, for example, that, despite all appearances, you are a committed radical. I also know that you were not, as you pretend, on your estate at the time of the December uprising two years ago. You were in Petersburg, and between the time of the death of Alexander and the events on Senate Square, you conspired with a number of the main players, including the late and unlamented Ryleev, Mikhail Bestuzhev, the Stenovskys, and others. I know from the record that you were a sworn member of the Northern Society and attended several meetings. You were prominent at Konstantin Chernov's funeral. You dined with Baron Rosen. You consorted with that liberal anglophile Kalinin, and you even bedded his colourful sister. You're in correspondence even now with a known English agent. You borrow banned publications from a man who is regularly silenced by the censor, and you allow him, illegally, to educate your serf.' Fedulov paused and shook his head. 'You know, Vasily Nikolayevich, there are now men working the Siberian mines who are less culpable than you.'

Vasily was tempted to say that their punishment had been wholly disproportionate to their crimes, but he resisted the impulse. His heart was now pounding, but he tried to calm himself as he considered Fedulov's words. Some of his comments were accurate, but others were not. He knew for a fact that, prior to his arrest, Ryleev had destroyed the records of the Northern Society. He had never met Rosen. Fedulov could well be bluffing.

'You're talking nonsense, Fedulov. I was on our Moscow estate. I was ill in bed. The police report confirmed it.'

'But their report is based on a lie. I know it's a lie because you were seen. I have a witness to the fact that you visited Ryleev in Petersburg on the evening of 12th December, just two days before the uprising. A number of other conspirators joined you.'

That, of course, was true. He had indeed been there. Vasily's stomach clenched. His collar felt damp with sweat. The smoke of the candle troubled him. He must control himself and admit to nothing.

His chance encounter with Ryleev might well have been observed, but even if that were the case, he didn't think that he had been recognised on other occasions. There had been no social events following the death of the Emperor, and the theatres had been closed. He had visited Irina's apartment almost every evening and sometimes dined there. He had once met Mikhail at an almost-empty tavern. Otherwise, he had remained at home. He had, of course, acted as a go-between, gone to the Naval barracks at Kronstadt, but the man to whom he had delivered papers was now in Siberia. He doubted that he would remember the dark-cloaked courier who had met him briefly in the shadowy gatehouse. Of course, anyone might have seen him in the street. But it had been winter, and he had been well muffled up.

'You say nothing,' Fedulov said.

'I have nothing to say, Leonid Sergeyevich. Whoever your witness was must have been mistaken.'

'I don't think so. The man is very reliable. He saw you quite clearly at around five o'clock in the evening. You were in the street outside the Russian American House. You had visited Ryleev, of course.'

'I can't have been seen since I wasn't there.' He had to brazen this out. 'Besides, had I been there, you've no way to prove it. Poor Ryleev isn't in a position to comment. I'm sorry, Fedulov, that won't stick.'

'Something else was brought to my attention quite recently. It seems that same night, a prisoner left St Petersburg. I have seen the register at the barrier. Strangely, however, there is no evidence of a pass being issued, nothing in the police records about the transportation, no escort recorded, no police wagon signed out. Were you that prisoner, Belkin?'

Vasily forced a smile. Fedulov had done some digging, it was clear, but did he really have proof that he was the prisoner in question? Convicts were regularly transported in secrecy, under cover of night without the knowledge of the police.

'Look, Fedulov, I thought you said that I was in St Petersburg at the time of the uprising, not masquerading as a prisoner two days beforehand. I will confess to you that I was in sympathy, remain in sympathy, with the aims of the Northern Society. But you have, as far as I can see, no proof of anything. If you do, I suggest you have me arrested.'

'I wouldn't be too hasty to turn yourself in, Belkin.'

'Who said anything about turning myself in? I repeat if you think you have a case, find Strogov. Have him arrest me.'

'You really wouldn't like that, Belkin.' Fedulov picked up a bronze paperweight and banged it softly and repeatedly on the desk as he spoke. 'Things have changed a good deal since State Prisoner Stenovsky and his friends made their journey to the east. They had carriages and travelled in relative comfort, although their shackles, which I understand they are still obliged to wear, must have been inconvenient. Those arrested now don't enjoy the same privileges. Vasily Kolesnikov, for example, has had to walk the whole way with common criminals. He'll still be on his journey, I suppose, if he hasn't been murdered. No, you don't want to be arrested, Vasily, and you know I wouldn't want that either. I'm sure that if you are open with me we can reach a happy compromise, come to some arrangement.'

So Fedulov wasn't interested in seeing him behind bars, at least not yet. He wanted to frighten him, punish him for the insults of the past, and blackmail him. The Count's lavish lifestyle couldn't possibly be supported by his salary or the receipts from his impoverished estate. His game was extortion, and he was his latest victim.

This made the response simpler. 'Well, Leonid Sergeyevich, if that's all, I need to get home.' He rose to his feet.

'Where do think you're going? I haven't finished!' Fedulov gripped the paperweight.

'I think you have, Count. *I* certainly have nothing further to say to you.'

Vasily moved the smoking candle so that it illuminated Fedulov's face. Fedulov sprang to his feet and pushed the candle away. It crashed to the floor. He glowered down at Vasily, who took a step backwards and forced himself to meet his gaze.

'If you feel you must, Fedulov, call on Strogov in the morning; present your evidence. If he believes it, I'm sure he'll be happy to arrest me. You can tell him that I'll be at home. Otherwise, I may be a little late in.'

'Don't think you've heard the last of this, Belkin.' Vasily caught the latent frustration. 'I could make a case against you now, as you know full well. As time goes on, I'll find more evidence. My next stop will be your estate. There will be someone there who remembers when you arrived before Christmas two years ago.'

'I strongly advise you to avoid my grandmother, Fedulov. She's unlikely to warm to you. And now if you'll excuse me…'

Vasily moved towards the door. He heard Fedulov's steps behind him and turned to face him once more. The man's eyes were pebble-dark, his breathing heavy and erratic. He still clutched the paperweight. Was he going to strike him? After a few seconds, Fedulov lowered his arm and looked away.

'Good evening, Fedulov. I'll leave you to lock up.' As Vasily walked through the outer office he heard the hollow chime of metal on plaster as the paperweight hit the wall.

Vasily stayed at home the next day. He had lain awake most of the night, reliving his encounter with Fedulov. Had his instincts failed him? Perhaps the man did have enough evidence to have him seized? If so, the heavy hand of the Gendarmes, or worse, the city police, could fall on him at any time. The more he thought about it, however, the more confident he felt that, although Fedulov knew something of the truth, he had little or no real proof of his guilt.

In the mid-afternoon, there was a loud knock on the door. Vasily's heart turned over. Had he been wrong? Had they come for him? He rose to his feet and took a deep breath. He must keep calm and confess to nothing.

Yakov was already in the hallway. 'Oh! Good afternoon, sir.'

'Is Vasily Nikolayevich at home?'

It was Chudov's voice. He didn't usually call at this hour. He seemed to be alone, so he probably hadn't come to detain him, but was he here to prepare him for the worst? Aching with apprehension, Vasily stood up.

Chudov was grinning as he removed his hat. 'Good news, Vasily! He's gone!

'Who's gone?'

'His excellency, the Count…'

'Who? Fedulov?'

''Yes, he didn't come to the office this morning, but we didn't think much of it. Later, he was seen being driven away at great speed from his lodgings in a hired tarantass. He took the road to Mtensk, so must be on the way to Moscow. He said nothing to his clerk. I suppose we shall have to send any outstanding papers after him.'

Vasily's head spun and his knees felt weak. It seemed he had seen the man off, for now, at least.

'Why do you think he's gone in such a hurry?'

'No idea, but we knew that his inspection was almost complete. He might have had the courtesy to tell us he was leaving, I suppose, but Fedulov wasn't long on courtesy. More snow is likely; perhaps he wanted to beat the weather.'

'Would you like tea? Some food?' Vasily would have liked to discuss this startling development further.

Chudov shook his head. 'No, I'm going to spend the evening with my family. You and I shall celebrate tomorrow. I'll book a table at the hotel!'

He disappeared and, within a few moments, Vasily heard him laughing with his children next door. It was dusk. There was a thin covering of snow outside, and, as he watched, flakes like small plump birds started to fall once again. Yakov was lighting the samovar and the bitter whiff of smoking charcoal filled the room. Matvey returned from school. They lit the lamps.

Vasily closed his eyes. His pulse slowed, and his muscles relaxed. This reprieve was welcome, but he was not yet safe. Fedulov had clearly been in a hurry to leave. He was probably on his way to Dubovnoye. The Count would ask questions there to try to pick holes in his story. His grandmother would probably see the man off, but he couldn't be entirely sure. A letter of warning would not arrive in time and might be intercepted. His only course was to wait and pray.

CHAPTER FORTY
Winter 1827/8 – The Province of Oryol

ON THE EVENING of Fedulov's departure, the snow persisted for several hours, the first of many heavy falls that interwove the dark months of that long winter. By early December, the town of Oryol lay under a white fleece. By March, vast heaps of icy sweepings blocked every street corner, roofs fell in and fences collapsed under the weight of snow. Country roads became dangerous to travellers, who risked hours stranded in their carriages as drifts piled up around them. Lives were disrupted and letters were lost or delayed; even the couriers' sledges, generally reliable, sometimes failed to get through. Vasily struggled along the icy streets to the Governor's House in the morning and back in the afternoon. Sometimes he took a droshky even though the distance was short.

Many of the tasks mandated by Fedulov remained undone as the Oryol office reverted to normal. Chudov had examined the hole in the wall of his office inflicted by the paperweight and, not for the first time, made ugly comments about the Court Councillor's habits. Vasily's fears that Fedulov had gone to Dubovnoye seemed to be unfounded. He received a letter from Karl Feodorovich that made no mention of him. All was well at the estate; his grandmother was in good heart, but heating the house was even more troublesome than usual.

Shortly after Vasily received this welcome news, it became apparent that Fedulov had disappeared. The Count, it seemed, had never reached Moscow. When the papers that had been sent after him arrived at the Ministry, an urgent note came in return asking if Fedulov had turned back, but nothing had been seen of him. Later, further inquiries came from St Petersburg.

Mystified but relieved, Vasily fell into a routine that, on the whole, satisfied him. He continued to work on behalf of petitioners, some deserving, some less so. At Strogov's behest, he spent time at the courthouse trying to expedite proceedings and seeking to give such advice as he could to poorer tradesmen and workers who were awed and confused by the proceedings. He ruefully recalled that Kondraty Ryleev had done similar work in St Petersburg.

Yevgeny's departure for Turkey was delayed, and he and Vasily attended some balls and receptions and also visited the theatre. Vasily had enjoyed brief flirtations with a number of girls from the local gentry, but he was aware that his service uniform did not have the allure of the hussars' fur-edged dolmans and in any event he did not want to encourage greater intimacy. There were also parties of a less polite nature, from which he extracted some fleeting pleasure.

Yevgraf, the steward from the Laptev estate, had struggled into Oryol on a couple of occasions with news. Boris continued to work on his painting of the Kukarin family, helped by his son Petya. Progress had been slow, but it seemed that the artist was in better spirits, cheered by the prospect of work from the military. The Countess had taken advantage of a brief dry spell to take her sister and daughter to Moscow, where Count Laptev had joined them at the home of his relations. They intended to spend the winter there. To Yevgeny's regret, Miss Roberts had accompanied them.

———

The months passed. In early April, the snow and ice sometimes relaxed into a thaw. On one of those warmer days, a message came from Yevgraf: there was trouble at the estate; could Vasily Nikolayevich come at once?

It would have been good to know the nature of the trouble. The Laptev family was still away in Moscow. Vasily decided to be cautious, although the serfs were unlikely to be restive in winter when the family was absent. The Gendarmes were involved in an exercise at the prison, so Chudov sent a request for a small escort of hussars. Vasily ordered a carriage.

The journey out to Bashkatovo took longer than usual. The going was difficult; the icy surface of the road was breaking up, revealing potholes and creating pools of water. When Vasily finally arrived, Yevgraf came out to meet him and, in silence, led him to the outbuildings close to the church. They stopped outside the carpenters' hut. The steward looked at his feet.

'It's Boris. I'm afraid he's in here, sir.'

'Boris? What's happened to him?'

Yevgraf shook his head. 'You'd best take a look.'

Vasily entered the workshop. Blinded by the sunlight, he couldn't at first make out the human form that swayed beneath the creaking central beam. But then, as his eyes adjusted to the shadows, he saw the body, all that remained of Boris, his teacher, and, latterly, his friend. He stood transfixed as the scene took shape: the rope, the bent neck, the face swollen and suffused with blood, and, below the feet, the overturned stool.

He heard voices outside, clear in the bright air. People were running from the house or the village, their footsteps muffled by a cover of icy slush. There was a shout as someone opened the wooden shutters and light shafted into the hut.

He realised that they looked to him to take control. He turned to the soldiers. 'Secure the door and order the serfs to return to their work.'

The tallest of the hussars stepped out into the yard, his hand on his pistol, his polished boots crushing the straw-strewn mix of mud and snow. His companions moved to join him. The noise outside seemed to fade but then was rekindled by the sound of a woman's cries. Yevgraf wavered, hesitating by the door. His hands trembled as he removed his cap.

'His wife,' he said.

'Try to keep her out of here.'

Vasily watched the steward push past the peasants gathering outside the door. Now alone, he looked around. Propped along one wall were panels of sinuous fretwork, decoration for the windows of peasant izbas. Beyond the joist and its heavy burden, the half-finished copy of a dining chair in the English style stood among curled wood shavings. In the far corner on an old armoire lay a palette and a scatter of spent paint bladders.

The noise outside the workshop had abated; the soldiers' presence had subdued the crowd. Edging past the body, he walked to an easel that leaned against the wall and turned over a sheet of paper resting on it. It was a sketch, a study for a larger work. He recognised the roughly drawn head of the Countess. After a moment's hesitation, he replaced the drawing and scanned the workshop again. The displaced stool was the only sign of disorder. He could smell sawdust, linseed oil, and varnish. Along the wall hung the tools of the carpenter's craft: bradawls, lathes, and a range of saws, each lined up in its place.

Yevgraf stood in the doorway.

'The wife's gone away with her mother, sir,' he said, and

after a pause, continued: 'This should never have happened, Count Belkin. They should have let Boris do the work he was trained for. His talent was wasted. There was talk of freeing him, but it never came to anything. He needed someone to make the case on his behalf.'

Vasily nodded. Should he have foreseen this? Could he have done more to support Boris? Perhaps, but it was too late now. A cloud passed across the sun. The light in the workshop faded, and the air seemed to chill. He pulled his greatcoat closer about him and replaced his hat. The hussars had returned.

'If the crowd has dispersed, there's nothing more for us to do here,' he said. 'The death of a serf isn't the Ministry's concern. We should return to town. Have the body taken down, Yevgraf, and carried to his house. You should write to Moscow and inform Count Laptev.'

The steward watched the soldiers leave and followed them. Vasily looked more closely at the corpse. Feeling nauseous, he turned away and involuntarily clutched the carpenter's bench. He took several deep breaths; the cold air made him gasp. He squared his shoulders and walked out into the yard.

His official carriage stood by the stables, gleaming on its winter runners. The three horses shifted under their curved yoke, their nostrils steaming. There was no sign of the coachman. The man was probably taking tea, or something stronger, in the kitchen block, gossiping with the cooks.

'Can you find my driver?' he said to a young serf who was kicking through the drifted snow.

In a few minutes, the coachman hurried from the house, heaving his cloak onto his shoulders. Vasily climbed into the carriage and ordered the man to drive on. The troopers followed.

They passed the great manor house, square on the carriage sweep, the windows blinded and the portico deep in shade. The bushes and statues on the drive stood in their sacking shrouds. When the carriage turned onto the highway, its motion changed. The coachman steered the horses along the sides of the fields to avoid the deep-driven roughness. The only sounds in the silence were the clinking of harnesses and the whispering of runners on the melting snow.

CHAPTER FORTY-ONE

'ARE YOU ALRIGHT, Vasily?' asked Chudov as Vasily walked into his office. 'You look terrible.'

Vasily's head swam. It was warm inside after the drive through the snowy fields. He cleared his throat and fought back unbidden tears. 'The news from Bashkatovo isn't good. The artist at the estate, Boris Abramovich, has been found dead. It seems he hung himself.'

'He was a serf, wasn't he?'

'Yes. That was his problem.'

'Well, we can't do much about serfs' problems, as you know.'

'I feel I must go back out there tomorrow, Sergey. My cousins are away. There's no family at the house, just a few old retainers. I should at least visit the widow, pay respects to the body, and talk to his son.'

'He definitely killed himself?'

'Yes, I don't think there's much doubt.'

'Well, do what you think is right. Do you need another escort?'

'No, I'll take Yakov with me. I don't foresee any trouble.'

Vasily turned away. His heart ached for Boris. Again, he wondered if he could have done more, if he might have changed Count Laptev's views? The cause of Boris's death was plain. The artist had no enemies, no quarrel with anyone. An unhappy accident of birth, the scourge of serfdom itself, had created the demons that had destroyed him.

On the following day, Vasily and Yakov visited the neat wooden izba in the village that had been Boris's home. The body was laid out, but there was no icon on Boris's breast, no candles at his head and feet, and no priest intoning the psalms. There would be no Christian burial. By committing the worst of sins he had condemned himself to a state of perpetual torment.

Vasily remained with Boris's widow for over an hour. There were no other visitors and there was no sign of Petya, Boris's son. Vasily gave her money to cover the cost of the burial and ensured that she had the means to feed herself and her family. Once satisfied of this, he and Yakov made their way up to the mansion house. There was no doorman on duty. The house was ice-cold and silent, the furniture and lights all covered. Only a small breakfast room and the divan room were open and warm. An elderly retainer was reading in Laptev's study, huddled in a cloak. There was nothing for Vasily to do here.

Before they left, Vasily took Yakov to the studio at the north end of the house. He wanted to see it again. Perhaps now it would be dismantled? When they entered the room, they were surprised to be met by a gust of warm air. The stove was lit, the shutters were open, and the room was bright in the April sunlight.

Boris's large painting appeared to be finished. Prince Kukarin stood with a proprietorial air on a stone staircase, surveying his park. He was flanked by the Princess, his sons and his dogs. Petya was working on the canvas, applying a coat of varnish to the surface with careful strokes. When he saw Vasily and Yakov, he put down his brush and bowl. His eyes were red-rimmed and his smudged cheeks marked with tears. He tried to greet Vasily but started to weep once again. Vasily wrapped his arms about him. The boy sobbed for some time.

When he was released, Vasily sat down on the divan and invited Petya to sit beside him. Yakov had disappeared. 'It's good that you're finishing the picture, Petya. Your father would have been pleased.'

The boy nodded, dumb for a moment, and then he said, 'It's important to finish it, sir. We'll not get the fee else. My mother needs the money, you know, to live. I expect it's the last thing I'll work on. I've not yet got the skills to paint something like this.'

'So what will you do?'

'I don't know. Probably duties in the house, perhaps the fields. When Father was here, I worked with him for much of the time, but I'm not a good woodworker. It used to annoy the Count. He'll be on my case, now.'

Damn Boris! By killing himself he had probably deprived the boy of any chance to develop his talent. He would speak to Laptev about Petya when the Count returned to the estate, but he was doubtful of success.

Vasily remembered how bitter Boris had seemed when they had met at the Merchant's Court in November. Clearly, the Countess had proved a disappointment to him and hadn't promoted his work as she had promised. Had she also lost interest in his person? On his rare visits here before Fedulov's departure, it had been impossible to ignore Antonina's overblown lips whispering confidences into the Count's willing ear.

But he hadn't foreseen this tragedy. On the one or two occasions that he and Boris had met over the winter, the artist had seemed to be happier, cheered by the prospect of commissions from the garrison. Not every soldier was leaving town. Boris had drawn a fine sketch of Yevgeny for which the yunker had paid generously, and this had encouraged interest from others. The spring was coming. Why abandon hope now?

Yakov brought tea, hot and strong, which they sat and drank together. Time was getting on. They should return to town. Petya picked up his brush once more; he seemed a little brighter. Vasily sifted through some of Boris's sketches. Many were studies for the Kukarin painting, and there were also portraits: the Countess, Nadezhda, Yevgeny Filipovich, and even one of himself. Then he came to one that gave him pause.

The paper was quite unlike the rest. It was covered from top to bottom with images of a face he had tried to blot from his mind: a mélange of pictures of Count Fedulov, drawn in black ink, tiny and precise but unmistakable.

CHAPTER FORTY-TWO

April 1828 – The Province of Oryol

WHEN THE SPRING thaw with its attendant floods was past its peak, a herdsman from the Laptev farms rode out one morning from the estate. He was planning to inspect the condition of the summer pastures by the river on the far side of the Oryol to Mtensk Road. His shaggy broad-footed pony picked its way along the mud-clogged track between a patchwork of dark silt and bright floodwater. The rooks had returned. In places, the grass was drying out and flushing with green shoots. Pockets of snow remained in blue-shaded hollows.

When the herdsman was just a long stone's throw from the main road, he noticed a bulky object to the right. There was an oval pool here where he sometimes watered his herd in the summer months. Pitched down the slope between the water and the track was a small carriage, a tarantass. Its rear was in the pond and its shafts, now broken short, pointed up to the sky. Beside the carriage lay a dark shape, which on closer inspection proved to be the body of a horse decomposing in a tangle of harness.

The herdsman slid down the bank and lifted the flaps at the mouth of the vehicle's domed interior. He cried out and leapt back. Losing his footing, he tumbled sideways. Then, regaining his balance, he stood for a moment, gasping for breath and gripping the edge of the roof. He lifted the flap again. A body was half sitting, half lying under the hood. The corpse was covered in furs and seemed to have toppled slightly to one side. One of its arms was stretched out towards him, as if in supplication. The flesh of the face, the only skin that was visible, had a strange green hue, but the features were recognisably those of a man.

The herdsman remounted and turned his pony back to the estate house, intending to raise the alarm.

———

Some hours later, Chudov sent for Vasily and together they went to see Strogov. The police had reported that the body of the missing Court Councillor, Leonid Fedulov, had been found.

'It seems to have been an accident, your honours,' a police officer told them. 'A field serf from the Laptev estate found the vehicle this morning. The driver must have mistook his way because he was down a side track, not on the main road. He'd toppled the carriage down into a pond. Perhaps he knew he had taken the wrong road and was trying to turn? Snow drifts have hidden the carriage and the body all winter, but the thaw has revealed all. The Count left the city in late November, so he has been there for four months. There's no sign of the coachman and there was just one horse out of the three, lying dead at the scene. The others had been cut loose.'

'Do you know how Fedulov died?' Strogov asked.

'Seems he froze to death, but one of his legs were broken, presumably in the accident. That's the doctor's view. We have the body at the police house. Fedulov couldn't get out of the carriage, and we think the coachman went to fetch help. It seems he never returned. The Laptev estate house is only a verst or so away from the spot, but he never showed up there. On the day Fedulov left, the weather got steadily worse. Snow started to fall in the late afternoon, and then continued all night. There was a wind, some drifting. By the morning the carriage might well have have been buried.'

'Why wasn't the carriage discovered that day, or the next?' said Chudov. 'The road's a busy one, someone should have gone to help. Was there no marker? Didn't the driver tie a scarf or flag to the shafts to alert passers-by? That's the normal practice.'

'That would have been a problem, sir, because the shafts were damaged in the accident, it seems. The carriage wasn't far from the main road. It would have been visible had the shafts been erect.'

'I see. It must have been quite a smash. Thank you, officer.'

'Well,' said Chudov, 'that solves the mystery of the missing Court Councillor. I don't think he'll much be missed. The facts look pretty clear. It's strange that he's been lying here just a few versts from town all this time. I thought he might have had an accident on the way to Moscow, but I also thought it possible that someone with a grudge had caught up with him. He wasn't popular.'

'No, he was a strange fellow,' said Strogov. He paused for a moment. 'I'd like to send a man out there, take a look at the site, at the vehicle, organise a search for the driver. That's a bit of a loose end. We need to investigate properly, not take the Police's word that it's an accident. The Minister will want to know what happened to his man. I expect I'll have to write a report, or at least arrange one. Do you want to go, Sergey Ivanovich?'

'Not much,' said Chudov. 'The roads will be deep in mud. It will be hell going out there in a carriage, it's too late for a sleigh, and I'm not one for riding out on horseback at this time of year. Send young Belkin here. He likes to get out of town, don't you, Vasily? He can write your report for you.'

Vasily rode out the next morning with one of the gendarmes. As the horses picked their way between deep puddled potholes and patches of mud, he was buoyed by a sense of relief. Fedulov would never now go to Dubovnoye asking awkward questions. In truth, it was hard to regret the Count's death.

When they reached Bashkatovo, Vasily and the gendarme called into the estate office and told Yevgraf their business. The steward had his horse saddled, and together they rode down the drive, a little way along the main road, and then took a track to the left. The tarantass had been moved and was pulled up on the sodden grass.

Vasily inspected it. He climbed inside. All of Fedulov's possessions and the furs that had wrapped him had been removed. Just wisps of old straw remained. There was no blood, nothing of interest as far as he could see. He clambered out and looked at the front. The reins hung in coils from the box. Two had been cut to let the horses loose.

'Have you got any strange horses in your stables, Yevgraf?'

'No, I have not! At least...'

'Can you check?'

'I would have thought that if some unknown beasts had trotted in, the grooms would know about it, but honestly, you never know. There are so many.'

'Can you check, anyway?'

Vasily ran his hand along the shafts. They certainly had been damaged, snapped off about half the way along. But had they been snapped off? Or had they been cut? He looked at them closely. The breaks were clean, the wood smooth. He thought he could see the marks of a saw. Surely, if they had broken from the impact of the accident, the wood would be rough, splintered, and irregular, and the broken shafts wouldn't be of equal length.

'Look, Yevgraf,' he said. 'I think these shafts have been cut through by someone. That's strange, isn't it? Why would someone do that?'

Yevgraf shrugged.

Vasily walked back to the point where the carriage had left the track. The pond had thawed completely, and a breeze furrowed the surface. He looked around. There was no sign of the sawn shafts, although some discarded reins trailed down the slope and a shattered carriage lamp lay some distance away on the bank. Then he noticed something under a bush at the side of the pond. It was a scarf. A red scarf, the sort that might be used to attract the attention of passers-by on the road, to alert them to an accident, to a carriage under the snow.

Vasily put the scarf into his pocket and said, 'I think I've seen enough now, Yevgraf. You say there's no sign of the driver?'

'No, sir, not as far as I know.'

'If you find his body, send word immediately.'

———

'I think Fedulov's death might not have been an accident, sir.'

Vasily was sitting in Strogov's office. His trousers were spattered with mud.

'How so?'

Vasily told the Colonel about the sawn-off shafts. Someone, he suggested, had not wanted the wrecked tarantass to be found. Someone had wanted Fedulov to die, buried in the snow.

'You mean the accident was staged? Was deliberate?'

'It's possible. Either someone arranged to have the Count driven out into the snow and abandoned, making it look like an accident, or, alternatively, someone opportunistically took advantage of an accident that had already occurred. Either way, Fedulov was injured in the crash and was unable to get out of the carriage. Remaining there in freezing temperatures would mean certain death. There had been some snow already, and more was expected. The vehicle would soon be buried. What the killer didn't want was some Good Samaritan to come along the Mtensk Road and see the carriage, or its shafts sticking out of the snow. As it happened, of course, the tarantass lay concealed for the whole winter.'

'I find the first theory more persuasive than the second,' said Strogov. 'The way Fedulov was seen leaving town at speed might suggest he had been taken against his will. The coachman, presumably the hired killer, has disappeared, as of course he would. The idea of a passer-by coming across the carriage and deliberately leaving the passenger to die is less likely, although it could have been an opportunistic robbery, I suppose. There are thieves along that road.'

And now, to Vasily's concern, Strogov continued, his cheeks pink with excitement. 'I think we must bring Golovkin in for questioning! And there are others, too, who would like to see Fedulov gone. While he was here, he visited several of the names on our list of potential troublemakers. And then there's Chudov! There may have been something that Fedulov discovered in the course of his investigations here. Chudov must be questioned, too!'

'Well sir, I know that Fedulov had been investigating Golovkin's activities, I told you that myself. But the man's not young and you've read his letters yourself. You know he's pretty harmless. And as for Chudov…'

Vasily would have liked to say that Chudov, who had trouble getting out of bed in the morning, was incapable of arranging the murder of anyone. However, it was true that several people had had motives to dispose of Fedulov, including, of course, himself. But he knew he was innocent, of this crime at least.

Strogov, waving his pipe in the air as he spoke, continued to indulge in a torrent of speculation. It was clear he found the prospect of a full-blown police investigation inspirational. 'We don't know, Vasily. I'm not suggesting Golovkin drove the man out there himself. There are plenty of rough types down by the Orlik who would do the job for a song, you know. I do know that Fedulov had quite a large file on Golovkin and his contacts. One of his correspondents was a man who was recently arrested and put in a St Petersburg guardhouse for a month!'

Vasily shook his head.

'I don't think it was Golovkin, sir; neither do I think it can have been a robbery. I checked Fedulov's possessions at the police house. All his things seemed to be untouched, and his purse was full. Since he didn't announce his departure, he could have been abducted, as you suggest. But I think I know what happened to him. I need a day or so to collect the evidence. Forgive me if I don't enlighten you further at this stage. I may be wrong and don't want to make false accusations.'

Something was troubling the Colonel. He flushed and cleared his throat. 'Vasily Nikolayevich, the thing is this: I think it's possible that you, too, could have a motive for killing the Court Councillor.'

Vasily's heart contracted. What did Strogov know? Perhaps he should have let him believe that Fedulov's death had been an accident.

'If I let you go out to collect your evidence, Registrar, I want your word of honour that you won't seek to avoid questioning. In short, that you will come back.'

'You can send one of your men with me if you like,' Vasily said. 'Although my task would be easier if I were not escorted by a gendarme. Colonel, you have my word. I shall come back and then you can ask all the questions you want.'

'Very well, Vasily. You have three days.' Strogov turned to his papers.

Vasily went to find Chudov. 'The Colonel wants me to go out to Bashkatovo again, to make further inquiries.'

'Do you need an escort?'

'No, I'll take Yakov with me.'

Chudov waved a piece of paper at him. 'I've had a request from your highly elevated uncle in St Peterburg. He asks me to grant you some leave, a request I can hardly refuse. He says he needs to discuss family business. Well, Vasily, I suppose that's it. You won't be wanting to come back. He'll offer you a comfortable post in Petersburg at three times the salary.'

'Don't think that, Sergey. I'd like to get this business of Fedulov resolved, and then I'll go to the capital for a week or so, but, all being well, I intend working out my last eight months here. I'll only be at Bashkatovo for a couple of days. Let's talk about it when I get back.'

Vasily returned to his desk. He sat down heavily and contemplated his inkwell. Why did Strogov want to interview him? Did he just want to carry out a thorough investigation into everyone associated with Fedulov's inspection? The Count's report was unlikely to be flattering, but surely that was no reason to murder the man. Perhaps, more worryingly, the gendarme had learned something of Fedulov's suspicions about his own past. But if so, why had Strogov not tackled him before? Had he been waiting for conclusive proof? Whichever interpretation was correct, he must try to unravel the real cause of Fedulov's death without delay.

He hung his head and swore under his breath. Why had these complications arisen now? Now, when, at last, he could go to St Petersburg, make peace with his uncle, and finally, perhaps, resolve his doubts and uncertainties. Had his past finally caught up with him? Was Irina irrevocably lost? Would he now be condemned to permanent exile, or worse?

CHAPTER FORTY-THREE

Kalinin Estate
Bryansk
March 1828

Dear Alexander Petrovich,

The winter has been, as you know, very severe. We have been cut off much of the time since November. Few letters have arrived.

My cousin, Georgy, who you will remember was living here over the winter, has returned to Moscow and I think that the time has come to communicate with Vasily, and perhaps meet him, if only to discuss the future of our child.

Oryol is not too far distant from here, so perhaps if he has the time, and still has the desire, he can visit me. I should like to have things settled by the end of the summer. I may decide to go abroad, to the south, perhaps to Italy.

The days have been long and dark, but of course lighter than with you. We have kept warm and Sophia is a constant source of amusement. I will wait to hear from Vasily and, of course, from you.

Your, Irina.

———

My dear Irina Pavlovna,
Thank you for your letter. What a winter it has been!

We are expecting Vasily in Petersburg shortly. I have sent for him since I feel that he has suffered in the provinces for long enough. If you agree, I shall inform him of your whereabouts at that time. I feel sure he will make arrangements to come to you.

I assume you would prefer to tell him of Sophia yourself? May I suggest you write to him here? I do not anticipate that he will return to Oryol, but, as ever, his future remains somewhat undecided.

Having said that, before the winter set in we received some good reports about 'Registrar Belkin'. He has been commended for his diligence and courage by the new Provincial Chief of Gendarmes in a letter to Count Benkendorf. (I confess I cannot imagine what he has done to deserve that!). His superior at the Ministry has also reported well of him. He is likely to be promoted!

I was disturbed when I learned before New Year that Count Fedulov had been undertaking an inspection in Oryol and can only think he has been continuing to take an interest in Vasily, but as far as I can tell without any result. He left there in November and now seems to have vanished without trace. In the light of his disappearance I have felt able to open an inquiry into some of his activities, and it is hard to escape the conclusion that his misdeeds may well have caught up with him.

The Prince is well, although sometimes feels his age. My

sister-in-law, Maria, spends much of her time with Katya, Princess Polunina and Nikolay her little son. Another child is expected. I am thinking of retirement. I should like to see something of the world before I am too old.

Well my dear, I must have this taken to the courier. I wait to hear from you.

Your, Alexander

CHAPTER FORTY-FOUR
April 1828 – Oryol

THREE DAYS AFTER their last meeting, Vasily sat once again in Strogov's office. He tried to suppress a sense of unease. The Colonel had said nothing further of wanting to question him. Perhaps the evidence he had brought today would be enough to allay any suspicion.

The gendarme was examining three items: a carpenter's saw, a sheet of paper, and the red scarf that Vasily had found at the scene of the accident. He picked up each in turn, then looked up. 'Well let's hear your report, Registrar.'

'I left town with my man Yakov the morning after we last met, Colonel. The roads haven't improved, and it took us some time to get to the Laptev estate. The steward offered us accommodation at the mansion, which we were pleased to accept.

'You'll remember that the serf artist, Boris Abramovich, killed himself there a week or so ago. Thinking that this may be connected with Fedulov's death, I made inquiries at the estate office about Boris's activities around the time the Court Councillor departed from Oryol. It appears that on the day before Fedulov drove away, Boris went to the Kukarin estate to make some sketches of the family dogs. While there, he intended to adapt a frame for the family portrait that had been commissioned by the Prince. There's a record at the Laptev estate office that Boris used a pony and cart to take him the ten versts to the Kukarins on that day. The following day, both the pony and cart were marked as returned.

'Having established these facts, after some refreshment, we

set off to the Kukarin estate. We confirmed with the steward there that Boris had arrived and started on his work. He hadn't finished by the time it got dark. It was November and the days were short, so he stayed the night. He set off home the following day in the early afternoon. The steward remembered that Boris was anxious. There was already some snow on the ground, and the threat of more. He didn't want to get stranded on his way. If you remember, it snowed heavily from the late afternoon.

'I believe that when Boris was almost back at the estate he noticed that there had been an accident off the road to the right. He could see the shafts of the tarantass high in the air, with that red scarf attached as a signal. He went to investigate, and he found the vehicle upturned on the slope, its rear resting on the ice of the pond. Inside he found Leonid Fedulov, his leg broken, unable to get out.'

Vasily fell silent as he reimagined the scene: the artist, amazed and delighted at finding his rival entrapped. Fedulov's terror, his increasingly pathetic pleas as the artist refused to help him. Boris would have taunted Fedulov and laughed at his plight. He would have told the Count that he had ruined his life and that now he, Boris, was going to destroy his. He had hurled the scarf into the bushes as he started work on the shafts with his saw. What despair Fedulov must have felt as, left alone in the silent fields, he saw the snow mounting up in great drifts around him.

'I can't be sure that Boris intended to kill Fedulov, but he was certainly indifferent to his fate.' Vasily continued. 'Boris didn't know where the coachman had gone; help might have been on its way. But he wasn't acting rationally. As it happened, of course, there was no rescue.'

Strogov interrupted him: 'The coachman's body was found this morning, in a ditch near the driveway to the mansion,' he said. 'He had suffered a blow to the head and had a hip flask in his hand. He may have been injured in the accident, or by something or someone else. Boris could have overtaken him on his way home and killed him, I suppose. In any event, he died in the snow and was buried there. We know he never raised the alarm.'

Vasily nodded and continued. 'If the coachman had been drinking, that might explain why he took the wrong turn on the road and then tipped the tarantass into the pond. Perhaps he was drunk when he started. Witnesses said that Fedulov left Oryol at a furious pace. But, to continue the story, one of the loose horses was found in the Laptev stables. No one had noticed it. There are a lot of animals there. One more or less didn't much exercise them. The other horse is unaccounted for.'

Vasily picked up the saw. 'According to Boris's son Petya, this is the tool that Boris used to adapt the picture frame. We checked it against the incisions on the shafts of the carriage and they seem to correspond. Once they were cut, of course, the tarantass was no longer visible from the main road, and certainly not when it was covered with snow. We checked the viewpoints.'

'But why did the serf bear such a grudge against Count Fedulov? Why the desperate fury? The hatred?' asked Strogov.

Vasily told Strogov Boris's sad history. 'I think it was when Boris became intimate with the Countess that his hopes were revived once again.'

'Intimate?'

'Yes, I don't know when their affair started, or how long it continued. It's clear that while they were lovers, the Countess encouraged Boris to think that she could persuade her husband, to allow him to pursue his artistic career. He would be required to pay a portion of his earnings to the estate and become an artist full-time. She even hinted at the chance of complete freedom. She secured the commission with the Kukarins, which much pleased him. He had really begun to believe that he might be released from his other work. However, when Fedulov started visiting the house everything changed. Boris found himself back in the carpenters' shed. He was also required to serve at table. I was there on one occasion. It was terrible to see his humiliation. His hatred of Fedulov was understandable. The Countess had eyes only for the Count. Boris and all his dreams were forgotten.'

'Was the Countess, uh… intimate with Fedulov?'

'Opinions differ in the servant's hall. Yakov is an excellent source of information. If Fedulov and the Countess were lovers – and having observed them together, I sense they were – they were discreet.'

'But not so discreet that Boris didn't notice,' said Strogov. 'Count Laptev seems remarkably tolerant of his wife's behaviour.'

'Laptev's a strange man. I have to admit I find him hard to fathom. It's generally known, however, that he and his wife are not close. They seem to get along by tolerating one another's weaknesses. From September, the Count was away in Petersburg, which would have increased the opportunity for intimacy between the Countess and Fedulov.'

Strogov frowned. 'And the artist killed himself. I wonder why he left it so long after the event?'

'It was in part, I think, because he realised that the crime would shortly be discovered, and, for whatever reason, he had done nothing to try to conceal it. He killed himself at the first sign of the thaw. The carriage would soon come to light; the serfs would have gone out into the fields, and all would be revealed. That was probably the trigger but, you know, sir, Boris was a very disturbed man. I think what really caused his death was the collapse of his dreams, his disappointments both in love and in his vocation, his art. The crime was secondary, a symptom of his disease, if you like. But he certainly believed that Fedulov was to blame for the loss of the Countess's affection, and with it his hopes of freedom.

'I found this in his studio. It tells you something of his state of mind.' He showed Strogov the paper over which Boris had compulsively drawn the small studies of Fedulov's face.

Strogov was silent as he studied the paper. 'Well, Vasily Nikolayevich, you've a talent for investigation, I think.'

'It's easier when you know, or have known, the parties involved.'

'Possibly, but you've been very organised in your approach.'

'I assume you won't now be interviewing poor Golovkin.'

'No, probably not.' The gendarme looked downcast. He had been cheated of his investigation. 'Write it all down for me, Registrar and I'll consider the case in full.'

Vasily rose to leave. Strogov looked up. 'Oh, Vasily, there remains one matter I need to clear up.' Not inviting Vasily to resume his seat, Strogov drew a document out from his desk drawer. It was handwritten and not very long. 'Count Fedulov left this deposition in my office. It concerns you. He makes some serious allegations.'

Vasily met Strogov's gaze, then looked down.

'I think you probably know what this says,' Strogov was saying. 'Do you have any comments?'

Vasily cleared his throat. His mouth was dry. A tight knot of despair sat beneath his breastbone. He knew he couldn't lie about his past forever.

'I think I know what Fedulov alleges, and I am prepared to

admit, sir, that I sympathised with the cause of the men of the fourteenth. I knew a number of the conspirators personally; I briefly joined their circle. My closest friend is now in Siberia, as I think you know. I was lucky not to be arrested simply because of my association with him. Had I been in St Petersburg in the aftermath of the revolt, there is little doubt that I would have been questioned at least.'

Vasily swallowed. Remembering Mikhail, his voice had faltered, but as he forced himself to continue, the words came more easily. 'And I still stand by my convictions. Serfdom is a terrible evil. You only have to consider this case before you. In any other country, or at least in most other civilised countries, Boris Abramovich would have been free to follow his destiny. But here, he was used like a plaything, picked up for a moment's amusement, and then put down, humiliated and mistreated. And we've seen the tragic consequences. I can give you many other examples, but I don't think I need to.

'I must also confess that I believe that autocracy in Russia must end. Despotism holds the country back; it affects the well-being of all. It's impossible and inefficient for one man to be above the law, be its sole arbiter. You can see the chaos we experience every day here in Oryol. The system leads to inertia, favouritism and corruption.'

He looked directly at Strogov. The gendarme's face gave nothing away.

'If these views make me a criminal, sir, then you must detain me. With the help of Fedulov's "evidence", you could achieve a conviction. A court would probably find me guilty, were I to be given the benefit of a court. But I must tell you that if I was once a revolutionary, I was not much of one. I would no longer support a violent uprising and have never supported coercion and terror. The revolution in France showed how terror can beget terror. Most, but admittedly not all, of the December rebels were opposed to a similar outcome here.

'Had the revolt succeeded, I've come to believe that chaos and violence would have followed. Despite their best intentions the conspirators would have ended up fighting among themselves. There would have been civil war.'

'Yes, I fear you are right,' Strogov said.

'If I've learned anything during my year here, Colonel, it is that you can bring about change without resorting to armed insurrection. There are better, more certain, ways to make a difference. Even under the current repressive regime here In Russia, every man has the power to fight local injustice, right individual wrongs, perform small acts of kindness. Of course, I continue to hope that, in time, a true democracy and a sound rule of law will be established here, but in the meantime, there is plenty to be done.'

Strogov raised his hand. 'I think you've said enough.' He leaned back in his chair, reached for his pipe, filled it with tobacco and tamped it down. He turned towards the window and stared for several minutes at the clouded pane.

Vasily knew he must prepare for the worst. Surely this newly minted policeman wouldn't refuse the chance to detain a confessed revolutionary? At any moment, Strogov would shout to his men to seize him and take him away.

Strogov cleared his throat. 'That's a very eloquent defence, Count Belkin.' He stood up, drew a spill from a holder on his desk, and, opening the door of the stove, lit his pipe. He took a corner of Fedulov's denunciation and, holding it away from him, set fire to it. The paper flared and blackened and finally fell into the sand tray. The smell of burning filled the room.

Strogov deposited the smouldering remains into the stove. 'Sit down,' he said.

'Thank you, sir,' Vasily could hardly speak. He sat, hung his head, and closed his eyes. He felt Strogov's hand, firm on his shoulder. 'Let's forget about it, Vasily. If we exile all the good men, how will we stop the bad, eh?'

After some moments, Strogov walked back behind his desk. 'I hear that we are going to be losing you.' he said.

Vasily looked up. 'Who told you that, sir?'

'Chudov says you're off on leave, and that you are unlikely to be back.'

'I don't know why he says that, Colonel. I'm supposed to be here until February of next year. I'd intended to stay through this summer and possibly next.'

'He thinks that your family have other ideas for you.'

Vasily sighed. 'No doubt we'll discuss that when I'm in St Petersburg, but I'm in no hurry to change my life at present. I'm content in Oryol. I find St Petersburg too cold, too formal.'

'Yes, I never feel comfortable there. You could think about transferring to us, to the Gendarmes. We would welcome you. It's not easy to find the right people. You could probably come in as a lieutenant.'

'That's good of you, Colonel, and I will think on it, but as I've said I don't want to make any decisions now. I do have one project that might affect what I do, but aside from that it's my intention to return here.'

'Oh, yes. May I ask what that is?'

'There's a woman I need to find…'

Strogov threw back his head and laughed.

CHAPTER FORTY-FIVE

April 1828 – Chita Settlement, Eastern Siberia

My dear Vasya,

I write in haste. The men from the Stenovsky household, who accompanied me on my journey, and of course Vera, my dear brave maid, must return home tomorrow. I shall entrust this to them. Sadly there is no time for Mikhail to write since his letters must be inspected and approved.

The most important thing to tell you is that, with the greatest happiness, I write as a married woman! A condition of the Emperor's consent was that I could only meet Mikhail 'as his wife,' so on my arrival rapid arrangements were made for our wedding. The first time I set eyes on him for over a year was when he entered the small wooden church here with his brother. The prison Governor gave me away, while Nikita supported Mikhail.

When the prisoners approached, I was alarmed by the sound of their chains. They are obliged to wear them constantly, even at night. Mikhail's fetters were removed at the door since the priest insisted that he should not wear them during the ceremony, but they were quickly replaced. He says that he is used to them, despite the fact that they have injured his legs.

We were allowed half an hour alone together, but then all the men were obliged to return to prison. I shall see Mikhail again for three hours the day after tomorrow. The former Princes Volonsky and Trubetskoy and their wives both begged the Governor to allow us to meet sooner, but wives and husbands are only permitted to meet on two afternoons a week, and the Governor does not dare to change the rules.

Mikhail is very thin, but he is far healthier than he was when we met at the post house outside St Petersburg. For one thing he is no longer bald!. Alexandrine has told me that he has been more resilient, and in better spirits, than poor Nikita, who bitterly resents his fate. I will tell Mikhail more news of you when we meet again, but he asked me to send you his most sincere affection and to tell you that he is happy that you are safe and well. He did add that due to surveillance his letters are not really worth receiving.

We arrived here in Chita three days ago after a journey of over two months, largely by sleigh. The kibitkas provided to us by Madame Stenovsky withstood the long journey without too much difficulty although all needed some repair along the way. Our passage across the frozen lake Baikal, encounters with wolves, and our other adventures must wait until a later letter. In Tobolsk I met the Governor of Siberia, and, in order to proceed further, was obliged to sign a paper renouncing my noble status and rights of inheritance. I have also lost the right ever to return to Western Russia. I did not realise this would be the case, but I was hardly going to turn back on account of it!

I am living with Alexandrine in a small wooden house. It is comfortable and warm enough. The settlement supports just a few hundred souls and comprises two streets, the church, and the prison itself where the men live in conditions that are very overcrowded. Maria Volonsky has told me it is expected that in time the prisoners will be allowed to remove their chains, and those who are married spend more time with their wives, but permission is awaited from the Emperor through Count Benkendorf. It seems that I will have to learn to cook, since although local servants have been engaged they are not very skilled.

Well my dear Vasya, I must seal this and give it to my messenger, along with letters to my parents. I have to confess it is strange here, and I dread Vera's departure. She is my last link with home. I know life will be difficult at first, but I have no doubt that I was right to come, that I have made the right choice. More than that, I know I shall be happy, that my marriage is secure. Think of me sometimes, pray to God for both of us, and be sure to write. We both long to hear your news.

Farewell my dearest friend, I embrace you,

Lisa Stenovsky.

CHAPTER FORTY-SIX

May 1828 – Moscow

THEY APPROACHED MOSCOW from the south along the road from Podolsk. Vasily was not in a hurry. They had travelled in easy stages, sleeping in their carriage overnight and eating their own food.

He had left Oryol with regret. He had bid farewell to his colleagues, to Strogov and also to Golovkin, who remained unaware of the recent threat to his peaceful existence. War had been declared on Turkey in April, and Yevgeny had already departed, with reluctance, for the front.

It was good to be driving through open country. Matvey spent much of the journey on the box with the driver, engaging him in incessant talk, alive to the sights along the way. Yakov mainly slept. They intended staying two nights in the old capital before travelling on to St Petersburg. A colleague of Alexander Petrovich in the Moscow office of the Ministry would accommodate them.

They had to wait in line at the Serpukhov Barrier to be admitted to the city. After an hour or so, they showed their passes to the sentinel on duty. He asked their business and where they were staying, and then they were waved in between pillars topped by the imperial crest.

Signs still remained of the fire that had engulfed Moscow fifteen years before. A good deal of building was continuing, and the city streets were blocked by wagons. Vasily barely recognised the areas they passed through. The high-walled Kremlin was largely unchanged, but all the streets seemed different – straighter, wider. Stone buildings of classical design had been established or were still being built, and boulevards were being created in place of the old city fortifications. Little remained of the curious Muscovite architecture that Vasily remembered from his childhood. Just the churches stood, bright-coloured or whitewashed, beneath their burnished onion domes. Many of the temporary shops that used to edge the streets had been cleared away, but the stalls of the tallow-makers still huddled at the Varvarovka Gate, selling candles below the Kremlin wall. The air was alive with the sound of bells. That, at least, was as it had always been.

The following day, Vasily took Matvey on a walk around the city. They admired the gardens that had been established in the ditch that once surrounded the Kremlin. They went into the fortress itself, saw the guns and huge bell, and climbed the great Octagon Tower. From the top, they wondered at the sprawl of the city itself: its golden cupolas; its green and brown iron roofs; its bright lime trees; the Moscow River, a silver snake moving through the distant fields. Vasily pointed out the road along which Napoleon had marched on the city in 1812. They saw the markets, the Merchant Court, and the new Theatre. They walked past the site of the Belkins' former home. A Palladian-style palace was rising on the plot. Vasily tried not to care but failed.

At last, exhausted, Vasily took Matvey for dinner at an eating house, where he was fascinated by the red smocks and wide-topped boots of the waiters. He chattered continually and ate a good deal: soup, fish, cabbage, and a honey cake, and when he got back to their rooms, he fell asleep immediately. Vasily looked down at the sleeping boy. How devoted and loyal he had been. Matvey's care during his illness had probably saved his life. Somehow, he must make sure that his dedication was rewarded.

Vasily yawned. He would have liked to sleep as well, but he had business to complete before he could rest. He pulled on his uniform.

———

Count and Countess Laptev were staying with relations in a house to the west of Tverskaya Street. Vasily sent up his card, and, since he had sent ahead to say that he was coming, was irritated to be kept waiting for almost half an hour.

He was not, as he had expected, shown to one of the main reception rooms, but was taken up two flights of stairs to the Laptev's private suite. The Count and Countess were seated in a cramped sitting room. They rose and greeted him cordially, but the Count repeatedly swept his brow with his kerchief and Antonina Stepanova could not meet Vasily's eye. She seemed somehow reduced, her shoulders narrowed, her whole bearing shrunken.

'Vasily Nikolayevich,' the Count said, 'It is good of you to call on us on your way to Petersburg. You were lucky to catch us here. We intend returning to Bashkatovo shortly.'

'I know you don't like to be far from the estate for too long,' Vasily said.

'No, indeed, we didn't expect to be from home until now.'

'You won't want to miss another hunting season, I dare say, sir.'

'No, no, indeed, although the lack of hunting last—'

Antonina Stepanova frowned and interrupted him. 'You find us still in distress, cousin. The news, as you know, from

Oryol has been most upsetting. Two deaths on the estate within two weeks!'

'Yes,' Vasily said. 'And I have to confess I find it somewhat strange that you at least, Count, haven't yet returned home.'

Gavril Ivanovich raised his eyebrows and again mopped his brow. 'We shall go when we're ready.' He settled his feet firmly on the carpet. 'The discovery of the body of Count Fedulov was a surprise to us, of course, but we believed he'd left the area. We didn't think that he'd had an accident on our doorstep. As for the shameful self-murder of the serf, well, I don't see that as a reason for precipitate return. We had nothing to do with either death. And, actually, Vasily, I don't see what business it is—'

The Countess interrupted once again. 'Boris Abramovich was always moody and highly strung, you know.'

'I see you haven't been appraised of the full details of what has happened on your estate while you've been absent,' Vasily said. 'That surprises me.' He was not, in fact, surprised at all, but he had wanted the Laptevs to remain in ignorance until he confronted them. Strogov had agreed to this deceit with reluctance.

'It seems that the deaths were not actually a coincidence.'

'What do you mean?' Count Laptev's chin twitched up.

Vasily outlined the sequence of events. He noticed the Count catch his wife's eye before she looked down and remained staring at the floor. Her hands weaved and twisted, swivelling her rings.

'The conclusion that must be reached is that your serf, Boris, murdered the Court Councillor, and possibly his driver, before killing himself some months later. One can speculate about his reasons, but there was clearly bad blood between the serf and Fedulov. Colonel Strogov is anxious to speak with you. He is concerned that public morality may have been compromised, but I can't really say more.' Vasily paused. 'Therefore, in my capacity as an officer at the Ministry of the Interior, I have come to inform you that Colonel Strogov requires you to return home as soon as possible so that you can throw what light you can on the matter.'

Count Laptev stirred in his seat, failing to hide his agitation. The Countess had turned pale. Vasily rose to go. Then, as if having second thoughts, he sat down again.

'I did wonder, Gavril Ivanovich, what arrangements you are intending to make for the artist's family? I think that you would receive a good deal of approbation if you were seen to be helping them at this difficult time. They'll suffer a great drop in income. Boris was beginning to build a following. You're probably unaware that Prince Uspensky had secured some commissions for him from the garrison.'

'Well I wasn't intending...' the Count began, and then he said, 'I didn't realise that. What do you suggest, Vasily Nikolayevich? I can see that there are those who might think that we are in some way connected to these sad events. In some way implicated. But I can't imagine why.'

'No, of course not, sir. But people do talk, and, were the facts to emerge... It would be better, I'd say, for the investigation to remain confidential. Don't you think so? Had the serf not killed himself, had he been brought to trial, that would have been impossible, but as things stand... So, I repeat, sir, how are you going to help Boris's family? I think you said you were hoping to stand for election once again this year for the role of Marshal of the Nobility? It would be an excellent way to demonstrate your compassion.'

Laptev was silent.

'I have an idea, sir,' Vasily said.

'Do you?'

'Well, you know, Boris has a son, Petya. It did occur to me—'

'Absolutely not,' said the Count.

The Countess raised her eyes. 'Gavril, do listen to our cousin. I think he has our best interests, the interests of the family, at heart. Listen for my sake, for both our sakes, and think of Nadya! She already has a sister who has made, shall we say, an unusual marriage. The circumstances surrounding the death of Count Fedulov might indeed be misinterpreted...'

'What are you asking me to do, Count Belkin?' Laptev dropped his kerchief and bent forward to retrieve it.

'Allow the son to fulfil his father's promise. Boris told me once that the boy is very talented. Petya is of the right age to follow his father to Stupin's school. It's still in operation. Alternatively, you could send him to Venetzianov's new establishment in Tver. And if you were, in time, minded to grant Petya his freedom, there are now groups of benefactors who will pay a good sum to free boys with talent and send them on to the Academy. It may end up costing you very little.'

'Apart from my principles,' the Count said.

'Gavril, please!'

After a pause, the Count said, 'And you think that this gesture of generosity would mean that any investigation will remain private?'

'I can't guarantee it, but the Colonel is a discreet man and does go out of his way to avoid creating – what shall we call it? – unnecessary trouble.'

The Count still seemed to hesitate.

Vasily felt a stir of impatience. These two privileged people had each, in their own way, played games with the life of a sensitive and talented man and had destroyed him. He didn't care what would become of them, what rumours about them would be spread around the town, what positions in the local administration Count Laptev would fail to secure. However, if some good could come out of all this, he would play the game and be content.

But now the Count, finally, was agreeing with his proposal. The Countess had appealed to him again.

Vasily rose to his feet.

'Won't you come downstairs to meet my cousin, Vasily?'

'No, Count, we have an early start in the morning. I'm anxious to see my family after so long. I expect to return to Oryol in a month or so. We shall meet again there I'm sure, and you can tell me what arrangements you have made for the boy's future.'

'Yes, yes, I quite understand.'

Vasily bowed his way out. As he walked down Tverskaya, he took off his hat and, to the surprise of passers-by, threw it high into the air.

CHAPTER FORTY-SEVEN
May 1828 – St Petersburg

Kalinin Estate

Bryansk Oblast

April 1828

Vasily Nikolayevich,

Alexander Petrovich has written that you wish to contact me. I now must communicate with you. Contrary to what you have been led to believe, I have been living here on our estate in Bryansk for some time.

Your uncle may by now have told you that it was I who interfered with your plans two and more years ago. I know that informing him of your involvement in the December plot might seem to you, even now, to have been an unforgivable intervention, but I hope you understand that I acted for your own good. I thought you to be in danger of ruin, and I think that I was right. I would do the same again. There is more to say more about this but I would prefer not to do so in a letter.

I also write to you, Vasily, because I should no longer keep a matter of great importance from you. You and I have a daughter, Sophia. She was conceived at about the time of the ball at the French Embassy in November 1825 and will be two years old in August. She is a lively and beautiful child who seems to have inherited your sense of humour.

It is right that you should meet your daughter, so I am asking you to come to me here when you can this summer. We should discuss her future. Perhaps we should *also discuss our own, although the Baron lives on and I am still not free.*

I will of course understand if you do not wish to come, but I would be pleased if you could tell me if you will not. I am minded to go abroad in the autumn. I do not feel strong enough to face another winter here. The forests are extraordinary, but they are empty and silent. It is hard to enjoy them alone.

For my part, Vasya, I will be plain with you. I want nothing more than to see you once again. I was almost overcome by grief when you came to our estate last year and I could not greet you. I was concerned that to do so may still endanger you, and, besides that, my cousin was strongly opposed to it.

I love you, Vasya. I will always love you. I have loved you from the moment we met in the Summer Garden, but this must be your choice.

Your, Irina

Vasily read the letter through twice. Alexander stood with his back to him, apparently transfixed by something in the stable yard. The apartment was quiet. His uncle had been alone when they had arrived from Moscow, and Vasily had sent Yakov and Matvey out to eat in the city.

'How long have you known about our child?'

Alexander half turned towards him. 'Since before she was born. I've kept in touch with Irina Pavlovna since the night you left here.'

'And you thought it right to keep it from me?'

'She didn't want me to tell you. That was her right. I've done what I can to support her. I knew she must tell you eventually.'

'She says it was she who informed you of my part in the conspiracy. Is that true?'

'Yes, she came to me at the Ministry on the morning that I forced you to leave here.'

'But how did she find out? I never mentioned the plot to her.'

'Well she discovered the truth somehow, and just in time, incidentally. She didn't know very much, few details. I suspect Kalinin let something slip, and she put two and two together. She came to me because she thought she wouldn't be able to persuade you to leave, to abandon the cause, your friends. She knew that I had the power and the resources to oblige you to go.'

'And what of Kalinin? Do you know what his plans for me actually were?'

'No. We still have unfinished business, which now includes unravelling what he was expecting of you. But that's a story for another day, I think. He disappeared from Petersburg just before the rising. I suppose he was concerned for his own safety, thought he might be implicated in the plot. But, even now, despite his known liberal views, he still seems to come and go to Russia as he pleases, continues to work for the diplomatic service. Perhaps he left because he thought the rebels might succeed. God alone knows what really drives the man and who pays for his fine English boots.'

'And the tale you concocted about Irina? You told me that her brother used her as bait to lure me into his schemes, that she had lied about her marriage.'

'Vasily, I had to get you out of St Petersburg that night. Surely you must see that? You were surprisingly obdurate. You seemed determined to see me as your enemy when my only aim was to get you to safety before it was too late. It was Irina's sole wish, too.'

'You said she was a harpy!'

Alexander held up his hand in defence. 'When she told me of your involvement in the conspiracy she knew that when I confronted you I would not paint an attractive picture of her behaviour and motives. She didn't want you to stay here for her sake, and, yes, I confess I told lies about her and her brother to confuse you, to weaken your resolve. Afterwards, she was sure that all would be over between you, that she would have lost your trust and of course your love. But Vasily, you have to know that she believed it could be for the best. She never thought your relationship could last. She was not free to marry and had always feared for your reputation.'

Alexander was silent for a moment. His face was flushed. He cleared his throat and continued: 'But you should not have any doubts now about her love for you, Vasily. Seeking my help to save you was a truly selfless act. She left Petersburg shortly after her brother. She went to Kalinin's estates in the south. I think she intended to disappear from your life, from both our lives, but then, when she discovered she was with child, she wrote to me. She realised that you must meet again.'

'But why did she leave it so long to contact me? My daughter is two years old!'

'Initially, we both considered that it simply wouldn't be safe. Fugitives were still being arrested. Nicholas's reaction to the affair was extreme, far more savage than I anticipated. Even now, he won't let the matter lie; he often refers to his 'friends of the fourteenth.' He takes an interest in every detail of the exiles' imprisonment, and the report of the Commission of

Inquiry lies on his desk to this day. It seemed best for you to remain, if not in actual hiding, somewhere obscure and out of the way. Less than a year ago, Fedulov visited her, you know, probing, asking questions. It seems he knew something of the truth but, happily, not enough.'

'But now she wants to see me.'

'Irina found this last winter difficult. I think she wants to settle matters between you and her one way or another. She is, I know, concerned that, knowing what she did, you might think that she interfered in your life and then deserted you when you needed her most, but I know that she entertains the hope that you will understand her true motives.'

'I shall go to her, to them both,' Vasily said. 'We've wasted too much time apart.'

'Yes, you must do that.' Alexander turned away and again stared down into the yard.

Vasily noticed that his uncle's hair was hatched with grey. He had aged since they had last met at Dubovnoye. He walked over to the window and reached out to take his arm. 'Uncle, I'm sorry. I know you've tried to do the best for me. You always have. I am truly sorry. I didn't understand. I thought that you were punishing me...'

'I can't pretend that when I discovered your involvement with the conspirators I wasn't angry and disappointed in you, Vasya. But I wasn't so disappointed that I wanted to see you imprisoned, in exile, your life ruined. That would truly have broken my heart.'

They embraced. Enclosed by the comfort and familiarity of his home, Vasily remembered poor Ryleev, buried, it was said, in an unmarked grave on an island in the Gulf. He thought of Mikhail, his brother Nikita, and the other men in Siberia. He thought of the fugitive that he had seen taken. Did he really regret not sharing their fate?

'You still have my picture on your wall' he said, looking up. 'I thought you'd remove it. I planned to have another painted in Oryol, but…' Vasily took a chair and told Alexander the full story of Boris, Fedulov and the Laptevs.

'Yes,' Alexander said when he had finished, 'some members of your mother's family are… well, let's say they don't know how to behave. And as for Fedulov, all sorts of ugly facts have emerged about him since his most timely accident.' His uncle pursed his lips. Then he shrugged his shoulders and smiled; he almost laughed.

They sat together until it was time to go down to the Prince for dinner. The family was expected, as well as Thomas Maltby and Madame Stenovsky. Ivan was back from the Caucasus and would be there, too.

As they walked to the door, they heard Yakov and Matvey returning. Alexander greeted them: 'You're looking very respectable, Matvey. I hardly recognised you,' he said. 'Your master tells me that you are progressing well with your lessons. We must decide what we are going to do with you. Do you have any ideas?'

'I should like to be an architect or a law agent, sir.'

'Well, there's plenty of call for their skills at the moment. We'll be able to hire you out at an excellent rate!'

Vasily looked sharply at his uncle. Was this a joke? As ever, it was hard to tell.

'Mr Maltby will be here this evening, Matvey. He says he'd like to see you later,' Alexander said. Matvey smiled. His fear of Alexander Petrovich seemed to have evaporated.

———

As in the past, after dinner, Vasily walked down to the English Embankment. It was a warm evening, and a light breeze blew from the west. He could smell the sea and, as he passed the gardens, lime trees and lilac in bloom. Couples and families were promenading, taking the air beside the stone-edged river.

He walked past the Polunin Palace, its elaborate façade now in shade. He reached the door of Kalinin's apartment and looked up at the windows. There was no sign of life. On impulse, he sought out the doorman who generally sat in the hallway. He recognised Vasily and, for a small consideration, admitted him.

The air in the apartment was close and dusty, the furniture covered, and the drapes drawn. He went into Irina's bedroom and pulled back the curtain. Soft light filled the room. He lay down on the bed. The white sheet was cool. There was a faint scent of soap, of lemons.

He had not been able fully to consider Irina's letter. He certainly hadn't yet absorbed the idea of their child. But, as he had dined with his family and friends that evening, he had enjoyed a new sense of certainty. He hadn't lost her. He knew that she loved him, that he loved her and, of course, that he would love their daughter.

In a few days, his duties to his family would be fulfilled. In a few days, he would go to her. He wouldn't return to St Petersburg; he needed more time away, space in which to consider his way ahead... their way ahead. Perhaps Irina might agree to come to Oryol while he completed his term of service, but, if not, Bryansk was not so distant. Whatever the future held, his life couldn't be entirely conventional. He would stay with Irina, married or not, and find different ways to make the world a better place.

He almost slept. He rose and shook himself. Dust flecks rose from the bed and shone in the air. He opened a drawer in the chest. Everything was still here: a razor, a spare shirt, cologne, a sketch pad, some chalks. He pulled out the pad and opened it. Irina lay as he had drawn her on the morning after the ball. Naked, beautiful and, then, of course, entirely his. Half asleep, she cradled her head with one arm, a barely perceptible smile on her lips.

For a moment, he felt a twist of doubt. The last two and a half years must have changed him. Was he still the man she thought she loved? Perhaps when they met she would no longer care for him? He didn't think he could bear to lose her now. But then he remembered the words of her letter. Surely all would be well.

He stepped into the drawing room and let in some light. The ice on the river was long gone, and the city was hazed in pale amber. A small boat with red sails tacked back and forth on the broad waters before the Fortress. In the soft sunlight of evening, the walls of the prison had lost their dumb menace.

An English ship was making its way up the river towards the city. Perhaps it was the *Virtuous*? With one sail set, she nosed upstream towards the Customs House. The vessel was early, but soon they would open the pontoon bridge and she would pass into the inner basin of the Neva. Wind-lashed and scourged with salt from her long voyage, the ship would return to harbour.

HISTORICAL NOTE

MOST OF THE characters who appear in *Small Acts of Kindness* are fictional, but many of the events described are based on historical events often as described in personal memoirs.

The principal historical character in the novel is the poet and revolutionary, Kondraty Ryleev (1795–1826), whose character and activities have been well described not only by his fellow conspirators and in his own writings but also in a literary biography by Patrick O'Meara (see below). Another historical character included in the action is Staff Captain of the Moscow Regiment, Mikhail Bestuzhev (1800–1871), a rebel who wrote engaging and detailed memoirs. Some of the activities of both these characters are necessarily imaginary.

Among the Romanovs and other historical grandees, Grand Duke Mikhail Pavlovich (1798–1849), has a ride-on part. The incident involving the serf who was unfortunate enough to run in front of his horse is true, but the actual perpetrator of the crime was his older brother, Emperor Alexander (1777–1825), and the incident, which is described in his memoirs by the Decembrist I.D. Yakushin (1793–1857), took place a few years earlier.

The character of Mikhail Stenovsky is loosely based on that of Alexander Mikhailovich Murav'ev, the younger brother of Nikita Murav'ev, a prominent leader of the Decembrist Movement. Like Mikhail, Alexander was only twenty-three at the time of the rising. The main liberty that I have taken with his story is the fiction of his betrothal to Lisa Laptev, which is based on the real-life experience of Count Ivan

Annenkov (1802–1878), a fellow officer in the Chevalier Guard. Annenkov's fiancée was permitted by Nicholas I to follow him into exile. Annenkov's story was the basis of Alexander Dumas's novel, *The Fencing Master*. Dumas met and interviewed the Annenkovs when they were allowed to move from Siberia to Nizhny Novgorod. Alexander Murav'ev, in fact, married the Estonian governess employed by Prince Volonsky in Irkutsk in 1839 and had two children with her.

The character of the gendarme Strogov is based on the officer of the same name, Erazm Ivanovich Strogov (1797–1880), the author of *Notes of a Gendarme Staff Officer in the Epoch of Nicholas 1st*. Some of the activities of the Gendarmes described in the novel are based on his experiences.

The character Boris Abramovich is based on serf artists who were unable to fulfil their artistic vocations in Imperial Russia. There are records of at least two who ultimately took their own lives, most famously Grigory Soroka (1823–1864). The story of the serf artist sold as part of a dowry is based on the experience of the artist Vasily Tropinin (1776–1847). Both Stupin's and Venezianov's provincial art schools, which admitted serfs, existed.

The 'winking' Governor of Oryol is based on an actual governor at the time.

SOURCES

THERE IS NO up-to-date book in English solely dedicated to the Decembrist Rising. The standard work remains *1825, The First Russian Revolution* by Anatole Mazour, published in the 1930s by California University Press. A good recent account can be found in the early chapters of Daniel Beer's book, *The House of the Dead: Siberian Exile Under the Tsars*.

The Decembrist Revolt is well documented. Many of the men involved were highly educated and wrote extensive memoirs about their experiences. However, since these accounts were written by different hands, often many years after the event, perspectives on what actually occurred before, during, and after the confrontation on Senate Square on 14 December 1825 (Old Style) inevitably differ.

For the description of the rising itself, I have principally relied on the memoirs of Mikhail Bestuzhev and the lucid and accurate writings of Baron Andrey Rosen (1799–1884), both of whom led rebel troops in St Petersburg on the day. The arrests and interrogations that took place immediately after the event are well described by both Rosen and also in the short but informative notes that were published by Alexander Murav'ev. He also wrote about his appearance before the Commission of Inquiry, as did the ex-soldier I.D. Yakushin.

The description of the Chernov affair is taken from the memoirs of Prince Yevgeny Obolensky (1796–1865). Additional detail about the duel and its aftermath can be found in O'Meara's biography of Ryleev (K.F. Ryleev, *A Political Biography of the Decembrist Poet*, Princeton, 1984).

The departure of the Stenovsky brothers to Siberia and the meeting with their mother and Nikita's wife on the road into exile is based on a scene described by Alexander Murav'ev.

The description of the prison settlement in Chita, eastern Siberia, relies on several Decembrist accounts. The details of Mikhail's (Annenkov's) wedding in the church at Chita are described in the memoirs of N.V. Basargin (1799–1861).

The descriptions of the town of Oryol, Count Kamensky's serf theatre, and the hussar regiments stationed in the town were informed by the memoirs of the historian Count Mikhail Buturlin (1807–1876). Buturlin served as a yunker in the Pavlogradsky hussar regiment in Oryol in 1827, the year that the hero of the novel, Vasily Nikolayevich, arrives there. The character of Yevgeny Uspensky is in part based on Buturlin's experiences, including his inability to speak Russian and the incident in which he is thrown out of the theatre.

The descriptions of Moscow and St Petersburg are derived from accounts of contemporary visitors to the cities: Robert Ker Porter, Augustus Bozzi Granville, and William Wilson.

The practice of alerting passers-by to carriages that might be buried in the snow is described in *A Siberian Journey: The Journal of Hans Jakob Fries*. Fries was a Swiss doctor who travelled through Russia in the late eighteenth century.

A description of the organisation and scope of the provincial civil service in Russia in the 1820s can be found in *Decentralization and Self-Government in Russia, 1830–1870*, by Frederick S. Starr.